THE
SKEIN
OF
LAMENT

Chris Wooding

GOLLANCZ
LONDON

The right of Chris Wooding to be identified as the
author of this work has been asserted by him in accordance
with the Copyright, Designs and Patents Act 1988.

First Published in Great Britain in 2004 by
Gollancz
An imprint of the Orion Publishing Group
Orion House, 5 Upper St Martin's Lane
London WC2H 9EA

A CIP catalogue record for this book is
available from the British Library

ISBN 0 575 07443 4 (cased)
ISBN 0 575 07444 2 (trade paperback)

Typeset at The Spartan Press Ltd,
Lymington, Hants

Printed in Great Britain by
Clays Ltd, St Ives plc

THE

SKEIN

OF

Also by Chris Wooding in Gollancz:

The Weavers of Saramyr:
Book One of The Braided Path

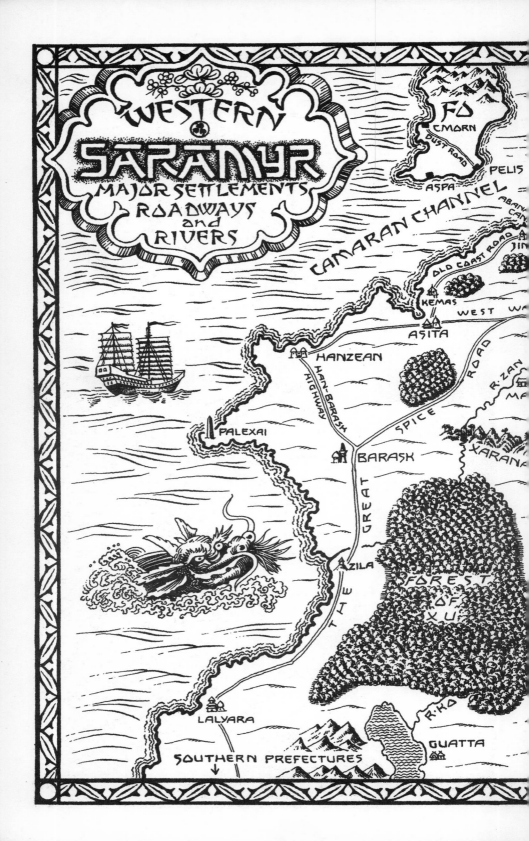

One

The air, cloying and thick from the jungle heat, swam with insects.

Saran Ycthys Marul lay motionless on a flat boulder of dusty stone, unblinking, shaded from the merciless sun by an overhanging chapapa tree. In his hands was a long, slender rifle, his eye lined up with the sight as it had been for hours now. Before him a narrow valley tumbled away, a chasm like a knife slash, its floor a clutter of white rocks left over from a river that had since been diverted by the catastrophic earthquakes that tore across the vast, wild continent of Okhamba from time to time. To either side of the chasm the land rose like a wall, sheer planes of prehistoric rock, their upper reaches buried beneath a dense complexity of creepers, bushes and trees that clung tenaciously to what cracks and ledges they could find.

He lay at the highest end of the valley, where the river had once begun its descent. The monstrosity that had been chasing them for weeks had only one route if it wanted to follow them further. The geography was simply too hostile to allow any alternatives. It would be coming up this way, sooner or later. And whether it took an hour or a week, Saran would still be waiting.

It had killed the first of the explorers a fortnight ago now, a Saramyr tracker they had hired in a Quraal colony town. At least, they had to assume that he had been killed, for there was never any corpse found nor any trace of violence. The tracker had lived in the jungle his whole adult life, so he had claimed. But even he had not been prepared for what they would find in the darkness at the heart of Okhamba.

After him had gone two of the indigenous folk, Kpeth men, reliable guides who doubled as pack mules. Kpeth were albinos, having lived for thousands of years in the near-impenetrable central areas where the sun rarely forced its way through the canopy. Sometime in the past they had been driven out of their territory and migrated to the coast, where they were forced to live a nocturnal existence away from the blistering heat of the day. But they had not forgotten the old ways, and in the twilight of the deepest jungle their knowledge was invaluable. They were willing to sell their services in return for Quraal money, which meant a life of relative ease and comfort within the heavily defended strip of land owned by the Theocracy on the north-western edge of the continent.

Saran did not regret their loss. He had not liked them, anyway. They had prostituted the ideals of their people by taking money for their services, spat upon thousands of years of belief. Saran had found them eviscerated in a heap, their blood drooling into the dark soil of their homeland.

The other two Kpeth had deserted, overcome by fear for their lives. The creature used them later as bait for a trap. The tortured unfortunates were placed in the explorers' path, their legs broken, left cooking in the heat of the day and begging for help. Their cries were supposed to attract the others. Saran was not fooled. He left them to their fates and gave their location a wide berth. None of the others complained.

Four more in total had been killed now, all Quraal men, all helpless in the face of the majestic cruelty of the jungle continent. Two were the work of the creature tracking them. One fell to his death traversing a gorge. The last one they had lost when his *ktaptha* overturned. The shallow-bottomed reed boat had proved too much for him to handle in his fever-weakened state, and when the boat righted itself again, he was no longer in it.

Nine dead in two weeks. Three remaining, including himself. This had to end now. Though they had made it out of the terrible depths of central Okhamba, they were still days from their rendezvous – if indeed there would even *be* a rendezvous – and they were in bad shape. Weita, the last Saramyr among them, was still shaking off the same fever that had claimed the Quraal man, and he was exhausted and at the limit of his sanity. Tsata had picked up a wound in his shoulder which would probably fester unless he had a chance to seek out the necessary herbs to cure himself. Only Saran was healthy. No disease had brushed him, and he was tireless. But even he had begun to doubt their chances of reaching the rendezvous alive, and the consequences of that were far greater than his own death.

Tsata and Weita were somewhere down the valley in the dry river bed, hidden in the maze of moss-edged saltstone boulders. They were waiting, as he was. And beyond them, similarly invisible, were Tsata's traps.

Tsata was a native of Okhamba, but he came from the eastern side, where the Saramyr traders sailed. He was Tkiurathi, an entirely different strain to the albino, night-dwelling Kpeth. He was also the only surviving member of the expedition capable of leading them out of the jungle. In the last three hours, under his direction, they had set wire snares, deadfalls, pits, poisoned stakes, and rigged the last of their explosives. It would be virtually impossible to come up the gorge without triggering something.

Saran was not reassured. He lay as still as the dead, his patience endless.

He was a strikingly handsome man even in this state, with his skin grimed and streaked with sweat, and his chin-length black hair reduced to sodden, lank strips that plastered his neck and cheeks. He had the features of Quraal aristocracy, a certain hauteur in the bow of his lips, in his dark brown eyes and the aggressive curve of his nose. His usual pallor had been darkened by long months in the fierce heat of the jungle, but his complexion remained unblemished by any sign of the trials he had endured. Despite the discomfort, vanity and tradition forebade him to shed the tight, severe clothing of his homeland for attire more suited to the conditions. He wore a starched black jacket that had wilted into creases. The edge of the high collar was chased with silver filigree which coiled into exquisite openwork around the clasps that ran from throat to hip along one side of his chest. His trousers were a matching set with the jacket, continuing the complex theme of the silver thread, and were tucked into oiled leather boots that cinched tight to his calves and chafed abominably on long walks. Hanging from his left wrist – the one which supported the barrel of his rifle – was a small platinum icon, a spiral with a triangular shield, the emblem of the Quraal god Ycthys from whom he took his middle name.

He surveyed the situation mentally, not taking his eye away from the grooved sight. The point where the gorge was at its narrowest was laden with traps, and on either side the walls were sheer. The boulders there, remnants of earlier rockfalls, were piled eight feet high or more, making a narrow maze through which the hunter would have to pick its way. Unless it chose to climb over the top, in which case Saran would shoot it.

Further up the rising slope, closer to him, the old river bed spread out and trees suddenly appeared, a collision of different varieties that jostled for space and light, crowding close to the dry banks. Flanking the trees were more walls of stone, dark grey streaked with white. Saran's priority was to keep his quarry in the gully of the river bed. If it got out into the trees . . .

There was an infinitesimal flicker of movement at the far limit of Saran's vision. Despite the hours of inactivity, his reaction was immediate. He sighted and fired.

Something howled, a sound between a screech and a bellow floating up from the bottom of the slope.

Saran primed the rifle again in one smooth reflex, drawing the bolt back and locking it home. He had a fresh load of ignition powder in the blasting chamber, which he counted as good for around seven shots under normal conditions, maybe five in this humid air. Ignition powder was so cursedly unreliable.

The jungle had fallen silent, perturbed by the unnatural crack of gunfire. Saran watched for another sign of movement. Nothing. Gradually, the trees began to hum and buzz again, animal whoops and birdcalls mixing and mingling in an idiot cacophony of teeming life.

'Did you hit it?' said a voice at his shoulder. Tsata, speaking Saramyrrhic, the only common language the three survivors had left.

'Perhaps,' Saran replied, not taking his eye from the sight.

'It knows we are here,' Tsata said, though whether he meant because Saran had fired at it or not was unclear. He was a skilled polyglot, but not adept enough at the intricacies of Saramyrrhic inflection, which were practically incomprehensible to someone who was not born there.

'It already knew,' murmured Saran, clarifying. The hunter had shown uncanny prescience thus far, having managed to get ahead of them numerous times, guessing their route and ignoring the decoys and false trails they had left. It was only Tsata who had even seen it at all, two days ago, heading after them into the gorge. Neither Tsata nor Saran had been under any illusion that their traps would catch it by surprise. They could only hope that it would simply be unable to avoid them.

'Where is Weita?' Saran asked, suddenly wondering why Tsata was here and not down among the boulders, where he was supposed to be. Sometimes he wished Okhambans had the same ingrained discipline as Saramyr or Quraal, but their anarchic temperament meant that they were never predictable.

'To the right,' Tsata said. 'In the shadow of the trees.'

Saran did not look. He was about to form another question when a dull blast thundered up the gorge, making the trees shiver and the rocks tremble. From the midst of the river bed, a thick cloud of white dust rose slowly into the air.

The echoes of the explosion pulsed away into the sky, and the jungle was silent once again. The absence of animal sounds was eerie; in the months they had been travelling, it had been a constant background noise, and the quiet was an aching void.

For a long moment, neither of them moved or breathed. Finally, the shifting of Tsata's shoe on stone broke the spell. Saran risked a glance back at the Tkiurathi, who was crouching next to him on one knee, hidden against the smooth bark of the chapapa that sheltered them both.

No words were exchanged. They did not need them. They simply waited as the rock dust cleared and settled, then resumed their watch.

Despite himself, Saran felt a little more at ease with his companion at his side. He was strange in appearance and even stranger in attitude, but Saran trusted him, and Saran was not a man who trusted anyone easily.

Tkiurathi were essentially half-breeds, born of the congress between the survivors of the original exodus from Quraal over a thousand years ago, and the indigenous peoples they found on the eastern side of the continent. Tsata had the milky golden hue that resulted, making him seem alternately healthy and tanned or pallid and jaundiced, depending on the light. Dirty orange-blond hair was swept back along his skull and hardened there with sap. He wore a sleeveless waistcoat of simple greyish hemp and trousers of the same, but where he was not covered up it was possible to see the immense tattoo that sprawled across him.

It was a complex, swirling pattern, green against his pale yellow skin, beginning at his lower back and sending tendrils curling up over his shoulder, along his ribs, down his calves to wrap around his ankles. They split and diverged, tapering to points, rigidly symmetrical on either side of the long axis of his body. Smaller tendrils reached up his neck and under his hairline, or slid along his cheek to follow the curve of his eye sockets. Two narrow shoots ran beneath his chin, hooking over to terminate at his lip. From within the tattoo mask that framed his features, his eyes were searching the gorge beneath them, their colour matching the ink that stained him.

It was perhaps an hour later that Weita joined them. He looked sickly and ill, his short dark hair lustreless and his eyes a little too bright.

'What are you doing?' he hissed.

'Waiting,' Saran replied.

'Waiting for what?'

'To see if it moves again.'

Weita swore under his breath. 'Didn't you see? The explosives! If they didn't kill it, then one of the other traps must have.'

'We cannot take the chance,' Saran said implacably. 'It may be only wounded. It may have triggered the trap intentionally.'

'So how long do we sit here?' Weita demanded.

'As long as it takes,' Saran told him.

'Until the light begins to fail,' Tsata said.

Saran accepted the contradiction without rancour. Privately, he was worried that the creature had already slipped up the gorge under cover of the boulders and made it to the treeline, although he counted it unlikely that it could have done so without him catching a glimpse of it. After sunset, it would have the advantage of shadow, and even Tsata's dark-adapted eyes would be hard pressed to pick it out at such a distance.

'Until then,' Saran corrected himself.

But though insects bit them and the air dampened until it took noticeably more effort to breathe, their vigil went unrewarded. They did not see another sign of their pursuer.

Weita's protests fell on deaf ears. Saran could wait forever, and Tsata was content to be as safe as possible in this matter. His concern was the welfare of the group, as it always was, and he knew better than to underestimate their pursuer. But Weita griped and complained, eager to get down among the rocks and see the corpse of their enemy, eager to dispel the fear of the creature that only Tsata had seen so far, the invisible agent of vengeance that had grown in Weita's imagination to the stature of a demon.

Finally, an hour before sunset, Tsata shifted against the trunk of the chapapa and murmured. 'We should go now.'

'At last!' Weita cried.

Saran got up from where he had been lying on his chest for almost the entire day. In the early days of the expedition, Weita had marvelled at the endurance of the man; now it merely irritated him. Saran should have been racked with pain by now, but he seemed as supple as if he had just been for a stroll.

'Weita, you and I will spread out through the rocks and come in from either side. You know where the traps are; be careful. The explosion may not have set them all off.' Weita nodded, only half-listening. 'Tsata, stay high. Go over the top of the boulders. If it tries to shoot or throw anything at you, drop down and head back here as fast as you can.'

'No,' said Tsata. 'It may already be in the trees. I will be an easy target.'

'If it has escaped the gorge, then we are all easy targets,' Saran answered. 'And we need someone up there to look out for it.'

Tsata thought for a moment. 'I understand,' he said. Saran took that to mean he agreed with the plan.

'Do not let your guard down,' Saran advised them all. 'We must assume it is still alive, and still dangerous.'

Tsata checked his rifle, refilled and primed it. Saran and Weita hid theirs in the undergrowth. Rifles would only be a hindrance in the close quarters of the river bed. Instead, they drew blades, Weita a narrow, curved sword and Saran a long dagger. Then they moved out of hiding and went among the rocks.

The heat was worse in the narrow passageways between the boulders. The stifling air was trapped, without wind to stir it. Slanting light cut across the faces of the explorers as they slipped through the sharp dividing lines between bright sun and hot shade and back again. The floor was strewn with rubble, though much of the lesser debris had been washed away in the rainy spells that restored the river to a ghost of its former glory for a few fleeting weeks at a time. What remained was too heavy for the flow to move: ponderous lumps of whitish stone, cracked and smoothed by sun and water.

Saran slid from rock to rock, a succession of blind corners, relying on his sense of direction to keep him going the right way. Somewhere above them, obscured by the boulders, Tsata was keeping to high ground, jumping over the narrow chasms with his rifle held ready, watching for movement. He could hear Weita by the sound of his feet scuffing. The Saramyr man was never capable of being silent; he did not have the grace.

'You are nearing the traps,' Tsata said from overhead.

Saran slowed, looking for the scratched signs they had left in the saltstone, coded signals to warn them where the snares and pits were. He spotted one, looked down, and stepped over the hair-thin wire that hovered an inch above the ground.

'Can you see it?' Weita called. Saran felt a twinge of exasperation. Weita's idea of stealth was pitiful.

'Not yet,' said Tsata, his voice floating down to them. He was already so exposed that he need not worry about endangering himself further by talking.

The boulders did not crowd quite so close here, and Saran caught a glimpse of his Tkiurathi companion, some way distant, picking his way with utmost care.

'Which way should I go?' Weita called again.

'Do you see the boulder to your right? The one that is broken in half?' Tsata asked.

Saran was edging past a concealed pit when he realised that Weita had not answered. He froze.

'Weita?' Tsata prompted.

Silence.

Saran felt his heart begin to accelerate. He stepped to safety and flexed his fingers on the hilt of his dagger.

'Saran,' said Tsata. 'I think it is here.'

Tsata knew better than to expect a response. Saran saw him slip from view and thump to the ground, dropping into the cover of the boulders. Then he was alone.

He brushed his lank hair back from his face in agitation, strained his ears for a sound, a footfall: anything that might give away the location of the creature. Weita was dead, he was sure of that. Not even he would be stupid enough to play a trick on them at a time like this. It was how *silently* he had died that was disturbing.

Better not to stay still. Moving, Saran might at least gain the advantage of surprise. He padded further into the jumble of saltstone boulders, squeezing through a crack where two of them had rolled together. The cursed thing had outwaited them, lured them in here. There was no question of escape now. They would not stand a chance.

He almost missed a coded sign in his mounting trepidation, catching it just in time to avoid setting off a deadfall. Glancing upward, he saw the props balancing a rock above his head. He ducked underneath the chest-high tripwire and stepped over the second one at ankle-height placed just beyond it.

Now he had reached the outskirts of the debris thrown by the explosion. He marvelled that the deadfall had stayed intact. Small stones and dust were scattered underfoot. He went carefully onward.

The quiet was terrifying. Though the sounds of the jungle were loud in the world outside the dim, uneven corridors of light and shade that he stalked through, within it was all stillness. Beads of sweat dripped from his jaw. Was Tsata even alive now, or had the thing caught him too?

A pebble rattled.

Saran reacted fast. The creature moved a fraction faster still. He did not even have time to see it before instinct had pulled his head back and to the side. Its claws were a blur, carving a shallow pair of furrows down the side of his neck. The pain had yet to register before the follow-up strike came, but this time Saran had his blade up, and the thing shrieked and darted backward, coming to rest with its weight evenly spread, momentarily at bay.

Two clawed fingers fell to the ground between the combatants in a puff of white dust.

Saran was stanced low, his blade hidden behind his leading arm so as to disguise his next angle of attack. The wound at his throat was beginning to burn. Poison.

His gaze flickered over his opponent. Its shape was humanoid, and yet not so, as if some manic potter had taken the clay of a man and moulded it into something awful. Its face seemed to have been pulled back over its elongated skull, features stretched, its black shark-eyes set in slanted orbits and its nose flat. Its teeth were perfectly straight and even, a double row of needles the thickness of a quill nib, dark with fresh blood and set into an impossibly wide mouth. Slender limbs were bunched with wiry muscle beneath smooth grey skin, and vestigial frills of flesh like fins ran along its forearms, thighs, and along the monkeylike prehensile tail that curled from its coccyx.

Saran had seen Aberrants in Saramyr that were fouler in shape than this, but they were accidents. This thing had been *made* this way, fleshcrafted in the womb for a fearsome appearance, its attributes altered to streamline it towards one purpose: to be the consummate hunter.

There was a knife in its hand now, a wickedly hooked jungle blade, but it was making no move to attack as yet. It knew it had scored a strike on its opponent, and was waiting for the venom on its claws to take effect.

Saran stumbled back a step, his posture sagging, his eyes drooping heavily. The creature came for him, knife angled to open his throat. But Saran's throat was not where the blade struck; he had already dodged aside, dagger sweeping up towards the creature's narrow chest. Saran was not half so weakened as he had pretended. Taken by surprise, it barely dodged; the tip of Saran's blade sliced a long track down its ribs.

There was not an instant's pause. It came back again, faster this time, less assured of its victim's weakness. Saran parried the strike with a harsh chime of metal and punched at the creature's neck. But his opponent flowed like water, and the blow hit nothing and left Saran dangerously overstretched. The creature grabbed his wrist in an iron grip and flung him bodily over its shoulder; he went sailing through the air for a sickening moment before he crashed into the hard ground, his knife skittering free across the stone. Unable to stop his momentum, he tumbled, feeling a pair of sharp tugs on his body as he came to a halt.

Tripwires.

He pushed off with his feet and backward-rolled a split second before the deadfall smashed to the ground where his head had been. In one smooth motion he was on his feet, but his opponent was springing over the debris of the trap even before the dust had settled, utterly relentless. Saran had barely time to realise that he had lost his dagger; he blocked upward with his hand inside the sweep of the creature's blade, catching it on the inside of the wrist, but already another knife was coming from nowhere, his *own* knife, slicing towards his face. He pulled away fast, the cutting edge missing the bridge of his nose by a whisker, but something caught at his ankle and he toppled backward, his balance deserting him. As he fell there was a harsh hiss of movement, and something blurred past his eyes, stirring his hair with the wind of its passage; then there was a dull, wet impact, and a moment later he crashed flat to the earth, supine and all but helpless against his opponent's killing strike.

But no strike came. He looked up.

The creature stood lifelessly before him, its body limp, supported in the air by the vicious row of wooden spikes that had impaled it through the chest. Saran had literally been tripped by a tripwire, and the bent sapling that was released had passed before his face as he fell backward and caught the creature instead. He lay in a long moment in disbelief, and then began to laugh convulsively. The fleshcrafted monstrosity hung like a marionette with its strings cut, its head lolling, black eyes sightless.

Tsata found Saran dusting himself off and still laughing. The sheer exhilaration of the moment had made him giddy. The Tkiurathi took in the scene with puzzlement on his face.

'Are you hurt?' he asked.

'A little poison,' Saran replied. 'Not enough. I think I will be sick for a while, but not enough. That thing counted on it finishing me off.' He began to laugh again.

Tsata, who was acquainted with Saran's remarkable constitution, did not question further. He studied the creature that had been caught in the spike trap.

'Why are you laughing?' he inquired.

'Gods, it was so fast, Tsata!' he grinned. 'To face something like that and *beat* it . . . it feels . . . *exhilarating.*'

'I am glad,' said Tsata. 'But we should not celebrate yet.'

Saran's laughter died to an uncertain chuckle. 'What do you mean?' he said. 'It is dead. There is your hunter.'

Tsata looked up at him, and his pale green gaze was bleak. 'There is *a* hunter,' he corrected. 'It is not the one I saw two days ago.'

Saran went cold.

'There is another,' Tsata said.

Two

The cracked moon Iridima still hung low in the north as dawn took the eastern sky in a firestorm.

It began as a sullen red mound, growing wider and glowering ever fiercer as it slid over the curve of the horizon. Beneath it, the sea, which had brooded under the glow of Iridima and the vast, blotched face of her sister Aurus during the night, took up the sun like a tentative choir picking up a melody. Scattered glints prickled the distance, flashing in rhythm with the tug and ebb of the waves. They began to infect the neighbouring swells, which glittered a counterpoint, lapping to a different time as they were stirred by underlying currents and the memory of the chaotic twin gravities of the moons. The sky overhead began to blend from black into a deep, rich blue, the stars fading by degrees.

The final stages came in a rush. The calm, gradual process collapsed into disorder as it came to crescendo, and the upper rim of Nuki's eye peeped over the edge of the planet, a blazing arc of white that ignited the breadth of the ocean. The light reached past the sea, over the tiny specks of Saramyr junks that plied towards the westward coast, and it spread over the land beyond: a colossal swathe of green as all-encompassing and apparently endless as the sea that foundered on its shores. Okhamba.

The port of Kisanth lay within the sheltered cradle of a lagoon, separated from the sea by a towering wall of ancient rock. The frowning black mass kept the lagoon waters safe from the ravages of the storms that lashed the eastern coast at this time of year, while myriad subterranean channels allowed a plentiful supply of fish through from the open ocean. Uncountable ages of erosion had widened one of these channels until it undermined the rock overhead and caused a section of it to collapse, forming a tall tunnel wide enough to allow through even large commercial trading ships.

The *Heart of Assantua* slid into that cleft, its fanlike sails sheeted close. It passed from the heat of the early morning sun into cold, dank shade, where the ceiling dripped and echoed, where lanterns cast a pitiful glow against the gloom and rope walkways ran along the walls. The interior of the tunnel was just as rough and uneven as it had been all those years ago when it was formed, before the settlers had ever fled here from the burgeoning Theocracy in Quraal, before they had ever discovered what kind of primitive nightmare they were casting themselves into.

Sharp eyes guided their slow way through the eerie half-light. Minute adjustments to the rudder were made as instructions were hollered from the prow. Dozens of men stood on the decks with long push-poles, ready to use their combined weight to avert the course of the bulky junk if it should drift too close to the sides. For a few long minutes, they passed through the strange, enclosed world that linked the port and the ocean; and then the end of the tunnel slipped over them and they were out, the blue sky above them again. The lagoon was still two-thirds in the shadow of the rock wall, but its western side was drenched in light, and there lay Kisanth, and the end of a long journey.

The port sprawled gaudily along the edge of the lagoon and up the steep incline of the forested basin that surrounded it. It was a heady riot of wooden jetties, gangways, brightly painted shacks and peeling warehouses, counting-houses and cathouses. Dirt tracks had been planked over and were lined with inns and rickety bars. Stalls sold foodstuffs from Saramyr and Okhamba in equal measure or combination. Small junks and *ktaptha* glided out from the beaches on the north side, cutting through the wakes of the larger vessels that lumbered towards the spidery piers of the dock. Shipwrights hammered at hulls on the sand. Everything in Kisanth was daubed in dazzling colours, and everything was faded from the scorching rays of the sun and the onslaught of the storms. It was a vivid world of warped boards and steadily flaking signs that tried to disguise its constant state of decay by distracting the eye with brightness.

The *Heart of Assantua* spread its smaller sails for the last, leisurely stretch across the lagoon, found an empty pier and nosed alongside it. The push-poles were gone now, and thick ropes came snaking down to the waiting dockhands, who made them fast to stout posts. The junk came to a standstill and furled itself like peacock.

The disembarkation formalities took most of the morning. Kisanth being a Saramyr colony, there were rigorous checks to be carried out. Robed officials and clerks logged cargo, checked passengers against the list, recorded any dead or missing in transit, asked what the travellers' purpose in Kisanth was and where they were staying or going. Routine though their questions were, the officials carried themselves with a fierce zeal, believing themselves the guardians of order in this untameable land, bastions against the brutal insanity that reigned outside the perimeter of their town. When all was accounted for to their satisfaction, they returned to the dock-master, who would check the list again and then hand it to a Weaver. At the end of the week, the Weaver would pass the information on to a counterpart in Saramyr, bridging the gulf between continents in the span of a thought, and the receiving Weaver would inform the dock-master there of the safe arrival of their dependant merchants' vessels. It was an eminently well-structured and effective system, and typically Saramyr.

Not that it concerned two of the passengers, however, who were travelling under assumed names with falsified papers, and who passed through the multitude of checks without raising the suspicions of anyone.

Kaiku tu Makaima and Mishani tu Koli walked amongst the crowd of their fellow travellers, exchanging goodbyes and empty promises of further contact as they dispersed at the end of the pier and headed away into the wooden streets. After a month aboard ship, legs were unsteady and spirits were high. The journey from Jinka on the north-western coast of Saramyr had shrunk their world to the confines of their luxurious junk. Largely ignored by the busy sailors, and with little else to do, the passengers had got to know each other well. Merchants, emigrants, exiles, diplomats: they had all found common ground in their journey, forming a fragile community that had seemed precious at the time, but which was already collapsing as their world expanded again and people remembered the reasons that they had crossed the sea in the first place. Now they had their own affairs to attend to, affairs that were important enough to spend a month in transit for, and they were forgetting hasty friendships or ill-advised trysts.

'You are far too sentimental, Kaiku,' Mishani told her companion as they wandered away from the pier.

Kaiku laughed. 'I might have known I would hear that advice from you. I suppose *you* feel no regret at seeing any of them go?'

Mishani glanced up at Kaiku, who was several inches the taller of the two. 'We lied to them the entire journey,' she pointed out dryly. 'About our lives, our childhoods, our professions. Did you honestly entertain the hope of meeting them again?'

Kaiku tilted her shoulder in what might have been a shrug, a curiously boyish gesture from a lithe, pretty woman nearing her twenty-sixth harvest.

'Besides, if all goes well we will be away from here within a week,' Mishani continued. 'Make the most of your time.'

'A week . . .' Kaiku sighed, already dreading the prospect of getting aboard another ship, another month back across the ocean. 'I hope this spy is worth it, Mishani.'

'They had better be,' Mishani said, with uncharacteristic feeling in her voice.

Kaiku took in the sights and sounds of Kisanth with fascination as they made their way up steps and along boardwalks, losing themselves in the belly of the town. Their first steps on a foreign continent. Everything around them felt subtly different and indefinably new. The air was wetter, somehow more fresh and raw than the dry summer they had left behind at home. The insect sounds were different, languid and lugubrious in comparison to the rattling chikikii she knew. The hue of the sky was deeper, more luxuriant.

And the town itself was like nowhere she had ever visited before, at once recognisably Saramyr and yet indisputably foreign. The hot streets creaked and cracked as the sun warmed the planking underfoot, which had been laid to keep the trails navigable when the rain turned the sides of the basin to mud. It smelt of salt and paint and damp earth baking, and spices which Kaiku did not even have a name for. They stopped at a streetside stall and bought *pnthe* from the wizened old lady there, an Okhamban meal of deshelled molluscs, sweetrice and vegetables wrapped up in an edible leaf. A little further on, they sat on a broad set of steps – having observed others doing the same – and ate the *pnthe* with their hands, marvelling at the strangeness of the experience, feeling like children again.

They made an odd pair. Kaiku projected vibrancy, her features lively; Mishani's face was always still, always controlled, and no emotion registered there if she did not desire it. Kaiku was naturally attractive, with a small nose and mischievous brown eyes, and she wore her tawny hair in a fashionable cut that hung in an artfully teased fringe over one eye. Mishani was small, plain, pale and thin, with a mass of black hair that hung down to her ankles in a careful arrangement of thick braids and ornaments tied in with strips of dark red leather, far too impractical for anyone but a noble and carrying all the attendant gravitas. Kaiku's clothes were unfeminine and simple, whereas Mishani's were elegant and plainly expensive.

They finished their meals and left. Later, they found a lodging-house and sent porters to fetch their luggage from the ship. Their time together in Kisanth would be short. In the morning, Kaiku would be leaving to head into the wilds while Mishani stayed to arrange their return to Saramyr. Kaiku hunted down a guide and arranged for her departure.

They slept.

★

The message that had come to the Fold eight weeks earlier had been of the highest priority and utmost secrecy, and neither Kaiku nor Mishani were even aware of it until the two of them had been summoned by Zaelis tu Unterlyn, leader of the Libera Dramach.

With Zaelis was Cailin tu Moritat, a Sister of the Red Order and Kaiku's mentor in their ways. She was tall and cold, clad in the attire of the Order, a long black dress that clung to her figure and a ruff of raven feathers across her shoulders. Her face was painted to denote her allegiance: alternating red and black triangles on her lips and twin crescents of light red curving from her forehead, over her eyelids and cheeks. Her black hair fell down her back in two thick ponytails, accentuated by a silver circlet on her brow, and where it caught the light it glinted blue.

Between the two of them, they had told Kaiku and Mishani about the message. A coded set of instructions, passed through many hands from the north-western tip of Okhamba, across the sea to Saramyr, and thence to the Xarana Fault and the Fold.

'It comes from one of our finest spies,' Cailin said, her voice like a blade sheathed in velvet. 'They need our help.'

'What can we do?' Mishani had asked.

'We must get them off Okhamba.'

Kaiku had adopted a querying expression. 'Why can they not get *themselves* off it?'

'Travel between Saramyr and Okhamba has been all but choked by the Emperor's ruinous export taxes,' Mishani explained. 'After he raised them, the Colonial Merchant Consortium responded by placing an embargo on all goods to Saramyr.'

Kaiku made a neutral noise. She had little interest in politics, and this was news to her.

'The crux of the matter is, our spy cannot get across the ocean back to Saramyr,' Cailin elaborated. 'A small trade still exists from Saramyr and Okhamba, since the scarcity of Saramyr goods has driven up the price enough for a tiny market to survive there; but next to no ships pass the other way. The merchants tend to travel on from there to Quraal or Yttryx. They are weathering the storm abroad, where the money still flows.'

Mishani, ever the quick one, had second-guessed them by now. 'You have passage over to Saramyr,' she stated. 'But you have no ship back. And for that, you need me.'

'Indeed,' said Cailin, studying her intently for a reaction and getting none.

Kaiku looked from one to the other, and then to Zaelis, who was thoughtfully running his knuckles over his close-cropped white beard. 'You mean she would have to go to the coast? To show her face in a port?' she asked, concern in her voice.

'Nothing so simple,' Mishani said with a wan smile. 'Arranging it from this end would be next to impossible. I would have to travel to Okhamba.'

'No!' said Kaiku automatically, flashing a glare at Cailin. 'Heart's blood! She is the daughter of one of the best-known maritime families in Saramyr! Somebody else can go.'

'That is exactly why she must go,' said Cailin. 'The name of Blood Koli carries great weight among the merchants. And she has many contacts still.'

'That is exactly why she must *not* go,' Kaiku countered. 'She would be recognised.' She turned to her friend. 'What of your father, Mishani?'

'I have evaded him these five years, Kaiku,' Mishani replied. 'I will take my chances.'

'I cannot impress upon you enough the importance of this person,' Zaelis said calmly, squaring his shoulders. 'Nor the information they carry. Suffice to say that since they asked for assistance from us at all, there must have been no other option left to them.'

'No other option?' Kaiku exclaimed. 'If this spy is as good as you seem to think they are, then why can they not make their own way back? There must be *some* ships, even if they are only running passengers. Or why not take the Quraal route? It would take a few more months, but—'

'We do not know,' Zaelis interrupted her, raising a hand. 'We only have the message. The spy needs our help.'

Mishani laid a hand on Kaiku's arm. 'I am the only one who can do it,' she said quietly.

Kaiku tossed her hair truculently, glaring at Cailin. 'Then I am going with her.'

The ghost of a smile touched the taller lady's lips. 'I would hardly expect otherwise.'

Three

The pre-dawn twilight on Okhamba was a serene time, a lull in the rhythms of the jungle as the nocturnal creatures quieted and slunk away to hide from the steadily brightening day. The air was blood-warm and still. Mist hazed the distance, stirring sluggishly along the ground or twining sinuously between the vine-hung trunks of the trees. Moonflowers which had turned in the night to track the glow of bright Iridima now furled themselves to protect their sensitive cells from the blazing glare of Nuki's eye. The deafening racket of the dark hours trailed away to nothing, and the silence seemed to ache. In that hour, the land became dormant, holding its breath in tremulous anticipation of the day.

Kaiku left Kisanth in that state of preternatural peace, following her guide. The port was surrounded by an enormous stockade wall on the rim of the basin where the lagoon lay, with a single counterweighted gate to let travellers in and out. Beyond there was a wide clearing, where the trees had been cut back for visibility. A dirt road crawled off along the coast to the north, and a thinner one to the north-west, their edges made ragged as the undergrowth encroached on them. A prayer gate to Zanya, the Saramyr goddess of travellers and beggars, stood in the midst of the clearing. It was a pair of carved poles without a crossbeam, their surfaces depicting Zanya's various deeds in the Golden Realm and in Saramyr. Kaiku recognised most of them at a glance: the kindly man who gave his last crust to a fellow beggar, only to find that she was the goddess in disguise and was richly rewarded; Zanya punishing the wicked merchants who flogged the vagrants that came to the market; the ships of the Ancestors leaving Quraal, Zanya sailing ahead with a lantern to light the way. The gate was too weathered to make out what detail had once been there, but the iconography was familiar enough to Kaiku.

She offered a short mantra to the goddess, automatically adopting the female form of the standing prayer posture: head bowed, cupped hands held before her, left hand above the right and palm down, right

17

hand palm up as if cradling an invisible ball. The guide – a leathery old Tkiurathi woman – stood nearby and watched disinterestedly. Once Kaiku was done and had passed through the gate, they headed into the jungle.

The journey to the rendezvous was only a day's walk, a spot chosen – Kaiku guessed – because it lay almost equidistant from three towns, one of which was Kisanth while the other two lay alongside a river that led shortly thereafter to another sea port. The spy had selected this place to be deliberately vague about their place of departure, in case anyone decoded all or part of the message that had been sent to the Fold. Kaiku found herself wondering about this person she was meant to meet. She did not know their name, nor whether they would be male or female, nor even if they were Saramyr at all. When she had protested at being kept in the dark by Zaelis and Cailin, they had merely said that there were 'reasons' and refused to speak further on it. She was not used to having her curiosity frustrated so. It only piqued her interest further.

From the moment they left the perimeter of man's domain, the land became wild. The roads – heading away to other settlements and to the vast mountainside crop fields – were going in the opposite direction to that in which Kaiku wanted to go, so they were forced to travel on foot and through the dense foliage. The way was hard, and there were no trails to speak of. The terrain underfoot was uncertain, having been moistened by recent rains. Kaiku's rifle snagged on vines with annoying regularity, and she began to regret bringing it at all. They were forced to scramble their way along muddy banks, clamber up rocky slopes that trickled with water, hack their way through knotted walls of creepers with *knaga*, a sickle-like Okhamban blade used for jungle travel. But for all that, Kaiku found the jungle breathlessly beautiful and serene in the quiet before the dawn, and she felt like an intruder as she went stamping and chopping through the eerie netherworld of branches and tangles.

The land warmed about them as they travelled, bringing with it a steadily growing chorus of animal calls, creatures hooting at each other from the meshed ceiling of treetops high above. Birds, with cries both beautiful and comically ugly, began to sing from their invisible vantage points. Frogs belched and croaked; the undergrowth rustled; fast things flitted between the trunks of the trees, sometimes launching themselves across the travellers' path. Kaiku found herself unconsciously dawdling, wanting to soak up the sensations around her, until her guide hissed something sharp in Okhamban and she hurried to catch up.

Kaiku had harboured initial doubts about the guide she had found, but the old woman proved far stronger than she looked. Long after Kaiku's muscles were aching from trudging along cruel inclines and chopping the omnipresent vines that hung between the trees, the Tkiurathi forged unflaggingly onward. She was tough, though Kaiku guessed she must have been somewhere past her fiftieth harvest. Okhambans did not count years, nor keep track of their age.

Conversation was limited to grunts and gestures. The woman spoke very little Saramyrrhic, just enough to agree to take Kaiku where she wanted to go, and Kaiku spoke next to no Okhamban, having learned only a few words and phrases while at sea. In contrast to the excessive complexity of Saramyrrhic, Okhamban was incredibly simple, possessing only one phonetic alphabet and one spoken mode, and no tenses or similar grammatical subtleties. Unfortunately, the very simplicity of it defeated Kaiku. One word could have six or seven discrete applications depending on its context, and the lack of any specific form of address such as *I*, *you* or *me* made things terribly hard for one who had grown up speaking a language that was unfailingly precise in meaning. Okhambans traditionally had no concept of ownership, and their individuality was always second to their *pash*, which was roughly translatable as 'the group'; but it was a very slippery meaning, and it could be used to refer to a person's race, family, friends, those who were present, those they were talking to, loved ones, partners, or any of a dozen other combinations with varying degrees of exclusivity.

As the heat climbed and the midges and biting insects began to appear, Kaiku sweltered. Her hardwearing and unflattering clothes – baggy beige trousers and a matching long-sleeved shirt with a drawstring collar – were becoming itchy with sweat and uncomfortably heavy. They stopped for a rest, during which time the guide insisted that Kaiku drink a lot of water. She produced a leaf-wrapped bundle of what seemed to be cold crab meat and a spicy kelp-like plant, and shared it with Kaiku without her asking. Kaiku brought out her own food and shared it with the guide. They ate with their hands.

Kaiku stole glances at the woman as she chewed, eyes roaming over the pale green tattoos that curled over her cheeks and poked from her shirt collar, wondering what thoughts passed through her head. She had not wanted any payment for her services as a guide; indeed, it was an insult to offer any. Mishani had explained that since the guide lived within the town of Kisanth, then at some level that was her *pash* and thereby she would willingly offer her services to anyone within that town who needed them and expect the same courtesy to be offered to her. Kaiku had been warned to be very careful about asking anything of an Okhamban, as they would almost unfailingly oblige, but they would become resentful if their nature was abused. Okhambans only asked for something when they could not do it themselves. She could not pretend to understand their ways, but she thought it seemed a strangely civilised and selfless lifestyle in a people who were generally thought of as primitive in Saramyr.

Night had just deepened to full dark when they arrived at the Aith Pthakath. They came at it from below, following a narrow stream bed until the trees abruptly fell back and exposed the low hilltop hidden in amongst the surrounding jungle. No trees grew on the hill, but in their place were the monuments of ancient Okhamba, built by a dead tribe long before any people's history had begun to be recorded.

Kaiku caught her breath. Aurus and Iridima shared the sky for a third successive night, lighting the scene in a wan white glow. Aurus, pale but patched with darker shades, loomed massive and close to the north. Iridima, smaller and much brighter, her skin gullied with bluish cracks, took station in the west, above and behind the monuments.

There were six of them in all, bulky shadows against the sky with the curves of their faces limned in moonlight. The tallest of them stood at thirty feet, while the smallest was a little over fifteen. They were sculpted from a black, lustrous stone that was like obsidian in quality, set in a loose ring around the crest of the hilltop, facing outward. The largest squatted in the centre, looking over Kaiku's head to the east.

The guide grunted and motioned at Kaiku to go on, so she stepped out of the trees and into the clearing, approaching the nearest of the monuments. The riotous sound of the jungle had not diminished one bit, but she felt suddenly alone here, in the presence of a humbling antiquity, a place sanctified by a long-dead people before any of what she knew existed. The statue she approached was a squatting figure hewn out of a great pillar, features grotesquely exaggerated, a prominent mouth and huge, half-lidded eyes, its hands on its knees. Though the rain of centuries had battered it and smoothed its lines so that they were indistinct, and though one hand had broken away and lay at its feet, it was incredibly well preserved, and its blank, chilling gaze had not diminished in authority. Kaiku felt minuscule under its regard, this forgotten god.

The others were no less intimidating. They were seated or squatting, with swollen bellies and strange faces, some like animals that Kaiku had never seen, some in disturbing caricatures of human features. They guarded the hill, glaring balefully out at the trees, their purpose alien and subtly unsettling.

Kaiku hesitated for a few moments, then laid her hand on the knee of one of the idols. The stone was cool and brooding. Whatever power this place had once seen had not been entirely dispersed. It retained a sacred air, like an echo of distant memory. No trees had encroached here, nor had any animals nested in the crooks and folds of the statues. She wondered if there were spirits here, as there were in the deeper forests and lost places at home. The Tkiurathi did not seem to be pious at all, from the accounts of the travellers she had talked to on the *Heart of Assantua*. Yet here was the evidence that there had once been worship in this land. The weight of ages settled on her like a shroud.

She became conscious that the guide had joined her, and removed her hand from the statue. She had forgotten the reason she came here in the first place. Looking around, it became evident that the spy was not here yet. Well, she was early. The rendezvous was at midnight on this date. They had cut it extremely fine on the crossing, slowed by unfavourable moon-tides caused by some inept navigator's mis-calculation of the orbits, but at least she was here now.

'Perhaps we should look around the other side of the hill,' she suggested, more to herself than the guide, who could not understand. She made a motion with her arm to illustrate, and the guide tilted her chin up in an Okhamban nod.

In that instant, a thick arrow smashed through her exposed throat, spun her sideways in a geyser of blood and sent her crashing to the earth.

Kaiku was immobile for a few long seconds, her mouth slightly open, barely certain of what had just happened. Flecks of blood trembled on her cheek and shoulder.

It was the second arrow that broke the paralysis. She felt it coming, sensed it slipping through the air; from her right, from the trees, heading for her chest.

Her *kana* blazed into life inside her. The world became a shimmer of golden threads, a diorama of contours all interlinked, every vine and leaf a stitchwork of dazzling fibres. The pulsing tangles that were the statues of the Aith Pthakath were watching her with dark and impotent attention, aware, *alive* in the world of the Weave.

She swept her hand up, the air before her thickening invisibly to a knot, and the arrow shattered two feet from her heart.

Sense finally caught up with instinct and reaction, and she exhaled a frantic breath. Adrenaline flooded in. She barely remembered to rein her *kana* before it burst free entirely. If it had been a rifle and not an arrow, if it had been her and not the guide that they had aimed at first, would she have been fast enough to repel it?

She ran. Another arrow sliced from the trees, but she felt it going wide of her. She stumbled, her boot sliding in the soil and smearing dirt up the leg of her trousers. Cursing, she scrambled to her feet again, tracing the route of the arrow in her mind. Her irises had darkened from brown to a muddy red, seeing into the Weave, tracking back along fibres torn into eddies by the spin of the arrow's feathered flight. Then – having established the rough location of her attacker – she was racing for cover once more. She slid behind one of the idols as a third arrow came at her, glancing off its obsidian skin. A flood of silent outrage rippled out from the statues at the desecration.

Find them. Find them, she told herself. She wanted to cringe under the weight of the idol's gaze, its ancient and malicious interest in her now that she had stirred the Weave; but she forced herself to ignore it. They were old things, angry at being abandoned by their worshippers and ultimately reduced to observers, incomprehensible in purpose and meaning now. They could not harm her.

Instead she sent her mind racing along the tendrils of the Weave, scattering among the trees to where her attacker was, seeking the inrush of breath, the knitting of muscle, the heavy thump of a pulse. The enemy was moving, circling around; she felt the turbulence of its passing in the air, and followed it.

There! And yet, *not* there. She found the source of the arrows, but its signature in the Weave was vague and meaningless, a twisted blot of fibres. If she could get a purchase on her attacker she could begin to do them harm, but something was defeating her, some kind of protection that she had never encountered before. She began to panic. She was not a warrior; with her *kana* out of the equation, she was no match for anyone who could shoot that accurately with a bow. Shucking her rifle from her shoulder, she primed it hurriedly, tracking the hidden assailant with half her attention as they dodged through the under-growth without a whisper.

Get away, she told herself. *Get into the trees.*

And yet she dared not. The open space around her was the only warning she had of another attack. In the close quarters of the jungle, she would not be able to run and dodge and keep track of the enemy at the same time.

Who is it out there?

She raised her rifle and leaned around the edge of the idol, aiming at where she guessed her attacker would be. The rifle cracked and the shot puffed through the trees, splintering branches and cutting leaves apart.

Another arrow sped from the darkness. Her enemy had gained an angle on her already. She pulled herself reflexively away as the point smacked into the idol near her face, sending her stumbling backward. She noticed the next arrow, nocked and released with incredible speed, an instant before it hit her in the ribs.

The shock of the impact sent sparkles across her vision and almost made her pass out. She lost control, her *kana* welling within, all Cailin's teachings forgotten in the fear for her life. It ripped up out of her, from her belly and womb, tearing along the threads of the Weave towards the unseen assassin. Whatever protection they wore stopped her pinpointing them, but accuracy was not necessary. There was no subtlety in her counterstrike. Wildly, desperately, she lashed out, and the power inside her responded to her direction.

A long swathe of jungle exploded, blasted to matchwood, rent apart with cataclysmic force and lighting the night with fire. The sheer force of the detonation destroyed a great strip of land, throwing clods of soil into the air like smoking meteorites. The trees nearby burst into flame, leaves and bark and vines igniting; stones split; water boiled.

In a moment, it was over, her *kana* spent. The jungle groaned and snapped on the fringes of the devastation. Sawdust and smoke hung in the air, along with the faint smell of charred flesh from the birds and animals that had been unfortunate enough to live there. The surrounding jungle was silent, stunned. The terrible presences of the idols bore down on her more heavily than ever, hating her.

She teetered for a moment, her hand going to her side, then dropped to one knee in the soil. Her rifle hung limply in her other hand. Her irises were a bright, demonic red now, a side-effect of her power that would not fade for some hours. In past times, when she had first discovered the awful energy within her, she had been unable to rein it in at all, and each use would leave her helpless as a newborn afterward, barely able to walk. Cailin's training had enabled Kaiku to shut off the flow before it drained her to such a state, but it would be some time before her *kana* would regenerate enough to allow her to manipulate the Weave again. She had not unleashed it so recklessly for years; but then, it had been years since she had been in such direct danger.

Kaiku panted where she knelt, scanning the destruction for signs of movement. There was nothing except the slow drift of powdered debris in the air. Whoever had been aiming at her had been in the middle of that. She'd wager there was not much left of them now.

A movement, down the hill at the treeline. She spun to her feet, snatched up her rifle and primed the bolt, raising it to her eye. Two figures burst into the clearing from the south. She sighted and fired.

'No!' one of them cried, scrambling out of the way. The shot had missed, it seemed. Ignoring the ache and the insidious wetness spreading across her side, she reprimed. 'No! Libera Dramach! Stop shooting!'

Kaiku paused, her rifle targeted at the one who had spoken.

'Await the sleeper!' he cried. It was the phrase by which the spy was to have been identified.

'Who is the sleeper?' Kaiku returned, as was the code.

'The former Heir-Empress Lucia tu Erinima,' came the reply. 'Whom you yourself rescued from the Imperial Keep, Kaiku.'

She hesitated a few moments longer, more in surprise at being recognised than anything else, and then lowered her rifle. The two figures headed up the hill towards her.

'How do you know who I am?' she asked, but the words came out strangely weak. She was beginning to feel faint, and her vision was still sparkling.

'I would not be much of a spy if I did not,' said the one who had spoken, hurrying up towards her. The other followed behind, scanning the trees: a Tkiurathi man with the same strange tattoos as her guide, though in a different pattern.

'You are hurt,' the spy stated impassively.

'Who are you?' she asked.

'Saran Ycthys Marul,' came the reply. 'And this is Tsata.' He scanned the treeline before turning his attention back to Kaiku. 'Your display will have attracted anyone hunting for us within twenty miles. We have to go. Can you walk?'

'I can walk,' she said, not at all sure whether she could. The arrow had punctured her shirt and she was certainly bleeding; but it had not stuck in her, and she could still breathe well enough, so it had missed her lungs. She wanted to bind herself up here and now, terrified of the moist stain that was creeping along the fabric under her arm; but something in the authority of Saran's voice got her moving. The three of them hurried into the forest and were swallowed by the shadows, leaving behind the grim sentinels of the Aith Pthakath, the body of Kaiku's guide and the smouldering crackle of the trees.

'What was it?' Kaiku asked. 'What was it out there?'

'Hold still,' Saran told her, crouching next to her in the firelight. He had slid off one arm of her shirt, exposing her wounded side. Beneath the sweat-dirtied strap of her underwear, her ribs were a wet mess of black and red. Unconsciously, she had clutched the other half of her shirt across her chest. Nudity was not something that most Saramyr were concerned about, but something about this man made her feel defensive.

She hissed and flinched as he mopped at her wound with a rag and hot water.

'Hold *still!*' he told her irritably.

She gritted her teeth and endured his ministrations.

'Is it bad?' she forced herself to ask. There was a silence for a few moments, dread crowding her as she waited for his answer.

'No,' he said at last. Kaiku exhaled shakily. 'The arrow ploughed quite a way in, but it only scraped your side. It looks worse than it is.'

The narrow cave echoed softly with the sussuration of their voices. Tsata was nowhere to be seen, out on some errand of his own. The Tkiurathi had found them this place to hide, a cramped tunnel carved by an ancient waterway in the base of an imposing rock outcropping, concealed by trees and with enough of a bend in it so that they could light a fire without fearing that anyone outside would see. It was uncomfortable and the stone was dank, but it meant rest and safety, at least for a short time.

Saran set about making a poultice from crushed leaves, a folded strip of cloth and the water that was boiling in an iron pot. Kaiku pulled her shirt tight around her and watched him silently, eyes skipping over the even planes of his face. He caught her glance suddenly, and she looked away, into the fire.

'It was a *maghkriin*,' Saran said, his voice low and steady. 'The thing that tried to kill you. It got here before us. You are lucky to be alive.'

'Maghkriin?' Kaiku said, trying out the unfamiliar word.

'Created by the Fleshcrafters in the dark heart of Okhamba. You cannot imagine what the world is like there, Kaiku. A place where the sun never shines, where neither your people nor mine dare to go in any number. In over a thousand years since the first settlers arrived, what footholds we have made in this land have been on the coasts, where it is not so wild. But before we came, *they* were here. Tribes so old that they might have stood since before the birth of Quraal. Hidden in the impenetrable centre of this continent, thousands upon thousands of square miles where the land is so hostile that civilised society such as ours cannot exist there.'

'Is that where you have come from?' Kaiku asked. His Saramyrrhic was truly excellent for one who was not a native, though his accent occasionally slipped into the more angular Quraal inflections.

Saran smiled strangely in the shifting firelight. 'Yes,' he said. 'Though we barely made it. Twelve went in; we two are the only ones who came out, and I will not count us safe until we are off this continent entirely.' He looked up at her from where he was grinding the leaves into a mulch. 'Is it arranged?'

'If all goes well,' Kaiku said neutrally. 'My friend is in Kisanth. She intends to have secured us passage to Saramyr by the time we return.'

'Good,' Saran murmured. 'We cannot stay in towns any longer than necessary. They will find us there.'

'The maghkriin?' Kaiku asked.

'Them, or the ones that sent them. That is why I needed somebody

25

to facilitate a quick departure from Okhamba. I did not imagine I could take what I took and not be pursued.'

And what did you take, then? Kaiku thought, but she kept the question to herself.

He added some water to the paste of leaves and then leaned over to Kaiku again, gently peeling her sodden shirt away from the wound. 'This will hurt,' he warned. 'I learned this from Tsata, and in Okhamba there is very little medicine that is gentle.' He pressed the poulticed cloth against her wound. 'Hold it there.'

She did so. The burning and itching began almost immediately, gathering in force and spreading across her ribs. She gritted her teeth again. After a time, it seemed to level off, and the pain remained constant, just on the threshold of being bearable.

'It is fast-acting,' Saran told her. 'You only need hold it there for an hour. After you remove it, the pain will recede.'

Kaiku nodded. Sweat was prickling her scalp from her effort to internalise the discomfort. 'Tell me about the Fleshcrafters,' she said. 'I need to keep my mind off this.'

Saran hunkered back and studied her with his dark eyes. As she looked at him, she remembered that her own eyes were still red. In Saramyr, it would mark her as Aberrant; most people would react with hate and disgust. But neither Saran nor Tsata had seemed concerned. Perhaps they already knew what she was. Saran had certainly seemed to recognise her; but the fact that she was under the tuition of the Red Order – and hence an Aberrant – was not widely known. Even in the Fold, where Aberrants were welcomed, it was best to keep Aberration a secret.

'I cannot guess what kind of things dwell in the deepest darknesses of Okhamba,' Saran said. 'They have men and women there with crafts and arts foreign to us. Your folk and mine, Kaiku, our ways are very different; but these are utterly alien. The Fleshcrafters can mould a baby in the womb, sculpt it to their liking. They take pregnant mothers, captured from enemy tribes, and they change the unborn children into monsters to serve them.'

'Like Aberrants,' Kaiku murmured. 'Like the Weavers,' she added, her voice deepening with venom.

'No,' said Saran, with surprising conviction. 'Not like the Weavers.'

Kaiku frowned. 'You're defending them,' she observed.

'No,' he said again. 'No matter how abhorrent their methods, the Fleshcrafters' art comes from natural things. Herblore, incantations, spiritcraft . . . Natural things. They do not corrupt the land like the Weavers do.'

'The maghkriin . . . I could not . . . I could not find it,' Kaiku said

at length, after she had digested this. 'My *kana* seemed to glance off it.'
She watched Saran carefully. Years of caution had taught her that
discussing her Aberrant powers was not something done lightly, but
she wanted to gauge him.

'They have talismans, sigils,' Saran said. 'Dark arts that they trap
within shapes and patterns. I do not dare imagine the kind of tricks
they use, nor do I know all that the Fleshcrafters can do. But I know
they place protections on their warriors. Protections that, apparently,
work even against you.'

He brushed the fall of dirty black hair away from his forehead and
poked at the fire. Kaiku watched him. Her gaze seemed to flicker back
to his face whether she wanted it to or not.

'Are you tired?' he asked. He was not looking up, but she sensed that
he knew she was staring. She forced her eyes away with an effort of
will, flushing slightly, only to find that they had returned to him again
an instant later.

'A little,' Kaiku lied. She was exhausted.

'We have to go.'

'Go?' she repeated. 'Now?'

'Do you think you killed it? The one that attacked you?' he asked,
straightening suddenly.

'Certain,' she replied.

'Don't be,' Saran advised. 'You do not know what you are dealing
with yet. And there may be more of them. If we travel hard, we can be
at Kisanth by mid-afternoon. If we stay and rest, they will find us.'

Kaiku hung her head.

'Are you strong enough?' Saran asked.

'Strong as I need to be,' Kaiku said, getting to her feet. 'Lead the
way.'

Four

'Mistress Mishani tu Koli,' the merchant said in greeting, and Mishani knew something was wrong.

It was not only his tone, although that would have been enough. It was the momentary hesitation when he saw her, that fractional betrayal that raced across his features before the facade of amiability clamped down. Beneath her own impassive veneer, she already suspected this man; but she had no other choice except to trust him, for he appeared to be her only hope.

The Saramyr servant retreated from the room, closing the folding shutter across the entryway as she left. Mishani waited patiently.

The merchant, who had seemed slightly dazed and lost in thought for a moment, appeared to remember himself. 'My apologies,' he said. 'I haven't introduced myself. I'm Chien os Mumaka. Please, this way.' He motioned to where the study opened onto a wide balcony over-looking the lagoon.

Mishani accompanied him out. There were exotic floor mats laid there, woven of a thick, soft Okhamban fabric, and a low table of wine and fruits. Mishani sat, and Chien took position opposite. The merchant's house was set high up on the slope of the basin that surrounded Kisanth, a sturdy wooden structure raised on oak pillars to make its foremost half sit level. The view was spectacular, with the black rocks of the coastal wall rearing up to the left and Kisanth to the right, lying in a semicircle around the turquoise-blue water. Ships glided their slow way from the docks to the narrow gash in the wall that gave out onto the open sea, and smaller craft poled or paddled between them. The whole vista was smashed with dazzlingly bright sunlight, making the lagoon a fierce glimmer of white.

She sized up her opponent as they went through the usual greetings, platitudes and inquiries after each other's health, a necessary preamble to the meat of the discussion. He was short, with a shaven head and broad, blocky features matched by a broad, blocky physique. His clothes were evidently expensive though not ostentatious; his only concession to conceit was a thin embroidered cloak, a very Quraal affectation on a Saramyr man, presumably meant to advertise his worldliness.

But appearances meant nothing here. Mishani knew him by reputation. Chien os Mumaka. The *os* prefix to his family name meant that he was adopted, and it would stay attached to his natural children for two generations down, bestowing its stigma upon them too, until the third generation reverted to the more usual *tu* prefix. *Os* meant literally 'reared by', and whereas *tu* implied inclusion in the family, *os* did not.

None of this appeared to have hampered Chien os Mumaka's part in his family's meteoric rise in the merchant business, however. Over the last ten years, Blood Mumaka had turned what was initially a small shipping consortium into one of only two major players in the Saramyr-Okhamba trade route. Much of that was down to Chien's daring nature: he was renowned for taking risks which seemed to pay off more often than not. He was not elegant in his manners, nor well educated, but he was undoubtedly a formidable trader.

'It's an honour indeed to have the daughter of such an eminent noble Blood come visit me in Kisanth,' Chien was saying. His speech patterns were less formal than Mishani's or Kaiku's. Mishani placed him as having come from somewhere in the Southern Prefectures. He had obviously also never received elocution training, which many children of high families took for granted. Perhaps he was passed over due to his adopted status, or because his family were too poor at the time.

'My father sends his regards,' she lied. Chien appeared pleased.

'Give him mine, I beg you,' he returned. 'We have a lot to thank your family for, Mistress Mishani. Did you know that my mother was a fisherwoman in your father's fleet in Mataxa Bay?'

'Is that true?' Mishani asked politely, though she knew perfectly well it was. She was frankly surprised he had brought it up. 'I had thought it only a rumour.'

'It's true,' Chien said. 'One day a young son of Blood Mumaka was visiting your father at the bay, and by Shintu's hand or Rieka's, he came face-to-face with the fisherwoman, and it was love from that moment. Isn't that a tale?'

'How beautiful,' said Mishani, thinking just the opposite. 'So like a poem or a play.' The subsequent marriage of a peasant into Blood Mumaka and the family's refusal to excise their shameful son had crippled them politically; it had taken them years to claw back their credibility, mainly due to their success in shipping. That Chien was talking about it at all was somewhat crass. Chien's mother was released

from her oath to Blood Koli and given to the lovestruck young noble in
return for political concessions that Blood Mumaka were still paying
for today. That one foolish marriage had been granted in return for an
extremely favourable deal on Blood Mumaka shipping interests in the
future. It had been a shrewd move. Now that they were major traders,
their promises made back then kept them tied tightly to Blood Koli,
and Koli made great profit from them. Mishani could only imagine
how that would chafe; it was probably only the fact that they had to
make those concessions to her family that prevented them from
dominating the trade lane entirely.

'Do you like poetry?' Chien inquired, using her absent comment to
steer her in another direction.

'I am fond of Xalis, particularly,' she replied.

'Really? I would not have thought his violent prose would appeal to
a lady of such elegance.' This was flattery, and not done well.

'The court at Axekami is every bit as violent as the battlefields Xalis
wrote of,' Mishani replied. 'Only the wounds inflicted there are more
subtle, and fester.'

Chien smiled crookedly and took a slice of fruit from the table.
Mishani exploited the gap to take the initiative.

'I am told that you may be in a position to do a service for me,' she
said.

Chien chewed slowly and swallowed, making her wait. A warm
breeze rippled her dress. 'Go on,' he prompted.

'I need passage back to Saramyr,' she said.

'When?'

'As soon as possible.'

'Mistress Mishani, you've only just got here. Does Kisanth displease
you that much?'

She was not surprised. He had checked the shipping logs. Easy to do
for a man of his connections, and it at least meant that he had made the
effort and took her seriously. She could only hope that his connections
overseas were not so good.

'Kisanth is a remarkable place,' she replied, evading the thrust of the
question. 'Very vibrant.'

Chien studied her for a long moment. To press her further on her
motives for returning would be rude. Mishani kept her features glacial
as the silence drew out uncomfortably. He was evaluating her; she
guessed that much. But did he know that the front she presented was a
charade?

Her connection to Blood Koli was tenuous at best. Though she was
officially still part of the family – the shame in having such a wayward
daughter would damage their interests – they shunned her now. Her

betrayal had been carefully covered up, and though the rumours inevitably spread, only a few knew the truth of it.

The story went that Mishani was travelling in the east, across the mountains, furthering the interests of Blood Koli there. In reality, her father had been relentlessly hunting for her since she had left him. She was in little doubt what would happen if he caught her. She would become a prisoner on her own estates, forced to maintain the show of solidarity in Blood Koli, to conform to the lie that they had spun to hide the dishonour she had brought upon them. And then, perhaps, she would be quietly killed.

Her nobility was a sham, a bluff. And she suspected that Chien knew that. She had hoped that a merchant trader would not have access to the kind of information that would expose her, but there was something odd about the way he was acting, and she did not trust him an inch. Her father would be a powerful friend, and he would be greatly indebted to anyone who delivered his daughter back to him.

'How soon do you have to leave?' Chien said eventually.

'Tomorrow,' she replied. In truth, she did not know how urgent their departure really was, but it was best to appear definite when bargaining.

'Tomorrow,' he repeated, unfazed.

'Can it be done?' she asked.

'Possibly,' Chien told her. He was buying himself time to think. He looked out over the lagoon, the sun casting shadows in the hollows of his broad features. Weighing the implications. 'It will cost me considerably,' he said at length. 'There will be substantial unused cargo space. No, three days from now is the absolute earliest we can be outfitted and under sail.'

'Good enough,' she said. 'You will be reimbursed. And you will have my deepest gratitude.' How convenient that a phrase like that, implying that he would be owed a favour by a powerful maritime family, could still be true when it meant literally what it said and nothing more. She did have money – the Libera Dramach would spare no expense to get their spy home – but as far as favours went, she had only what she could give, which was not much to a man like Chien. She almost felt bad about cheating him.

'I've a different proposition,' he said. 'Your offer of reimbursement is kind, but I confess I have matters to deal with in our homeland anyway, and money is not an issue here. I'd rather not hold a family as eminent as yours in my debt. Instead, I've a somewhat presumptuous request to make of you.'

Mishani waited, and her heart sank as she listened, knowing that she could not refuse and that she was playing right into his hands.

★

Later, it rained.

The clouds had rolled in with startling speed as the humidity ascended, and in the early afternoon the skies opened in a torrent. Out in the jungle, thick leaves nodded violently as they were battered by fat droplets; mud sluiced into streams that snaked away between the tree roots; slender waterfalls plunged through the air as rain ramped off the canopy and fell to earth, spattering boughs and rocks. The loud hiss of the downpour drowned the sound of nearby animals hooting from their shelters.

Saran, Tsata and Kaiku trudged through the undergrowth, soaked to the skin. They walked hunched under *gwattha*, hooded green ponchos woven of a native fabric that offered some protection against light rain, but not enough to keep them dry in such an onslaught. Kaiku had been given one by her guide before they set out, and had kept it rolled in a bundle and tied to her small pack; the other two had their own. Setting foot in the jungle without one was idiocy.

The rain slowed an already slow pace. Kaiku stumbled along with barely the strength to pick up her feet. None of them had slept, and they had been travelling through the night. Under ordinary conditions, Kaiku would have found this endurable; however, the long month of inactivity aboard the *Heart of Assantua*, the wound in her side and the detrimental effects of unleashing her *kana* had combined to severely curtail her stamina. But rest was out of the question, and pride forbade her from complaining. The others had trimmed their pace somewhat, but not by much. She kept up miserably, leaving it to Saran and Tsata to look out for any pursuers. Without sleep, her *kana* had not regenerated and her senses had dulled. She told herself that her companions were alert enough for the three of them.

She brooded on the fate of her guide as they made their way back to Kisanth. It saddened her that the Tkiurathi woman had never told Kaiku her name. Saramyr ritual dictated that the dead must be named to Noctu, wife of Omecha, so that she could record them in her book and advise her husband of their great deeds – or lack of them – when they came hoping for admittance to the Golden Realm. Even though the woman had most likely not believed at all, it worried at Kaiku.

Saran and Tsata conferred often in low voices and scanned the jungle with their rifles ready, the weapons wrapped in thick rags and strips of leather to keep their powder chambers dry. The downpour – which would hamper anyone following by obliterating their trail – had not seemed to ease their fears one bit. Despite Saran's reservations, Kaiku was certain that she had incinerated the assassin at the Aith

Pthakath. And if there *was* a maghkriin still hunting them, Saran seemed to believe its tracking ability was nothing short of supernatural.

She found herself wondering why this man was so important, what he knew, what was worth risking her life for. She felt galled that her curiosity had not been satisfied yet. Of course, he was a spy, and she should have expected that he would not reveal his secrets easily, but it annoyed her that she should be going through all this without knowing the reason why.

Kaiku had tried to engage Saran in conversation occasionally throughout the morning, but was frustrated by his distractedness. He was too intent on watching out for enemies and jungle animals, which could be deadly even out near the coast where the land was a little more civilised. He barely listened to her. She found that it piqued her unaccountably.

By the time they stopped, exhaustion and the rain had combined to make her fatalistic. If a maghkriin was going to come, let it come. They could do nothing about it.

However, the cause of the halt was not the rest that Kaiku had hoped for.

It was Tsata who saw it first, a little way up the incline which rose to their left, overlooking their route. He darted back in a flash and pointed through the trees. Kaiku squinted through dewed lashes, but she could only see grey shadows in amid the shifting curtains of rain.

'Who is that?' Tsata asked her. Saran was at their side in a moment.

'I cannot see,' Kaiku said. The unspoken question: how should *she* know? She tried to pick out movement, but there was nothing.

Saran and Tsata exchanged a glance. 'Stay here,' Saran told her.

'Where are you going?'

'Just stay,' he said, and he disappeared into the undergrowth with a light splashing of mud. She caught a few glimpses of him heading up the incline towards where Tsata had pointed, and then he was swallowed.

She brushed her sodden fringe back and threw off her hood, suddenly feeling enclosed by it. The warm rain splashed eagerly onto her head and dribbled through to wet her scalp.

When she looked around, Tsata was gone.

The jolt of alarm woke her savagely out of her torpor. Her earlier fatalism was chased away. She drew a breath to call out for her companions, but it died in her lungs. Shouting would be a foolish thing to do.

Hurriedly, she scrambled her rifle off her back and into her arms. The lack of visibility terrified her; she would not have time to react against an attack. She had barely survived when she was out in the open back at the Aith Pthakath, and now she did not even have her *kana* as protection: she was too exhausted to open the Weave.

The pounding rain and constant, disharmonious sounds of running or dripping water masked all but the loudest noises. She blinked and wiped her eyes, glancing around in agitation.

They would be back. Any moment, they would be back, and she would be angry at the way they had deserted her with barely a warning. A branch fell behind her, and she started and whirled, narrowly missing tangling her rifle in a hanging vine. Staring intently into the rain-mist, she looked for movement.

Her sword would be better at close quarters like this, but she had never been much of a swordswoman. Most of the training she had received had built on her natural skills, learned from her constant competition with her older brother back in the Forest of Yuna. They would fight to outride, outshoot, outwrestle each other, for she always was the tomboy; but swords were never a favourite of either of them, and too dangerous to spar with. The rifle was impractical here, but it was comforting. She shifted her grip on the underside of the weapon and scanned the trees.

Time passed, drawing out slowly. They did not come back. Kaiku felt a cold dread creeping along her bones. The effort of waiting here, so exposed, was too much for her. She needed to know what was happening.

Her eyes fell again on the grey shadow that Tsata had pointed out. It still had not moved. She thought on his earlier words. *Who is that?* What did he mean?

Action, any action, was better than cowering in the rain. Even crossing the small distance that would bring her close enough to that half-obscured blot to see what it was. With one last look around, she began to tread warily up the incline, her boots sinking into the mud as she went, rivulets of water diverting to fill up the holes that she left.

The leather wrapped around the powder chamber of her rifle was sodden on the outside. She hoped that none of it had got in to wet the powder, or her rifle would be merely an expensive club. She wiped her hair away with her palm and cursed as it flopped back into her eyes. Her heart was pounding in her chest so hard that she felt her breastbone twitch with each pulse.

The grey shadow resolved all of a sudden, a gust of wind blowing the rain aside like a curtain parting with theatrical flair. It was revealed for only an instant, but that instant was enough for the image to burn itself into Kaiku's mind. Now she understood.

Who is that?

It was the guide, lashed by vines in a bundle as if she had been cocooned by a spider. She hung from the stout lower boughs of an enormous chapapa tree. Her head lolled forward, eyes staring sightlessly down, the arrow still buried in her throat. Her arms and legs were wrapped tight together, and she swayed with the sporadic assault of the rain.

Kaiku felt new panic clutch at her. The maghkriin had left it as a message. Not only that, it had predicted exactly the route its prey would take and got ahead of them. She stumbled back from the horror, slid a few inches in the dirt. Intuition screamed at her.

A maghkriin was here. Now.

It came at her from the left, covering the ground between them in the time it took her to turn her head. The world seemed to slow around her, the raindrops decelerating, her heartbeat deepening to a bass explosion. She was wrenching her rifle up, but she knew even before she began that there was no way she would get the muzzle in between her and the creature. She caught only a sharp impression of red and blackened skin, one blind eye and flailing ropes of hair; then she saw a hooked blade sweeping in to take out her throat, and there was nothing in the world she could do about it in time.

Blood hammered her face as she felt the impact, the maghkriin smashing into her and bearing her to the ground in a blaze of pain and white shock. She could not breathe, could not breathe

– drowning, like before, like in the sewers and a filthy, rotted hand holding her under –

because the air would not get to her lungs, and there was the taste of her own blood in her mouth, blood in her eyes blinding her, blood everywhere

– spirits, she couldn't breathe, couldn't breathe because her throat had been opened, hacked like a fish, her throat! –

Then movement, all around her. Saran, Tsata, pulling the weight off her chest, wrenching away the limp corpse of her attacker. She gasped in a breath, sweet, miraculous air pouring into her lungs in great whoops. Her hand went to her neck, and found it blood-slick but whole. She was being pulled roughly up out of the mud, the rain already washing the gore from her skin and into her clothes.

'Are you hurt?' Saran cried, agitated. 'Are you hurt?'

Kaiku held up a hand shakily to indicate that he should wait a moment. She was badly winded. Her eyes strayed to the muscular monstrosity that lay face-down and half-sunk in the wet earth.

'Look at me!' Saran snapped, grabbing her jaw and pulling her face around roughly. 'Are you *hurt?*' he demanded again, frantic.

She slapped his arm away, suddenly angry at being manhandled. She still did not have enough breath in her to form words. Palm to her chest, she bent over and allowed the normal airflow to return to her lungs.

'She is not hurt,' Tsata said, but whether it came out accusatory, relieved or matter-of-fact was lost amid his inexperience at the language.

'I am . . . not hurt,' Kaiku gasped, glaring at Saran. He hesitated for a moment, then retreated from her, seemingly perturbed at himself.

Tsata reached down into the mud and hauled the maghkriin over onto its back. This one was more humanoid than the last, its clothing burned away in rags to reveal a lithe body slabbed with lean muscle beneath ruddy, tough skin. Only its face was bestial: what of it there was left, anyway. One side was charred and blistered by fire; the other had splintered into bloody pulp by a rifle ball. In between the damage were crooked yellow teeth and a flat nose, and its hair was not hair at all but thin, fleshy tentacles that hung flaccid from its scalp.

Kaiku looked away.

'It was the one that you burned,' said Tsata. 'No wonder it was slow.'

'You shot it?' Kaiku asked numbly, trying to make sense of the confusion. Had he said it was *slow?* The pounding rain had cleansed the blood from her face now, but pink rivulets still raced from her sodden hair. Mud clung to her back and arms and legs. She didn't notice.

Tsata tilted his chin up. It took a moment for Kaiku to remember that this was a nod.

'You left me,' she said suddenly, looking from one to the other. 'You both left me, and you knew that thing was out there!'

'I left you with Tsata!' Saran protested, glaring at the Tkiurathi, who returned with a cool green stare, his tattooed features calm beneath his hood.

'It made sense,' Tsata said. 'The maghkriin would have hunted for you, Saran, as you went away alone. But if we were *all* alone, it would choose the most dangerous or the most defenceless prey first. That was her, on both counts.'

'You used me as *bait?*' Kaiku cried.

'I was hidden, watching you. The maghkriin did not suspect that we would willingly endanger one of our own.'

'You could have missed!' Kaiku shouted. 'It could have killed me!'

'But it did not,' Tsata said, seemingly unable to comprehend why she was angry.

Kaiku glared in disbelief at Tsata, then at Saran, who merely held up his hands to disavow any knowledge or responsibility.

'Is this some Okhamban kind of logic?' she snapped, her face flushed. She could not believe anyone would casually gamble with her life that way. 'Some spirit-cursed primitive matter of *pash?* To sacrifice the individual for the good of the group?'

Tsata looked surprised. 'Exactly that,' he said. 'You are quick to learn our ways.'

'The gods damn your ways,' she spat, and pulled her hood up over her head. 'It cannot be far now to Kisanth. We should go.'

The remainder of the journey was undertaken in silence. Though Saran's and Tsata's alertness had not diminished in the slightest, the danger seemed to have passed now, at least for Kaiku, who nursed her fury all the way to Kisanth. When they emerged again from the jungle it was in front of Zanya's prayer gate. The sight of the pillars brought a flood of relief and weariness over Kaiku. She walked slowly over to it and gave her thanks for a safe return as ritual dictated. When she was done, she saw that Saran was doing so as well.

'I thought you of Quraal did not give credit to our heathen deities,' she said.

'We need all the deities we can get now,' he replied darkly, and Kaiku wondered if he was serious or making fun of her. She stepped through the gate and stalked onward toward the stockade wall of Kisanth, and he followed.

Five

Axekami, heart of the empire, basked in the heat of late summer. The great city sat astride the confluence of two rivers as they merged into a third, a junction through which most of the trade in north-western Saramyr passed. The Jabaza and the Kerryn came winding their ways across the vast yellow-green plains from the north and east to enter the sprawling, walled capital, carving it up into neat and distinct districts. They met in the centre of Axekami, in the Rush, swirling around a hexagonal platform of stone that was linked across the churning water by three elegant, curving and equidistant bridges. In the middle stood a colossal statue of Isisya, Empress of the gods and goddess of peace, beauty and wisdom. Saramyr tradition tended to depict their deities obliquely rather than directly – as votive objects, or as animal aspects – believing it somewhat arrogant to try to capture the form of divine beings. But here tradition had been ignored, and Isisya had been rendered in dark blue stone as a woman, fifty feet high, robed in finery and wearing an elaborate sequence of ornaments in her tortuously complicated hair. She was gazing to the north-east, towards the Imperial Keep, her expression serene, her hands held together and buried in her voluminous sleeves. Beneath her feet, in the Rush, the Jabaza and the Kerryn mixed and mingled and became the Zan, an immense flow that pushed its way out of the city and headed away in a great sparkling ribbon to the south-west.

As the political and economical centre of Saramyr, Axekami was an unceasing hive of activity. The waterside was lined with docks and warehouses, and swarmed with nomads, merchants, sailors and labourers. On the south bank of the Kerryn, the colourful chaos of smoke-dens, cathouses, shops and bars that crowded the archipelago of the River District were trafficked by outrageously-dressed revellers. To the north, where the land sloped upward towards the Imperial Keep, gaudy temples crowded against serene library domes. Public squares thronged with people while orators and demagogues expounded their beliefs to passers-by, horses crabstepped between creaking carts and lumbering manxthwa in the choked thoroughfares of the Market District, while beneath their bright awnings traders hawked all the goods of the Near World. From the sweat and dust of the roads it was possible to escape to one of the many public parks, to enjoy a luxurious steam bath or visit one of a dozen sculpture gardens, some of them dating from the time of Torus tu Vinaxis, the second Blood Emperor of Saramyr.

North of the Market District, the Imperial Quarter lay around the base of the bluff which topped the hill, surmounted by the Imperial Keep itself. The Quarter was a small town in itself, inhabited by the high families, the independently wealthy and patrons of the arts, kept free from the crush and press of the rest of the city. There, the wide streets were lined with exotic trees and kept scrupulously clean, and spacious townhouses sat within walled compounds amid mosaic-strewn plazas and shady cloisters. Ruthlessly tended water gardens and leafy arbours provided endless secret places for the machinations of court to be played out in.

Then there was the Keep itself. Sitting atop the bluff, its gold and bronze exterior sent blades of reflected sunlight out across the city. It was shaped like a truncated pyramid, its top flattened, with the grand dome of the Imperial family's temple to Ocha rising in the centre to symbolise that no human, even an Emperor, was higher than the gods. The four sloping walls of the Keep were an eye-straining complexity of window-arches, balconies and sculptures, a masterwork of intertwined statues and architecture unequalled anywhere in Axekami. Spirits and demons chased their way around pillars and threaded into and out of scenes of legend inhabited by deities from the Saramyr pantheon. At each of the vertices of the Keep stood a tall, narrow tower. The whole magnificent edifice was surrounded by a massive wall, no less fine in appearance but bristling with fortifications, broken only by an enorm-ous gate set beneath a soaring arch of gold inscribed with ancient blessings.

Inside the Keep, the Blood Emperor of Saramyr, Mos tu Batik, glowered at his reflection in a freestanding wrought-silver mirror. He was a stocky man, a few inches shorter than his width would suggest, which made him barrel-chested and solid in appearance. His jaw was clenched in barely suppressed frustration beneath a bristly beard that was shot through with grey. With terse, angry movements, he arranged his ceremonial finery, tugging his cuffs and adjusting his belt. The afternoon sun angled through a pair of window-arches into the chamber behind him, two tight beams illuminating bright dancing motes. Usually the effect was pleasing, but today the contrast just made the rest of the room seem dim and full of hot shadows.

'You should compose yourself,' creaked a voice from the back of the room. 'Your agitation is obvious.'

'Spirits, Kakre, of course I'm agitated!' Mos snapped, shifting his gaze in the mirror to where a hunched figure was moving slowly into the light from the darkness in the corner of the room. He wore a patchwork robe of rags, leather and other less easily identifiable materials, sewn together in a haphazard mockery of pattern and logic, with stitchwork like scarring tracking randomly across the folds. Buried beneath a frayed hood, the sun cut sharply across the lower half of an emaciated jaw that did not move when he spoke. The Emperor's own Weaver, the Weave-lord.

'It would not do to meet your brother-by-marriage in this condition,' Kakre continued. 'You would cause him offence.'

Mos barked a bitter laugh. 'Reki? I don't care what that bookish little whelp thinks.' He spun away from the mirror and faced the Weave-lord. 'You know of the reports I received, I assume?'

Kakre raised his head, and the radiance of Nuki's eye fell across the face beneath the hood. The True Mask of Weave-lord Kakre was that of a gaping, mummified corpse, a hollow-cheeked visage of cured skin that stretched dry and pallid over his features. Mos had found his predecessor unpleasant enough, but Kakre was worse. He would never be able to look at the Weave-lord without a flinch of distaste.

'I know of the reports,' Kakre said, his voice a dry rasp.

'Yes, I thought you would,' Mos said poisonously. 'Very little goes on in this Keep without you finding out about it, Kakre; even when it's not your concern.'

'Everything is my concern,' Kakre returned.

'Really? Then why don't you concern yourself with finding out why my crops fail year after year? Why don't you do something to stop the blight that creeps through the soil of my empire, that causes babies to be born Aberrant, that twists the trees and makes it dangerous for my men to travel near the mountains because the gods know what kind of monstrosities lurk there now?' Mos stamped across to where a table held a carafe of wine and poured himself a generous glassful. 'It's almost Aestival Week! Unless the goddess Enyu herself steps in and lends us a hand, this year is going to be worse than the last one. We're on the edge of famine, Kakre! Some of the more distant provinces have been rationing the peasants for too long already! I *needed* this crop to hold out against the damned merchant consortium in Okhamba!'

'Your people starve because of *you*, Mos,' Kakre replied venomously. 'Do not apportion blame to the Weavers for your own mistakes. You started the trade war when you raised export taxes.'

'What would you have preferred?' he cried. 'That I allowed our economy to collapse?'

'I care little for your justifications,' Kakre said. 'The fact remains that it was your fault.'

He drained the glass and glared balefully at the Weave-lord. 'We took this throne *together*,' he snarled. 'It cost me my only son, but we took it. I fulfilled my part of the deal. I've made you part of the empire. I gave you land, I gave you *rights*. That was my half of our agreement. Where is yours?'

'We have kept you on your throne!' Kakre replied, his voice rising in fury. 'Without us, your ineptitude would have seen you deposed by now. Do you remember how many insurrections I have warned you of, how many plots and assassination attempts I have unearthed for you? Five years of failing harvests, crumbling markets, political disarray; the high families will not suffer it.' Kakre's voice fell to a quiet mutter. 'They want you gone, Mos. You and me.'

'It's *because* of the failed harvests that this whole damned mess has come about!' Mos cried, choking on his frustration. 'It's this spirit-cursed blight! Where is the source? What is the cause? *Why don't you know?*'

'The Weavers are not all-powerful, my Emperor,' croaked Kakre softly, turning away. 'If we were, we should not need you.'

'There he is!' grinned the Empress Laranya, slipping away from her fussing handmaidens and hurrying across the small chamber to where Mos had just entered. She swept into the Emperor's arms and kissed him playfully, then withdrew and smoothed his hair back from his face, her eyes roaming his.

'You look angry,' she said. 'Is anything wrong?' She smiled suddenly. 'Anything that I could not fix, anyway?'

Mos felt his bad mood evaporate in the arms of his lover, and he bent to kiss her again, with feeling this time. 'There's nothing that you couldn't fix with that smile,' he murmured.

'Flatterer!' she accused, darting out of his grasp with a flirtatious twist. 'You're late. And your clumsy paws have ruffled my dress. Now my handmaidens will have to put it right. Everything must be in order in time to receive my brother.'

'My apologies, Empress,' he said, bowing low with mock sincerity. 'I had no idea that today was such an important day for you.'

She gasped in feigned disbelief. 'Men are so ignorant.'

'Well, if I'm going to be insulted so, I may go back to my chambers and get out of your way,' Mos teased.

'You will stay here and make ready with me!' she told him. 'That is, if you still want to have an Empress by tomorrow.'

Mos acceded graciously, taking his place by his wife and allowing his own handmaidens to see to his appearance. They began spraying him with perfumed oils and affixing the paraphernalia that tradition demanded of his station. He endured it all with a lighter heart than before.

The pomp and ceremony involved in being Blood Emperor taxed his patience at the best of times; he was a blunt man, not given to subtlety and with little time for ritual and age-old tradition. The process of welcoming an important guest for an extended stay was complex and layered in many levels of politeness and formality, depending on the status of the guest in relation to the Imperial family. Too little preparation, and the guest might be offended; too over-blown, and they would be embarrassed. Mos wisely left all such matters to his advisers and latterly to his new wife.

The chamber around him was aswarm with retainers clad in their finest robes, Imperial Guards in white and blue armour, servants carrying pennants and elegant courtesans tuning their instruments. Handmaidens ran to and fro, and Mos's Cultural Adviser sent runners here and there to fetch forgotten necessities and make last-minute adjustments. The entrance hall was only the surface gloss to the entire operation. Later, there would be theatre, poetry, music and a myriad other entertainments that were all but interminable to a man of Mos's earthy tastes. Only the feast that would signal the end of the ceremony held any interest for him at all. But despite his own feelings about their visitor, this was Laranya's brother, to whom she was very close, and what made her happy made him happy. He steeled himself and resolved to make an effort.

As the final touches were being made to his outfit, he stole glances at Laranya, who pretended not to notice. How strange the ways of the gods, that they should have brought him a creature as fine as her at this time in his life, approaching his fifty-fifth harvest. Surely divine approval for his assumption of the role of Blood Emperor. Or, he reflected with a twinge of his former black mood, perhaps it was merely redressing the balance for taking his son Durun from him.

It had begun as a simple matter of politics. With his only heir dead and Blood Batik as the high family, Mos needed a child. His first wife, Ononi, was past child-bearing age, so Mos annulled his marriage with her and sought a younger bride. There was no acrimony on either side, since there had been no passion there in the first place; it had been a marriage of mutual advantage, as were most amid the high families of Saramyr. Ononi remained to oversee the Blood Batik estates to the north, while Mos moved into the capital and began to look for potential matches.

He found one in Laranya tu Tanatsua, daughter of Barak Goren of Jospa, a city in the Tchom Rin desert. Forging ties with the eastern half of Saramyr was a sensible move, especially when the mountains that divided them were becoming ever more treacherous to cross and increasingly the only way to communicate between the west and the east was through Weavers. Laranya was eminently eligible and beautiful with it, dark-haired and dusky-skinned, curvaceous and fiery. Mos had liked her immediately, better than the slender, demure and subservient women he had been offered up until then. In a move of outrageous audacity, Laranya had made him come to her, had made him travel all the way to Jospa to assess her suitability for marriage. Even when he had done so, intrigued by her brazen nerve, she had acted as if it were *she* choosing *him* for a suitor, much to her father's chagrin.

Perhaps it was then that she had captured his heart. She had certainly captured his attention. He took her back with him to Axekami, and they were married amid great ceremony and celebration. That was three years ago, and at some point over the intervening time he had fallen in love with her, and she with him. It was unusual, but not unheard of. That she was over twenty harvests his junior was not an issue. Both of them were stubborn, passionate and used to getting their own way; in each other, they met their match. Though their arguments were legendary among the servants of the Keep for their violence, so their affection for each other was immeasureable and obvious. Despite the misfortune that had dogged every step of his way as Blood Emperor, he felt blessed to have her.

There had been only one shadow over their marriage these past years, and the root of most of their fights. Though the physical attraction between them made for energetic and frequent bedplay, no child had come of it. Laranya wanted nothing more than to bear him a son, but she could not conceive, and the bitterness and frustration began to pool like oil beneath their words over time. Unlike his son Durun – who had gone through the same ordeal with his own wife, the murdered former Blood Empress Anais tu Erinima – Mos knew that he was not barren of seed. Yet he knew also that an heir was needed, and Laranya would not graciously step aside as Ononi had to allow him to remarry again. Even if he had wanted to.

Then, miraculously, it had happened. Two weeks ago, she had told him the news. She was pregnant. He saw it already in her manner, the new flush to her cheeks, the secret smiles she kept to herself when she thought he was not looking. Her world had turned inward, to the child in her womb, and Mos was at once mystified and entranced by her. Even now, though she was far from showing her condition, he watched her unconsciously lay a hand on her pelvis, her eyes distant while the handmaidens chattered and worked around her. His child. The thought brought a fierce and sudden grin to his face.

He straightened himself as a horn lowed outside the Keep, and the handmaidens scattered, leaving the Emperor and Empress standing on a low platform at the top of a set of three steps, facing down an aisle of immaculately presented retainers and Guards. The hall whispered with the shuffle of people arranging themselves in their places. The red-and-silver pennants of Blood Batik rippled softly in the hot breeze from the window-arches above the gold-inlaid double doors. Reki had arrived.

Laranya took Mos's hand briefly and smiled up at him, then let it drop to assume the correct posture. The Blood Emperor's heart warmed until it was like a furnace. He thought of the gruelling day ahead, and then of the life growing in his wife's belly.

He was to be a father again, he thought, as the double doors swung open and let in the blazing light from outside, silhouetting the slight form of Laranya's brother at the head of his retinue. For that, he would endure anything.

The coals in the fire-pit at the centre of Kakre's skinning chamber bathed the room in arterial red. Deep, insidious shadows lay all around, cast by the steady glow. At the Weave-lord's insistence, the walls had been stripped down to naked stone and the black, semi-reflective *lach* chiselled away from the floor to reveal the gullied, rough bricks beneath. Overhead, the octagonal chamber rose high above in a lattice of wooden beams, its upper reaches lost in darkness. Chains and hooks hung from there, appearing out of the lofty shadows and hanging down to the level of the floor, where they brushed this way and that in the rising warmth, quietly clinking.

Strange shapes swayed gently between the beams, half-seen things turning slowly and silently. Some of them were hung close enough to the firelight to make out details, underlit in glowering red. Kites of skin, human and animal, stretched across wicker frameworks of terrible ingenuity. Some were mercifully unrecognisable, simple geometric shapes from which it was difficult to determine the donor of the material that surfaced them. Others were more grotesque and artistic. There was a large bird stitched from the skin of a woman; distorted, empty features were still appallingly identifiable over the head and beak, hollow breasts pulled flat between the outspread wings, long black hair still spilling from her scalp. Something that had once been a man hung in a predatory pose, outstretched bat-wings of human skin spread behind him and his face constructed of sewn-together strips of snake scales. A mobile of small animals rotated next to him, each one skilfully peeled on the left side of its front half and the right side of its rear, particoloured sculptures of fur and glistening striations of muscle.

Closer to hand, placed on the walls like trophies, were works in progress or pieces that Kakre was particularly fond of. Black pits that were once eye sockets stared blindly across the chamber from wicker skulls. No matter how changed the form of the being, it was impossible to forget where that dry, stretched surface had been robbed from, and each horror was magnified by the memory. An iron rack stood near the firepit, diabolical in its craftsmanship, capable of being adapted to suit any type of body shape and any size. The stones beneath it were dyed a deep, rusty brown.

Kakre sat cross-legged by the fire-pit, a ragged heap of clothes with a dead face, and Weaved.

He was a ray: a flat, winged shape, infinitesimal in an undulating world of black. He hung in the darkness, rippling slightly, making the tiny adjustments necessary to maintain his position while he probed out along the currents in search of his route. Above and below him and to either side were whorls and eddies, riptides and channels, currents that he could only feel and not see, a violent, lethal churning that could pick him up and dash him apart. He sensed the vast and distant leviathans that haunted the periphery of his senses, the inexplicable denizens of the Weave.

He was blind here in this sightless place, but the water rushed around and through him, over his cold skin and into his mouth, out past his gills or down to his stomach, diffusing into his blood. In his mind, he saw how the currents twisted and corkscrewed and curled in ways impossible for water or wind, tracing each one to where it intersected another, junctions in the chaotic void.

In an instant he had plotted a route of staggering mathematical complexity, a three-dimensional tunnel of currents that flowed in his favour, leading him to where he had to go in the shortest time and with the least effort. Not that physical distance had any bearing in the world of the Weave, but it was a human trait to impose order on the orderless, and this was Kakre's way of understanding a process that could not be understood.

The raw stuff of the Weave was too much for a man's sanity to bear, too alluring and enticing. A proportion of apprentice Weavers were lost every year to the terrifying ecstasy of being opened to the bright fabric of creation, the sheer and overwhelming beauty of it. It was a narcotic beyond anything that the organic world could provide, and in that first rush only the strongest were resilient enough to avoid being swept away, lost to the Weave, mindless phantoms blissfully wandering the stitchwork of the universe while their vacated bodies became vegetative. Weavers were taught from the very first to visualise the Weave in a way that they could cope with. Some thought of it as an endless series of spider's webs; some as a pulsing mass of branching bronchioli; some as a building of impossible dimensions in which any door could lead to any other; some a sequential dream-story in which the process of getting from the start to the finish mirrored the effect that their Weaving was intended to accomplish.

Kakre found it most accommodating like this. More fluid, more dynamic, and never once letting him forget how dangerous the Weave was. Even now, after so many years, he found himself having to rattle hypnotic mantras around in the back of his mind to ward off the constantly encroaching sense of wonder and awe at his surroundings. He knew well that such feelings were merely a sly route to the addiction that would follow if he relaxed his self-control, and once lost he would never be regained.

Now he had the route mapped in his consciousness, and with a tilt of his wings he dropped down into the current beneath him. It threw him forward with a breathless rush, accelerating faster than thought, swifter than instinct. Into a cross-current he dived, riding the maelstrom smoothly, and was flung out again at even greater velocity. Now switching again, more cross-currents, dozens of them coming so rapidly that they were virtually continuous. He was flicking like a spark through the synapses of the human brain, seeing every ebb and flow and countering or riding them with exhilarating grace, quicker and quicker until—

—the world blossomed outwards, sight returning to him, crude human senses replacing the infinitely more subtle ones employed in the Weave. A room; a room built with uneven walls, lines measured by an idiot's hand in a mockery of symmetry. Thin needles of sculpted rock broke through the floor like stalagmites, a forest of strange obelisks marked in nonsense-language. Lamps rested in sconces, some new and burning sullenly, some cold and webbed over. It was dark and shadowy and steeped in an ancient awareness that bled from the walls. He felt the shift and stir of the abominations that haunted the mines far beneath. He sensed the strange delirium of the other Weavers. Here at Adderach, mountain monastery, stronghold and founding-place of the Weavers, the colossal singularity of purpose that united all the wearers of the True Masks resonated more powerfully than ever.

He was a ghost in the chamber, hanging in the air, a hunched and blurred comma. Only his Mask appeared in sharp focus; the hood and rags that surrounded it became progressively less clear with distance. Three other Weavers stood before him, a random trio whom he had never met before. All wore their heavy patchwork robes, their clothing made unique by the lack of rhyme or reason in its construction. They had responded to his summons and awaited him here. They would listen, and advise, with the voice of the entity that was the Weavers, the guiding gestalt presence that even the Weavers themselves, in their insanity, could not identify. These three would then disseminate what information he had to give across the network.

It was time to set things in motion.

'Weave-lord Kakre,' began one them, who wore a Mask of leather and bone. 'We must know of the Emperor and his actions.'

'Then I have much to tell you,' Kakre said hoarsely, his ruined throat making his voice raw and flayed.

'The harvest fails again,' said the second of the trio, whose face was shaped from thin iron, in the shape of a snarling demon. 'Famine will strike. How do we stand?'

'The Blood Emperor Mos loses patience,' Kakre replied. 'He is frustrated at our lack of progress in stopping the blight that twists his crops. He still has no inkling that it is we who are *causing* it. I had hoped that the harvest would hold for longer than this, but it seems the change in the land is more rapid than even we had guessed.'

'This is grave,' said the first Weaver.

'We cannot disguise this,' Kakre said. 'The damage is becoming too pronounced to ignore, and too obvious to hide. Several have already traced the blight to its source; more do so with each passing year. We cannot continue to silence them all. Questions are being asked, and by people that we do not dare to coerce.' Kakre shifted in the air, blurring in and out of focus.

'If it were known that the famine is our doing, it would be the excuse that all Saramyr has been waiting for to destroy us,' said the Weaver with the iron Mask.

'Could they? Could they destroy us?' demanded the first.

'Unlikely,' Kakre croaked. 'Five years ago, maybe.'

'You are overconfident, Kakre,' whispered the third Weaver, wearing an exquisite wooden Mask with an expression of terrific sadness. 'What of the Heir-Empress? What of the presence that Vyrrch warned us of, the *woman* that could play the Weave? You have not found either, in five years of searching.'

'There is no indication the Heir-Empress is alive at all,' Kakre replied slowly, his words crossing the Weave and arriving as a sonorous echo. 'There remains the possibility that she perished in the Imperial Keep and was burned. She may have died after she escaped. I am under no illusion as to how dangerous she is, but she is considerably less dangerous now that we have disposed of her mother and she no longer stands to inherit the throne.'

'She is still a rallying point for discontent,' argued the first and most vocal Weaver. 'And the people may even prefer an Aberrant on the throne to Mos when the famine begins to bite.'

'We would not allow that,' Kakre said calmly. 'The Heir-Empress, and the woman that beat the Weave-lord Vyrrch, are dangers that we can do nothing about now, and unquantifiable. They have evaded our best attempts to find them. Put these matters aside. We must decide what to do *now*.'

'Then what do you propose?' murmured the third Weaver.

Kakre's ghost-image turned to face the one who had spoken. 'We cannot afford to wait any longer. We must embark upon our schemes in earnest. Mos's unpopularity will bring civil war again, and we cannot stand with him without revealing our hand. That we will not do. He has served his purpose; he is worthless to us now.'

There was a murmur of agreement from those assembled.

'Mos's time as Blood Emperor is becoming short,' Kakre continued. 'Blood Kerestyn are rebuilding their forces, and forming secret alliances with the other high families. The people stir in discontent, and superstition is rife. Some believe that the Weavers should never have been given power, that the gods have cursed the land because of it. It is a movement that is gaining much sympathy in the rural areas beyond the cities.' He swept them all with his gaze. 'We must see to our own survival.'

'You have a plan, then?' prompted the bone-and-leather Mask.

'Oh, indeed,' replied Kakre.

Six

Screams.

Lan hadn't imagined anything so awful could emerge from a human throat, never believed that such a naked shriek of animal terror could be made by an intelligent being. Never dreamed he would be hearing it from his own mother.

It was a perfect day, the occasional sparse train of tiny, puffy clouds freckling what was otherwise a clear blue sky, blending to a turquoise hue near the horizon. The *Pelaska* lazed down the centre of the Kerryn, the huge paddle-wheels at either side idle while the current took the lumbering barge westward from the Tchamil Mountains, heading towards Axekami. They were ahead of schedule, perhaps a half-day east of the fork where the river split and its southward channel became the Rahn, flowing into the wilds of the Xarana Fault. It had begun to seem that nothing would go wrong.

The journey had been a nervous one. Lan had wanted to beg his father not to take the Weaver and his cargo, but he would have been wasting his breath. They had no choice.

And now his mother was screaming.

They had been moored up in the tiny town of Jiji, at the feet of the mountains, loading in metals and ores and surplus equipment from the mines to deliver to Axekami. It was their bad luck that theirs was the only barge there with sufficient capacity for the Weaver's needs.

The Weavers ran their own fleet of barges, which plied the rivers of western Axekami and were viewed with mistrust by all. The barge-masters were cold-eyed, taciturn and strange, and tales circulated up and down the waterways about these damned men who had made pacts with the Weavers in return for riches and power. Exactly where the riches and power came from was unclear: the barges hardly turned a profit, trading enough only to cover their operating costs. For the rest of the time, they passed silently by the ports and rarely docked, running secret errands of their own.

The Weaver commandeered the craft and crew and demanded passage, declaring that he had an urgent delivery to make and that none of the Weavers' own barges were near. Lan's father, Pori, accepted his fate stoically. Their patron would be furious at having one of his barges commandeered; but being of the peasant class, the barge-folk's lives were a Weaver's to command, or to take.

Lan was terrified of their new passenger. Like most people of Saramyr, he had attended the sporadic gatherings that occurred throughout his childhood when a Weaver arrived in town to preach. The fascination never waned. These strange, fearful, enigmatic men, hidden behind their grotesquely beautiful Masks and clothed in patchwork furs and fabrics, were a sight to see. They talked of Aberrants: evil, deformed monstrosities that desired to subvert the Saramyr way. Aberrants came in many guises. Some wore their deformities on the outside, twisted or crooked, limbless or lame. Others were more subtle and hence more dangerous: those who looked like normal people, but who harboured within them strange and terrible powers. The Weavers taught them how to recognise the taint and what to do when they found it. Execution was the most lenient of recommendations.

Root out the evil, the Weavers urged. Let nothing stop you. Aberrants are a corruption of humanity. It was a message that had been repeated for generations now, and was as ingrained in the Saramyr consciousness as the virtues of tradition and duty that underpinned their society.

But in those gatherings Lan had been one of a crowd, safe in their numbers, able to leave whenever he chose. There had been tales told of the Weavers' terrible appetites, but nobody was sure how much was truth and how much fancy. There was a shiver of danger about them, but nothing more.

Now, however, they were forced to live with a Weaver for at least a week, maybe longer, for they had no idea where their passenger wanted to go and he would not tell them beyond an indication that they were heading downriver. A week spent in fear of some insane whim or demand, trapped within the confines of the barge, avoiding the blank gaze of that dry grey sealskin Mask with its puckered eyes and sewn-up mouth.

And if the Weaver were not bad enough, there was the question of the cargo that he would bring aboard. Instead of loading up at Jiji, they had been informed that they would be stopping along the way. Pori asked where, and had been backhanded across the face for his trouble.

They were forced to set off immediately. Thankfully they already had most of their own goods loaded, mainly barrels of surplus ignition powder from the mines, where it was used for blasting. They were selling it back to the city, where the civil unrest was pushing prices of firearms and powder up as demand increased. The trip might not be entirely wasted; if the Weaver were agreeable they could stop in Axekami to deliver it and fulfil their contract. But then, they had no idea how much space this mysterious new cargo would take up, nor whether they might have to throw out some of their own en route to accommodate it.

The Weaver took the cabin that belonged to Pori and his wife Fuira. That was to be expected; it was the best. Pori was the master of the *Pelaska*. They moved without complaint to the crew's quarters, where Lan slept along with the bargemen and wheelmen. Lan might have been the master's son, but when they were on the river he was no more than another barge-boy, and he swabbed decks with the rest of them.

The first night they were underway, the Weaver brought them to a stop on the port side of the river and made them moor up against the bank. There was nothing there but the trees of the Forest of Yuna crowding in, with the Kerryn carving a trail through what was otherwise a dense wall of undergrowth and foliage. The night was dark, with only one moon riding in the sky, and the current was treacherous there. By the pale green light of Neryn, they managed to secure the craft against the bank with ropes and anchors, and lower a gangplank. When they were done, they glanced at each other and wondered what was in store for them next.

They were not left to wonder long. The Weaver ordered them all below decks, into the crew quarters, and locked them in there.

Lan listened to the griping of the sailors in breathless silence while his father and mother sat calmly next to him on a bunk. Their curses and anger were practically blasphemous. He could not believe they dared to criticise a Weaver; nor did he think it was safe to do so, even out of their target's earshot. But they went on damning the name of the Weavers, pacing their cramped quarters like caged animals. They might have been bound by law and duty to do as the Weaver said, but they did not have to like it. Lan cringed, half-expecting some indefinable retribution to descend upon them; but all that happened was that his father leaned over to him and said softly: 'Remember this, Lan. Five years ago, men like these would not have dared say such things. Look how a mistreated man's anger can make him overcome his fears.'

Lan did not understand. Until this journey, the only thing on his mind had been the upcoming Aestival Week which would mark his fourteenth harvest. He had the sense that his father was imparting some grave wisdom to him, some instinct that told him the comment meant more than it appeared to. But he was only a barge-boy.

It was dawn when the Weaver released them. Most of the bargemen had gone to sleep by then. Those that had stayed awake had heard strange cries from the forest that had made them swear hurried oaths to the gods and make warding signs. The decks were too thick to hear the sounds of the cargo being loaded, but they had to presume that whatever was being put aboard had been brought out of the depths of the forest, and that there were more hands than the Weaver's alone at work. Yet when the lock clicked back and the men were released, there was only the Weaver on the deck, his grey mask impassive in the golden light of the newly rising sun. Despite their furious words of the previous night, the bargemen were less than belligerent as they emerged under the cold gaze of their sinister passenger. None of them dared to ask what had occurred the previous night, nor what kind of cargo now resided in the belly of the barge that was too secret to allow them to lay their eyes on it.

The Weaver took Pori aside and spoke to him, after which Pori addressed the crew, and told them what they had all been expecting. None of them would be allowed to go down to the cargo hold. It was locked, and the Weaver had the key. Anyone attempting to do so would be killed.

After that, the Weaver retreated to his cabin.

The next few days passed without incident. The Weaver stayed inside, seen only when his meals were delivered or his chamber pot was emptied. The sailors listened at the door of the hold and heard scrapes of movement inside, strange grunts and scuffles; but no one dared try to get in and see what was making them. They grumbled, aired their superstitions, and cast suspicious and fearful glances at the cabin where the Weaver had entrenched himself, but Pori hounded them all back to work. Lan was glad of it. Mopping the decks meant he could keep his mind off the baleful presence in his parents' bed and the secret cargo below decks. He found that by not thinking about them, he could pretend that they were not there. It was remarkably effective.

Nuki's eye shone benevolently down over the Kerryn with the pleasant heat of late summer. The air was alive with dancing clouds of midges. Pori walked the barge, ensuring everyone was doing his part. His mother Fuira cooked in the galley, occasionally emerging to share a few words with her husband or give Lan an embarrassing kiss on the cheek. Hookbeaks hovered over the water, floating in the sky on their smoothly curved wings, searching the flow for the silver glint of fish. As time drifted past in the slow wake of the *Pelaska*, it was almost possible to believe that this was a normal voyage again.

Not any more.

The Weaver must have grabbed her as she came to deliver his

midday meal. Pori had always been uncomfortable with his wife having any contact with the Weaver at all, but she had told him not to be silly. She handed out the meals to everyone else on the barge; it was her duty to feed their unwanted guest as well. Perhaps he had just finished Weaving, sending his secret messages or completing some other unfathomable task; Lan had heard that some Weavers became very violent and strange after they used their powers. He could imagine her standing there, ringing the brass chime for permission to enter, and the Weaver appearing, all fury and anger, dragging her inside. The Weaver was small and crooked as most of them were, but Fuira would not dare to fight and besides, they had ways to make people do as they wanted.

Then, the screams.

The cabin door was shut, and the bargemen were gathered around it in fear and impotent rage. Lan stood with them, trembling, his eyes fixed on the spilled tray of food on the deck. He wanted to get away from there, to dive off the side of the *Pelaska* and silence her cries in the dull roar underwater. He wanted to rush in and help her. Instead he was paralysed. Nobody could interfere. It would mean their lives.

So he listened to his mother's suffering, numb and detached from the reality of the situation, and did not dare to think what was being done to her in there.

'*No!*' came his father's voice from behind him, and there was a rush of movement as the bargemen hurried to restrain him. '*Fuira!*'

Lan turned and saw Pori in the midst of four men, who were pulling a rifle out of his grip. He was flailing and thrashing with the strength of the possessed, his face contorted in rage. The rifle was torn free and slid across the deck, and then suddenly there was a scrape of steel and the bargemen fell away from him, one of them swearing and clutching a long, bleeding cut on his forearm.

'*That's my wife!*' Pori screamed, spittle flying from his lips. A short, curved blade was in his hand. He glared at them all, his face a deep red, then he plunged through the crowd and shoved open the door of the cabin with a cry.

The door slammed shut behind him, through whether by his hand or some other force Lan never knew. He heard his father's shout of rage, and a moment later something heavy smashed into the inside of the door, splintering the thick wood. There was a beat of silence. Then a new scream from his mother, long, sustained, ragged at the edges. Blood began to seep through the cracks in the door, and crawled slowly down to drip onto the deck.

Lan stood where he was, immobile, as the Weaver went back to work on his mother. He was watching the slow, dreadful path of the blood. Disbelief and shock had settled in, hazing his mind. At some point, he turned and walked away. None of the bargemen noticed him go, nor did they notice him picking up his father's rifle on the way. He did not really know where he was heading, motivated only by some vague impulse that refused to cohere into a form he could understand. He was barely aware of moving at all until he found himself standing in front of the door to the cargo hold, hidden in the shade at the bottom of a set of wooden stairs, and he could go no further.

He raised his rifle and fired into the lock, blasting it to shards.

There was something in here, something that he was looking for, but whenever he tried to picture it he only saw that insidious blood, and his mother's face.

His father was dead. His mother was being . . . *violated.*

He was here for something, but what? It was too terrible to think about, so he didn't think.

The cargo hold was hot and dark and spacious. He knew from memory the dimensions of the place, how high the ribbed wooden ceiling went, how far back the bow wall lay. Crates and barrels were dim shadows nearby, lashed together with rope. Thin lines of sunlight where the tar had worn away on the deck above provided meagre illumination, but not enough to see by until his eyes had adjusted to the gloom from the blinding summer's day outside. Absently, he reprimed the bolt on his father's rifle, taking a step into the hold, searching. There were running footsteps overhead.

Something stirred.

Lan's eyes flickered to the source of the sound. He squinted into the gloom.

It moved then, a slow flexing that allowed him to pick out its shape. The blood drained from his face.

He staggered backward, holding his rifle defensively across its chest. There were *things* down here. As he watched, more of them began to creep from the shadows. They were making a soft trilling sound, like a flock of pigeons, but their predatory lope made them seem anything but benign, and they approached with a casually lethal gait.

Shouts behind him. Bargemen running down the steps to the hold, attracted by the sound of the rifle.

Fuira shrieked distantly, a forlorn wail of loss and agony and fear, and Lan suddenly recalled what he was here for.

Ignition powder. The cargo.

A tidy stack of barrels lay against the stern wall, by the door where the other bargemen had rushed into the hold. They scrambled to a halt, partially because they had remembered the Weaver's edict, mostly because they thought Lan's gun was levelled at them. The darkness made it hard to see. He was aiming at the barrels. Enough there to blast the *Pelaska* to flinders and leave barely a trace of any of them.

It was the only way to end his mother's suffering. The only way.

Behind him, there was the sound of dozens of creatures breaking into a run, and the trilling reached shrieking pitch in his ears.

He whispered a short prayer to Omecha, squeezed the trigger, and the world turned to flame.

Seven

The Xarana Fault lay far to the south of the Saramyr capital of Axekami, across a calm expanse of plains and gentle hills. In stark contrast to its approach, the Fault itself was a jagged, rucked chaos of valleys, plateaux, outcrops, canyons and steep-sided rock masses like miniature mountains. Sheer walls abutted sunken rivers; hidden glades nestled in cradles of sharp stones; the very ground was a shattered jigsaw which rose and fell to no apparent geological law. The Fault was a massive scar in the land, over two hundred and fifty miles from end to end and forty at its thickest point, cutting west to east and slanting slightly southwards on its way.

Legend had made it a cursed place, and there was more than a little truth in that. Once, the first Saramyr city of Gobinda had been built there, before a great destruction – said to be the wrath of Ocha in retribution for the pride of the third Blood Emperor Bizak tu Cho – had wiped it away. Restless things remembered that time, and still roamed the hollows and deeps of the Fault, preying on the unwary. It was shunned, at first as a symbol of Saramyr's shame but later as a place where lawlessness abounded, where only bandits and those foolhardy enough to brave the whispered terrors within would go.

But for some, the Fault was a haven. Dangerous though it was, there were those who were willing to learn its ways and make their home there. At first it was a place for criminals, who used it as a long-term base from which to raid the Great Spice Road to the west; but later, more people came, fleeing the world outside. Those under sentence of death, those whose temperament made them too alien to live among normal people, those who sought the deep riches exposed at the bottom of the Fault and were prepared to risk anything to get it. Settlements were founded, small at first but then becoming larger as they amalgamated or conquered others. Aberrants – who would be executed on sight in any lawful town – began to appear, looking for sanctuary from the Weavers who hunted them.

The home of the Libera Dramach was one such community. It was known to its inhabitants as the Fold, both to imply a sense of belonging and because of the valley in which the settlement was built. It was constructed across an overlapping series of plateaux and ledges that tumbled down the blunt western end of the valley, linked together by stairs, wooden bridges and pulley-lifts. The Fold cluttered and piled up on itself in a heap, a confusing mishmash of architecture from all over Saramyr, built by many hands and not all of them skilled. It was an accretion of dwellings raised over twenty-five years to no overarching plan or pattern; instead, newcomers had made their homes wherever they would fit, and in some cases they only barely did.

Off the dirt tracks that wound haphazardly across the uneven terrain, rickety storefronts sold whatever the merchants could get this far into the Fold. Bars peddled liquor from their own stills, smoke-houses offered amaxa root and other narcotics for those who could afford it. Dusky Tchom Rin children in their traditional desert garb walked alongside Newlandsmen from the far northeast; an Aberrant youth with mottled skin and yellow eyes like a hawk's kissed deeply with an elegant girl from the wealthy Southern Prefectures; a priest of Omecha knelt in a small and sheltered shrine to make an offering to his deity; a soldier walked the streets, lightly tapping the pommel of his sword, alert for any trouble.

Amid the immediate clutter of houses were the fortifications. Guard-towers and outposts rose above the crush. Walls had been built, their boundaries overrun by the growing town, and newer ones constructed further out. Fire-cannons looked east over the valley. On the rocky rim, which sheltered the Fold from prying eyes, a thick stockade hid between the pleats and dips of the land. In the Xarana Fault, danger was never very far away, and the people of the Fold had learned to defend themselves.

Lucia tu Erinima stood on the balcony of her guardian's house, on one of the uppermost levels of the town, and fed crumbs to tiny piping birds from her cupped hand. A pair of ravens, perched on the guttering of the building opposite, watched her with a careful eye. From within the house, sharing a brew of hot, bitter tea, Zaelis and Cailin watched her also.

'Gods, she's grown so much,' Zaelis sighed, turning away to face his companion.

Cailin smiled faintly, but the black-and-red pattern of alternating triangles on her lips made her look like a smirking predator. 'If I were a more cynical woman, I would think that you engineered the kidnapping of your erstwhile pupil all those years ago just so you could adopt her for yourself.'

'Ha!' he barked. 'You think I haven't been over *that* in my mind enough times?'

'And what did you decide?'

'That I worry far more since I became her surrogate father than I ever did in all the years since I started the Libera Dramach.'

'You have looked after them both admirably,' Cailin said, then took a sip from the small green tea-bowl in her hand.

Zaelis gave her a surprised look. 'That's unusually kind of you, Cailin,' he said.

'I am occasionally capable of being so.'

Zaelis turned his attention back to the balcony where Lucia stood. Once, she had been the heir to the Saramyr Empire. Now she was just a girl a few weeks from her fourteenth harvest, standing in the sun in a simple white dress, feeding birds. Her blonde hair, once long, was cut short and exposed the nape of her neck, from which terrible burn scars ran down her back. He wished she would grow her hair again; her scars were easy enough to conceal. But when he asked her she would only give him that fey, dreamy look of hers and ignore him. She was pretty as a child, and now that the bones of her face and body were lengthening it was already easy to see that she would be beautiful as a woman, with the same petite and deceptively naïve features that her mother had. But in those pale blue eyes there was a strangeness that made her unfathomable to him, to *anyone*. He had known her longer than anyone alive, but he still didn't know her.

'I worry also,' Cailin said eventually.

'About Lucia?'

'Among other things.'

'Then you mean her . . .' – Zaelis searched for a word with an expression of faint disgust – '*followers.*'

Cailin shook her head once, her black ponytails swinging gently with the movement. 'I will admit they are a problem. It is far harder to keep her secret from those who would harm her when rumour spreads from the mouths of those who would keep her safe. Yet they do not concern me overly, and they may eventually prove to serve a purpose.'

Zaelis sipped his tea meditatively and stole a glance at Lucia. Several of the birds were perched on the balcony rail now, looking at her like children attentive to a master. 'What troubles you, then?'

Cailin stirred and stood. At her full height, she was tall for a woman, and of deliberately fearsome appearance. Zaelis, from where he sat cross-legged on a mat by the low table, followed her up with his eyes. She walked a few paces across the room and stopped, looking away from him.

'We are short of time,' she said.

'You know this?' Zaelis asked.

Cailin hesitated, then made a negative noise. 'I feel it.'

Zaelis frowned. It was not like Cailin to be so indefinite with him. She was a practical woman, little given to flights of fancy. He waited for her to continue.

'I know how that sounds, Zaelis,' she snapped irritably, as if he had accused her. 'I wish I had more evidence to present you.'

He got up and stood with her, favouring one leg. His other was weak; it had been badly broken long ago and never quite healed. 'Tell me what you feel, then.'

'Things are building to a head,' Cailin replied after a short pause to marshal her thoughts. 'The Weavers have been too quiet these past years. What have they gained from their alliance with Mos? Think, Zaelis. What moves they had to make, they could have made directly after Mos took power. They had nobody to oppose them then. But what did they do instead?'

'They bought land. They bought land, and shipping companies on the rivers.'

'Legitimate enterprises,' Cailin said, throwing a slender hand up as if to dash the words away. 'And none that turn any kind of profit.' Her frustration was evident in her tone. The Libera Dramach had been unsuccessful at gaining any further information on the Weavers' curious purchases. The Weavers had defences that ordinary spies could not penetrate, and Cailin dared not use any of the Red Order for fear of revealing them. One captured Sister could bring the whole delicate network down.

'This is old news, Cailin,' Zaelis said. 'Why is it bothering you now?'

'I do not know,' Cailin replied. 'Perhaps because I cannot see their plan. There are too many unanswered questions.'

'Yours has been the loudest voice arguing for secrecy these past years,' he reminded her. 'We have been content to consolidate, to build our strength and hide ourselves while Lucia grows. Perhaps we have been too careful. Perhaps we should have been harrying them every step of the way.'

'I think you overestimate us,' Cailin said. 'We hide because we must. To reveal our hand too early would be the death of us all.' She paused, mused for a time, then went on: 'The Weavers *appear* to be consolidating also, but look closer: they knew from the start that their term in power was finite. They knew the very blight their witchstones cause would poison the earth, and they must have known Mos would be blamed for it. Mos is their champion; without him, they will not only be torn from power, but punished for trying to usurp the system. The nobles plot to be rid of him.'

'But who has the strength to do it?' Zaelis asked. 'The only one who even *might* be a contender is Blood Kerestyn, in alliance with Blood Koli. They could stir up an army that would trouble the Blood Emperor. But even they could not defeat him in Axekami, with the Weavers behind him. In a few years, perhaps, but not now. They would not dare attack, no matter what outrages Mos commits. And what chance does an assassin have with Kakre guarding his life?'

'But now there is the famine, and the prospect of poor harvest. The very *people* will rise against Mos sooner or later,' said Cailin. She turned to Zaelis, her gaze cool. 'Do you not see, Zaelis? There was no way that the Weavers could have thought this rise to power was a permanent position, since it is their blight that is undermining their benefactor. They were *buying time*.'

'They have had hundreds of years to do whatever you suspect they are doing,' Zaelis argued, his phlegmy voice as persuasive and author-itative as ever.

'But they have only been able to move freely these past five,' Cailin said. 'They are letting the empire slide towards ruin, because they have no interest in maintaining it. They are up to something, Zaelis. And if they do not play their hand now, it may be too late.'

Zaelis studied his companion. Seeing her so perturbed was pro-foundly unsettling. She was usually a picture of cold elegance.

'Perhaps our spy from Okhamba will have new insight,' he said to placate her.

'Perhaps,' Cailin said, unconvinced. She looked over at Lucia, who had not moved. 'And in the meantime the spirits in the Fault become more hostile, and we lose more men and women to them than we can afford. They sense the change in the earth and grow bitter. We are being penned in, Zaelis. Soon we will be surrounded by enemies, unable to move within the Fault and unable to leave it.'

This struck closer to Zaelis's heart. Two of his best men had disappeared only last week while scouting west along the Fault. He wondered if this place would soon be too dangerous to inhabit, and what they could possibly do if it became so.

'She can help us,' Zaelis said, following Cailin's eyes. 'She can calm the spirits.'

'Can she?' Cailin mused darkly. 'I wonder.'

The world was full of whispers to Lucia.

It had been that way ever since she could remember. The wind soughed in a secret language, flitting wisps of meaning piquing her attention like catching her name in someone else's conversation. Rain pattered nonsense at her, teasing her with an incipient form that always washed away before she could grasp it. Rocks thought rock thoughts, slower even than the trees, whose gnarled contemplations sometimes took years to complete. Darting between them were the lightning-fast minds of small animals, ever alert, only relaxing their guard in the safety of their burrows and hidey-holes.

She was an Aberrant, a perversion of nature, and yet she was closer to nature than anyone alive, for she had the ability to decipher its many tongues.

She walked along a grassy, well-worn trail that dipped and curved around an overhanging cliff face to her right. To her left, the ground fell suddenly sheer away, leaving her looking out over an enormous canyon half a mile wide or more. On the far side, where the wall was sloped, tall spines of rock and stone pillars stood crookedly, dusty red in the slanting evening sun, casting spindly finger-shadows. The air was dry and hot and smelled of baked earth.

Before her went Yugi and another Libera Dramach guard; behind her, Cailin and Zaelis, and two more armed men. Venturing beyond the lip of the valley where the Fold lay was not a light undertaking these days.

They followed the trail upwards as it bent away from the edge of the chasm and into a long ditch with a thin ribbon of a stream flowing down the middle. Trees meshed tightly overhead. Bees droned in the warm shade, harvesting nectar from the rare flowers that thrived here. Lucia listened to their quiet, comforting industry, and envied their singularity of purpose and unquestioning loyalty to the hive, the simple pleasure they gleaned from serving their queen.

After a short time, they came to a glade, where the ditch ran up against a crumbling rock wall. The trees were driven back here by the pebbly soil, and Nuki's eye peeped in to brighten it. Water splashed through a narrow gash in the orange stone, pooling in a basin where it overflowed and drained off into a muddy channel that meandered away in the direction they had come.

'You,' Yugi indicated his companion. 'Stay here with me. You two, take station further down the ditch. Call if you see anything bigger than a cat.'

The men grunted and complied, their footfalls thudding away as they departed. Yugi scratched under the sweaty rag that he had wrapped around his forehead to keep his dirty brown-blond hair back from his eyes. He gave those assembled a mischievous grin and said: 'Well, here we are again.'

Lucia smiled. She was fond of Yugi. Though his duties with the Libera Dramach meant that she did not see him as often as Kaiku or Mishani, he was always an entertaining rascal, even though she sensed sometimes that he was not as happy as his manner would suggest. She knew she would only make him uncomfortable if she pried. Whereas once she would have asked the question, now she kept her silence. Wisdom was only one way in which she had grown since they had first met.

Zaelis knelt down in front of her, his calloused hands gripping her upper arms tightly. 'Are you ready, Lucia?'

Lucia held his gaze for a moment and then looked away, to the pool. She gently pried his fingers off her and walked over to it. Crouching at its edge, she stared into the water. It was only a few inches deep, and clear enough to see the eroded curve of the basin beneath. As she watched, a tiny minnow slipped from the cut in the rock and plopped into the pool. It made a few disorientated circuits and then allowed itself to be washed over the pouting lip of the basin, and into the stream that ran along the ditch, little realising that its path would take it plunging over the edge of the canyon in a few short minutes.

Lucia watched it go. She would not have warned it, even if she could and even if it would have listened. Its path was chosen for it, like hers.

Once, she had lived in the Imperial Keep, a prisoner in a gilded cage. Five years ago she had been rescued from that confinement and brought to the Fold, only to discover that it was merely a different prison, and in its way as constricting as the last. Instead of walls, she was suffocated by expectation.

The Libera Dramach had taken that struggling settlement eleven years ago and turned it into a thriving fortress town, using the steadily growing population as recruitment grounds for their own secret cause. It was a carefully organised, well-oiled operation. And it was all for her.

'I saw what would happen,' Zaelis had told her once. 'When you were still an infant, I came to be your tutor, and even then we knew you were Aberrant. You were speaking at six months old, and not only to us. Your mother thought she could hide you, but I knew you couldn't be hidden. That was when I began. I moved in scholars' circles, seeking out those who might be sympathetic with Aberrants, sounding them out; and then, when I was sure, I would tell them about you. It was treason, but I told them. They saw then what you were, what you meant. If you took the throne, if an *Aberrant* ruled the empire, then it would undermine everything the Weavers had stood for. How could the Weavers consent to give service to an Aberrant Blood Empress? Yet to refuse would be to go against all the high families, who would owe you their loyalty. The stranglehold they have on us would be broken.'

And so here she was. Though she was allowed to roam and play free in the valley, there was always someone keeping an eye on her. They had vested all their hopes, all their ambitions in Lucia. Without her as a figurehead, they were merely a treasonous group of subversives. She was their reason to exist. They protected her, hid her, jealously guarding their dispossessed Heir-Empress until she could grow in power and influence, investing their time against the day when she would return to claim her throne.

Nobody had asked her if she even *wanted* to claim the throne. Not in all these years.

'Is everything well, Lucia?' Cailin asked. Lucia looked up at her fleetingly, then returned her gaze to the pool.

'She's probably wishing we had chosen to build the Fold nearer a stream she could talk to,' Yugi quipped. 'I've heard the brooks in our valley curse like soldiers.'

This brought a faint smile to Lucia's lips, and she gave him a grateful glance. He was half right. It was dangerous to go outside the valley, but this was the closest body of water that flowed directly from the Rahn, and its language was less muddied by the ancient ramblings of subterranean rocks and deeper, darker things. She cupped her hands in the water and lifted it carefully, not spilling a drop.

Listen.

Her head bowed, her eyes closed, and the physical world fell quiet to her ears. The rustle of the leaves in the sluggish wind dimmed and the sound of calling birds diminished to a distant staccato. Her heartbeat slowed; her muscles loosened and relaxed. Each exhalation made her sink deeper into unreality. She focused only on the feel of the water in her palm, the trembling of the liquid from the slight movement of her hands, the way it slid into the minuscule gullies in her skin and filled the whorls of her fingertips. She let the water feel her in return, the warmth of her blood, the throb of her pulse.

Everything natural had a spirit. Rivers, trees, hills, valleys, the sea and the four winds. Most were simple, merely an existence of life: an instinctive thing, as incapable of reason as a foetus and yet just as precious. But some were old, and aware, and their thoughts were massive and unfathomable. This water came from the belly of the Tchamil Mountains, flowing along the Kerryn for hundreds of miles until it had split off into the Rahn and travelled southward to the Fault. The great rivers were ancient, but beneath their incomprehensible consciousness they thronged with many more simple spirits. Lucia would not dare try to communicate with the Rahn itself; that was a magnitude of mystery beyond her. But here, at this place, she could sift out something that was within her capabilities. And gradually, while she kept practising like this, she was gaining the control that might one day let her make contact with the true spirit of the river.

She let the water trickle through her fingers, allowing it to carry the feel of her into the pool, tentatively announcing herself. Then, gently, she let her hands rest on the surface, her touch turning it to a chaos of ripples.

Something coming.

Something—

It rushed shrieking at her, a black wave of horror that forced its way into her throat, her lungs, choking. Death and pain and atrocity, washed downriver in the water. And with it something cold, cold and corrupt, a blasphemy against nature, a monstrous clawing thing that rent at her. A terror on the river, *terror on the river*, and the spirits were *screaming!*

Her mind blanked out, overwhelmed by the unimaginable ferocity of the onslaught, and she tipped backwards onto the pebbly floor of the glade without a sound.

Eight

The *Servant of the Sea* drifted in an endless black, the lanterns along its gunwale and atop its mast casting lonely globes of light in the abyss. A single gibbous moon stood sentry in the sky overhead: Iridima, her bright white surface spidercracked with blue like a shattered marble. Thick, racing bands of cloud obscured her face periodically, extinguishing stars in their wake.

An unseasonably chilly wind fluttered across the junk, setting the lanterns swaying and making Kaiku hug her blouse tighter to her skin as she picked out constellations on the foredeck. There was the Fang, low in the east – a sure sign that autumn was almost upon them. Just visible through the cold haze of Iridima's glow was the Scytheman, directly above her: another omen of the coming end to the harvest. And there, to the north, the twin baleful reds of The One Who Waits, side by side like a pair of eyes, watching the world hungrily.

It was late, and the passengers were asleep. Those men that kept the junk sailing through the night were quiet presences in the background, their voices low. But Kaiku had not been able to rest tonight. The prospect of arriving at Hanzean tomorrow was too exciting. To set foot on Saramyr soil again . . .

She felt tears start to her eyes. Gods, she never thought she would miss her homeland this much, after it had treated her so badly. But even with her family dead and she an outcast, destined to be shunned for her Aberrant blood, she loved the perfect beauty of the hills and plains, the forests and rivers and mountains. The thought of coming home after two months brought her more joy than she would have ever imagined it could.

Her gaze was drawn to the face of Iridima, most beautiful of the moon-sisters and the most brilliant, and she felt a chill of both awe and fear. She said a silent prayer to the goddess, as she always did when she had a moment like this to herself, and remembered the day when she been touched by the Children of the Moons, brushed by a terrible majesty of purpose that humbled her utterly.

'I thought it would be you,' said a voice next to her, and she felt the chill turn to an altogether more pleasant warmth that seeped through her body. Turning her head slightly, she favoured her new companion with an appraising glance.

'Did you?' she answered him, making it less of a question and more an expression of casual disinterest.

'Nobody else wanders the decks at night,' Saran replied. 'Except the sailors, but they have a heavier tread than you.'

He was standing close to her, a little closer than was proper, but she made no move to lean away. After a month of seeing each other every day, she had given up trying to conceal her attraction, and so had he. It had become a delicious game between them; both aware of the other's feelings to some extent, neither willing to give in and be the one to make the next move. Waiting each other out. She suspected that part of it was the allure of the message he carried, the implied air of mystery which it lent him. She was desperately curious about the nature of his mission, yet he always evaded her probing, and the frustration only added to how tantalising he was.

'You are thinking of home?' he guessed.

Kaiku made a soft noise in her throat, an affirmation.

'What is there for you?' he persisted.

'Just home,' she said. 'That is enough for the moment.'

He was silent for a time. Kaiku suddenly realised that she had been callous, and misinterpreted the pause. She laid a hand on his arm.

'My apologies. I had forgotten. Your accent has improved so much, sometimes you seem almost Saramyr.'

Saran gave her a heartbreaking smile. As usual, he was immaculately dressed and not a hair out of place. He might have been vain – something Kaiku had learned over the past weeks – but he certainly had something to be vain about.

'You should not apologise. Quraal is not my home, not any more. I have been away a long time, but I do not miss it. My people are blinkered and reluctant to leave their own shores, afraid that mingling with other cultures is offensive to our gods, afraid that the Theocrats might accuse them of heresy. I do not think that. Those Quraal that do deal with foreigners stay aloof, but I find beauty in all people. Some more than most.'

He was not looking at her as he delivered the final sentence, nor was it weighted any more that its predecessors, but Kaiku felt a blush anyway.

'I thought that way once,' she said quietly. 'I suppose I still do, but it is not so easy nowadays. Mishani tells me I need a harder heart, and she is right. To think too much of someone only makes a person vulnerable. Sooner or later, one will disappoint or betray the other.'

'That is Mishani's opinion, not yours,' Saran said. 'And besides, what of Mishani herself? You two seem close as kin.'

'Even she has wounded me in the past, and that hurt went deeper than any had before it,' Kaiku murmured.

Saran was silent for a time. They stood together, listening to the sussurant breathing of the sea, looking out over the darkness. Kaiku had more she wanted to say, but she felt she had already said too much, revealed too great a portion of herself to him. She kept her inner self guarded; it was her way, and experience had taught her that there was little point in trying to change it. Somehow, whenever she let her defences down, she always chose the wrong person; yet if she kept them up, she drove people away from her.

She had fallen into two relationships since she had lived in the Fold, both fulfilling at the time but ultimately proving empty. One man she was with for three years before realising that she stayed with him to alleviate the guilt she felt over the death of Tane, who had followed her into the Imperial Keep out of love and had died there. The other lasted six months before he revealed a terrible temper, made worse by the fact that he could not physically overpower her since she was an apprentice of the Red Order. She did not see the rage building until it burst out. He hit her once. She used her *kana* to crush the bones in his hand. Unfortunately, despite his other failings, he had been a skilled bomb engineer and a great asset to the Libera Dramach, but Kaiku's actions had put paid to that. She felt more sorry about causing trouble for Zaelis's organisation than about maiming him.

But there was one other, who had got under her skin a long while ago and would not be dislodged, persistent as the whispers from her father's Mask that sometimes woke her in the night with their insidious temptations.

'I miss Asara,' she said absently, her eyes unfocused.

'Asara tu Amarecha?' Saran said.

Kaiku's head snapped around to meet his gaze. 'You know her?'

'I have met her,' he said. 'Not that she was going by that name, but then, she never did keep to one identity for too long.'

'Where? Where did you meet her?'

Saran raised a sculpted eyebrow at the urgency in Kaiku's voice. 'Actually, it was in the very port that we are docking at tomorrow. Several years ago, now. She did not know me, but I knew her. She was wearing a different face, but I had intelligence of her arrival.' He smiled to himself, enjoying Kaiku's attention. 'I made contact with her. We are both, after all, on the same side.'

'Asara is on nobody's side,' Kaiku said.

'She chooses her allegiances to suit herself,' Saran said, then turned away from her and into the wind, flicking his hair away from his face with a flourish. 'But you of all people should know that she is helping the Red Order and the Libera Dramach.'

'She *was*,' said Kaiku. 'I have not seen her since Lucia was—' She stopped herself, then remembered that Saran already knew. Brushing her fringe back in an unconscious imitation of him, she continued more carefully. 'Since Lucia came to the Fold.'

'She spoke highly of you,' Saran told her, pacing slowly about the foredeck. He stood too rigid, too straight, and Kaiku felt that his movements and speech were pretentiously theatrical. He annoyed her when he became like this. Suddenly, now that he knew he had information she wanted, he was showing off, making the most of his advantage. She should have deflated him and feigned disinterest, but it was too late. Quraal were legendarily arrogant, and Saran was no exception. Like many people who were naturally beautiful, he did not feel he had to cultivate the finer points of his personality since women would fall at his feet anyway. What irked Kaiku more than anything was that she *knew* that, and yet she still kept coming back to him.

Saran wanted her to ask what Asara had said about her, but she would not give him the satisfaction this time.

He leaned on his elbows against the bow railing, the moon at his shoulder, and studied her with his dark eyes. 'What were you two to each other?' he asked eventually.

Kaiku almost felt that she did not want to tell him; but tonight she felt reflective, and it did her good to talk.

'I do not know,' she said. 'I never knew who she was, or *what* she was. I knew she could . . . shift her form somehow. I knew she had watched over me for a long time, waiting for my *kana* to show itself. She could be cruel, or kind. I think maybe she was lonely, but too obsessed with being independent to admit it to herself.'

'Were you friends?'

Kaiku frowned. 'We were . . . more than friends, and less than friends. I do not know what she thought of me, but . . . there is a piece of her still in me. Here.' She tapped her breastbone. 'She stole the breath of another and put it into me, and some of her went with it. And some of me went into her.' She became aware that Saran was watching her coolly, shook her head and snorted a laugh. 'I do not expect you to understand.'

'I think I understand enough,' Saran said.

'Do you? I doubt it.'

'Did you love her?'

Kaiku's eyes flashed in disbelief. 'How dare you ask me that?' she snapped.

Saran gave an insouciant shrug. 'I was merely asking. You sounded like—'

'I loved what she taught me,' she interrupted him. 'She made me accept myself for what I am. An Aberrant. She helped me to stop being ashamed of myself. But I couldn't love *her*. Not as she was. Deceitful, selfish, heartless.' Kaiku checked herself, realising that she had raised her voice. She flushed angrily. 'Does that answer your question?'

'Quite adequately,' Saran said, unruffled.

Kaiku stalked to the other side of the foredeck and stood with her arms crossed, glaring at the moon-limned waves, furious with herself. Asara was still an open wound that refused to heal. She had told Saran far more than she intended. It would be better to cut her losses and leave now, but she stayed.

After a moment, she heard him walk over to her. His hands touched her shoulders, and she turned around, her arms unknitting. He was standing close to her again, his dark eyes piercing in the shadowed frame of his face, heavy with intent. She felt her pulse quicken; a salty wind blew between them. Then he bent to kiss her, and she turned her mouth away. He drew back, hurt and angry.

Kaiku slipped from his grasp and turned her back again, her arms once more folded beneath her breasts. She could feel his frustrated confusion prickling at the back of her neck. She countered with a coldness in the set of her shoulders, an impassable resolve. Finally, she heard him leave.

Kaiku stood alone again, watching the stars, and added another brick to the barrier around her heart.

They arrived at Hanzean early in the morning of the next day. The harbour town was bathed in a pink light. Far to the east, the Surananyi was blowing, great hurricanes throwing up the red dust of the Tchom Rin desert to tinge Nuki's eye.

As was customary, the sailors enacted a small ceremony around a tiny shrine that they brought up from its usual place belowdecks, and made offerings of incense to Assantua, goddess of the sea and sky, for their safe passage. All the Saramyr folk attended, but Saran and Tsata were notably absent.

Hanzean was less hectic than Jinka to the north, which took most of the traffic from Okhamba, but though the journey was slightly longer it was the home port of Blood Mumaka's fleet. It was the most picturesque of the western coastal towns, and the oldest, being the first Saramyr settlement ever on this continent. Ninety miles to the south-west stood the Palexai, the great obelisk that marked the point where landfall was first made. Though Hanzean had never blossomed into Saramyr's first capital – the cursed Gobinda had held that title – it remained an influential place, steeped in its own history.

Mishani had visited Hanzean several times, in the days before her estrangement from her family. She was fond of its quiet alleyways and ancient plazas; it reminded her of the Imperial Quarter in Axekami, but a little less carefully kept, a little rougher around the edges. Somehow more *real*. Now, however, the sight of the smooth stone towers and the red skirts of ornamental guttering around the market-dome made her feel a strange mix of relief and trepidation. Their journey had been bought at a price, but what kind of price she could not yet tell. Chien had not been interested in money; instead, he had exacted a promise from her, one that courtesy demanded she grant in such a situation, even if it was not in return for such a heavy favour as the merchant had done them.

'You must be my guest at my townhouse in Hanzean,' he said.

On the surface, it seemed innocent enough; but surfaces, like masks, covered over the truth beneath. Though no time had been set, etiquette demanded that Mishani stay for at least five days. And in that five days, anything could happen. She was far too close to Blood Koli's estates in Mataxa Bay for her comfort.

She examined all the angles, looked for hidden meaning in every-thing. It was a necessary habit with Mishani, and she was particularly talented at it.

Chien was not an idiot; he could have negotiated great advantage for himself out of the deal. She knew what she would do in his shoes. If he truly had heard about the rift in her family, then he was aware that she had nothing to offer him, and he probably knew that Barak Avun was secretly searching for his daughter. He would simply trade her into the arms of her enemy.

Then why am I letting him? she asked herself, as she mouthed the words of the mantra to Assantua and paid attention to the sailors' ceremony with only a small fraction of her mind.

Because she had made a promise. It was her refusal to compromise her honour that had made her an outcast in the first place; she would scarcely abandon it now. Chien knew she could not refuse his invitation without insult, and it would have revealed that she suspected him. He was probably just as puzzled about her motives as she was of his. What had she been doing on Okhamba? Why risk herself that way?

She had told him nothing, though they had talked often on the journey. His uncertainty was her advantage, and she had to keep hold of it. When they got to his townhouse, then she would see what could be done about her situation.

She had not shared her fears with Kaiku. Though Kaiku had initially had the same suspicions as Mishani, she had been calmed by assurances that Chien was trustworthy. It was, of course, a lie, but Kaiku was in no position to help anyway. She had to take Saran and his Tkiurathi companion back to the Fold, and her passionate outbursts would be counterproductive to Mishani's intrigues.

Kaiku was content to let it drop, in the end. Mishani's intention had always been to head south when they returned from Okhamba, anyway; Kaiku knew that. Mishani was next to useless in the Fold, except when Zaelis or Cailin called on her for advice or Lucia needed a sisterly hand. No, she had other errands to run, assuming she had liberty to run them after Chien was done with her. She was going to Lalyara, to meet with the Barak Zahn tu Ikati. Lucia's true father.

They disembarked on Chien's private jetty, after which he insisted that they come to his townhouse and dine with him before they set off. Saran appeared reluctant to Mishani's practised eye, but he made no complaint. Kaiku, who was eager to put off her farewells to her friend, was happy to accept. Tsata and Chien exchanged a few words in Okhamban – in which the merchant was apparently fluent – and then he, too, acquiesced. Not being bound by Saramyr manners, Kaiku had feared he would say something rude; but Chien knew how to deal with Tkiurathi.

They were met at the jetty and taken by carriage through the quiet streets of Hanzean. Slender cats watched them curiously from rooftops; sun-browned women stepped aside as they passed, and then returned to sweeping the dust away from their doorsteps with reed brooms; old men sat outside streetside restaurants with cups of wine and cubes of exotic cheese; startled birds took flight from where they bathed in ancient fountains. Kaiku was rapt, enjoying the simple glory of being back in Saramyr and off that ship. Mishani wished she could do the same. She had noted that the carriage was taking a very indirect route to wherever it was going, heading down narrow, winding thoroughfares and doubling back on itself several times. The others had not noticed, or appeared not to; but for one who knew Hanzean well, it was obvious.

Chien's townhouse was not particularly ostentatious. It was a squat, three-storeyed building like a crushed pagoda, with scalloped tiling on its skirts and a sculpted effigy of a spirit on each corner serving as a gargoyle. Enclosed within was a small garden, with colourful rockeries arranged with typical care and forethought. The grounds were small and tidy, merely a lawn within the compound wall and a few cultivated areas of flowers and trees, where stone benches were placed and a small brook ran. It was located in a wealthy district, on a street of compounds that were a similar size, and it stood out not at all from its neighbours.

The theme continued on the inside. While he was a man of undoubted wealth, Chien had chosen comfort and simplicity over opulence, and the only real displays of his merchant prowess were the rare and valuable Okhamban stone icons that rested on pedestals in some of the rooms. Kaiku shivered at the sight, remembering the dreadful awareness of the idols at the Aith Pthakath.

The meal was exquisite, and doubly so after the preserved food that they had been getting on board the ship. Pot-cooked slitherfish, seasoned saltrice in delicate cakes wrapped in strips of kelpweed, a stew of vegetables and grilled banathi, and – most delicious of all – jukara berries, that only flourished in the last few weeks of the harvest, and were ruinously hard to cultivate. They ate and talked and joked, united in the common relief of being back on dry land. Laughing, reminiscing about the journey, they cut and speared food with silver finger-forks worn on the second and third digit of the left hand, and their counterpart finger-blades on the right. Occasionally they switched to delicate spoons, held between the unencumbered thumb and forefinger. Neither Saran nor Tsata appeared to have any trouble with the technique, nor with the rituals of politeness at the table. Mishani guessed that the quiet Tkiurathi was a lot more well-educated than she had initially thought.

Finally, the meal was over. Chien, as was expected, asked Mishani's companions to stay and they, as was equally expected, regrettably refused. Chien did not insist; but he did offer to put a carriage at their disposal to take them out of the town.

They went out to the small lawn of the compound together, strolling idly in the muggy heat of the afternoon. The cooling breezes of approaching autumn had died off and left the air still and humid. Mishani walked ahead with Kaiku, the former as poised as ever, the latter as casual.

'I will miss you, Mishani,' Kaiku said. 'It is a long way to the Southern Prefectures.'

'I shall not be gone for ever. A month, two at most, if my errands are well.' She gave her friend a wry smile. 'I thought after this trip you would have had enough of me.'

Kaiku returned the smile. 'Of course not. Who else would keep me out of trouble?'

'Cailin tries, but you do not let her.'

'Cailin wants me as a pet,' Kaiku said derisively. 'If she had her way,

I would spend every day studying, and by now I would have been putting on that ghoulish make-up and that black dress as part of the Red Order.'

'She does have a lot of faith in you,' Mishani pointed out. 'Most masters would not put up with such an errant pupil.'

'Cailin looks after her own concerns,' Kaiku replied, shading her eyes and squinting up absently into the sun. 'She trained me to harness what I have inside me – for that, I will always be grateful – but I never agreed to spend the rest of my life as one of her Sisters. She does not understand that.' Kaiku dropped her gaze. 'Besides, I am pledged first to a higher power than her.'

Mishani laid a hand on her elbow. 'You have done much to help the Libera Dramach over these past years, Kaiku. You have played an important part in many of their operations. Everything you do for them hurts the Weavers, even in a small way. Do not forget that.'

'It is not enough,' Kaiku murmured. 'My family are still unavenged; my promise to Ocha unfulfilled. I have waited, and waited, but my patience is growing thin.'

'You cannot defeat the Weavers on your own,' Mishani told her. 'Nor can you expect to undo two and a half centuries of history in half a decade.'

'I know,' said Kaiku. 'But that does not help.'

They said their goodbyes, then Saran, Tsata and Kaiku departed in a carriage, leaving Mishani with Chien.

'Shall we go inside?' he offered, after they had left. Mishani acquiesced politely, and went with him, more aware than ever now that she was alone, and very likely walking into a trap.

Nine

Mos sat in the Chamber of Tears, and listened to the rain.

He had never been to this room before. That was not unusual; many of the upper levels of the Imperial Keep were almost entirely empty. It had been built as a somewhat impractical gesture of appeasement by the fourth Blood Emperor of Saramyr, Huita tu Lilira, in recompense to Ocha for the hubris of his predecessor. But not even the Imperial Family needed a building of the sheer size and complexity of the Keep. Even if Mos had summoned all his distant relatives to live there – which was hardly possible, since it was always necessary to have bloodline scattered about the country to oversee the diverse affairs of Blood Batik – they would have had trouble filling all the rooms. When the great fire of five years ago had destroyed large areas of the interior, the inhabitants had simply moved to new sections and carried on quite comfortably while the repairs were made.

The upper levels, where Mos had found the Chamber of Tears, were the least practical to get to, and their *lach* corridors held only hollow echoes. Laranya had said once that there could be people living up here, a whole community of lost wanderers that might have gone undiscovered for centuries. Mos had laughed and told her that she was being fanciful. Though they were deserted, they were not covered in dust or neglected, and he suspected that one of his advisers' duties was to ensure that servants did not let any part of the Keep go to ruin.

The sound of falling water had brought him here as he wandered, seeking solitude, carrying his third bottle of wine. It was a wide, circular chamber with a domed roof, in the centre of which was a hole through which the rain fell onto the tiled floor and drained away through small grilles. The floor was slightly slanted towards the centre to keep the water there, so that it was possible to sit just outside the curtain of droplets and remain dry. A crafty system of guttering on the roof funnelled water down through secret channels to the statues that stood in alcoves at the periphery of the chamber, and tears ran from their eyes and down their faces, collecting in stone basins at their feet.

It was dusk, and no lanterns had been lit. The room was gloomy and sultry with the remainder of the day's heat. The rain was unusual for this time of year, but it suited Mos's mood, and he was drawn to it. He sat in one of the many chairs that formed a circle around the room, and watched the column of droplets come down, the carpet of tiny explosions they made as they struck the shallow pool in the middle of the chamber. The only light was the fading glow of Nuki's eye, coming through the hole in the dome, outlining Mos's brow and bearded jaw and the edge of the bottle he held. He took another swig, without finesse, a bitter and angry draught.

'You should not be alone,' croaked Kakre from the doorway of the chamber, and Mos swore loudly.

'Gods, you are the *last* person I want to see now, Kakre,' he said. 'Go away.'

'We must talk,' the Weave-lord insisted, coming further into the room.

Mos glared at him. 'Come closer then. I'll not talk to you while you're lurking over there.'

Kakre obliged, shambling into the light. Mos didn't look at him, watching the rain instead. The vaguely cloying scent of decay and animal fur reached him even through the haze of the wine, like the smell of a sick dog.

'What must we talk about?' he sneered.

'You are drunk,' Kakre said.

'I'm never drunk. Is that what you had to say to me? I have a wife to scold me, Kakre; I don't need you for it.'

Kakre bridled, a wave of anger emanating from him that made the hairs of Mos's neck stand on end.

'You are too insolent sometimes, my *Emperor*,' Kakre warned, loading the title with scorn. 'I am not one of your servants, to be dismissed or mocked as you choose.'

'No, you're not,' Mos agreed, taking another swig from his bottle. 'My servants are loyal, and they do what they're supposed to. You don't. It makes me wonder why I even keep you around at all.'

Kakre did not reply to that, regarding him in malicious silence instead.

'What do you have to tell me, then?' Mos snapped, casting Kakre an irritated glance.

'I have news from the south. There has been a revolt in Zila.'

Mos did not react, except that his frown deepened and his brow clouded.

'A revolt,' he repeated slowly.

'The Governor has been killed. It was a mob, mainly peasants and townsfolk. They stormed the administration plaza. One of my Weavers sent me the news, before he too was killed.'

'They killed a Weaver?' Mos exclaimed in frank surprise.

Kakre did not see any need to answer that. The spatter of the rain filled the void in the conversation while Mos thought.

'Who is responsible?' the Emperor asked eventually.

'It is too early to say,' rasped the Weave-Lord. 'But the peasants were organised. And my agents in Zila had been reporting a rise in sympathy for that somewhat persistent cult that has been a constant diversion of our resources these past few years.'

'The Ais Maraxa? It was *them*?' Mos cried in sudden fury, flinging his bottle across the room. It smashed against one of the weeping statues, mixing red wine into the rainwater that collected in the basin at its feet.

'Perhaps. I have warned you often that they would manage something like this eventually.'

'You were supposed to prevent this kind of thing from happening!' The Emperor stood up violently, knocking his chair away behind him.

'They know about the harvests,' Kakre said. He was not intimidated, even though he was physically dwarfed by the larger man. 'Here in the north-west we can disguise the damage somewhat, but Zila lies on the edge of the Southern Prefectures. Down there, they see the blight destroying their crops before their very eyes; and all bad news travels through Zila on its way up the western coast. The Weavers are powerful, my Emperor, and we have many subtle ways; but we cannot see all plans, not when the very country turns against us. You should have let me tackle the Ais Maraxa when we first heard of them.'

'Don't shift the blame, Kakre!' Mos raged. 'This is *your* fault!' He grabbed the Weaver roughly by his patchwork robe. 'Your fault!'

'*Do not touch me!*' Kakre hissed, and Mos felt his body seized, his chest gripped as if by an iron hand. The strength flooded out of him, replaced by sudden panic. His hands spasmed open, releasing the Weave-lord, and he staggered backward, his throat bubbling with phlegm and his breath short. Kakre seemed to loom, becoming huge and terrifying in his mind: a hunched figure with emaciated white hands clenched into claws, held over him like the hands of a puppeteer over a marionette. Backing away, Mos slipped and fell into the column of rain, splashed into the shallow pool where he cringed, whimpering. Kakre seemed to fill the room, his Mask shadowed and cadaverous, and the very air seemed to crush Mos down to the floor.

'You overstep your boundaries,' said the Weave-lord, his voice dark and cold as the grave. 'You will learn your place!'

Mos cried out in fear, unmanned by Kakre's power, his natural courage subverted by the insidious manipulation of his body and mind. The rain fell, soaking him, dripping from his beard and plastering his hair.

'You need me, Mos,' Kakre told him. 'And I, regrettably, need you. But do not forget what I can do to you. Do not forget that I hold the power of life and death over you at every moment. I can stop your heart with a thought, or burst it within your breast. I can make you bleed inside in such a way that not even the best physicians could tell it was not natural. I can drive you insane in the time it takes for you to unsheathe your sword. *Never* touch me again, or perhaps I shall do something more permanent to you next time.'

Then, gradually, Kakre seemed to diminish, and the terrible energy in the air slackened. Mos found his breath again, gasping. The room returned to what it once had been, gloomy and spacious and echoing, and Kakre was once again a small, twisted figure with a bent back, buried in badly sewn rags and hide.

'You will deal with the revolt in Zila. I will deal with its causes,' he rasped, and with that he departed, leaving Mos lying on his side in the rain, overlit by the fading dusk, angry and fearful and beaten.

The Empress Laranya and her younger brother Reki collapsed through the elliptical doorway, wet and breathless from laughing. Eszel raised a theatrical eyebrow as they blundered into the pavilion, and said wryly to Reki: 'Anyone would think you had never seen rain before.'

Reki laughed again, exhilarated. It was not far from the truth.

The pavilion lay in the middle of a wide pond, joined to the rest of the Imperial Keep's roof gardens by a narrow bridge. Its sides were carved wood, a thin, hollow webwork of leaf shapes and pictograms that allowed those inside to look through them and out over the water. Baskets of flowers hung from the drip-tiles on the sloping roof, and at each corner were stout stone pillars painted in coral red. Eszel had lit the lanterns that hung on the inner sides of the pillars, for night had newly fallen outside. It was small, but not so small that eight people could not sit in comfort on its benches, and with only the three of them there was plenty of room.

Reki flopped down and looked out through the wooden patterns, marvelling. Laranya gave him an indulgent kiss on the cheek and sat beside him.

'Rain is something of a novelty where we come from,' she explained to Eszel.

'I gathered as much,' Eszel replied, with a quirk of a grin.

'Spirits!' Reki exclaimed, his eyes flickering over the dark and turbulent surface of the rain-dashed pool. 'Now I know what Ziazthan Ri felt when he wrote *The Pearl Of The Water God.*'

Eszel looked at the young man with newly piqued interest. 'You've read that?'

Reki became shy all of a sudden, realising that he had been boasting. Ziazthan Ri's ancient text – containing what was generally recognised as some of the greatest naturalistic writing in the Empire – was extraordinarily rare and valuable. 'Well . . . that is . . .' he stammered.

'You precious thing! You must tell me about it!' Eszel enthused, rescuing him. 'I've seen copied extracts, but never known the whole story.'

'I memorised it,' said Reki, trying to sound as modest as possible. 'It is one of my favourites.'

Eszel practically squealed: 'You *memorised* it? I would *die* to hear it from beginning to end.'

Reki beamed, the smile lighting up his thin face. 'I would be honoured,' he said. 'I have never met anyone who has even heard of Ziazthan Ri before.'

'Then you haven't met the right people yet,' Eszel told him with a wink. 'I'll introduce you around.'

'Now wait there,' Laranya said, springing from Reki's side to sit next to Eszel. She grabbed his arm possessively, dripping all over him. 'Eszel is mine! I'll not have you stealing him away from me with your dry book-learning and conversations about dead old men.'

Eszel laughed. 'The Empress is jealous!' he taunted.

Laranya looked from her brother to Eszel and back. She held great fondness for both of them. The two could not be more different, yet they seemed to be getting on better than she had hoped. Reki was grey-eyed and intense, his features oddly accentuated by a deep scar that ran from the outside of his left eye to the tip of his cheekbone. His chin-length hair was jet-black, with a streak of white on the left side from the same childhood fall that had marred his face. He was quiet, clever, and awkward, never seeming to quite fit the clothes that he wore or to feel comfortable in his own skin.

Eszel, in contrast, was flamboyant and lively, very handsome but very affected; he seemed like he belonged in the River District rather than the Imperial Keep, with his bright eye make-up and his hair dyed in purple and red and green, tied with ornaments and beads.

'Perhaps a little jealous,' she conceded mischievously. 'I want you both to myself!'

'Rank has its privileges,' Eszel said, standing up and making an exaggerated bow. 'I am yours to command, my Empress.'

'Then I demand that you recite us a poem about rain!' she said. Reki's eyes lit up.

'I do so happen to have one in which rain forms something of a key element,' he said. 'Would you like to hear it?'

'I would!' said Reki. He was somewhat awed by Eszel, who Laranya had told him was a brilliant poet. He was a member of the Imperial Court on the suggestion of Mos's Cultural Adviser, who believed that with a few years' patronage Eszel would be turning out poems good enough to make him a household name in Axekami, and a prestigious figure to be associated with the Imperial family.

Preening himself outrageously in the lantern-light, Eszel took up position in the middle of the pavilion and cleared his throat. For a few moments, the only sound was the hiss and trickle of the rain, and he basked in the rapt attention of his audience. Then he began to speak, the words flowing across his tongue like molten silver. High Sara-myrrhic was a wonderfully complex language, and lent itself well to poetry. It was capable of being soft and sibilant or jarring and sharp, layered with meanings that could be shifted and manipulated in the mouth of a wordsmith to make them a sly puzzle to unlock and a joy to hear. Eszel was extremely talented, and he knew it; the pure beauty of his sentences entranced the listener.

The poem was only obliquely about rain, being rather the story of a man whose wife had been possessed by an achicita, a demon vapour that had stolen in through her nostrils as she slept and was turning her sick inside. The man's heartbreak made him mad, and in his madness he was visited by Shintu, the trickster god of luck, who persuaded him to carry his wife outside their house and lay her in the road for three days, at the end of which time Shintu would drive out the demon. Then Shintu asked his cousin Panazu to bring three days of rain, to test the man's faith, for his wife was already weak and would likely not survive three days of being soaking wet. After the first day of sitting by his wife in the rain, the villagers, thinking the man insane, locked him up and put his wife back to bed, where she continued to sicken.

Shintu, having played his trick, thought it was over and promptly turned his attention to something else. He forgot about the whole affair, at which time it came to the attention of Narisa, goddess of forgotten things, who saw how terrible and unjust it was that this couple should suffer so. She appealed to Panazu to put things right, since he too had played a part in this. Panazu, who loved Narisa – and whose love would later draw Shintu's attention and result in the birth of the bastard child Suran by Panazu's own sister Aspinis – could not refuse her, and so he relieved the wife of the achicita and sent lightning to break open the man's jail cell. Freed and reunited, they were both pronounced cured, and found their happiness together once again.

Eszel was just coming to the end of his tale, and was gratified to see tears standing in Reki's eyes, when suddenly Mos came stamping in out of the rain. The poet faltered at the sight of the Blood Emperor, whose face was like a thunderhead. He stood there dripping, surveying the scene before him. Eszel fell silent.

'You all seem to be enjoying yourselves,' he said, and even Eszel could tell that he was spoiling for a fight, and wisely remained quiet. The Blood Emperor did not like him, and made no disguise of the fact. Eszel's somewhat effeminate ways and showy appearance offended a man of his earthy nature. In addition, it was plain that Mos resented the friendship between Eszel and Laranya, for she often sought him out when Mos was too busy with affairs of court to attend to her.

'Come and join us, then,' said Laranya, getting up and holding out her hands for Mos to take. 'You look like you need some enjoyment.'

He ignored her hands and glowered at her. 'I have searched for you, Laranya, because I thought I might find some solace from my wife after the ordeal I have suffered. Instead I find you . . . soaking wet and playing childish games in the rain!'

'What ordeal? What are you talking about?' Laranya asked, but in amid the concern there was already the spark of anger that had ignited in response to the Emperor's tone. Eszel sat down unobtrusively next to Reki.

'Don't concern yourself,' he snapped. 'Why is it that whenever I have to track you down, I find you with this abhorrent peacock of a man?' He waved a dismissive gesture at Eszel, who took the insult meekly. He could scarcely do any different. Reki looked in horror from Mos to Eszel.

'Do not take out your frustrations on your subjects, who cannot answer you back!' she cried, her cheeks becoming flushed. 'If your grievance is with me, then say so! I am not at your beck and call, to wait in your bedchamber until you decide you need *solace*.' She twisted the word to mock him, making him seem needy and ridiculous.

'Gods!' he roared. 'Am I to face hostility from all sides? Is there not one person with who I can exchange a kind word?'

'How persecuted you are!' she retorted sarcastically. 'Especially when you blunder in here like a banathi and begin insulting my friend, and embarrassing me in front of my brother!'

'Come with me, then!' Mos said, grabbing her wrist. 'Let me speak to you in private, away from them.'

She pulled her arm back. 'Eszel was reciting a poem,' she said, her voice taut. 'And I will stay to hear it finished.'

Mos glared balefully at the poet, almost shaking with rage. Reki could almost feel Eszel's heart sink. His sister meant well, but when incensed she was not subtle. In providing a reason to refuse Mos, she had turned his wrath back onto her defenceless friend.

'And how would you feel if your treasured poet was suddenly to find himself without a patron?' he grated.

'Then my treasured husband would find himself without a wife!' Laranya fired back. Once she had dug her heels in, she would give no ground.

'Does he mean so much to you, then?' Mos sneered. 'This half-man?'

'This *half-man* is more a man than you, since he can keep his temper, as a noble like you should be able to!'

This was too much. Mos raised his hand suddenly, a reflex of pure anger, drawing back to hit her.

She went suddenly cold, her passion taking her beyond mere fury and into a steely calm. 'I *dare* you,' she said, her voice like fingernails scraping on rusted metal.

The change in her stopped him. He had never raised his hand to her before, never lost control this way. Trembling, he looked into her eyes, and thought how achingly beautiful their arguments made her, and how much he loved and hated her at the same time. Then he cast one last glare of pure malice at Eszel, and stormed out of the doorway and onto the bridge, disappearing into the rainy night.

Reki let out a breath that he did not know he had been holding. Eszel looked miserable. Laranya's chin was tilted arrogantly, her breast heaving, fiercely pleased that she had faced her husband down.

The mood was spoiled now, and by unspoken consent they dispersed to their chambers. Later, Laranya would find Mos, and they would fight, and reconcile, and make frenetic love in the embers of their anger, unaware that then, as now, Kakre would be watching from the Weave.

Ten

Kaiku, Saran and Tsata arrived in the Fold in the early morning, having ridden hard from Hanzean. They had made their way along secret routes into the Xarana Fault under the cover of darkness and slipped into the heart of the broken land without alerting any of the hostiles that lived there. Their return was greeted with great activity by those who knew of Kaiku's mission and guessed who her companion was. By midday, an assembly of the upper echelons of the Libera Dramach and the Red Order had gathered to hear what their spy had to tell them, and Kaiku was included, both at Saran's insistence and at Cailin's. She felt a certain amount of relief. After giving two months of her life – and almost losing it – to bring this man back, the thought that the information he carried might be too sensitive to trust her with was too cruel.

They met on the top floor of a semicircular building that was unofficially the nerve centre of the Libera Dramach. It stood on one of the highest tiers of the Fold, its curved face looking out over the town and into the valley below. The uppermost storey was open to the view, with pillars to hold up the flat roof and a waist-high barrier of wrought iron running between them. The whole storey was a single room, used for congregations or occasional private theatrical performances or recitations, and like most of the buildings in the Fold it was functional rather than elegant. Its beige walls were hung with cheap tapestries and there was wicker matting to cover the floor, and little else except a prayer wheel in one corner and some wind chimes ringing softly in the desultory breeze, to ward off evil spirits. It was a quaint and ancient superstition that seemed somehow less comical here in the Xarana Fault.

There was no real formality about the meeting, but basic hospitality demanded that refreshments be served. The traditional low tables of black wood were scattered with small plates, and metal beakers of various wines, spirits and hot beverages were placed between them. Kaiku was sitting with Cailin and two other similarly attired members

82

of the Red Order, neither of whom she had met before, since the membership seemed to be constantly shifting and only Cailin provided any permanence. She was excessively paranoid about letting the numbers of the Red Order be known, and kept them scattered so that they might not all be wiped out at once by any disaster. Nearby sat Zaelis with Yugi, who was virtually his right-hand man. Yugi caught her look and gave her a reassuring grin; startled, she smiled back. Tsata sat on his own, away from the tables at the edge of the room.

Kaiku watched him for a moment. She had to wonder what the Tkiurathi was doing here at all. Why had he accompanied Saran so far? What was the relationship between them? Though her anger at the callous way he had risked her life had been ameliorated by the intervening month, she had learned little about him and Saran was strangely reluctant to fill in the details, claiming that it was Tsata's business and that he would tell her if he wanted. Kaiku could not decide if Saran was being diplomatic out of respect for his companion's foreign beliefs, or if he was just being obtuse to vex her.

Her thoughts turned from Saran to Lucia. She wished she had been given time to visit the former Heir-Empress before the meeting, but she supposed there would be time later. Still, something chewed annoyingly at her about the matter. When Kaiku enquired after her health to Zaelis, he had responded with a breezy comment and changed the subject; but thinking back on it, he never had answered her question. If she had been Mishani, she might have thought it suspicious; but being Kaiku, she assumed that it was her own fault for not pressing him.

Then silence fell, and Saran stood with his back to the railing, framed against the far end of the valley and outlined by the sun. It was time to learn what she had risked her life for, and to determine whether it was worth it.

'Only a few of you here know me,' he began, his voice clear and almost entirely free of Quraal inflections now. In his tight, severe clothes he looked like a general addressing his troops, and his voice had a similar authority. 'So I will begin with an introduction. My name is Saran Ycthys Marul. I have been a spy for the Libera Dramach for several years now, travelling far afield with one objective in mind: to discover all I could about the Weavers. My mission has taken me to the four countries of the Near World: Saramyr, Okhamba, Quraal and distant Yttryx. If you will indulge me, I will tell you now what I have found.'

He paused dramatically, and prowled left and right, sweeping the assembly with his gaze. Kaiku flinched inwardly at his grandstanding. It occurred to her suddenly that by delivering his message personally to so many people he was endangering himself in the future. The more people that knew he was a spy, the more likely he was to be discovered. She wondered what had brought on this recklessness; surely it was not that he was so conceited that he was willing to take the risk in exchange for this moment of glory?

'Saramyr has forgotten its history,' he said. 'So proud were you to settle this great continent that you did not think about what you were sweeping aside. In hunting the Ugati aboriginals to extinction, you wiped the slate clean, and lost thousands upon thousands of years of this land's memory. But other lands still remember. In Okhamba, tribes have lived untouched by outside civilisation for centuries. In Quraal, the repression of doctrine and the rewriting of history by the Theocracy was not thorough enough, and still there persists evidence from the darkest depths of the past, if a person knows where to look for it. And in Yttryx, where the constant internal wars have shifted the epicentre of power so often, documents have become so scattered that it is both impossible to find them all and impossible to destroy them all. History persists. Even here. And it seems we would do best not to forget it, for we never know when the events of the past may emerge to change the present.'

Some of the assembly shifted uneasily at the impertinence of this Quraal upbraiding them for their history, when it was the Quraal who had driven them to Saramyr in the first place; but Kaiku noted that Cailin wore a faint smile on her painted lips.

'I will be brief, and begin with the good news,' Saran continued, flicking back his hair and fixing Zaelis with a haughty eye. 'Later, I am sure, I will have an opportunity to give a more detailed account to those who wish to hear it.' He made an expansive gesture with his arm to encircle the assembly with his account. 'In all my travels throughout the Near World, I was looking for three things: firstly, evidence of the corruption that is spreading through your own land, that we now generally believe is a side-effect of the Weavers' witch-stones; secondly, the Weavers themselves, or beings analogous to them; and finally, the witchstones, since these are the source of the Weavers' powers.'

He began stalking back and forth again, his features profiled in the sunlight from outside. 'I am pleased to report that on two counts, I found nothing at all. Nowhere did I find any kind of blight that could not be accounted for by insect plague or other natural explanation, and none that possessed the insidious persistence of the one that affects Saramyr. And nowhere did I find anything that might be described as a

Weaver, except those few that reside in distant colonies on other continents. Certainly, there are those who possess abilities unusual to the common folk; our own priests are an example, having learned to communicate in a rudimentary fashion with the spirits of our land. The honourable Kaiku tu Makaima, here present, was witness to the abilities of the Fleshcrafters of Okhamba; and there are worse things even than Fleshcrafters in the hidden world of the deep jungle. In Quraal there are the Oblates, in Yttryx the Muhd-Taal. But however these talents are attained, it is through processes either natural or spiritual. Even the Aberrants, who were born from the corruption that the Weavers create, do not actively participate in its spreading.' He paused, ran a finger along his cheekbone. 'I found no Aberrants outside your own shores. There were the deformed, and lame, and crippled, but these are not Aberrants, merely the way of nature. In this land, most people do not differentiate any more; though if I may say, those in this room provide the exception to that rule, and I applaud you for it.'

Kaiku watched him as he held court, her mind wandering to the lean physique that she imagined underneath his strict black Quraal clothing. Why had she rejected him, anyway? It did not have to mean anything, to share a bed with him for a night. Why allow her mistrust of her own emotions to get in the way of enjoying herself?

She realised that she was drifting, caught herself and returned to the matter at hand.

'From this, we can surmise that the blight is responsible for Aberrancy,' Saran was saying. 'This we had already guessed, but now I believe it proven beyond doubt. There is no blight outside of Saramyr, and hence no Aberrants. But there *are* witchstones.'

This brought general consternation to the assembly. Kaiku ate a spiced dumpling and kept quiet, her eyes flickering over the suddenly animated audience.

'He plays his crowd well,' Cailin whispered, leaning over to her.

'He craves the attention, I think,' Kaiku murmured. 'It flatters his vanity.'

Cailin gave a surprised laugh and subsided with an insinuating glance at her pupil. Kaiku ignored it.

'But if the witchstones cause the corruption in our land, how is it that there are witchstones abroad, but no blight?' someone called.

'Because they have not been *found* yet,' Saran said, raising a finger. The assembly hushed. 'They lie deep in the earth. Dormant. Waiting. Waiting to be woken up.'

'Then what wakes them up?' asked the same man.

'Blood,' Kaiku said. She had meant to say it to herself, but it came out louder than she had intended and the assembly heard it.

'Blood. Indeed,' said Saran, giving her a disarming half-smile. 'Of all of us here, only Kaiku has seen a witchstone. She has witnessed the human sacrifice that feeds them. She has seen the heart.'

Kaiku felt suddenly embarrassed. Her account of her infiltration into the Weavers' monastery in the Lakmar Mountains on Fo was a subject of some skepticism among the Libera Dramach. Many argued, quite reasonably, that what she had seen in the chamber where the witchstone was kept could have been a hallucination. She had been weak from exhaustion and starvation, and had been wearing a Weaver's Mask for days, which was dangerous to anyone's sanity. But for all that, Kaiku knew what she saw and stuck by it. She had seen the great branches of stone that reached from the witchstone's main mass into the walls of the cavern, too organic to be formed by pressure or any other geological force. She had seen *into* the witchstone as it fed, seen the bright veins running through the rock, seen the pulsing core at its centre. Whatever the witchstones were, they were more than just inert matter. They were alive, like the trees were alive. They *grew*.

'How do you know the witchstones are there if they haven't been found?' Yugi asked Saran.

'At least one *has* been found, in Quraal, five hundred years ago or more,' Saran said. 'It is mentioned in texts I stole from the Librum of Aquirra's own vaults, which I brought here at great peril to myself. These texts tell of an incident in a rural province wherein a small mining village began exhibiting sudden and violent behaviour. When soldiers were sent in to quell the disturbance, they were overwhelmed, with survivors reporting strange bouts of insanity and displays of unholy abilities by the villagers, such as being able to move objects without touching them and killing men from a distance without using weapons. The Theocrats sent in a much greater force to stamp out the heretics, and they triumphed with heavy losses. In the mine beneath the town, they found evidence of an altar upon which blood sacrifices had been made. The soldiers later said how they had been drawn to the altar by evil temptations and promises, but their faith was strong enough to resist, and with explosives they destroyed the altar and pounded it to dust, then sealed the mine.' He tossed his black hair and looked around the room. 'I am certain that what they found was a witchstone.'

'So they can be destroyed?' Zaelis asked.

'If the account is to be believed, yes,' Saran replied.

'You said that *at least* one has been found,' another member of the assembly asked. 'Do you imply that there are others?'

'Consider this,' Saran said. 'There are four witchstones that we know of in Saramyr, and all of them the Weavers have built monasteries on. Two in the Tchamil Mountains: one beneath Adderach and one beneath Igarach on the edge of the Tchom Rin desert. Another in the Lakmar Mountains on the isle of Fo. The last in the mountains near Lake Xemit. We know that the witchstones are there, thanks to the efforts of Kaiku and her father Ruito, because these are the epicentres of the surrounding corruption. That is four in Saramyr alone. Why should our continent be the only one to have them?'

'Why shouldn't it?' asked Yugi. 'Unless you know what they are and how they came to be there, then who knows how they are distributed over the lands?'

'But I *do* know,' Saran said. He turned his back on his audience a moment, walking over to the railing, looking down onto the shambolic rooftops of the Fold, the narrow streets through which children ran, the bridges and pulleys and stairways. 'This may be hard for you to hear.'

Kaiku sat up straighter, a thin shiver passing through her. A subdued mutter ran around the room.

Saran turned and stood leaning on the railing. 'I found records of a fire from the sky,' he said, his handsome face grave. 'Many thousands of years ago, in Quraal, back when our language was young. A cataclysm of flaming rocks, annihilating whole settlements, boiling lakes, smashing the earth. We believed it a punishment from our gods.' He tilted his head slightly, the sunlight shifting to add new accents to his cheekbones. 'I found pieces of the same story in Okhamba, where there is no written history, only their legends. Tales of destruction and burning. The same in Yttryx; more coherent documents this time, for theirs was the first alphabet. There is even talk of primitive paintings somewhere in the Newlands of Saramyr, where the Ugati made their own records of the catastrophe. Every ancient culture in the Near World has their version of the event, it seems, and they all correspond.' His eyes darkened. 'Then, following the advice of a man I met in Yttryx, I returned to Okhamba and went deep into it, to its centre, and there I found this.'

He walked quickly over to a table, where he picked up a roll of what looked like parchment. He knelt on the wicker matting in the centre of the room and smoothed it open. The assembly craned for a closer look.

'Careful,' he said. 'This is over two thousand years old, and it was copied from a document even older than that.'

This drew a collective gasp from the audience. What had seemed to be parchment was in fact animal skin of some kind, cured by some forgotten technique and in remarkably good condition considering its incredible age.

'I will, of course, pass it to our allies in the Red Order to verify its authenticity,' Saran went on. 'But I myself am convinced. The Fleshcrafters of the tribe I stole it from certainly were. It cost the lives of ten men to bring that here to you.' He exchanged a look with Tsata, who was watching him expressionlessly, his pallid green eyes blank.

Kaiku moved around to get a better view. The picture itself was enough to make her uneasy. The main characters were all but unidentifiable, stylised and jagged horrors that might have been men dancing or animals rutting. There was a fire in the central foreground, its flames time-dimmed but still visible. Kaiku found herself marvelling at the preservation methods that had carried it through all the ages. If it were not for Saran's promise to let the Red Order verify it – which they could easily do, at least as far as telling how old it was – then Kaiku would have not believed it could be so ancient.

She looked around its border, which was inscribed with many strange patterns, searching for the clue that Saran wanted them to find. At the top, in the centre, was the blazing lower half of the sun, and below that, in a crescent shape, were the moons.

The moons!

'There are four moons,' Yugi said, before anyone else could.

Kaiku felt something deep shift inside her, an unpleasant stirring that made her feel slightly nauseous. He was right. There was Aurus, biggest of them all; Iridima, with her cracked skin; Neryn, the small green moon; and a fourth, the same size as Neryn, charcoal black and scratched with dark red lines like scuff marks. Kaiku's skin began to crawl. She frowned, puzzled at her own reaction, and then noticed that Cailin was looking at her inquiringly, as if she had noted Kaiku's discomfort too.

Saran folded his arms and nodded. 'There were clues. I found several references to an entity called Aricarat in Yttryx, and one in Quraal to Ariquraa. I had assumed they were different versions of the same root word, but I could not imagine to what they referred. Even though they were almost always used in conjunction with stories of the other moon-sisters, I did not guess. After all, it was always referred to as male. Then I found an old Yttryxian creation myth that made reference to Aricarat as being born from the same stuff as the other moons, and it suddenly made sense.' Saran bowed his head. 'Aricarat was the fourth moon. He disappeared thousands of years ago. The moon-sisters, it seems, had a brother.'

If Saran had expected a barrage of abuse or denial, he was disappointed. The Saramyr pantheon had never held anything but three moons, and the genealogy of the gods was something taught to all children at an early age. To accept what he was suggesting ran counter to more than a thousand years of belief. But the assembly looked merely dazed. A few belligerent dissenters said loudly that his idea was ridiculous, but soon quieted, finding little support. Kaiku had sat down, overwhelmed suddenly by a terrible, creeping dread that made her lightheaded and faint.

'Are you unwell?' Cailin asked.

'I do not know,' Kaiku said. 'Something . . . there is something about Saran's account that is troubling me.'

'You think he is wrong?'

'No, I think he is *right*. I am certain of it. But I do not know *why* I am certain.'

Zaelis stood up. 'I believe I understand,' he said, his molten voice commanding attention. 'You think the fourth moon . . . Aricarat?' Saran tilted his head in a nod. 'You think that Aricarat was destroyed somehow back when the world was young, and that it fell to earth in pieces. And these pieces are the witchstones.'

'Exactly,' Saran said.

'This is a wild theory, Saran.'

'I have evidence to support it,' the Quraal man said, unruffled. 'But that will bear close examination, and will take time. There are dry tomes and parchments that require translating from dead languages.'

'You will permit me to see this evidence?'

'Of course. I am convinced of its authenticity. Anyone who wishes can study it.'

Zaelis limped in a slow circle around Saran, his brow furrowed, his hands linked behind his back. The wind chimes rang softly into the silence. 'Then I will reserve judgement until I have done so; and I would urge you all to do the same.' This last was addressed to the general assembly. He returned his attention to Saran, stopped pacing, and put a curled forefinger on his white-bearded chin. 'There is one thing that puzzles me, though.'

'Please,' Saran said, inviting his inquiry.

'If pieces of the moon rained down all over the Near World all that time ago, then why are they only found in the mountains? Why not the deserts and the plains?'

Saran smiled. He had been anticipating this.

'They *are* in the deserts and the plains,' he said. 'You are looking at the matter from the wrong angle. First, we should be asking how we know where the witchstones are at all. It is only through the Weavers. How do the Weavers *find* them? That I do not know. But until five years ago, the Weavers were not allowed to own land in Saramyr; the only places they could inhabit were the mountains, where no land laws applied as there were no crops to be had. It is not easy for them to mine something out from so deep underground and keep it a secret; yet in the mountains, behind their shields of misdirection that our spies cannot penetrate, they have leisure to do so. The reason that the only witchstones we know of are in the mountains are because they are the only ones the Weavers have been able to *get* to.'

'But not any more,' Zaelis concluded for him.

'No,' Saran agreed. 'Now the Weavers have bought land all over Saramyr and guard it jealously, and on that land they erect strange buildings, and not even the high families know what they do there. But I believe *I* know. They are mining for witchstones.'

There was a grim attentiveness fixed on him now. It was not a new idea to them, but in conjunction with what Saran believed he had discovered about the origin of the witchstones, it made for an uncomfortably neat fit.

'But why seek out new witchstones?' Zaelis asked. 'They seem to have enough for the Edgefathers to make Masks.'

'I do not pretend to know that,' Saran said. 'But I am certain that they are seeking them. And that is not the worst of it.' He spun around melodramatically from Zaelis to face the audience again. 'Extrapolate from this. Since they first appeared, the Weavers have infiltrated society and made themselves indispensible. You pay a terrible price for their powers, but you cannot be rid of them. Now that they are part of the empire itself, they are even harder to dislodge. All of us know that the Weavers must be removed; all of us know that they desire power for themselves. But I ask you, what if the Weavers' sole purpose is to find these witchstones? What if they grow to dominate all of Saramyr? Even if they somehow subverted your entire continent, they would be stuck. No other land would permit Weavers onto its shores in any number; we have a healthy and sensible mistrust of them. So what then?'

'They invade,' Cailin said, standing up herself. All eyes turned to her. She walked slowly into the centre of the room to stand by Zaelis, a tower of darkness against the noon sun. 'Perhaps you extrapolate too far, Saran Ycthys Marul.'

'Perhaps,' he conceded. 'And perhaps not. We know nothing of the motives of the Weavers other than what history has shown us; and in that, they have proved to be as aggressive and acquisitive as they have been able while still at the mercy of the high families. But I believe soon the high families will be at the *Weavers'* mercy, and then there will be no stopping them. And there would be no stopping an invading army backed up by Weavers, either. No other country has any kind of defence against that.' He looked to Tsata again; Kaiku caught the brief glance. 'This is not only a threat to Saramyr; this is a shadow that could fall on the whole of the Near World. I would have you aware of that.'

His report concluded, Saran walked to where the tattooed Tkiurathi was and sat next to him. It had been a lot for the audience to digest, and it was uncomfortable for them. He could see some of them already dismissing his findings as ridiculous speculation: how could he make guesses like that, with the little they knew of the Weavers? But they were the voices that would bring down the Libera Dramach if they were allowed to prevail, for Saran knew better than to allow the Weavers even an inch of leeway, to let them have the benefit of any doubt.

'Saran's information sheds a somewhat more foreboding light on another piece of news I received this morning,' said Zaelis. 'Nomoru, please stand.'

It was a young woman of perhaps twenty winters who responded. She was wiry and skinny and not particularly attractive, with a surly expression and short, blonde-brown hair in a ragged, spiky tangle. Her clothes were simple peasant garb, and her arms were inked with pictures, in the manner of street folk and beggars.

'Nomuru is one of our finest scouts,' Zaelis said. 'She has just returned from the westward end of the Fault, near where the Zan cuts through it. Tell them what you saw.'

'It's what I *didn't* see,' Nomoru said. Her dialect was clipped and sullen, muddied with coarse Low Saramyrrhic vowels. Everyone in the room immediately placed her as being from the Poor Quarter of Axekami, and weighted their prejudices accordingly. 'I know that area. Know it well. Not easy to cross the Fault lengthways, not with all that's in between here and there. I hadn't been there for a long time, though. Years. Too hard to get to.'

She appeared to be uncomfortable talking to so many people; it was obvious in her manner. Rather than be embarrassed, she took on an angry tone, but seemed not to know where to direct it.

'There was a flood plain there. I used to navigate by it. But this time . . . this time I couldn't find it.' She looked at Zaelis, who motioned for her to go on. 'Knew it was there, just couldn't get to it. Kept on getting turned around. But it wasn't me. I know that area well.'

Kaiku could see what was coming, suddenly. Her heart sank.

'Then I remembered. Been told about this before. A place that should be there, but you can't get to. Happened to her.' She pointed at

Kaiku with an insultingly accusatory finger. 'Misdirection. They put it around places they don't want you to find.'

She looked fiercely at the assembly.

'The Weavers are in the Fault.'

Eleven

The Baraks Grigi tu Kerestyn and Avun tu Koli walked side by side along the dirt path, between the tall rows of kamako cane. Nuki's eye looked down on them benevolently from above, while tiny hovering reedpeckers swung back and forth seeking suitable candidates to drill with their pointed beaks. The sky was clear, the air dry, the heat not too fierce: another day of perfect weather. And yet Grigi's thoughts were anything but sunny.

He reached out and snapped off a cane with a twist of his massive hand; a puff of powder burst out from where it was broken.

'Look here,' he said, proffering it to Avun. His companion took it and turned it slowly under his sleepy, hooded gaze. There were streaks of black discolouration along its outer surface, not that Avun needed such a sign to tell it had been blighted. Good kamako cane was hard enough to be used as scaffolding; this was brittle and worthless.

'The entire crop?' Avun asked.

'Some can be salvaged,' Grigi mused, waddling his immense frame over to the other side of the dirt path and breaking off another cane experimentally. 'It's strong enough, but if word gets out that the rest of the crop is afflicted . . . Well, I suppose I can sell through a broker, but the price won't be half what it could be. It's a gods-cursed disaster.'

Avun regarded the other blandly. 'You cannot pretend that you did not expect as much.'

'True, true,' said Grigi. 'In fact, half of me had hoped for this. If the harvest had picked up this year, then some of our allies would be having second thoughts about the side they had chosen. Desperation makes weak links in politics, and they're easily undone when times turn.' He tossed the cane aside in disgust. 'But I don't like seeing thousands of shirets in market goods going to waste, whatever the cause. Especially not mine!'

'It can only strengthen our position,' Avun said. 'We have made preparations against this. Others are not so fortunate. They will see

93

that the only alternative to starvation is to oust Mos and put someone who knows how to run the empire on the throne.'

Grigi gave him a knowing glance. There was something else that they did not say, that they never spoke of any more than necessary. Getting Grigi on the throne was only part of the plan; the other part was getting the Weavers away from it. Neither of them had any particular animosity towards the Weavers – no more than any other high family had, anyway, in that they resented the necessity of having them – but they sensed the popular mood, and they knew how the common folk felt. The peasantry thought that the Weavers were responsible for the evil times that had befallen the empire, that their appointment as equals to the high familes was an affront against tradition and the gods. Avun did not know whether that was true or not, but it really didn't matter. Once Grigi was Blood Emperor, he would have to cut the Weavers down to size, or the same thing that was happening to Mos would happen to him.

But it was a dangerous game, plotting against the Weavers under their very noses. For like all the high families, Grigi and Avun had Weavers in their own homes, and who could tell how much they knew?

They walked on a little, until the dirt track emerged from the forest of kamako cane and curved left to follow the contours of a shallow hill. Below them, Grigi's plantation spread out like a canvas, uneven polygons of light brown tessellating with fields of green, where the cane had not yet been stripped and still retained its leafy aerial parts. In between were long, low barns and yards where harvesting equipment was left. Men and women, genderless beneath the wide wicker hats that protected them from the sun, moved slowly between the rows, cutting or stripping or erecting nets over the unblighted sections to keep off the persistent reedpeckers. From up here, all looked normal, and faintly idyllic. An untrained eye would not guess that there was poison in the earth.

Grigi sighed regretfully. He was being philosophical about his loss, but it still made him sad. Waste was not something he approved of, a fact evidenced by his enormous frame and ponderous weight. In Saramyr high society, it was usual to prepare more food than was necessary, and let diners pick and choose as they would; people ate only as much as they wanted and left the rest. That lesson had never taken with Grigi, and his fondness for fine meals and his reluctance to leave any on the table had made him obese. He wore voluminous robes and a purple skullcap, beneath which his black hair was knotted in a queue; a thin beard hung from his chin to give his fleshy face definition.

To look at him, it would not be easy to guess he was a formidable

Barak, and perhaps the only contender to the throne since he had annihilated Blood Amacha's forces. He appeared rather as a pampered noble, gone soft on luxury, and his high, girlish voice and passion for poetry and history merely corroborated the illusion. But gluttony was his only vice. Unlike many of the other Baraks, he did not indulge in narcotics, bloodsports, courtesans or any of the other privileges of rank. Beneath the layers of fat there was hard muscle on a broad skeleton well over six feet in height, a legacy of a ruthless regime of wrestling and lifting heavy rocks. Much like his companion Avun, whose languid, drowsy manner hid a brain as sharp and unforgiving as a blade, he was often underestimated by those who assumed that the weakness of character that led to such excess hinted at a weak mind.

If he had any fault, it was the one that his entire family shared: he was bitter about the twist of fate that had dethroned his father and allowed Blood Erinima to become the high family over a decade ago. If not for that, Kerestyn would still have been the head of the empire. It was his bitterness that led him to make an ill-advised assault on Axekami during the last coup; ill-advised because, despite his clever disposal of Blood Amacha, he had not counted on the cityfolk uniting to repel his invading force, and they kept him out long enough for Blood Batik to enter the capital at the east gate and take the throne themselves.

Now the people of Axekami wished they had let him in, he thought darkly.

But if it was fate that had torn Blood Kerestyn from the Imperial Keep, then it was fate that would put them back there. His father was dead now, and his two older brothers carried away by crowpox – so called because nobody ever survived it, and crows gathered around in anticipation of a meal. The mantle had passed to him, and now things were turning his way again. Nobles and armies flocked to his banner, supporting the only real alternative to the Blood Emperor Mos. This time, he vowed, he would not fail.

They ambled in the sun for a time, walking along the side of the hill to where the trail began to take them back through the fields of kamako cane, towards the Kerestyn estate. It was one of several that the family owned, and he and Avun had been using it as a base for the diplomatic visits they had been conducting among the highborn of the Southern Prefectures. The Prefects were gone now, rendered unnecessary by the Weavers, who made it pointless to appoint largely independent governors over distant lands when instantaneous communication meant that they could be overseen from the capital, and thus power kept with the Imperial family. But the Prefects' wealthy descendants remained, and they were appalled at seeing their beloved land rendered barren by the blight. They were eager to make promises to Grigi, if he could stop the rot in the land. Of course, he had no idea *how*, but by the time they knew that it would be too late.

'What news of your daughter, Avun?' he asked eventually, knowing that the Barak would walk in complete silence all the way back to the estate unless he spoke first.

'Her ship should have arrived several days ago,' he said offhandedly. 'I expect to learn of her capture very soon.'

'It will be something of a relief to you, I imagine,' Grigi said. He knew the whole truth behind Avun's rift with his daughter; in fact, he had been instrumental in spreading the smokescreen to save face for Blood Koli. 'To have her back, I mean.'

Avun's lip curled. 'I mean to ensure that she does not embarrass her family this way again. When I return to Mataxa Bay, I will deal with her.'

'Are you so confident that you have her, then?'

'Her movements have been known to me ever since she arrived in Okhamba,' he said. 'And my informant is extremely reliable. I do not predict any difficulties. She will be in very capable hands.'

When Kaiku arrived at Zaelis's study, she found Cailin already there. It was a small, close room with thick wooden walls to dampen sound from the rest of the house. One wall was crammed with ledgers, and a table rested in a corner with brushes scattered haphazardly across it and a half-written scroll partially furled. The shutters were thrown open against the afternoon sun, and the air was hot and still. Zaelis and Cailin were standing near the windows, their features dimmed by contrast to the bright external light. Birds peeped and chittered on the gables and rooftops below.

'How could I have guessed *you* would be first to offer your services?' Cailin said wryly.

Kaiku ignored the comment. 'Zaelis,' she began, but he raised a seamed palm.

'I know, and yes you may,' he replied.

Kaiku was momentarily wrongfooted. 'It appears that I have become somewhat predictable of late,' she observed.

Zaelis laughed unexpectedly. 'My apologies, Kaiku. Do not doubt that I am grateful to you for the good work you have done for us these past years; I'm glad that you still have the enthusiasm.'

'I only wish she were so eager to apply herself to her studies,' Cailin said, arching an eyebrow.

'This is more important,' Kaiku returned. 'And I have to go. I am the only one who can do it. The only one who can use the Mask.'

Cailin tilted her head in acquiescence. 'For once, I agree.'

Kaiku had not expected that. She had been ready for an argument. In truth, half of her *wanted* them to argue, to forbid her to go. Gods, just the thought of it made her afraid. Crossing the Fault was bad enough, between the terror of the spirits and the murderous clans and the hostile terrain; but at the end of it waited the Weavers, the most deadly enemy of all. Yet she had no option, not in the eyes of Ocha, to whom she had sworn an oath of vengeance. She did not want to throw herself into danger this way. She merely had to.

Zaelis stepped away from the window, out of the dazzling light. 'This may be more important than you imagine, Kaiku,' he murmured in his molten bass.

Kaiku had the impression that she had come in at the end of a grave conversation between the two of them, and she was unsure what she had missed.

'The Xarana Fault has always been our sanctuary,' he said. 'It has hidden us and protected us from the Weavers for many years now . . .' He trailed off, then looked up at her, his gaze shadowed beneath his white eyebrows. 'If the Fold has been compromised, all may be lost. We must know what they are planning, and we must know now. Go with Yugi and Nomoru; find out what the Weavers are hiding at the other end of the Fault.'

Kaiku made an affirmative noise, then looked expectantly at Cailin.

'I will not try and dissuade you,' Cailin said. 'You are too head-strong. One day you will realise the power you have and how you are squandering it with your negligence; then you will come back to me, and I will teach you how to harness what you have. But until then, Kaiku, you will go your own way.'

Kaiku frowned slightly, suspicious at this easy capitulation; but she did not have a chance to question it before Zaelis spoke again.

'It is all connected somehow, Kaiku,' he said. 'The Weavers in the Fault, the strange buildings they have constructed all over Saramyr, the information that Saran brought, what happened to Lucia . . . We have to act, Kaiku, but I do not know which direction to strike in.' He looked at Cailin. 'I think sometimes we have hidden too long, while outside our enemies have strengthened.'

But Kaiku had caught something in his explanation that chilled her. 'What *did* happen to Lucia?'

'Ah,' said Zaelis. 'Perhaps you had better sit down.'

Mishani lay awake in the guest bedchamber of Chien os Mumaka's townhouse, and listened to the night.

The room was simple and spacious, as Mishani liked it. A few carefully placed pots holding miniature trees or flowers stood on tall, narrow tables. Prayer beads hung from the ceiling, tapping softly against each other in the warm stir of the breeze that stole around the edges of the sliding paper screens. They were supposed to be left open, to provide a view of the enclosed garden beyond, but Mishani had kept them shut. Her attention was not on the external sounds of Hanzean: the distant hoot of an owl, the ubiquitous rattle of chikkikii, the occasional snatch of distant laughter or the creak of a cart. She was listening for sounds within the house: for a footstep, for the quiet hiss of a partition being drawn aside, for a dagger drawn from its sheath.

Tonight was the last night she was going to spend at Chien's hospitality. One way or another.

She had slept little and lightly these past four days. When Nuki's eye was in the sky it was almost possible to forget the danger she was in; Chien was an excellent host, and despite everything she had even begun to enjoy his company. They dined together, they had musicians perform for them, they wandered the grounds or sat in the garden and talked. But it was when the sun went down and she was alone that the fear came close enough to touch her. Then the immediacy of her situation struck home, and the air was full of whispered doubts. There were too many things wrong. Why so suspiciously generous in offering to provide passage from Okhamba? Why the convoluted route of the carriage from the jetty to the townhouse? And why did he never take her outside the walls of his compound, in all of these five days? In Hanzean there was theatre, art, spectacles of all kinds that a host was virtually obligated to show a visitor; and yet Chien had not offered any. On the one hand, Mishani was relieved at not being forced to parade around a port town, for any public exposure was dangerous; but the fact that Chien seemed to know that did not bode well for her.

If Chien was to make his play, she knew it would be tonight. This evening she had gone through the ritual of informing him of her departure on the morning of the morrow. It was perhaps a little inelegant to seem in such haste to leave after staying for the bare minimum of time that etiquette required, but her nerves had frayed enough so that she did not care. If she got away from this, she was unlikely ever to come across Chien again anyway. He was too well connected in the maritime industry to risk it. He had not seemed offended; but then, he was still frustratingly hard to read.

Tonight, she resolved, she would not sleep at all. She had asked one of the handmaidens to make her a brew of xatamchi, an analgesic with a strong stimulant side-effect usually taken in the morning to overcome menstrual pains. The handmaiden had warned her that she would be up all night if she took it so late in the day, but Mishani had said that she was willing to take that risk, and only xatamchi would do.

The handmaiden had not been exaggerating. Mishani had never taken xatamchi or anything similar before – her cycles were mercifully gentle, and had been all her life – but she knew now why she had been advised against it. She could not imagine being further from sleep as she was now, and she felt marvellously aware despite the late hour. In fact, the inactivity of lying on her sleeping-mat was chafing at her, and she longed to go out and stroll around in the garden at night.

She was just considering doing so when she heard a soft thud through the paper screens on the other side of the room. Someone else was in the garden, she realised with a thrill of fright; and she knew with a sudden certainty that her enemies were coming for her at last.

Her ears strained as she lay there, seeking another sound. Her heart had become very loud in her ears; she felt the pressure of her pulse at her temples. A whispered voice: a short, terse command from one to another, too quiet to make out. It was beyond doubt, then. Now she could only wait to hear the dreadful sound of the paper screens sliding back, to pray to the gods that they would pass by, change their minds somehow, just leave her where she lay.

Her eyes were closed, feigning sleep, when it happened. A whisper of wood sliding against wood, slow and careful so as not to wake her. A soft breeze from outside, carrying with it the fresh, healthy smell of the trees in the garden; and another smell, a faint metallic tang of sweat. Then, overwhelmingly, the stink of matchoula oil, a few breaths of which would render a person unconscious.

The creak of leather as one of them crouched down next to her mat.

She screamed at the top of her lungs, throwing her blanket aside in one violent movement and flinging the handful of red dust that she had kept gathered in her palm. The intruder, surprised, jerked back in alarm, and the dust hit him full in the face: abrasive bathing salts that she had smuggled into her bedroom. He cried out in pain as the scratchy crystals got into his eyes and bubbled on his tongue and lips, fizzing with the moisture there. The second shadow in the room was already lunging at her, but she had rolled off the mat and got to her feet. She was wearing an outdoor robe instead of nightclothes, and her curved dagger sheened in the wan moonlight.

'You tell your master Chien that I will not be taken so easily!' she hissed, surprising herself with the strength in her voice; then she cried: '*Intruders! Intruders!*' as loud as she could manage. The gods knew what good that would do – she doubted it would bring any aid, since it was the master of the house that had sent these men – but she was not going to allow herself to be stolen away in the night without making it known to everybody she could.

The one who was not blinded ran at her, oblivious to his companion's cries. He was wielding a pad of cloth that reeked of matchoula oil. They wanted her alive then, she thought, through the cold panic that was gripping her. That gave her an advantage.

She backed away as he came at her, and slashed wildly with her blade. She was no fighter: she had never been threatened with genuine physical violence in her life beyond the occasional slap from her father, and did not know how to react to it. The intruder swore as the dagger cut into the meat of his forearm, then he smacked her hand aside, and numbing force of the blow sent the blade skidding away. Though slender in build, he was much bigger and stronger than her, and she had no hope of overmatching him. She tried to run, but he grabbed at her, only half-catching her wrist; she spun and tripped on her hem, and in a flail of hair and robes she crashed through the paper screens and fell down the two short wooden steps to the townhouse's central garden.

She landed on the path that ran around the inside edge of the house, the paper screens falling around her. The impact was enough to bring tears to her eyes. She scrabbled to free herself from the light wooden frames of the screens. Her ankle-length hair was tangled and caught in everything, and she kept kneeling on it and having it wrench painfully at her scalp.

Then the screens were torn away from her, and there was her attacker. In the warm, moonlit night, she could see him better. He was dressed in bandit clothes, and his hair was unkempt, his face swarthy and angry. She slipped out from under his grip, another scream rising from her to wake the household. She got only a few paces across the garden before he caught her, hooking his foot under hers so that she tumbled again, rolling into a flowerbed and cracking her wrist on a rock. Then he was on her, pinning her hands with one arm while she thrashed and kicked.

'*Get off me!*' she cried through gritted teeth, and she felt the impact as one of her kicks connected and the man grunted. She thought for a moment that he might release her, but instead he knelt one leg agonisingly hard on her stomach, driving the breath from her, and he wadded the matchoula-soaked cloth in one hand and brought it to her face. Then she was being smothered, and his relentless palm was moving with the shaking of her head and would not be dislodged. The stinging reek was in her nostrils, on her lips, and her lungs burned for oxygen. She bucked and twisted in panic, but she was small and frail and she did not have the strength to get him off her.

Then, a shriek from somewhere in the house, and running feet thumping across the turf. The pad was pulled away suddenly, the knee released, and Mishani gasped as she sucked in the air, wild-eyed.

But the man who held her had only dropped the pad to pull a knife, and it was already driving towards her throat. Something deep and faster than thought made her shift her shoulders and shove with her knees, now that she had the purchase to do so. She bucked him forward enough so that he automatically put out his arms for balance, his knife-stroke arrested; and an instant later an arrow took him through the eye, the force of the shaft throwing him off her and sending him tumbling into a shallow pool at the base of a rockery.

She scrambled to her feet before he had come to rest, sweeping up the knife that he had dropped and brandishing it as she turned to face the ones who were running across the garden. Panting, dishevelled, her mass of black hair in a muddy mess, she glared at the shadows that came for her and held her blade ready.

'Mistress Mishani!' said Chien, the foremost of them. Behind him were three guards, one carrying a bow. At the sound of her name, she raised the dagger to throat-height, daring him to come closer. He scrambled to a halt with his hands raised placatingly before him. 'Mistress Mishani, it's me. Chien.'

'I know who you are,' she told him, an unforgivable tremble in her voice from the shock of being attacked in such a way. 'Stay back.'

Chien seemed confused. 'It's me,' he repeated.

'Your men have failed, Chien,' she said. 'If you want to kill me, you will have to do it yourself.'

'*Kill* you? I . . .' Chien said, lost for words. Behind her, she heard a guard call out. Chien looked over her shoulder. 'Are there more?' he asked her.

'How many did you hire?' she returned.

The second attacker was dragged out behind her into the garden. He was limp. Poison, she guessed. His employer would want no evidence left.

'Mistress Mishani . . .' he said, sounding terribly wounded. 'How could you think this of me?'

'Come now, Chien,' she said. 'You did not get to where you were without seeing all the angles. And nor did I.'

'Then you have not considered the right ones, it seems,' Chien said. He sounded desperate to convince her, almost wheedling. 'I had nothing to do with this!'

Mishani glanced around. There were no escape routes; guards were everywhere now. She could not fight her way out of here. If they wanted her dead, they could simply shoot her.

'Why should I believe you, Chien?' she asked.

'Put down the blade, and I will *tell* you why,' he said. 'But not here. Your business and mine is between us.'

Mishani felt a great weariness suddenly. She tossed the dagger away with an insultingly casual gesture, then gave the merchant a withering look. 'Lead on, then.'

'May we drop the façade now?' Mishani demanded, when they were alone.

They stood in Chien's accounting office, a sombre room heavy with dark wood and weighty furniture. Scrolls cluttered the shelves and lay across the desk where the merchant usually worked, heaped untidily against stacks of leather-bound tally books. The Blood Mumaka crest hung on one wall, a curving pictogram rendered in gold-edged calligraphy against a grey background. Chien had lit the lanterns in their brackets, and now the room was alive with a soft, warm glow.

'There is no façade, Mistress Mishani,' Chien said, then blew out the taper he was holding and put it back in the pot it had come from. He turned to her, and there was new strength in his voice all of a sudden. 'If I wanted you killed, I could have done it many times by now, and by subtler means. If I wanted to give you up to your father, I could have done that, too.'

'Why are you still playing this game?' Mishani said quietly. She might have been muddied and bedraggled, but her poise and gravitas had returned, and she seemed formidable for such a slight woman. 'Your words betray you. You know the state of play between myself and my father. You have known from the start. If you do not mean me any harm, then why insist on inviting me to stay at your pleasure? You have been well aware of the uncertainty and doubt I have suffered these past days. Does it give you joy to torment me? Your maliciousness shames you. Do with me as you will, since you seem to hold all the cards here; but give up this sham, Chien, for it is getting tiresome now.'

'You forget who I am and who you are, that you can throw insults around so lightly!' Chien snapped, his temper igniting. 'Before you waste another breath on calling me honourless, then listen to me. I *did* know that you were estranged from your father, and that he wanted you back. I also knew that your arrival in Okhamba had been marked by merchants in the Barak Avun's employ. You got away from Saramyr without being seen by his people, though the gods only know what luck you must have had; but the moment you showed up in Kisanth you were spotted. They were going to wait until you returned to Saramyr, watch what ship you were travelling on, and have someone there to meet you when you disembarked. Those were your father's men. I'm not. In fact, I've made a considerable risk on your behalf, and he most likely now counts me one of his enemies!'

Mishani was pleased that she had rattled him. She did seem to have a way of getting under his skin; she had learned that in the time they had spent together.

'Go on,' she said. This was suddenly interesting.

Chien took a steadying breath and stalked to the other side of the room. 'I had a carriage meet us at the docks, and brought you and your friends here before your father's men could get to you. It was necessary to take a circuitous route through Hanzean in case we were followed; I imagine you noticed that. The location of my townhouse isn't generally known.' He waved a hand to dismiss the point. 'I saw your friends to safety, but you I knew would not be safe. You said you were heading south. I couldn't let you. Not until I'd found out who your father had hired and what they knew. They would have been on you before you got ten miles down the Great Spice Road.' He gazed at her earnestly. 'So I have kept you here, under my protection, for these past days, while my men have been trying to divine just how much trouble you're in.'

'This was your *protection?*' Mishani said softly. 'I was almost killed, Chien. You will forgive me if my faith in you has been shaken somewhat.'

Chien looked pained. 'That is my shame. Not what you would imagine, Mistress Mishani. I have not tormented you or betrayed you. I have tried to safeguard you, and I failed.'

Mishani regarded him coldly. His explanation fitted, at least, but it seemed to her frankly unlikely. Still, she could not think why he would waste the effort on making it up, nor why, if he meant her harm, he had not done it to her by now. Why kill his own men? She supposed that it could be a trick – kill his men to win her trust; she had seen cleverer ploys than that in her time at court – but what advantage would that win him? She considered asking him why he was protecting her at all, then thought better of it. Any answer would likely be a lie. What was there that he thought she could do for him, what *point* was there in his winning her favour? He knew she was politically impotent.

'I didn't tell you before,' Chien said. 'If you realised that I knew about you and your father, you would have tried to get away from me as soon as you could. That would have only got you caught faster.'

Mishani had surmised this already, just as she had guessed why the intruders started off trying to kidnap her and ended up trying to kill her. Their orders were simple: alive if possible, dead if necessary. She was not in the least surprised at her father's ruthlessness.

Chien looked at her levelly, his blocky features even, the lantern light limning one side of his shaven head. 'Mistress Mishani, you may believe me or not, but I was going to tell you all this in the morning to try and prevent you from leaving. I left it too late, it seems. Your father's men found you, and nearly had your life.' He walked over to her. 'If there is anything I can do to atone for my failure to protect you, you have only to name it.'

Mishani studied him for a long moment. She *did* believe him, but that did not mean she trusted him. If he was in alliance with her father, or even if he wasn't, there was something down the line that he wanted from her, something that she did not even know she had in her power to give. Chien's attempt at an explanation had made him more puzzling than ever. Was this an elaborate trap, or something entirely unexpected? Was he telling the truth about her father's men?

It didn't matter. He owed her now, and she needed him.

'Take me south,' she said.

Twelve

The Fold was alive with celebration. The paths between the houses thronged with revellers in the heat of the late afternoon. The morning rituals were over, the noontime feast had been cooked and consumed, and now the people had taken to the streets, sated and merry and many of them already drunk. In the cities there would be fireworks as night drew in, but here in the Fault it was too dangerous to broadcast their presence with such fancies. Still, there would be bonfires, and another, more communal feast, and the revelries would go on past dawn.

Aestival Week had begun.

It was the biggest event in the Saramyr calendar: the last farewell to summer, the festival of the harvest. Since Saramyr folk counted their age in the amount of harvests they had lived through rather than the date on which they were born, everyone was a year older today. On the last day of Aestival Week, a grand ritual would see out the season, and autumn would begin with the next dawn.

The morning had seen a ceremony conducted on the valley floor for the whole town, by three priests of different orders. The denomination did not matter in any case, since Aestival Week was about thanking the gods and spirits alike. The bulk of the ceremony was an expression of gratitude for the simple joy and beauty of nature. Saramyr folk were particularly close to their land, and they had never lost their sense of the magnificence of the continent that they lived on. Everyone attended, for while most Saramyr picked and chose their godly allegiances piecemeal and prayed or attended temples as much as their conscience dictated, there were certain days when even the least pious person would not risk staying away if they could help it. And if there were some shreds of bleak and bitter irony in celebrating the harvest this particular year, they did not spoil the excitement that marked the beginning of the revels to come.

The midday feast was as much a tradition as the morning rituals, though its content differed wildly from region to region. The Fold's enterpreneurial importers had been stretched to their limit to fulfil the many and varied orders over the preceding weeks, and charged accordingly. Gazel lizards from Tchom Rin, lapinth from the Newlands, coilfish from Lake Xemit, shadeberries and kokomach and sunroot, wines and spirits and exotic beverages: one meal in the year had to be perfect for everyone, and this was it. Most people gathered in groups with family and friends, with the prestige of creating the meal going to best cook among them. Afterwards, small gifts were exchanged, vows between couples were renewed, promises were made between families.

Now the valley floor was a mass of preparations as tables and tents and mats were set for the enormous feast after dark. Bonfires were being built, pennants hung, a stage erected. But around the valley rim, the guards had been doubled, and they looked outward over the Fault, knowing that they dared not be caught off guard even now.

Kaiku walked with Lucia through the crowded, baked-dirt streets, along one of the higher ledges on which the town was built. It was a little quieter up here, and the streets were not yet so crammed that it was difficult to move. A few temporary stalls sold favours and streamers, or hot nuts, and groups of singing revellers would sweep by them every so often; but most people that they passed were either coming up from the main crush on the lower levels of the valley slope or going down to it. The two of them idled, sated with the memory of the wonderful meal cooked for them by Zaelis, who had revealed a somewhat startling culinary talent. They had shared their celebration with Yugi and a dozen others. Cailin was not to be found, and Saran and Tsata were also elsewhere, having not been seen since the day they arrived. They were not missed, though Kaiku did find herself glancing at the doorway every so often, expecting to see the tall, stern Quraal man there. She supposed that he and his Tkiurathi companion did not observe Aestival Week.

It had been a warm time, and their troubles had been forgotten in the uncomplicated atmosphere of happiness there. Kaiku sought to preserve that, and so she had wandered away before conversation could turn to weightier matters, and taken Lucia with her. Later, Lucia would undoubtedly find friends of her own age – despite her quietness, she had a magnetism that made her popular among the other children of the Fold – but for now, she was wonderful company for Kaiku, who felt contemplative and not a little emotional. Such a precious child. Kaiku could not imagine what she would have done if . . . if . . .

Lucia caught Kaiku looking at her fondly, and smiled. 'Stop worrying,' she said. 'I only fainted.'

'You fainted for *two days*,' Kaiku returned. Heart's blood, two days!

When Kaiku had learned of her strange experience with the river spirits, she had been frantic with concern. It was only because Lucia appeared to be fully recovered now that Kaiku had been placated. She dreaded to think what worse consequences could have come from Lucia's interfering in the unknown. Thank the gods that she seemed alright now.

'It was just something bad,' Lucia said, shedding no light on her ordeal at all. 'Something happened on the river. The spirits didn't like it. It gave me a shock.'

'I just want you to be careful,' Kaiku told her. 'You are still young. There is plenty of time to learn what you can and cannot do.'

'I'm fourteen harvests today!' Lucia mock-protested. 'Not so young any more.'

They came to a wooden bridge that arced between two ledges, vaulting over the rooftops of the plateau below, and there they rested, leaning their arms on the parapet and looking out into the valley. The whole haphazard jumble of the Fold was spread beneath them, and the raucous sounds of merriment drifted up from below. A few revellers on the rooftops saw them and waved. Nuki's eye looked down on it all from a cloudless sky that gave no hint that summer was ending.

'You're still worrying,' Lucia observed, looking sidelong at her friend. She was uncannily perceptive, and it was not worth hiding the truth from her.

'It is what Zaelis said that worries me,' Kaiku explained.

Lucia seemed to sadden a little. They both knew what she referred to. Earlier, Zaelis had toasted Lucia's recovery, and asked her when she would be ready to tackle the spirits again. Kaiku had responded somewhat irately on Lucia's behalf, telling him that Lucia was not some tool to be sharpened until she was useful enough to wield against an enemy. She had already suffered some unknown trauma that even she did not understand; Kaiku admonished Zaelis for even thinking about pushing her further. It had cast a momentary pall over the midday meal; but then Yugi had defused the situation with a well-chosen comment, and both Kaiku and Zaelis had dropped the matter. In retrospect, Kaiku felt that she had been overprotective, a reaction fuelled by her anger at the fact that she had not been told of Lucia's ordeal until after the assembly. Yet she could not stop fretting about it.

'Do not listen to him,' she said. 'I know he is like a father to you, but only you know your capabilities, Lucia. Only you know what you are willing to risk.'

Lucia's pale blue eyes were far away. She was not too much shorter than Kaiku these days. Kaiku's gaze flickered over the burns on the back of her neck, and she felt the familiar jab of guilt. Burns that Kaiku had given her. She wished that Lucia did not wear them so openly.

'We need to know,' Lucia said quietly. 'About what happened on the river.'

'That is not true,' Kaiku responded, her tone sharp. 'Heart's blood, Lucia! You know as well as anyone that the spirits are not to be trifled with. Nothing is worth risking yourself like that. Start small again, if you must. Work up to it.' She paused, then added: 'Zaelis is sending spies to investigate. Let them do their work.'

'We may not have time,' Lucia said simply.

'Are those Zaelis's words, or yours?'

Lucia did not give a reply. Kaiku felt her mood souring a little, but she was unwilling to let this go. She tried to keep the stridency out of her tone in the spirit of the occasion.

'Lucia,' she said softly. 'I know the responsibility you have to bear. But even the strongest backs bend under the weight of expectations. Do not let anyone push you. Not even Zaelis.'

Lucia turned to Kaiku with a dreamy expression on her face. She had heard, even if she seemed inattentive. A part of her was listening to the wind, and the ravens who watched her from their perches on the rooftops.

'Do you remember when Mishani came to you in the roof gardens of the Imperial Keep, carrying that nightdress for you?' Kaiku asked.

Lucia nodded.

'What did you think? When she offered it to you?'

'I thought it would kill me,' Lucia said simply.

'Would you have taken it?' Kaiku asked. 'Would you have worn it, even knowing what it was?'

Lucia turned away slowly, looking back out over the town. A clamour of drunken men staggered across the bridge behind them, hollering bawdy songs. Kaiku flinched in annoyance.

A silence stretched between them.

'Lucia, you are not somebody's sacrifice,' she said, her voice becoming gentle. 'You are too unselfish, too passive. You are not a pawn here, don't you see that? If you do not learn that now, then what will you be like in the years to come, when people will look to you with even greater hope in their eyes?' Kaiku sighed, and put her arm around Lucia's slender shoulders, hugging her companionably. 'I think of you as a sister. And so it is my job to worry about you.'

A grin touched the corner of Lucia's mouth, and she returned the hug with both arms. 'I'll try,' she said. 'To be more like you.' The grin spread. 'A big, stubborn loudmouth.'

Kaiku gave a gasp of spurious disbelief and pulled away from the hug. 'Monster!' she cried, and Lucia fled laughing as Kaiku chased her off the bridge and up the street.

Night fell over the Xarana Fault. Fires were started and paper lanterns were lit in warm constellations. The darkness lay muggy and sultry around the periphery of the celebrations, but within the light all was merriment. The communal feast was well underway. Many people had already left the table to make room for others, and had gone to watch the actors performing on the stage, or were dancing to an impromptu orchestra of six musicians who were improvising their way around old folk melodies. The mismatched instruments and varying skill of the players made for a controlled raucousness, raw-edged and visceral. The low, sawing drone of the three-stringed miriki was counterpointed by the glassy, plucked chimes of the reed harp and the mournful double-barrelled melodies of the two dewhorns. The rhythm was dictated by a swarthy man and his animal-skin drum, while over it all played the true talent of the group, a lady who had once been a courtesan for the Imperial family before the last coup. She played the irira, a seven-stringed instrument of leather and bone and wood that produced a hollow and fragile keening, and her achingly sweet touch on the strings almost made the air glimmer.

Kaiku, red-cheeked with wine and heat and laughter, danced a peasant dance with the young men and women of the Fold. It was much more energetic and less elegant than the courtly fashion, but far more fun. She spun and whirled from one man's arms to another, and then found herself with an Aberrant boy, whose skin was clammy as a dead fish and whose blank eyes were bulbous and blind. After the initial moment of surprise, she led him through the wild motions until someone else took his hand and they parted. Exhilarated and not a little drunk, she let the music sweep her up, and for once her cares were forgotten in the movement and the motion of the dance.

The song ended abruptly as she was being passed from one dancer to another, and she was surprised to find Yugi before her as the revellers rested in the pregnant silence between tunes. They were both breathing hard from the exertion, and exchanged a guilty grin.

'My timing is as good as ever, then,' he said. His eyes were very bright, his pupils huge. 'May I have the honour?' He held out his hand, inviting her to partner him for the next dance.

But Kaiku had seen a figure watching her on the edge of the lantern light, leaning against one of the wooden poles that held up the overhead banners.

'My apologies, Yugi,' she said, kissing him on his stubbled cheek. 'I have someone I have to see.'

And with that she left him, the music started up again behind her, and he was gathered up by a pretty Newlander girl and drawn into the heart of the dance. Kaiku left the noise and the warmth, walking out to where the darkness and quiet held ready to invade, and where Saran was waiting.

'Do you dance?' she asked, tilting herself flirtatiously.

'Regretfully not,' he replied. 'I do not think we Quraal have such loose joints as your folk seem to.'

It took her a moment to realise that it was a joke, delivered as it was in a tone dry as dust.

'Where have you been?' she asked. She wavered slightly, but the flush in her cheeks and her more inviting manner only heightened her allure to him.

'This is not my celebration,' he said, his features dark against the moonless night.

'No, I mean: where have you *been?*' she persisted. 'It has been days since the assembly. Have you forgotten me that soon? Could you not even muster a goodbye? Spirits, I am leaving the day after tomorrow to cross the Fault!'

'I know,' he said. 'Tsata is going with you.'

'Is he?' Kaiku asked. That was news to her. 'And what about you?'

'I have not decided yet.' He was silent for a long moment. 'I thought things would be awkward,' he said at last. 'So I stayed away.'

Kaiku regarded him for a time, then held out her hand. 'Walk with me,' she said.

He hesitated, studying her intensely; then he took it. Kaiku tugged him gently away from the pole he had been leaning on, and they made their way around the edges of the celebration, back towards the town. To their left, the valley was like a void, only defined by the lighter night sky that surmounted its rim. To their right, there was fire and laughter and feasting. They walked the line of the limbo in between, where the two sides met and blended and neither could quite find dominance.

'Part of me . . .' Kaiku began, then stopped, then began again. 'Part of me is glad to be going. I have been idle too long, I think. I have been helping the Libera Dramach in my own small way over the years, but these subtle increments of progress do not satisfy me.' She looked up at Saran. 'Nor do they satisfy Ocha.'

'The gods are patient, Kaiku,' he said. 'Do not underestimate the Weavers. You were lucky once. Most people do not get a second chance.'

'Is that *concern* I hear from you?' she teased.

Saran released her hand and shrugged. 'Why would you care for my concern?'

110

Kaiku's expression fell a little. 'I apologise. I did not mean to mock you.' She had forgotten how tender his pride was. They walked a little further.

'It is the Mask I fear,' she said, feeling it necessary to give a little to rekindle the moment that had existed between them. 'It has been five years since I wore it last, but it still calls to me.' She shivered suddenly. 'I have to wear it again, if we are to get past the Weavers' misdirection.'

'You are cold,' Saran said, unclasping his cloak and putting it around her shoulders. She wasn't, but she let him anyway, and as he fixed the clasp at her throat she put her hand over his. He paused, prolonging the contact, before drawing away.

'Why not have a Sister unravel the barrier?' he said. 'Why you?'

'Cailin dare not risk a fully-fledged Sister being discovered,' Kaiku said. 'And it would be unsafe to let anyone else use the Mask. The Weavers know nothing of the Red Order, and she would have it stay that way. The Mask is a Weaver device, and so the breach it causes in the barrier should raise no alarms.'

'But you have no idea if the Mask will even work this time,' Saran argued. 'Perhaps it was made only to work at the monastery on Fo.'

Kaiku made an expression of resignation. 'I have to try,' she said.

Saran brushed his sleek black hair behind his ear. Kaiku watched him sidelong, studying the lines of his figure beneath the severe cut of his clothes. A cautionary voice was warning her against what she was doing, but she ignored it. The pleasant glow of the wine she had drunk kept her mind resolutely in the present and refused to allow it to construct consequences.

Saran caught her looking, and she was a little too obvious in her haste to look away.

'Why is Tsata coming with us?' she asked, suddenly needing something to say. Then, realising that it was something she actually wanted to know, she added: 'What is he to you?'

Saran was silent a while, thinking. Kaiku could never decide if he was merely weighing his words or if he added these pauses in a conscious attempt at drama or gravitas. It was difficult to tell with Saran, whom she found annoyingly affected at times.

'He is nothing to me,' Saran said at last. 'No more than a companion. I met him in Okhamba, and he came with me into the heart of the continent for reasons of his own. By the same token he came to Saramyr. I do not know why he has asked to go with you across the Fault, but I can vouch for his worthiness. Of all those who I travelled with on my journeys across the Near World, there was none I would more readily trust with my life.'

By now they had reached the edge of the town, where it spilled onto the valley floor. The lowest steps formed a natural protective barricade, into which lifts had been built and gated stairways cut. The gates would be closed in times of war and the lifts drawn up to prevent enemies getting in.

They made their way upward along the less-travelled routes. Lanterns spilled bright islands into the darkness. They passed townsfolk kissing or singing or fighting, and once they almost walked into a parade which had gathered up hundreds in its wake and was marching them on a sinuous path to an uncertain destination. At some point, Kaiku took Saran's hand again. She thought she could detect him trembling slightly, and smiled secretly to herself.

'Do you have any doubts?' she said. 'About what you found?'

'The fourth moon? No,' Saran replied. 'Zaelis is convinced, too, now I have shown him the evidence and the Sisters have verified it. I had thought, perhaps, that the idea would be too outlandish for your people to accept; after all, you are the only people in the Near World who still worship the moons.' He flicked a strand of hair away from his forehead in a curiously effeminate manner. 'But it seems that I was wrong. In only the last thousand years, there have been other gods forgotten and lost in antiquity; it is only natural that you should not know of one that died before your civilisation was founded.'

'Perhaps he did not die,' Kaiku murmured. 'Perhaps that is the problem.'

Saran made a questioning noise.

'It is nothing,' Kaiku said. 'Just . . . I have an ill suspicion about all this. I was touched by one of the Children of the Moons; did you know that? Indirectly, anyway. It was Lucia they were helping.'

'I knew,' said Saran.

'This affair with Aricarat, it makes me . . . uneasy.' She could not put it better than that, but there was a faint nausea, a trepidation like the warning rumble of the earth before a quake, whenever she thought of that name. Would she have felt it if she had not once brushed against the unfathomable majesty of those spirits? She could not be sure.

'But more than that,' she continued. 'My friend Tane died trying to live out what he believed his goddess Enyu thought he should do. I almost shared that fate on Ocha's behalf, and tomorrow I set off to risk the same again. The Children of the Moons themselves intervened for Lucia. And now you tell me that the source of the Weavers' power, the true reason for this land's affliction and misery, are the remnants of another moon, a forgotten one?' She made an unconscious sign against blasphemy before continuing. 'I begin to believe that I have stumbled into a game of the gods, willingly or not; that we are part of some conflict beyond our power to see. And that we are all of us expendable in the eyes of the Golden Realm.'

Saran considered this for a moment. 'I think you put too much stock in your gods, Kaiku,' he said. 'Some people mistake their own courage for the will of their deities, and others use their faith as an excuse to do evil. Be careful, Kaiku. What your heart dictates and what your gods tell you may one day be in opposition.'

Kaiku was frankly surprised to hear such words from a Quraal, whose upbringing within the Theocracy generally made them rigid in their piety. She would have responded then, but she found herself suddenly before the door of the house that she shared with Mishani. It stood on one of the middle tiers of the Fold, a small and unassuming place with the rough edges of its construction smoothed over by some artful use of creepers and potted plants. Since it was hardly possible to recreate the elegant minimalism of the dwellings they had grown up in among all the surrounding chaos, they had decided to try and beautify it as much as possible. It was all Mishani's work, as was the interior, for Kaiku was hopeless at decorating; it was a very feminine art, and she had been too busy competing with her older brother to learn it.

There was a moment of shared intent, when Kaiku and Saran met each other's eyes and neither really considered saying goodbye to the other, when both feared that any advance might be rebuffed even though their senses told them it would not. Then Kaiku opened the door, and they both went inside.

The threshold that they crossed was more than physical. Kaiku had barely closed the door before Saran was kissing her, and she responded with equal fervour, her hands on his cheeks and in his hair, a warm flush seeping through her body as their tongues touched and slid. He pressed her against the wall, their lips meeting and parting, the hot gusts of breath the only sound between them. Kaiku moved her hips up against him, felt with lewd pleasure the bulge at his crotch. The cautionary voice had been swept away to the corners of her mind now, and there was no question of stopping what was going to happen.

Her hands were already working at his tight jacket, fumbling with the unfamiliar Quraal catches. She laughed at her own clumsiness; he had to help her with the last few before he slid his jacket off to reveal the bare torso underneath. She pushed him back from her a little way to see what she had uncovered. He was lean and muscled like an athlete, not an ounce of fat on his body. She ran her hands over the landscape of his abdomen, and he shivered in pleasure. She smiled to herself, coming in closer to place wet, languorous kisses on his neck and clavicle. His lips were in her hair, on the lobe of her ear.

Kaiku steered them over to a long settee and fell on to it, pulling him down on top of her. The night was close and shadowy, for the lanterns in the room had not been lit. The shutters were closed, muting the revelries outside. They kissed again, moving against each other, her hands running down the ridge of his spine to his lower back.

He stripped her blouse from her with fluid expertise, leaving it rumpled and discarded; then, without pause, he slipped off her upper undergarment, which caused Kaiku a twinge of disappointment. He was getting hasty in his ardour, and she liked her lovemaking to be slow and gradual. Anxious to interrupt him – for his hands were already moving towards her waist – she tipped him gently off the settee and onto the floor, rolling with him so that she came out on top.

Straddling his hips, she kissed his cheeks and forehead, and he leaned upward to take her breast in his hand and bring his mouth to her nipple, the hot, wet touch of his tongue sending minute trembles of delight through her. She reached behind herself and began to massage his erection through the fabric of his trousers with the heel of her hand. He was becoming excited, his breathing fast and shallow, and while part of her found it flattering that she elicited such a reaction in a man so rigidly calm and controlled, she was again a little concerned that he was getting too overeager. She sucked in her breath through her teeth as he bit her nipple hard enough to hurt.

He shifted her weight suddenly, turning her over so that he was on top now, and she saw that his face had become red and straining and ugly. Her heat faded, underpinned by something unpleasant that she saw in his eyes, an animal lust that went beyond the coupling of man and woman.

'Saran . . .' she began, not knowing what she would say, whether she would ride this out and hope that it was but a passing moment or if she would disappoint him and stop this. She was afraid of how he might react if she dared to do that. She did not want to hurt him, but she would if she had to.

He silenced her with a hard and savage kiss, one that bruised her lips with its ferocity, and suddenly there was a shift in the nature of the kiss, turning it from passion to something else.

Feeding.

Her *kana* uncoiled like a nest of snakes, bursting from her groin and her womb and tearing through her almost before she knew what was happening. There was a moment in which she felt something trying to pull free from her insides, as if her organs would rip from their tethers and crowd through her mouth and into Saran's, and then there was a blast of white and Saran was thrown back across the room, slamming into the opposite wall and landing in a heap.

It was just like last time. She had felt that hunger before.

'No . . .' she murmured, tears standing in her eyes as she got up. She had gathered her blouse across her breasts protectively. Her fringe fell over her face. 'No, no, no.' She whimpered it like a mantra, as if she could deny the magnitude of the betrayal she felt.

Saran was getting to his feet, his face a picture of anguish.

'Kaiku . . .' he began.

'No, no, *NO!*' she screamed, and the tears spilled over and down her cheeks. Her lip trembled. 'Is it you? Is it you?'

Saran did not speak, but he shook his head a little, not in denial but because he was begging her not to ask the question.

'Asara?' she whispered.

His expression tightened in a stab of pain, and that was all the answer Kaiku needed. She fell to her knees, her features crumpling as she began to cry.

'How could you?' she sobbed, then suddenly she found her anger and she shrieked: '*How could you?*'

His gaze was aggrieved, but they were Asara's eyes. He opened his mouth to speak, but there were no words. Instead, he picked up his jacket and walked out into the warm night, leaving Kaiku on the floor of the room, weeping.

Thirteen

D awn came to the Xarana Fault, a bleak and flat light muted by a blanket of unseasonable cloud that haunted the eastern horizon. Morning mists wisped in the hollows of the Fold, stirring gently among the creases and pits of the valley. The town was eerily silent, and not a soul walked the crooked streets except for an occasional guard, the creak of their hardened-leather armour preceding them along the empty passageways and dirt alleys. Aestival Week had begun two days ago now, and that first night the whole town had celebrated long past the dawn and into the morning. Last night, the festivities had been less raucous: people slept and recovered, and they would still be in bed for a long while yet.

But there were some whose purpose even Aestival Week could not be allowed to delay. They had gathered on the uppermost tier of the town, where a sheer wall of rock rose up on the western end of the valley, riddled with caves bored by the same ancient and long-dried waterways that had cut the plateaux and ledges below them. Blessings and etchings had been carved into the stone around the cave mouths, and small alcoves had been cut into the rock to serve as shrines. Even now, the musky smell of smouldering kama nuts and incense reached them faintly, the remnants of yesterday's offerings. Small hanging charms clacked and chimed.

Kaiku sat on the grass, her face pale and her eyes dark from sleeplessness, and gazed bitterly over the valley and into the east. She was vaguely aware of the other three behind her. They were tightening the belts on their backpacks, chambering ammunition in their rifles, murmuring softly as if loth to disturb the stillness of the dawn: Tsata, Yugi, and Nomoru, the surly scout whose report had inspired this expedition. Today they set out to cross the Fault, heading along it lengthwise to where the Zan cut through near its western end, and there to investigate the anomaly that Nomoru had found. There to seek out the Weavers once again.

She should have felt something more than this. After so long champing at the bit, the prospect of coming up against the Weavers, the murderers of her family whom she was oath-bound to oppose, should have fired something inside her. If not excitement, then at least fear or trepidation. But her heart felt dead in her breast, an ashen lump like a fire burned out, and she could not even summon the enthusiasm to care.

How could she not have known about Saran? How could she not have recognised the source of her attraction? Gods, she had stood there on the bow of Chien's ship and *told* him about how Asara brought her back from the brink of death, how that act had bonded them on some deep and subtle level, and all the time it had been that very bond that was drawing them together. All the time it had been Asara she had been talking to.

Spirits, Kaiku hated her. She hated her deceit, her trickery, her unbearable selfishness. Hated how she had allowed Kaiku to believe she was Saran, to dupe her into talking about Asara while Asara herself watched from behind those dark Quraal eyes; and then, worst of all, to allow Kaiku to seduce him, to make love to him, thinking he was a real person and not some cursed *counterfeit*. It made no difference that they had not completed the act. The betrayal was in the intention, not in the result: and it was total.

Kaiku knew now that her decision to sleep with him had not been one based on simple lust and the desire to enjoy him; she had been fooling herself there. She had opened herself to him, and in her mind the consummation would have been more than just bedplay but an affirmation of the feeling that she thought had grown between them. Not that she admitted it to herself, of course. She had never been an honest judge of her own emotions. It was only by the savagery of her grief that she realised how much she had secretly invested in Saran, and by then it was too late.

She had made herself vulnerable, and once again she had been cut to pieces. Staring balefully into the middle distance, she promised herself grimly that it would never happen again.

'It's time, Kaiku,' said Yugi, laying a hand on her shoulder.

She looked up at him slowly, hardly seeming to see him; then she got wearily to her feet, picked up her pack and rifle and shouldered them.

'I am ready,' she said.

They passed through the fortifications on the rim of the Fold and headed westward. Nuki's eye rose above the louring clouds to warm the canyons and valleys of the Xarana Fault. For a long while, nobody spoke. Nomoru led them into narrow pleats that angled down to the lower depths, where they could pass unobserved through the wild land about them. The jagged and bumped horizon was consumed by high walls of scree-dusted rock, rising before and behind and to either side. They passed out of Nuki's sight, and into the cool shadow.

The western side of the Fold was guarded by a tight labyrinth of fissures and tunnels known as the Knot. Here, ages ago, the same springs that had flowed east from the lip of the valley to sculpt the land on which the town was built had also flowed westward, gnawing through the ancient stone. As time passed the water would undermine some vital support, or the earth would be shaken by the tremors and quakes that ran through the Fault from time to time, and the rock above it would collapse and divert some of the tunnels elsewhere. Now the water was gone, but the paths remained, a maze of branching dead-ends that led tortuously downward. It was possible, and much faster, to go over the top of the Knot, where there was a bare hump of smooth stone a mile wide, like a horseshoe around the western edge of the Fold; but up there was no kind of cover and anyone attempting to cross it would be visible for miles around. In the Fault, secrecy was the watchword.

The dawn had grown into a bright morning by the time they emerged from the Knot. They clambered out of a thin crack onto the floor of a ravine, sloping gently upward ahead of them. Kaiku caught her breath as she saw it, and even through the weight of misery that she carried she felt a moment of awe.

The walls of the ravine rose sheer to over a hundred feet above their heads, a weathered mass of creases and ledges on which narrow swatches of bushes grew where they could find purchase. The floor was an untamed garden of trees and flowers, leaves of deep red and purple mixed in amid the green. A spring fed into a series of small pools. The sun was blazing over the rim at a shallow angle, throwing its light to the far end of the ravine and leaving the near end in shade. Bright birds nested in the heights, occasionally bursting out to swoop and tumble, chattering as they went. The air was still and hazed with a dreamlike glow. They had stepped into a secret paradise.

'This is the edge of our territory,' Nomoru said. It was the first anyone had spoken since they set out, and her harsh and ugly Low Saramyrrhic vowels jarred against Kaiku's mood. 'Not so safe from now on.'

The Xarana Fault was an ever-shifting mass of unacknowledged borders, neutral ground and disputed areas. The political geography of the place was as unstable as the Fault itself. Like gangs, each faction held their territory jealously, but from one month to the next entire communities might be sacked or overthrown, or defect to join a more powerful leader. The Fold was at constant war to keep its routes open to the outside world, and bandits preyed upon the cargoes that were smuggled in to supply the Libera Dramach. Other forces had other agendas: some were relentlessly expansionist, pursuing the hopeless ideal of dominating or uniting the Fault; others wanted merely to be left alone, and poured their efforts into defence rather than aggression; still others simply hid. The business of knowing what their neighbours were up to was a perpetual drain on the time and resources of Zaelis and the Libera Dramach, but it was vital for survival in the cut-throat world that they had settled in.

They headed onward with renewed vigilance. The terrain was hard, and Nomoru seemed to choose difficult routes more often than not, for the most inaccessible ways were often the safest. Within hours, Kaiku had utterly lost her sense of direction. She glared resentfully at the wiry figure leading them, blaming her for their ordeal; then she caught herself and realised how unfair that was. If not for Asara, she would have been glad to come on this expedition. If not for Asara.

She found herself lapsing into dark thoughts again in the absence of conversation. Yugi was unusually subdued, and Tsata rarely said anything unless it was worth saying, content instead to observe and listen with an alien and faintly unsettling curiosity. Had *he* known? Had he known that Saran was not who he appeared to be? What about Zaelis and Cailin; surely *they* had known? Cailin would have, certainly: she could sense Aberrants merely by looking at them. All the Sisters could.

In the aftermath of her discovery, in the rage that came after grief, she had wanted to face Cailin and Zaelis and demand to know why they had not told her. But it was useless; she already knew their arguments. Asara was a spy, and it was not their place to reveal her. Kaiku had spoken little enough to anyone but Mishani about Asara, and said nothing at all about her attraction to Saran. Why should they intervene? And besides, she would only be feeding Cailin ammunition for her demands that Kaiku apply herself to the teachings of the Red Order. If she had attended to her lessons instead of restlessly combing the land, she would have sensed Asara's true identity herself.

And yet she had not suspected. How could she, really? She had no idea of the extent of Asara's Aberrant abilities. She had witnessed her shift her features subtly, change the hue of her hair, even seen a tattoo on her arm that faded away; she had seen her repair the most horrendous burns to her face. But to change not only the form of her body but her *gender* . . . that had been beyond even Kaiku's notion of possibility. What kind of creature could do that? What kind of thing?

And what kind of thing can twist the threads of reality to shape fire or break minds? she asked herself pitilessly. *She is no more impossible than you. The world is changing faster than you imagine. The witchstones are remaking Saramyr, and all that once was is uncertain now.*

'You're brooding, Kaiku,' Yugi said from behind her. 'I can feel it from here.'

She smiled apologetically at him, and her heart lifted a little. 'Talk to me, Yugi. This will be a long journey, and if someone does not do something to lighten the mood then I do not think I will last the day.'

'Sorry. I've been a little remiss as the provider of good humour,' he said with a grin. 'I was suffering somewhat from last night, but the walk has cleared my head.'

'Over-indulged yourself, did you?' Kaiku prodded.

'Hardly. I didn't touch a thing. No wonder I feel so awful.'

She laughed softly. Nomoru, up ahead, glanced back at them with an irritable expression.

'You're troubled,' Yugi said, his voice becoming more serious. 'Is it the Mask?'

'Not the Mask,' she said, and it was true: she had entirely forgotten it until now, obsessed as she was with nursing the hurt Asara had done to her. It lay wrapped in her pack, the Mask her father had stolen and died for. She felt it suddenly, leering at her. For five years it had been hidden in a chest in her house, and she had never put it on again; for she knew well enough the way the True Masks worked, how they were narcotic in nature, addicting the wearer to the euphoria of the Weave, granting great power but stealing reason and sanity. Yet the insidious craving was undiminished, the tickle at the back of her mind whenever she thought of it. Calling to her.

Sometime in the afternoon, they rested and ate on a grassy slope beneath an overhang. They had passed out of the ravine and were skirting a sunken plain of broken rocks, bordered on all sides by high cliffs. Some of the rocks had thrust their way up from below in shattered formations like brutal stone flowers, their petals lined with quartz and limestone and malachite; others had fallen from the tall buttes that jutted precariously into the sky. The travellers had been darting from cover to cover for over an hour now, and while the progress they made was faster than it had been through the ravines, it was harder on the nerves. They were too exposed for comfort here.

'Why did we come this way? We're not in so much of a hurry,' Yugi asked Nomoru conversationally, as he ate a cold leg of waterfowl.

Nomoru's thin face hardened, taking umbrage at the comment. 'I'm the guide,' she snapped. 'I know these lands.'

Yugi was unperturbed. 'Then educate me, please. I know them too, though not so well as you, I'd imagine. There's a high pass to the south where—'

'Can't go that way,' Nomoru said dismissively.

'Why not?' said Tsata. Kaiku looked at him in vague surprise. It was the first he had spoken that day.

'It doesn't matter why not,' Nomoru replied, digging her heels in further. Kaiku was taken aback by the rudeness of her manner.

Tsata studied the scout for a moment. Hunkered in the shade of the rock, the pale green tattoo reaching tendrils over his arms and face, he looked strangely at home here in the Fault. His skin, which had been sallow in the dawn light, now seemed golden in the afternoon and he appeared healthier for it. 'You have knowledge of these lands, so you must share it. To withhold it hurts the *pash*.'

'The *pash*?' Nomoru sneered, uncomprehending.

'The group,' Kaiku said. 'We four are now travelling together, so that makes us the *pash*. Is that right?' She addressed this last to Tsata.

'One kind of *pash*,' Tsata corrected. 'Not the only kind. But yes, that is what I was referring to.'

Nomoru held up her hands in exasperation. Kaiku noted Nomoru's own tattoos on her arms as her sleeves fell back: intricate, jagged shapes and spirals, intertwining through emblems and pictograms symbolic of allegiances or debts owed and honoured. It was the tradition of the beggars, thieves and other low folk of the Poor Quarter in Axekami to ink their history onto their skin; in that way, promises made could not be broken. In poverty, need drove them to perform services for each other, a community of necessity. Mostly, their word was their bond; but occasionally, for more important matters, something greater was required. A tattoo was an outward display of their undertaking. Usually it was left half-drawn, and finished when the task was done. The Inkers of the Poor Quarter knew all faces and all debts, and they would only complete a tattoo once they had word the task had been fulfilled. An oathbreaker would soon be exposed, and they would not survive long when others refused to aid them.

How strange, Kaiku thought, that the need for honour increased as money and possessions decreased. She wondered if Nomoru had been an oathbreaker; but the meaning of the tattooes was incomprehensible to her, and any words she could see were written in an argot of Low Saramyrrhic which she did not know.

'Territories change,' Nomoru said, relenting ungraciously at last. 'But the borders aren't defined. Between territories, it's uncertain. Scouts, warriors sometimes, but no proper guards, no fortifications. So I've been taking you between the territories. Not so well guarded, easier to slip through.' She tilted her head in the direction of the rock-strewn plain. 'This place is a battlefield. Look at the terrain. Nobody owns it. Too many spirits here.'

'Spirits?' Kaiku asked.

'They come at night,' Nomoru said. 'Lot of killing here. Places remember. So we come in the day. Keep our heads down, we stay safe.'

She scratched her knee beneath her trousers, and looked at Yugi. 'The high pass got taken a month ago. There was a fight; someone lost, someone won.' She shrugged. 'Used to be safe. Now you'd be killed before you got a yard into it.' She raised her eyebrow at Tsata. 'Satisfied?' she asked archly.

He tipped his chin at her. Nomoru scowled in confusion, not knowing that it was the Okhamban way of nodding. Kaiku did not enlighten her. She had already decided that she disliked the tangle-haired scout.

It was late evening when their luck ran out.

The sky was a dull and glowering purple-red, streaked with shades of deep blue and ribboned with strips of translucent cloud. Neryn and Aurus were travelling together tonight, and they were already hanging low in the western sky, a thin crescent of green peeping out from behind the vast waxing face of the larger sister. Nomoru was leading them along a high spine of land, rising up above the surrounding miles of thin ghylls and narrow canyons. The ground here was broken into a jigsaw of grassy ledges which rose and fell alarmingly, so that they often found themselves having to climb around dark pits or clamber up thin, dizzying slopes with a terrible drop on either side. As hard as it was, it did have one advantage: they were well hidden within its folds, and nobody was likely to see them unless they ran into them.

They had almost reached the far end of the spine, where the land loomed glowering to meet them again, when Nomoru suddenly held her hand up, her fingers curved in the Saramyr gesture for quiet. It was something that all children learned, generally from their parents who used it often on them. Tsata either knew or guessed its meaning, but his movements were utterly silent anyway.

Kaiku strained to hear anything, but all that came to her were distant animal cries and the rising chorus of night insects. They had seen no evidence of human life so far, whether by chance or by Nomoru's skill, and only the occasional glimpse of a large predator in the distance had kept them from relaxing. Now the presence of danger tautened her, her body flooding with chill adrenaline, sweeping her brooding thoughts away.

Nomoru glanced back at them, indicating for them to stay. A

moment later, she had flitted up the side of the rock wall that faced them and disappeared over the top.

Yugi crept up alongside her in a crouch, his rifle primed in his hands. 'Do you sense anything?' he whispered.

'I have not tried,' she said. 'I dare not, yet. If it should be a Weaver, he might notice me.' She did not express her deeper fears on the subject: that she had never faced a Weaver in the battlefield of the Weave, that no Sister had except Cailin, and that she was terrified that one day the moment might arrive when she had to.

It was then she noticed Tsata was gone.

The Tkiurathi kept himself low, hugging close to the stone bulk rising to his left. On a level so basic that it did not even need conscious thought, he was aware of what angles he was exposed from and where he was covered. The thorny brakes to his right guarded his flank, and he would hear anyone coming through them, but there were shadowy spots high up on a thin finger of rock beyond that might provide a hiding place for a rifleman or an archer. He had gone to the right around the rise of stone where Nomoru had gone left, hoping to encircle the bulk and meet her on the other side, or clamber over the top if he could not get past it.

It was simple sense to him, born of a logic shaped over thousands of years of jungle life. One scout could be bitten by a snake, fall into a trap, break a leg, or be captured and be unable to warn the rest of the *pash* when enemies inevitably tracked back to where the scout had come from. Two scouts, taking different routes but still watching each other, were much harder to surprise, and if misfortune befell one then the other could rescue them or go for help. Above all, it was safer for the group.

Tsata was confounded over and over by the incomprehensible thought processes of foreigners, Quraal and Saramyr alike. Their motives baffled him. So much was not said in foreign society, a mass of implications and suggestions meant to hint at private under-standings. Their loveplay, for example: he had watched Saran and Kaiku fence around each other for weeks aboard Chien's ship. How was it that it was somehow unacceptable to say something that both of them knew, to admit their lust for one another, and yet it *was* acceptable to make it just as obvious through oblique means? Every one of them was so secretive, so locked into themselves, unwilling to share any part of their being with anyone. They hoarded their strength instead of distributing it, building themselves through words and actions for personal advancement rather than using what they had gained to benefit their *pash*. And so, instead of a community, they had this wildly unequal culture of many social levels in which inferiority was bestowed by birth, or by lack of possessions, or by the deeds of a man's father. It was so far beyond ridiculous that Tsata did not even know where to begin.

He felt some affinity with Saran, because Saran had been willing to sacrifice every man that accompanied him into the jungles of Okhamba to get himself out alive. That, at least, Tsata could understand, for he was working for the good of a greater *pash*, that of the Libera Dramach and the Saramyr people. The others on the expedition were merely interested in monetary gain or fame. Only Saran's motives seemed unselfish. But even Saran, like all of them, was so hidden in intention, and often tried to tell Tsata where to go and what to do. He had thought of himself as the 'leader' of their group, even though Tsata had taken no payment and joined of his own free will.

It was too much. He put it from his mind. Time to muse on these puzzling people later.

The stone bulk on his left was not showing any sign of rounding off and allowing Tsata's path to converge with Nomoru's, so he decided to chance climbing over it. It would leave him dangerously exposed for a few moments, but there was no help for that. In one lithe movement, he rose from his running crouch and sprang up to grip the rough sides of the rock, using his momentum and his dense muscles to pull himself up. He found a toehold and boosted himself to the top, spreading himself flat on the lumpy roof of stone. In the jungle of his homeland, his jaundiced skin and green tattoos served to camouflage him; now he felt uncomfortably visible. He crawled swiftly over the rock to the other side, staying close to what sparse vegetation grew up here. The waxing moons glared down at him as the light slowly bled from the sky to be replaced by a pale, green-tinged glow.

He was atop a long, thin ridge. Below and to its left, a ledge ran close, following the ridge's contours until it dropped away suddenly to a small clearing, which was hemmed in on three sides by other shoulders of land.

He could hear them and smell them even before he saw the men moving along the ledge towards where Kaiku and Yugi waited.

There were two of them. They were dressed in a curious assemblage of loose black clothing and dark leather armour, and their faces were powdered unnaturally white, with bruise-coloured dye around their eyes. Their clothes, hair and skin were dirty and striped with a kind of dark blue war-paint, and they were unkempt and stank of an incense that Tsata recognised as ritasi, a five-petalled flower which he understood the Saramyr often burned at funerals. They carried rifles of an early and unreliable make, heavy and grimy things, and there were curved swords at their waists.

Tsata shifted his own rifle, slung on a strap across his back, and loosed his *kntha* from his belt. *Kntha* were Okhamban weapons, made for close combat in jungles where longer weapons were unwieldy and likely to snag on creepers. They comprised of a grip of bound leather with a steel knuckle-guard, and two kinked blades a foot long, protruding from the top and bottom of the grip. The blades bent smoothly the opposite way from each other, about halfway along their length, tapering to a wicked edge. *Kntha* were used in pairs, one to block with and the other to slash, making a total of four blades with which to attack an opponent. They required a particularly vicious fighting style to use effectively. The Saramyr folk had a name for them that was easier for them to remember than the Okhamban: gutting-hooks.

He dropped down to the ledge like a cat, his landing soundless. Tkiurathi disdained any kind of ornamentation that might make a noise, for their skill was in stealth. The two men, intent on their own inept creeping, did not hear him come up behind them. They were easy prey.

He took them by surprise, sweeping at the neck of the rightmost, putting enough of his body weight behind it to behead the man cleanly. With his left hand he slashed out at the other one as he turned into the blow; it caught him square in the throat, not hard enough to decapitate him but enough to plough through thick muscle and lodge in his spine. As the first man fell, Tsata pressed his hide shoe into the second man's chest and used it as leverage to wrench his gutting-hook free. A spume of steaming blood came with it, followed by a belch of gore from the wound that spilled down his victim's chest. Tsata stepped back and watched him slump to the ground, his body still not seeming to realise that he was dead, his heart spasmodically pumping as he went.

Satisfied that the greater part of his *pash* was safe, his thoughts immediately turned to Nomoru. He wiped the blood off his blades and his sleeveless hemp waistcoat so as not to provide any scent-warning to an enemy, and then headed along the ledge in the direction the men had come from.

He found her in the sunken clearing at the end of the ledge. She was backed against a wall, facing him. There were two more with her, one with his knife pressed up under her chin, the other wielding a rifle and scanning the rim. In the last light of the day, Tsata was all but invisible as he watched from the shadow of the rocky ridge. He checked quickly for signs of any others nearby, but there was nothing, not even any sentries or lookouts on the high points surrounding the clearing. These were not warriors, however much they swaggered.

His priority was the man with the knife to Nomoru's throat. He would have liked to try and do it in silence, but the risk was far too great. Instead, he waited until neither of them were looking at him, then took aim with his rifle. He was just weighing the possibilities of taking the man out without him reflexively stabbing Nomoru when the scout spotted him with an infinitesimal flicker of her eyes. A moment later, she looked back at him again, hard. Purposefully. The man guarding her frowned as he noticed. She glared wide at Tsata, her eyes urging him.

Tsata held his fire. Clever. She was trying to turn her enemy's attention from her.

'Stop mugging, you fool,' the man hissed. 'I'm no idiot. You won't make me look away.' And with that, he slapped her. But he had to take his knife away a few inches to do it, and the instant he did so Tsata blew his brains out of the side of his head.

The last man turned with a cry, raising his rifle; but Tsata was already leaping down upon him, driving the butt of his weapon into the man's jaw. His enemy's rifle fired wild as he fell, and a second blow from Tsata stove his skull in.

The echoes of the gunshots rang across the Fault and into the gathering night.

There was a pause as Nomoru and Tsata looked at each other in the gloom, and then Nomoru turned away and scooped up her rifle and dagger, which had been taken from her.

'They'll be coming,' she said, not meeting his eye. 'More of them. We have to go.'

Fourteen

The echoes of the hunt floated distantly across the peaks.

Upon her return with Tsata, Nomoru had led them off the spine of land that they had been following, taking a north-westward route that descended hard. They were bruised and scratched from sliding down steep slopes of shale, and the exertion had tired them, for Nomoru had set a reckless pace for more than an hour. She seemed furious, though whether at herself or at them it was difficult to tell. She pushed them to their limits, guiding them down into the depths of the Fault, until the dark land reared all around them.

Finally, she called a halt in a round, grassy clearing that seemed to spring out of nowhere amid the lifeless rock that bordered it. A dank mist lay on the ground, despite the night's warmth, a sad pearly green in the light of the crescent moons. The clearing slid away down a narrow hillside to the west, but whatever was there was obscured by the contour of the land.

Yugi and Kaiku threw themselves down on the grass. Tsata squatted nearby. Nomoru stalked about in agitation.

'Gods, I could sleep right here,' Yugi declared.

'We can't stay here. Just take a rest,' Nomoru snapped. 'I didn't want to go this way.'

'We are going on?' Kaiku asked in disbelief. 'We have been travelling since dawn!'

'Why break our backs over this? There's no hurry,' Yugi reminded them again.

'They are tracking us,' Tsata said. When Yugi and Kaiku looked at him, he motioned up to where they had come from with a tilt of his head. 'They are calling to each other. And they are getting closer.'

Yugi scratched the back of his neck. 'Persistent. That's annoying. Who are they?'

Nomoru had her arms crossed, leaning against a wall of rock. 'Don't know their name. It's an Omecha cult. Not like in the cities. These are very extreme. They think death is the point of life.' She waved a hand

127

dismissively. 'Blood sacrifice, mutilation rituals, votive suicide. They look forward to their own deaths.'

'I expect Tsata was something of a pleasant surprise for them, then,' Yugi quipped, grinning at the Tkiurathi. Tsata laughed, startling them all. None of them had ever heard him laugh before; he had seemed utterly humourless until now. It was inexplicably strange to hear. Somehow, they had expected his expression of mirth to be different to a Saramyr laugh.

Nomoru did not appreciate the comment. She was already angry at herself for being captured, and perversely she was also angry with Tsata for rescuing her. 'They weren't supposed to be there,' she said churlishly. 'There were different ones there a week ago. We could have got past them. They didn't pay much attention.'

'Perhaps that was why they got driven off,' suggested Yugi.

She scowled at him. 'I didn't want to come this way,' she said again.

Kaiku, who was eating a stick of spicebread from her pack to re-plenish some energy, looked up at her. 'Why not?' she asked round a mouthful of food. 'What is this way?'

Nomoru seemed about to say something, a haunted look in her eyes; then she clammed up. 'Don't know,' she said. 'But I know not to come here.'

'Nomoru, if you have heard something about this place, then tell us!' Kaiku said. Her reticence was more alarming than if she had spoken out.

'Don't know!' she said again. 'The Fault is full of stories. I hear them all. But there's bad rumours about where we're going.'

'*What* rumours?' Kaiku persisted, brushing her fringe back from her face and giving Nomoru a hard look.

'Bad rumours,' said the scout stubbornly, returning the glare.

'Will they follow us in there?' Yugi asked, trying a different tack.

'Not if they have any sense,' Nomoru said; then, tiring of questions, she told them to get up. 'We have to go. They're getting close.'

Yugi looked to Tsata, who confirmed it with a grim tip of his chin. He hauled himself to his feet, and offered a hand to Kaiku to help her do the same. Their legs were aching, but not so much as they would be tomorrow.

'We have to go *now!*' Nomoru hissed impatiently, and she headed off down the narrow grass slope to what lay beyond.

The slope tipped gently into a broad, flat marsh; a long, curving alley flanked by walls of black granite that trickled and splashed with thousands of tiny waterways. The air was inexplicably chill; the travellers felt their skin pimpling as they descended. Humps of grass and ragged thickets rose like islands above the dreary, funereal ground mist. Strange lichens and brackens streaked the dark walls or straggled from the mire, swathes of sombre green and red and purple. Under the mournful glow of Aurus and Neryn, it lay dismal and quiet, disturbed only by the occasional shriek or croak of some unseen creature.

The terrain underfoot became steadily wetter, and water welled up in their bootprints. By the time the slope had levelled off enough to become the marsh floor, Yugi was expressing concerns over whether they could cross it at all. Nomoru ignored him. The sounds of their pursuers calling to each other in some dark, sacred cant provided all the reply she needed to give. Though the air around them seemed to dampen sound and foil echoes, it was evident that the cultists were not far away.

They forged on into the marsh, and the disturbed mist wrapped around their legs and swirled sullenly up to their knees. Already, the water had found ways in through their boots, and their feet squelched with every step. They trudged in single file, the mud sucking at them in an attempt to rob them of their footwear. Tsata took the rear, his rifle in his hands, glancing often back at the slope to the clearing, where he expected at any moment to see more of the dirty figures appear.

'We are too exposed here,' he said.

'That's why we're hurrying,' Nomoru said tersely, then stumbled and cursed. 'They'll never hit us if we're too far ahead.'

It was too late to argue the call now, so they laboured through the doleful marsh as fast as they could, following Nomoru's lead. She seemed uncannily sure-footed, and though a misstep often landed them in the watery sludge that lay to either side of the paths she chose, as long as they walked in her footprints they found relatively solid ground there.

Suddenly, Tsata clicked his tongue, a startlingly loud snap that made Kaiku jump. 'There they are,' he said.

Nomoru looked back. On the crest of the slope: four men and a woman, two with rifles. They were calling to companions out of sight. As she watched, one of the riflemen aimed and fired. The sharp crack was swallowed by the thick marsh air. Kaiku and Yugi ducked automatically, but the shot went nowhere near them.

Nomoru slipped back along the line to where Tsata was, unslinging her rifle. For the first time, Kaiku noticed how incongruous the weapon was in comparison with the woman that carried it. Whereas Nomoru was scrawny and scruffy and uncouth, her rifle was a thing of beauty, with a sleek black lacquer on its stock and body, inscribed with tiny gold pictograms, and a swirling silver intaglio along the length of its barrel.

'Stop worrying,' she told Kaiku and Yugi, as another cultist fired and they cringed from the shot. 'They'll never hit us. We're out of their range.'

'So what are you doing?' Yugi asked. Standing still in the open while somebody shot at them, no matter how distant, was fundamentally unnerving; yet he did not dare move without Nomoru leading them, for he had already gained a healthy respect for the dangers of the marsh.

Nomoru settled her rifle against her shoulder, took aim, and squeezed the trigger. A moment later, one of the cultists collapsed, shot through the forehead.

'They're not out of *my* range,' she said. She pulled the bolt back into position to reprime the rifle, swung the barrel fractionally to the left, and fired again. Another cultist went down.

'Heart's blood . . .' Yugi murmured in amazement.

The remaining cultists were hurriedly retreating now, back into the clearing and out of view.

'Now they've got something to think about,' Nomoru said, shouldering her rifle. 'Let's go.'

She made her way to the head of the line and trekked onward. The others followed her as best they could.

It was not long before Kaiku began to sense a change. At first, it was too subtle for her to identify, merely a feeling of unease. Gradually it grew, until it made the fine hairs on her arms prickle. She glanced at the others to see if anyone shared her discomfort, but nobody showed any sign. She had the slightly unreal sensation of being sealed off from her companions, of existing on a level apart from them, as if she was a ghost that they were powerless to see or touch or interact with. Her *kana* stirred within her.

The sensation was emanating from the marsh, from the very ground that they walked on. A feeling of steadily intensifying awareness, as if the land was slowly waking up around them. And with that awareness, malevolence.

'Wait,' she said, and they stopped. They were midway through the marsh, stranded far from any place of safety, and still the sensation grew, the colossal, rank *evil* that seemed to bleed from the air. 'Gods, wait. The marsh . . . there's something in the marsh . . .' Her voice sounded thin and weak and trancelike, and her eyes were unfocused.

As if her warning was a signal, there was a sudden gust of foul-smelling wind, whipping the mist at their feet high above their heads. The wind passed, dying as quickly as it came; but the vapour stayed hanging there, a white, hazy veil that turned the world around them to grey shadow. From being able to see the length and breadth of the marsh, they found their vision sharply curtailed, and the sensation of being shut in was alarming.

'What had you heard about this place, Nomoru?' Tsata demanded suddenly.

'It was the only way we could go,' she snapped defensively. 'They were just rumours. I didn't know they—'

'*What had you heard?*'

The quiet Tkiurathi's voice was rarely ever raised, but his frustration at Nomoru was getting too much. She was a complete loner, disappearing on her own without telling anyone why, stashing nuggets of information instead of sharing them so that she could keep control of the group, meting out what knowledge she had as it suited her. It was anathema to Tsata. And now her evasions were endangering the *pash*, and that could not be borne. If necessary, he would threaten her to find out what she knew.

There was a silence for a moment, a battle of wills between the two of them. Finally, it was Nomoru who relented. 'Demons,' she said resentfully. '*Ruku-shai.*'

A distant rattling sound cut through the mist, like hollow sticks being knocked together, rising to a crescendo and then dropping away. Yugi let out a breath, turning it into an unpleasant oath.

'It was the only way we could go,' Nomoru said again, more softly this time. 'I didn't believe the rumours.'

Yugi ran his hand through his hair in exasperation, adjusted the rag tied around his forehead, and shot her a disgusted look. 'Just get us out of here,' he said.

'I don't know which way *out* is!' she cried, sweeping a hand to encompass the murk that surrounded them.

'Guess!' Yugi shouted.

'That way,' said Tsata calmly. He had kept his bearings, for he had not turned or moved since the mist came down.

'They're coming!' Kaiku said, looking around in a panic. Her irises had darkened from brown to a deeper, richer shade of red.

They did not waste any more time. Nomoru took the lead, following Tsata's direction, and she headed across the marsh as fast as she dared. The mist was not thick enough to make it impossible to see nearby objects, but the accumulation of it over distance rendered anything beyond twenty feet away as an indistinct blur. They waded through the muck in long strides, eyes and ears alert. The rattling came from all around them now, a rhythmic clicking noise that swayed from slow and sinister to rapid and aggressive. The mist ruined any hope they had of pinpointing it. They went with guns ready, knowing that the iron in a rifle ball was the only weapon they had against demons, knowing also that it could do no more than deter them.

'Kaiku,' said Yugi from behind her. She did not seem to hear him;

her gaze was on something beyond what they could see. 'Kaiku!' he said again, putting his hand on her shoulder. She looked up at him suddenly, as if shaken from a dream. Her eyes were wild, and she trembled. She was remembering other demons, and the terror she had suffered at their hands.

'Kaiku, we need you,' Yugi said, staring hard at her. She did not seem to comprehend. He smiled suddenly, unexpectedly, and brushed her hair back from where it lay over one side of her face. 'We need you to protect us. Can you do that?'

She searched his face for a second, then nodded quickly. His smile broadened encouragingly, and he gave her a companionable pat on the upper arm. 'Good girl,' he said, using an affectionate diminutive that Kaiku would have found insultingly patronising in any other situation. Now, however, she found it strangely heartening.

'Come on!' Nomoru barked from up ahead, and they hurried to catch her.

Kaiku was in a different world to the others. She had slipped into the Weave, maintaining herself on a level midway between the realm of the senses and the unearthly tapestry that ran beneath human sight. But her heightened perceptions made her open to more sensations than the simple fear that the others had to deal with. She brushed against the enormity of the demon minds, the dimensionless pathways of their thoughts, and it threatened to crush her. She fought to shut it out, to keep herself from slipping off that knife-edge into the yawning void that waited if she should try to understand it. This was of a different order to the moment when she had glimpsed into the world of the Children of the Moons. Kaiku had been overwhelmed then by her own insignificance, how unimportant she was to that incomprehensible consciousness. The ruku-shai were not even close to the power of those terrible spirits, but they *hated*, and she quailed at the force of it. Their attention was bent upon her now.

Saramyr legend had it that demons were unclean souls cursed to corporeal form for their terrible offences against the gods in life; neither living nor dead but condemned to the torment of limbo. But in that moment, Kaiku knew that it was not true, that her people would never know their origins, for they were so far from human that it was impossible to believe they had ever walked the earth, that they had loved and lost and smiled and cried like she had.

She could see through the mist, through the lazily swirling threads of glittering gold; and there she watched the demons pulling themselves up from the mire, their shapes a black, knotted tangle against the purity of the Weave. She could not make out details, but their forms were clear to her. Their bodies were sinuous and snakelike, ending in sharp, cord-like tails. Six slender legs radiated from their underbellies, thrusting upward and outward and then crooking down at a spiked knee joint. They crept onward slowly, high-stepping with exaggerated care, placing their two-toed forefeet delicately. And all the time, there was that horrible rattling as they clicked together the bones in their throat, communicating in their dreadful language.

'Three of them,' she said, then stumbled and went thigh-deep into a brackish pool of foul-smelling water. Tsata caught her under her arm before she could topple in any further, and lifted her out as if she weighed nothing at all. 'There's three of them,' she repeated breathlessly.

'Where?' Tsata demanded, urging her into motion once again.

'On our left.'

Yugi looked over automatically, but there was only the grey shroud of the mist. Nomoru was forging on, almost too far ahead to see.

'Nomoru, wait!' he cried, and there was an explosive oath of exasperation from up ahead. When they caught her up, she was furious; but it was obvious by now that the anger was merely a thin sheen to contain the raw fear that bubbled underneath and threatened to spill over. As soon as they were close enough, she headed off again, setting a cruel pace.

'How far are we from the edge of the swamp?' Yugi asked Kaiku.

'Too far,' she said. She could sense the demons prowling unhurriedly towards them, content to let them wear themselves out, like dogs hunting antelope. They had been on their feet since dawn, and it told in their tired steps and frequent stumbles. The ruku-shai only had to wait, and pick their moment.

And with that realisation, she halted. She had run from other demons in the past, from the relentless shin-shin. She had spent days and nights hiding from Aberrants in the Lakmar Mountains on Fo, creeping and huddling. She had slunk through the corridors of a Weaver monastery in terror of discovery. Always running, sneaking, shying from the notice of beings more powerful than she was. But those were the days before she had been taught to use her *kana* by Cailin, before her schooling had made it a weapon she could wield instead of a random and destructive thing. She was not so defenceless any more.

'What *now?*' Nomoru cried.

Kaiku ignored her, turning her face to the blank mist and the demons beyond which were approaching with their languid, mincing gait. Her irises darkened to blood-red, and a wind stirred her hair and ruffled her clothes, momentarily blowing back the gloomy vapour.

'I will not run,' she said, heady with a sudden recklessness. 'We have to stand.'

Her *kana* burst out from her, a million fibrous tendrils winding away into the golden diorama of the Weave, invisible to the eyes of her companions. The barrage smashed into the nearest of the ruku-shai, and Kaiku's consciousness went with it. It was like being plunged into freezing, foetid tar. For a few fractions of a second – though in the world of the Weave they seemed like minutes – she was suffocating, her senses encased in the cloying foulness of the demon, flailing in panic at the unfamiliar brutality of the sensation; and then her instincts took over, and she found her bearings and oriented herself. The demon had been as confused and unprepared for the attack as Kaiku was, but the advantage was lost now, and they tackled each other on equal footing.

Nothing in the Sisters' training could have prepared her for this. Nothing in her carefully orchestrated sparring had come close to the frantic sensation of meeting another being in combat within the Weave. Some part of her had thought that she could simply rip the demon apart, tear its fibres in a blast of flame as she had done to several other unfortunates that had crossed her path in the days after her power awakened; but demons and spirits were not so easily despatched.

They met in a scrabbling mesh of threads, bursting apart and arcing in on each other again like a ball of serpents chasing one another's tails. The demon fought to track the threads back to her body, where it could begin to do her damage; she strove to foil it while simultaneously attempting the same thing. Suddenly, she was everywhere, her mind fractured and following a thousand different tiny conflicts, here knotting a strand to block the oncoming blackness that slipped along it, there skipping between fibres and probing weaknesses in the demon's defences. She used tricks Cailin had taught her, finding to her surprise that they came to her as if she had known them all her life. She broke and fused threads to form loops which turned the ruku-shai's advance back on itself; she created stuttered tears in the fabric of their battleground which her enemy was forced to work around while she sent darts of *kana* to harry at its inner defences.

She feinted and probed, now drawing all her threads into a bundle, now scattering them and engaging the demon on many fronts at once. With each contact she felt the hot, dark reek of her enemy, the frightening singularity of its hatred. Again and again she was forced to retreat to sew up a gap that the ruku-shai had opened, to corral its quick advances before it could get to her and touch her with the awful energy that composed it. She shrank before it, rallied and drove it back, then was driven back in turn by its sheer presence. It used maneouvres unlike anything that the Sisters had schooled her in, patterns of demon logic that she could never have thought of.

And yet, they were evenly matched. Their struggle swayed one way and another, but essentially they were at a stalemate. And gradually, Kaiku became accustomed to the conflict. Her movements became a little more assured. She felt less like she was floundering, and more in control. If the demon had thrown all its strength at her in the beginning, she might have been defeated; but she was learning its ways now, for its methods were few and often repeated. She found with a fierce delight that she could spot the demon's tricks and prevent them. The ruku-shai's inroads into her defences became less frequent. She realised that, untested as she was, she was quicker and more agile on the strings of the Weave than the creature she faced, and only her inexperience had allowed it to hold her back thus far.

She began to think she could win.

She gathered the threads under her control into a tight ribbon and went spiralling skyward, dragging her enemy with her like the tail of a comet. She took the demon dizzyingly high and fast, keeping it snared with hooks and loops, and it was bewildered by this strange offensive and slow to react. Dogging it with swift attacks, she drew its attention far from the core of its consciousness; then, nimbly, she cut it loose and plunged, skipping onto different threads and racing back towards the demon's body, circumventing the battle front entirely. The ruku-shai, realising that it had been lured away from the place it was meant to be defending, followed as rapidly as it could. But Kaiku used all her speed now, and her enemy was not quick enough. She crashed up against its inner defences like a tidal wave, utilising the full force of her *kana*, and they crumbled. Then she was in, racing through the fibres of the ruku-shai's physical body, scorching through its muscles and veins, suffusing herself into every part of its alien physiology.

There was no more time for subtlety. She simply planted herself inside it, and tore apart the black knot of its being.

The demon emitted an inhuman clattering from its throat as it ruptured from the inside. A cloud of fire belched from its mouth, its limbs and belly distended, and then it exploded into flaming chunks of sinew and cartilage. Kaiku felt the rage and pain of its demise come washing over her as she withdrew her *kana*, an aftershock across the Weave that stunned her with its force. She snapped back into reality, her *kana* retreating into the depths of her body again, recoiling from the backlash of the demon's ending.

She blinked, and suddenly she was no longer seeing the Weave but the grey mist, and her companions staring at the muted bloom of flame that had suddenly lightened it on one side. Perhaps a second had passed for them, if that; but Kaiku felt as if she had fought a war singlehanded.

Her momentary elation at being the winner of that war disappeared as she heard the rhythmic gallop of the approaching demons. She had beaten one, but its companions were enraged, and they were no longer content to wait on their prey. Their rattling took on a harsher pitch that hurt the ear. The dank curtains of vapour coalesced into two monstrous shadows. She did not have time to gather her *kana* again before the ruku-shai were upon them.

They burst from the gloomy haze, their six legs propelling them in a strange double-jointed run. They were seven feet high from their wickedly hoofed toes to the knobbed ridge of their spines, and over twelve feet in length, a drab green-grey in colour. Their torsos were a mass of angles, plates of bony armour covering their sides and back. It grew in sharp bumps and spikes like a coat of thorns, smeared with rank mud and trailing straggly bits of marshweed. Their heads were similarly plated around their sunken yellow eyes and forehead, and when they opened their jaws a cadaverous film of skin stretched across the inner sides of their mouth.

They smashed into the group, catching them off-guard with their unexpected speed. Kaiku threw herself aside as one of them thundered past her, lashing its tail in a blur at her head. She fell awkwardly, tripping on a clump of long grass and going down full-length into a vile slick of sucking mud. Her attacker pulled up short, rearing on its back four legs, and drew its front ones up like a praying mantis, spearing her with a deadly regard. Then a rifle sounded, and the ball sparked off the armour on its cheek. The demon recoiled, and Kaiku felt Yugi's arm on her, pulling her back to her feet.

She found her balance just in time to catch sight of the other ruku-shai over Yugi's shoulder. It had also reared in a mantis position, and as Kaiku watched in horror it jabbed a blow at Tsata with its hoofed foreleg, faster than the eye could follow, sending the Tkiurathi reeling back in a spray of blood to collapse against a marshy hillock. An instant later, it came for them.

'Yugi! Behind us!' she cried, but she was too late. The demon's cord-like tail whipped Yugi across the ribs as he turned to respond to her warning. He sighed and fell forward onto Kaiku, his muscles going slack all at once. She caught him automatically; then she heard another rifle shot, and the angry, clattering snarl of a demon. She threw Yugi's limp weight down, registering momentarily that the demon who had stung him was now flailing in agony at a wound in its neck where Nomoru's rifle had pierced its armour.

But the ruku-shai who had first attacked them was looming over her now, its forelegs held before it and its mouth open, crooked and broken fangs joined by strings of yellow saliva as they stretched apart. A sinister rattle came from deep in its throat.

She had only an instant to act, but it was enough. With an effort of desperate will, she marshalled her *kana* from within, and throwing out her hand at the demon she projected herself into a furious attack. The Weave erupted into life around her as she narrowed her energies into a tight focus, driving into the demon's defences like a needle through stitchwork, leaving nothing back to protect herself. The ruku-shai was not quick enough to mount an effective counter, overcome by the suicidal audacity of the maneouvre, and Kaiku lanced into its core in the space of an eyeblink and ripped it apart.

The force of the explosion scorched her muddied face as the demon was destroyed. Somewhere behind her, Nomoru was swearing, foul curse words in a gutter dialect thrown at the last demon as she fired again and again, repriming between each ball as she pumped shot after shot into the creature. Ignoring Yugi, Kaiku turned from the flaming remains of her victim and stumbled to the scout's aid.

Nomoru was standing over the prone form of Tsata on the hillock, holding the ruku-shai at bay. Each time she hit it, the creature writhed in pain as the iron in the rifle ball burned its flesh; but each time it came for her again, and Nomoru's ammunition could not last forever.

Kaiku cried out in challenge. She was wading through the marsh towards it, her irises a deep red and her expression grim. The sight of her approach robbed the demon of the last of its spirit, and with a final rattle it plunged away into the mist.

Nomoru squeezed the trigger for a parting shot, and her rifle puffed uselessly. Her ignition powder had burned up. She glanced at Kaiku with a flat expression, revealing nothing; then she crouched down next to Tsata, and rolled him over.

'Get the other one,' she said to Kaiku, not looking up.

Kaiku did as she was told. The air was becoming less oppressive, the evil departing like an exhaled breath, the mist thinning around them. She felt numb. The demons were gone, but she was racked with tiredness, and the sudden departure of adrenaline from her system left her trembling.

Yugi lay sprawled face-down, his shirt torn open where the tail of the ruku-shai had hit him. Blood welled through from beneath. Kaiku knelt down by his side, her heart sinking. She pulled off his pack, then turned him over and shook him. When that produced no response, she shook him again, his head lolling back and forth as she did so.

Puzzlement turned to alarm. He had not been hit hard. What was wrong with him? She had no training in herbcraft or healing; she did not know what to do. The cushioning folds of exhaustion were not enough to suppress the new horror rising up inside her. Yugi was her friend. Why was he not waking up?

Omecha, silent harvester, have you not taken enough from me already? she prayed bitterly. *Let him live!*

'Poison,' said a voice by her shoulder, and she looked round to see Tsata crouching by her. His face was bloodied with a deep gash, and his right eye was swollen shut. When he talked, his bruised lips made a smacking noise.

'Poison?' Kaiku repeated.

'Demon poison,' Nomoru said, from where she stood over them. 'The ruku-shai have barbs in their tails.'

Kaiku remained staring at the face of the fallen man, which was turning steadily a deep shade of purple as they watched.

'Can you help him?' Kaiku said, her voice small.

Tsata put his fingers to Yugi's throat, feeling for a pulse. Kaiku did not know to do that. It was not part of a high-born girl's education. 'He is dying,' Tsata said. 'It is too late to remove the poison.'

The mist had almost sunk back to the ground now, and in some peripheral part of her mind Kaiku realised that they were three-quarters of the way through the marsh. The cultists on the other side were gone.

'You get it out,' said Nomoru. It took Kaiku a moment to realise who she was addressing.

'I do not know how,' she whispered. She did not trust the power inside her enough. Suddenly she felt a crushing regret for all those years she had spurned Cailin's advice to study, to learn to master her *kana*. Wielding it as a weapon was one thing, but to use it to heal was a different matter entirely. She had almost killed Asara with it before, and later she had almost killed Lucia, all because of her lack of control. She would not have Yugi's death on her hands, would not be responsible for him.

'You're an apprentice,' Nomoru persisted. 'An apprentice of the Red Order.'

'I do not know *how!*' Kaiku repeated helplessly.

Tsata grabbed her collar and pulled her towards him, glaring at her with his good eye.

'*Try!*'

Kaiku tried.

She threw herself into Yugi before her fear could overwhelm her again, placing her hands on his chest and squeezing her eyes shut. The veined film of her eyelids did nothing to block the Weave-sight as the world turned golden again. She plunged into the rushing fibres of his body, knitting past the striations of muscle and into the weakening current that kept him alive.

She could sense the poison, could *see* it as it blackened the golden threads of his flesh. The slow thunder of his heart throbbed through her.

She did not know where to start or what to do. She had hardly any formal knowledge of biology and none of toxicology. She did not know how to defend against the poison without destroying it and Yugi with it. Indecision paralysed her. Her consciousness hung within the diorama of Yugi's body.

Learn from your surroundings. Mould yourself to them.

The words that came to her were Cailin's. A lesson taught long ago. If all else failed, go limp and let the flow of the Weave show you how to move.

Yugi's body was a machine that had run efficiently for over thirty years now. It knew what it was doing. She only had to listen to it.

She began a mantra, a meditation designed to make her relax. Against all odds, it began to ease her, and the rigid form of her consciousness began to disseminate, to melt like ice into water. Kaiku was startled by how easily her *kana* responded to her command. What had moments ago seemed an impossible task became simple. She allowed herself to be absorbed into the matrices of Yugi's body, and let nature instruct her instincts.

It made perfect sense: the circulation of the blood, the flickering of the synapses in his brain, the tiny pulses through his nerves. By becoming part of it, she found his body as familiar to her as her own. She found that she knew what to do on a subconscious level rather than a conscious one, so she let her *kana* guide her.

The poison spread like a cancer, with even the tiniest part blooming out evil threads of corruption if left unchecked. Kaiku was forced to move within the fibres of Yugi's body with the precision of a surgeon, tracking the dark coils amid the glowing tubes of his veins and capillaries, defending his heart from the insidious inward progress of the invader while simultaneously cleansing the befouled blood that passed through it with every weakening beat. The mental strain of trying to keep Yugi alive while neutralising the poison was immense, and more so because she had little idea of what she was doing; but she found herself gaining the upper hand, her *kana* working with a mind of its own, seeming to be only nominally under her control.

She chased the poison. She knotted and looped it to arrest its progress. She gently excised corrupted threads and sent them elsewhere, discharging harmlessly into the swamp around her. She erected tumorous barriers that it could not pass, and then took them down when the danger had gone. Twice she thought she had beaten it, only to find that a tiny shred of poison had been overlooked and was creeping inward again. Exhaustion threatened to overwhelm her, but her will held strong. She would not let him die. She would *not*.

Then, unexpectedly, it was done. Her eyes flickered open, irises deep crimson, and she was back in the marsh once again. Tsata was looking at her with something like awe in his gaze; even Nomoru bore an air of grudging respect. Yugi was breathing normally, his pallor back to its usual hue, sleeping deeply. She felt disoriented; it was a few moments before she realised where she was and what had happened.

Gods, she thought to herself in stark disbelief. *I did not realise. I did not see what I could do with the power inside me. Why did I not let Cailin teach me?*

A sense of elation more deep and profound than any she could remember touched her. She had saved Yugi's life. Not by bearing him out of danger, or protecting him in battle, but by physically drawing him back from the brink of death. She knew well enough the perilous euphoria of the Weave, but this was a different ecstasy, purer somehow. She had used her power to heal instead of to destroy; and what was more, she had done it without ever being taught how. A smile spread across her face, and she began to laugh with relief and joy. It was some time before she realised she was crying also.

Fifteen

The Blood Emperor Mos woke with a shout from a dream. He gazed wildly around, his meaty hands clutched tight to the gold sheets of his bed; then sense returned to him as he realised he was awake. But the dream lingered: the humiliation, the sorrow, the rage.

It was too hot. Past midday, he guessed, and the Imperial bedchamber was stifling despite the open shutters. The room was designed to be wide and airy, with a floor of black *lach* and a single archway leading to a balcony high up on the north-eastern side of the Imperial Keep. Smaller, oval windows flanked the archway, beaming painful brightness into the room.

Mos lay on the bed that formed the centrepiece. Most of the other furniture was for Laranya – dressing-tables, mirrors, an elegant couch – but this was his, a gift from an emissary of Yttryx that he had received near the start of his reign. At each corner of the bed, the ivory horns of some colossal Yttryxian animal formed the bedposts, six feet long and curving outward in symmetry, ringed with gold bracelets and studded with precious stones.

The room smelled of sour alcohol sweat, and his mouth tasted of old wine, befouled by the dry mucus in his throat and on his tongue. He was naked amid the tangle of covers that his nocturnal thrashing had displaced.

His wife the Empress was not in the bed with him, and by the absence of her perfume he knew she had not slept there the previous night.

Recollection came sluggishly. Aestival Week was still young. He remembered a feast, musicians . . . and wine, a lot of wine. Vague images of faces and laughter scattered across his mind. His head throbbed.

An argument. Of course, an argument; they seemed to be doing that more and more of late. When two firebrands clashed, sparks flew. But he had been in a conciliatory mood, still feeling faint tatters of guilt for that moment in the pavilion when he had almost struck her. He had made it up to her somehow, and they had celebrated through the night. Feeling that their temporary peace was fragile, he had even tolerated the terrible company she attracted, forsaking his more stolid and interesting companions for his wife's repellantly gaudy and theatrical friends.

Of course, Eszel was there, and her brother Reki. The bookworm seemed to have found his element among Laranya's lot. Mos remembered swaying drunkenly, not saying much, while they talked gibberish about inconsequential matters that seemed designed to exclude him from the conversation. What did he know of the ancient philosophers? What did he care for classical Vinaxan sculpture? Beyond occasional attempts by Laranya to rope him into the conversation, like throwing scraps to a starving dog, he had absolutely nothing to contribute.

He frowned as bits and pieces slotted into place. A feeling of resentment, that they were not paying attention to him, their Blood Emperor. Satisfaction that his presence was making both Reki and Eszel very uncomfortable. Ardour . . . that was very strong. He remembered wanting Laranya, a deep stirring that needed satisfaction. Yet he would not ask his own wife to come to bed with him, not in front of the peacocks she was mingling with. It offended his sense of manhood. She should come with him when he told her to; he would not beg. Heart's blood, he was the Emperor! But he feared an embarrassing rejection if he commanded her, and she was too wilful to be sure of a yes.

He wanted to go, and he wanted her to come with him. He did not want to leave her here. Sometime during the night, in a moment of drunken clarity, he realised that he did not want to leave her with Eszel. He did not trust what they might do, once he was gone.

Dawn was the last thing he could recall. By then, unable to keep awake beneath the smothering blanket that wine had laid over his senses, he announced loudly and awkwardly that he was going to bed, gazing pointedly at Laranya as he did so. The peacocks all bade him farewell with the usual graceful rituals, and Laranya kissed him swiftly on the lips and said that she would be there soon.

But she did not come. And Mos's dreams had been bad that night, and uncommonly vivid. Though he could recall only one, he could not shake the feelings it had evoked. A dream of hot, red rutting, of walking invisibly into a room and finding his wife there, fingers clawing the back of the man who thrust between her legs, gasping and moaning the way she did when Mos was with her. And he was powerless in his dream, impotent, unable to intervene or to see the face of the man that was cuckolding him. Weak and pathetic. Like that moment when Kakre had loomed over him, cowed him like a child.

He lay back down in his bed, his jaw clenched bitterly. First the Weave-lord, now his own wife? Did they conspire to humiliate him? Sense told him that Laranya was probably still where he left her, still celebrating with the inexhaustible zest for life that was one of the things he loved in her. But he would never know what had gone on in those lost hours since dawn, and his dream tormented him as he waited angrily for her return.

The townsfolk of Ashiki had learned to fear the coming of the night.

Aestival Week had been a cursed time for them. There were no celebrations now. They were only a tiny community, and new to the Fault. Scholars and their families, mainly, though their personal wealth had been used to hire soldiers as guards. In the past few years, there had seemed to be more and more people fleeing to the Xarana Fault to escape the oppressive atmosphere in the cities, the sense of slowly rising tension. The Weavers' eyes were everywhere except here, and the scholars and thinkers who had founded Ashiki had feared persecution for their radical ideas more than they feared the tales they heard of the Fault.

They had not heard the right tales.

Their arrival in the Fault had been blessed with good luck. Guided by Zanya or Shintu or both, they had happened upon a secluded vale near the east bank of the Rahn, at the foot of the great falls. Initially it had appeared to be an ill omen, a charnel-house of corpses that horrified them; but they were pragmatic people, and not superstitious, and soon they realised what had happened here and understood that it was the perfect place for a town. Here, two warring factions had wiped each other out fighting over one another's territory, and the remainder had scattered. The land was unclaimed, and so the scholars claimed it.

They did not know the extent of their fortune. Most new arrivals in the Fault did not last a week before some other force, already well entrenched, consumed them. But the great battle had emptied the land for a mile in every direction, and they managed to create a small community unhindered and unnoticed, hiding in their picturesque vale while they built crude fortifications and homes.

This was to have been their first Aestival Week in the Fault, and despite the hardships they felt like explorers on a new frontier, and they were glad.

Then, on the second night of Aestival Week, people started to disappear.

Lulled by their apparent safety, the revellers in Ashiki had allowed their security to become lax amid the celebrations. Four people were nowhere to be found by the morning. Their absence was hardly noted at first; when it was, it was thought that they had fallen asleep somewhere, drunk. By nightfall, their families and friends were concerned, but the rest of the town were not worried enough about a few missing people to curtail their festivities. In all probability they had simply gone off to find themselves a place to couple or to get a much-needed break from the community at large. It was not unknown.

That night, six people disappeared. Some of them from their beds.

This time the town took notice. They sent out search parties to comb the surrounding area. When they returned, they were two men short.

Now, as night came on the fourth day of Aestival Week, nobody slept. The silent demons and spirits that were stealing them away had made them mortally afraid, and they clustered in their houses or hid behind their stockade walls and dreaded what the dawn might bring. They did not know that their demon had done its work, and departed now. It had all the victims it needed.

The entity that Kaiku knew as Asara brooded in a cave, still wearing the shape of Saran Ycthys Marul. Kaiku would not have recognised him, however. He was massive and swollen, his skin a webwork of angry red veins that hung loosely off him in folds as if all the elasticity had gone out of it. His strict Quraal clothes lay discarded at his side, next to a different set of clothes that he had stolen for the purpose of his new guise. The once-muscular body was grotesque and sagging now, spilling over his folded knees. His eyes were filmed with white and speckled with shards of dark iris which floated freely around in myopic orbs. The components of his body were breaking themselves down, reordering themselves in a genetic dance of incredible precision, changing bit by bit to ensure that all functions kept working while the miracle of metamorphosis occurred. He was altering his very structure, being reborn within his own skin.

The cave was dank and pitch-black, well hidden. By firelight, it would have been a small, pretty grotto, dominated by a shallow pool surrounded by stalagmites, its walls glinting with green and yellow mineral flecks. But he had lit no fire, for he needed no heat. He had chosen the cave for its inaccessibility, and had made sure it was well away from any settlement in the Fault. It reeked of a choking animal musk. The occupant had been killed and removed by Saran a few days ago, but the stink would serve to keep other animals away. He had barricaded the entrance with stones, to be sure.

In the days it would take him to change, he was vulnerable. His muscles had already wasted to the point where he could barely move. He was effectively blind and deaf. Alone in the dark, there was only the gradually slowing tide of his thoughts to keep him company, decelerating towards the hibernation state in which he would spend the bulk of his transformation.

What thoughts still swirled around in the bottom of his mind were bitter dregs.

Asara had taken on the body of Saran Ycthys Marul with entirely innocent intentions. It had been a necessary guise to facilitate her mission in Quraal. Under the rigidly patriarchal Theocracy, women were not allowed to move between provinces without special dispensation, and foreign women were not even allowed to set foot in the country. Taking on the form of a Quraal male was the only realistic way of performing any kind of investigation there. It was distasteful to her, but not entirely unpleasant. She had spent a few years as a man before, during her years of wandering and searching for the sense of identity that had ever eluded her. This time around, she found she was better accustomed to it, and she fit easier in her own skin. Still, she could not help sometimes feeling that she was acting as she thought a man should, rather than the behaviour coming naturally to her. Such moments manifested themselves as moments of grandiose gravity or flair that, unbeknownst to her, seemed somewhat forced and ridiculous.

He had kept the guise for that last visit to Okhamba. Partially it was because he had got used to it, but it was also because it would be easier to gather men for a dangerous trip if he himself was a man: there would be no tiresome issues of gender, whether in preparation for the journey or during it. Men were apt to either feel disdain towards a woman who sought to risk herself – thinking arrogantly that she was trying to measure up to a man by doing so – or they felt protective, which was worse. They were as predictable as night and day.

But there was another, more important reason. To effect a change of his entire body meant that he was forced to glut himself, to steal the breath and the essence of others until he was gorged to the limit of endurance. The forge of change, the organ that he felt nestling between his stomach and spine – which he imagined as a coil, though he really had no anatomical comparison to draw against – had to be stocked with fuel enough to keep it burning throughout the metamorphosis. That required many lives of men and women.

Not that Saran felt guilt about taking what he needed. He had long since learned that he was unable to feel more than a passing regret in killing, no more than a butcher would in slaughtering a banathi. But he had lived to eighty-six harvests by being careful, and a dozen deaths in quick succession would always arouse terror and suspicion among the survivors. Sometimes they thought it was a mysterious plague, the Sleeping Death that they had heard of, for his victims were found dead without a mark on them as if they had simply stopped breathing; but other times, they sought a scapegoat, and if they found him in mid-transformation, they would tear him apart.

Usually he did not change his whole body any more than he absolutely had to. But this time was an exception.

A violent loathing had taken him. This form, this skin, was tainted now. Saran Ycthys Marul would be sloughed away, and with it perhaps some remnant of the responsibility for the memories it bore.

How could he have known that they would send Kaiku to meet him? Of all people, why her? Though they had been separated for five years, the same cursed attraction existed between them in whatever form he took, and now it was strengthened by the simplicity of being between man and woman. He wished he had never saved Kaiku's life now. It had exacted a heavy price on one who prided himself on his utter independence.

Yet for a time, he had believed that fortune had turned his way. Why tell her? he had thought. He did not owe her the knowledge. It was his prerogative to change his identity whenever he pleased, and he did not feel that he was betraying a trust if he chose to lie about his past. Then, after Kaiku had told him what she thought of Asara, his mind had been made up. Better to begin again. Kaiku would never have to know.

And then came the time, the moment of joining; but his body betrayed him as Asara's had done before him. The desire to take her, to be inside her, was stronger than the act of making love could satisfy. At a primal level he wanted to *consume* her, to reclaim the lost part of himself and to assimilate her very being in the process. Once again, he had lost control.

Now he had ruined everything. He knew Kaiku too well: she was as stubborn in her grudges as in everything else. She would not forgive him, ever. His deception, which had seemed justifiable at the time, now seemed abhorrent when mirrored through Kaiku's eyes. What a pitiful vermin he was, taking on shapes to reinvent himself over and over, to erase past mistakes with different faces. A being with no core, and no soul, stealing his essence from others, vapid inside.

He had gone to Cailin, and they had spoken of a new task for him, one that would require him to take a new form. He was only too glad to take it.

He could bear himself no longer. It was time to change.

Zaelis found Lucia sitting with a young boy her own age in the lee of a rocky jut that protruded from the side of the valley. It was midday, and Nuki's eye was fierce overhead, pummelling the world in dazzling light. Lucia and the boy lay in what little shade the rock provided, he on his back, she on her belly reading, kicking her legs absently. Several small animals busied themselves nearby, strangely nonchalant in their activities: a pair of squirrels dug for nuts, darting quickly about but never straying far; a raven prowled up and down the jut like a lookout; a black fox sat worrying at its brush, glancing back occasionally at the two adolescents who lounged under its protection.

Zaelis halted for a time, watching them from downslope. His heart softened at the sight. It was like a painting, a moment of childhood idyll. Lucia's posture and manner was more girlish than he had ever seen her. As he thought this, she turned to the boy and said something about the book she was studying, and he burst into explosive laughter, startling the squirrels. She grinned at him in response; a carefree, genuine smile. Zaelis felt gladdened, then suddenly sad. Such moments were too rare for Lucia, and now he came to ruin it for her. He almost turned back then, resolving to talk to her later; but he reminded himself that there was more at stake than his feelings or hers now. He limped up the hill towards them.

He knew that boy, he realised, as he got closer. His name was Flen; the son of one of the few professional soldiers that the Fold possessed. His father was a Libera Dramach man. Zaelis remembered meeting him once or twice. Of all the people that Lucia spent her time with, Flen was the one she preferred; or so his informers told him, anyway. Caution had driven him to keep a watch on the former Heir-Empress's activities as she grew.

He found himself disliking the boy already. He had warned Lucia against making her abilities overt, for fear of revealing herself. Even though nobody knew the Heir-Empress of Blood Erinima was even alive, much less the strange affinity with nature that she bore, it was too great a risk. Yet she did not conceal them around Flen. Only Flen. Out of all her friends, what made *him* special?

Careful, Zaelis, he told himself. *She is fourteen harvests old now. No longer a little girl. No matter what you may prefer to think.*

Flen noticed him then, though the animals – and hence Lucia – had spotted him a long time ago. They did not scatter as animals should, but held their ground with a peculiarly insolent air.

'Master Zaelis,' he said, getting to his feet and bowing swiftly in the male-child fashion, hands linked behind his back.

'Flen,' he replied, with a mere dip of his head. 'May I have a private word with Lucia?'

Flen glanced at Lucia as if to seek her approval; it irritated Zaelis inexplicably. But she was still reading her book as if neither of them were there.

'Of course,' he said. He seemed about to say some words of farewell to Lucia, but then decided against it. He walked away hesitantly, unsure of whether he should stay nearby or leave, and then made a decision and struck out towards the town.

'Daygreet, Zaelis,' Lucia said, not looking up. It was the first time they had met today, for she had left the house before he had awoken, making the pleasantry an appropriate one.

He sat down next to her, his damaged leg out straight before him. He could manage the traditional cross-legged position when he needed to, but it made his knee ache. His eyes wandered over the puckered and grooved skin on the nape of her neck, the appalling burn scars revealed by her short hair. She looked up at him over her shoulder, narrowing her eyes against the glare of the sun, and waited expectantly.

Zaelis sighed. Talking to her was never easy. She gave so little back.

'How are you feeling?' he asked.

'I'm fine,' she said casually. 'And you?'

'Lucia, you should really be using a more formal mode by now,' he told her. Her language had subtly evolved into a hybrid of girl-child form and woman-form, which was usual for adolescents as they became embarrassed about using a diminutive mode and began to copy adults; but the dialect she had picked up from the mass of influences among the people of the Fold did not seem appropriate for the child of an Empress.

'I am quite capable of adopting a far more elegant mode, Zaelis,' she said, in crisply elocuted, chilly syllables. She sounded eerily like Cailin. 'But only when I need to,' she finished, reverting to her usual style.

Zaelis abandoned that line of conversation. He should never have brought it up.

'I see you have been communicating with the wildlife of the valley again,' he said, indicating the black fox, which glared at him.

'They come to me whether I talk to them or not,' she said.

'Does this mean that you are well recovered from your incident with the river spirits?' he asked, absently running his knuckles over his close-cut white beard.

'I told you I was,' she replied.

Zaelis looked out across the valley, framing his next sentence; Lucia, surprisingly, spoke up first.

'You want me to try again,' she said. It was a flat statement.

Zaelis turned back to her, his expression set as a grim affirmative. There was no point evading it; she was far too incisive.

Lucia got up and sat cross-legged, arranging her dress over her knees. She seemed so tall and slender suddenly, Zaelis thought. Where was the little girl he had tutored, the little girl he had built a secret army around?

'It will do no good,' she said. 'What happened on the river has been forgotten now, at least by any spirits that I could contact.'

'I know that,' said Zaelis, although he really hadn't for sure until Lucia told him. 'But *something* happened there, Lucia. I sent spies to investigate, after what happened to you. The river towns are talking of nothing else.'

Lucia studied him with her fey blue eyes, her silence prompting him to continue.

'A barge was destroyed on the Kerryn,' he said, shifting himself awkwardly. 'Carrying explosives, apparently, and they must have gone off and blown it to pieces. But there were . . .' He hesitated, wondering if he should share this with her. 'There were bits washed up, bits of the people that had been on the barge. That, and bits of *other* things. That barge was carrying something when it exploded, and it wasn't human.'

Still Lucia did not speak. She knew he was getting to his point.

'Cailin believes that things are building to a head. The failing crops, Blood Kerestyn's armies, Saran's report, the thing you sensed on the river, the Weavers in the Fault. I have grown to believe her. We have little time left.'

He intentionally left out the revolt in Zila, though intelligence had reached him long ago about that. He tried to keep the doings of the Ais Maraxa as far from Lucia's ears as possible.

He laid a hand on his adopted daughter's knee. 'I have come to realise that we have no clear idea of what we are truly facing, and ignorance will kill us. We have to know what is going on *now*,' he said. 'We have to know what we are dealing with. The source of all of this.'

Her heart sank as she felt the inevitability of what was to come.

'Lucia, we need you to tell us. To go to Alskain Mar, contact one of the great spirits. We need to know about the witchstones.' He looked pained as he said it. 'Will you do it?'

You are not a pawn here. Kaiku's words came back to her then, spoken on the first day of Aestival Week. But they seemed hollow, brittle under the weight of necessity. She knew in her heart that she was not capable of a meeting of minds with a spirit such as dwelt in Alskain Mar, and that she would be placing herself in grave danger by trying; and yet, how could she refuse? She owed her life to Zaelis, and she loved him dearly. He would not ask her if it was not a matter of utmost importance.

'I will,' she said, and the day seemed suddenly a little darker.

Sixteen

A estival Week passed, but for Mishani there had been no celebration this year. For seven days now she had been riding
through the Saramyr countryside, and for one not used to
long journeys on horseback it was a gruelling test. Yet despite saddle-
sores and fatigue, and the endless watchfulness, she never made a
complaint, never let her mask slip even a little. Though she was
surrounded by men whom she mistrusted, though she headed south
in secret to an uncertain end, though her own father was trying to have
her killed, she was calm and serene. It was her way.

They had left Hanzean soon after the attempt on Mishani's life,
timing their departure to coincide with the beginning of the harvest
celebrations so as to take advantage of the confusion and slip away
unnoticed. Chien had insisted on personally accompanying her as
escort, to make reparations for the shame of allowing assassins to
menace his guest. Mishani had expected no less. Whatever Chien's
plans for her, she was sure that he would want to be present to see
them carried out.

Nevertheless, their journey was far from safe, despite the retinue of
eight guards who went with them; the merchant put himself at
considerable risk by travelling with her. Transport by sea was not an
option, since all boats would be watched by Barak Avun's men and
their arrival logged in their destination port. That left land travel,
which was more fraught with minor perils but which would make
evading her father a much simpler task. Anyone seeking them from
Hanzean would have no idea which way they went, since nobody knew
their destination but Mishani.

Still, the need for secrecy carried its own disadvantages. Mishani
was accustomed to travelling by carriage; but they were forced to
stay off the roads, and that meant horses, and camping under the
stars. Though Chien expended every effort to make her comfortable,
providing her with sheets and an elegant tent which the grumbling
guards had to put up for her each night, it was still somewhat irksome

151

for the child of a Barak. Mishani liked her little luxuries, and she did not share Kaiku's readiness to forsake them. But at least she still had her luggage with her from her trip to Okhamba, so she had her clothes and scents, and plenty of diversions.

They had struck out south from Hanzean for several days before turning south-east to meet the Great Spice Road below Barask, which ran almost exactly a thousand miles from Axekami to Suwana in the Southern Prefectures. They did not dare use the Han-Barask Highway, one of only two major routes out of the port, and even when they found the Great Spice Road they stayed well off it, keeping to the west of the thoroughfare until the northern reaches of the Forest of Xu began to loom to their left, and they were forced to join the road to take the Pirika Bridge across the Zan. There they were warned about the revolt in Zila and told to go back if they could and find another route to their destination.

Few heeded the warning: there was no other way. The vast and fearful forest crowded them to the east, spirit-haunted and ancient, while to the west was the coast. There were no ports of a size capable of supporting passenger craft unless they went back to Hanzean, and to go around the forest would require a detour of some nine hundred miles, which was insanity. Instead, most travellers were heading off the road, skirting the Forest as closely as they dared and passing to the east of Zila. With no option left to them, Mishani and her retinue took that route also.

By nightfall of their seventh day of travel, they were camped twenty-five miles to the south-east of the troubled city, near a shallow semicircle of black rocks that knuckled out of the flat plains. It was the last day of summer, and in Axekami the final ritual of Aestival Week would be at its height, welcoming in the autumn. There was no question of hiding out here, unless they cared to go within the borders of the forest which glowered a mile to their east. But their camp was anonymous among many scattered across the plains: other travellers heading south like them and forced to brave the bottleneck that Zila commanded.

Mishani sat cross-legged on a mat near the fire, her back to the rocks that ran along one edge of their campsite, and watched the guards building her small tent nearby. A slender book lay closed on the ground next to her. One of her mother's. It was a gift from Chien: the latest volume of Muraki tu Koli's ongoing series of fictions about a dashing romantic named Nida-jan and his adventures in the courts. Muraki's creation had made her moderately famous among the high families, and her stories had spread by word of mouth to the servant classes and peasantry as well. Handmaidens would beg their masters and mistresses to read them the tales of Nida-jan, which were printed in High Saramyrrhic, a written language taught to high-borns, priests and scholars but incomprehensible to the lower classes. They would then eagerly pass the stories on to their friends, embellishing here and there, and their friends would do the same for *their* friends.

Nida-jan was everything Mishani's mother was not: daring, adventurous, sexually uninhibited and confident enough to talk his way out of any situation, or able to fight his way out if words failed. Mishani's mother was quiet, shy, and fiercely intelligent, with a strong moral compass; she lived her life in her books, for there she could shape the world any way she saw fit instead of having to deal with the one that was presented to her, a place that was often too cruel and hurtful for a woman so sensitive.

Mishani took after her mother in appearance, but her father in temperament. Muraki was a lonely woman, too introverted to connect with those around her, and though she was pleasant company, it was easy to forget that she was there at all. When her father Avun began grooming Mishani in the ways of the court, Muraki dropped out of the picture almost entirely. While Mishani spent all her time in Axekami with her father, Muraki stayed at their Mataxa Bay estates and wrote. When Mishani had fled to exile in the Xarana Fault, she had not considered her mother's feelings at all. Muraki showed them so rarely that it simply did not occur to Mishani that they might be affected.

Now Mishani had finished the book, and a deep sorrow had taken her. The stories were not the usual Nida-jan fare; instead, they were melancholy and tragic, an unusual turn for the irrepressible hero. They concerned Nida-jan's discovery that one of his courtly liasons had produced a son, who had been hidden from him, and whom he only learned of when the mother confessed it to him on her death-bed. But the boy had gone to the east, and had disappeared there some months before. Nida-jan was tortured by love for this unknown son, and set out to find him, becoming obsessed with his quest, spurning his friends when they told him it was hopeless. He set out on foolhardy adventures to seek clues to the boy's whereabouts. Finally he faced a great demon with a hundred eyes, and he blinded his enemy with mirrors and slew it; but as it died, the demon cursed him to wander the world without rest until he found his son, and until his son called him 'Father' and meant it.

So the book ended with Nida-jan condemned, his soul racked and his quest still incomplete. Loss bled from every line. Each story had, directly or indirectly, been about a parent's yearning for their child. Mishani's mother may have been introverted, but she had not been cold. She poured out her pain on to the pages, and Mishani grieved to read it. Suddenly, she missed her mother like a physical ache in her stomach. She missed her father too, the way he had been, before she made herself an enemy to him. She wanted desperately to wipe away the years that separated them, to return to the time when she was her father's pride, to embrace her mother and tell her how sorry she was that they had never been closer, that she had not realised how Muraki felt.

All the years of hiding bore down on her, living in fear of being recognised, terrified of her own family. She would have cried, had she been alone.

She was looking up at the moonless sky when Chien sat down next to her. The air, though warm, seemed unnaturally clear and brittle tonight, and the light of the stars was sharp and hard.

'You're thinking of your mother, aren't you?' Chien said, after a time.

Mishani supposed that was a guess based on the book lying by her side. She did not wish to answer him, so she avoided the question.

'The Grey Moth is out tonight,' she said, gesturing upward. Chien looked.

'I don't see it,' he said.

'It is very faint. Most nights it cannot be seen at all.'

'I only see the Diving Bird,' the merchant said, counting off nine stars in the constellation with one stubby finger.

Mishani lowered her head, her hair falling forward over her shoulder with the movement. 'It is there,' she said. 'Hidden to some and visible to others. That is part of its mystery.'

Chien was still trying to find it, eager to be included in her experience. 'Is it an omen, do you think?'

'I do not believe in omens,' Mishani replied. 'I merely find it appropriate to my mood.'

'How?'

Mishani looked up at him. 'Surely you know how. Do you not remember the story of how the gods created our world?'

Chien's blocky face was blank. 'Mistress Mishani, I was adopted. They don't teach adopted children the finer points of religion, and academia hasn't played a great part in managing my family's shipping business. I know about the tapestry, but nothing about moths.'

Mishani studied him, sidelit as he was by the fire of their camp. He seemed earnest, at least, but she half-suspected he was feigning ignorance simply to engage her in further conversation. He was sometimes hard work to be around, since he had none of the ease of spirit which allowed most people to sit in comfortable silence with each other. He always had to talk when he was with her, always had to have something to say. She could feel him squirming awkwardly when he did not.

'The story goes that the gods were bored, and Yoru suggested they weave a tapestry to amuse themselves,' Mishani began. 'This was in the time before his enforced vigil at the gates of the Golden Realm, before Ocha discovered his affair with Isisya and banished him there.'

'That part I *do* know,' Chien said with a crooked smile.

'Each god or goddess would stitch their own piece,' Mishani continued. 'But they had nothing to make it out of, so Misamcha went to her garden and gathered caterpillars. The caterpillars made silk at her touch, and she wrapped them up into skeins and gave them to the gods, who made their tapestry. When the work was done, all agreed that it was the most wonderful tapestry they had ever seen, the richest and the most detailed. Since they liked it so much, Ocha decided to give it life, so they could watch their tapestry grow. Each god or goddess became reflected in their favourite aspect. Some took physical things: the sea, the sun, the trees, fire and ice. Others took less tangible matters: love, death, revenge, honour. And so the world was created.'

'You've told me of caterpillars now,' said Chien, 'but not of moths.'

Mishani looked back up at the night sky, where the Grey Moth hung, seven dim stars surrounding an abyss of perfect void. 'The gods wanted the tapestry to be perfect. But after it was sewn and the world made, the caterpillars changed into beautiful coloured moths. All but one, and that one was grey and sickly. For no thing is utterly perfect, not even that which the gods create, not even the gods themselves.'

She turned her gaze to the fire, and it danced in the pupils of her eyes. 'The grey moth had produced a silk that was corrupt, a thread that the gods had used along with all the others to make their tapestry, interwoven with the other threads. And in that silk was all the evils of the world, all the jealousy and hatred and foulness, all the sadness and grief and hunger and pain. Once the gods saw what had been done, they were appalled; but it was too late to undo their work. They loved the world a little less after that.' She paused for a time, considering. 'They called the silk of that caterpillar the Skein of Lament, and then they put the image of the Grey Moth in the night sky as a reminder.'

'A reminder? Of what?' Chien asked.

'A reminder that we should never relax our vigilance. That even the gods could not make something perfect without it becoming corrupted, and humankind is more fallible than they. If we cease to be watchful, then evil slips into our lives, and it will undermine us and bring us down.' She met Chien's gaze, and she let her eyes show her weariness, and a fraction of her melancholy. 'I do not think we have been watchful enough of late.'

Chien regarded her strangely for a few moments, his plain features blank with incomprehension. Mishani did not feel inclined to elaborate any further. Presently, Chien began fiddling with the hem of his cloak, a sure sign that he was becoming uncomfortable. She let him suffer until he spoke again.

'We've passed Zila,' he said, 'and the way south widens again. Perhaps it's time you told us where you're going now. We need to decide if we have to stop for supplies and choose the best route.'

Mishani acceded with a tilt of her head; Chien would, after all, be unable to do anything about it now, even if he had wished to betray her somehow.

'I will go to Lalyara,' she said. 'There you may leave me, and I will count your obligation fulfilled with honour.'

'Not until I have you safely delivered to your ultimate destination, Mistress Mishani,' Chien insisted. 'Into the care of someone who will take responsibility for your welfare.'

Mishani laughed. 'You are kind, Chien os Mumaka; but there is nobody in Lalyara who will do that. My business must remain my own, and I am bound by other promises not to tell you.'

Chien bore the news well enough. She had expected him to be crestfallen – he was curiously childlike at times – but he smiled faintly in understanding. 'Then I will treasure these last days we will spend in each other's company,' he said.

'As will I,' Mishani replied, though more because it was expected than because she meant it. In truth, against her better judgement, she did like Chien. It was wise not to feel affection for a potential opponent, but that tension was the part of their relationship that she found most interesting, and she had to admit that he had grown on her. He had a quick brain and a sharp wit, and Mishani could not help but respect his achievements: how he had overcome the stigma of being adopted into a disgraced family to help raise Blood Mumaka back to power through his devious mercantile skills.

Still, for all that, it would be a great relief to be rid of him. She was constantly on edge, waiting for his hidden agenda to manifest itself.

But would her destination be any better?

He excused himself and got up to go and talk to his men, leaving Mishani to her thoughts. She found them wandering ahead of her, to what she had to do once he was gone.

She was to meet Barak Zahn tu Ikati, Lucia's true father. And if things went well, she was to tell him that his daughter still lived – and that Mishani knew where she was.

It would be a terribly delicate thing to achieve, and it would test her diplomatic skills more sorely than at any time past. The risk was immense, and the responsibility placed in her hands was greater still. Mishani dared not reveal that she knew anything about Lucia until she was sure that the Barak would react in the way that they wanted. If she misplayed her hand, she could find herself a hostage, held and interrogated, at the mercy of Zahn's Weaver. Zahn might demand to have his daughter brought to him, or he might marshal his troops and storm into the Fold, and that would be catastrophic.

His mental state over the last few years had been more and more distracted and lugubrious if accounts were to be believed. He had let the affairs of his family slip and retreated to one of his estates north of Lalyara. Popular rumour had it that he was mourning the death of his friend – and lover, so the gossips said with unwitting accuracy – the former Blood Empress Anais tu Erinima. Mishani knew better.

Zaelis had witnessed the moment when Zahn met Lucia for the first time in the roof gardens of the Imperial Keep, and both father and daughter had known at that moment what Anais had kept concealed all those years.

But if Zahn had ever intended to make a claim on his daughter, he missed his chance. The Blood Empress was slaughtered, and in amongst the confusion the little Heir-Empress disappeared. Though her body was never found, it was assumed that she had died in the fires and explosions that raged through the Keep on that day, her corpse charred beyond recognition. In reality, she had been snatched away by the Libera Dramach, but not even Zahn knew about that.

Zaelis had charged Mishani to make the decision whether to tell him or not. It was a heavy burden to bear. But they could not keep Lucia a secret for ever, and if they could get Zahn onto their side, then they would gain a powerful ally. It would take time to prepare the moment when Lucia would emerge from the shadows, years of planning; and it began here, with Mishani. After Zahn, she would approach Blood Erinima, who also had a vested interest, for Lucia was a living child of theirs that they had thought dead, and ties of blood were the strongest of all.

But first, Barak Zahn. One trick at a time.

A stirring in the camp brought her out of her musing. A few of the guards had got up hurriedly from around the fire, and were looking into the darkness over her head, past the shallow semicircle of black rocks. She felt a vibration in the ground, and a moment later the sound reached her ears. Hooves, pounding on the plains.

Approaching fast.

The first volley of shots cut down four of the eight men that Chien had brought to protect them. The defenders' night vision was destroyed by the fire, and the attackers were firing from the outside in, so

Chien's men were easy targets while the newcomers were impossible to see. Mishani scrambled into the shelter of the rocks a moment before six horses came leaping over them, one thundering to the ground mere inches from where she lay and trampling over the mat where she had sat. The attackers rode into the camp, swords chiming free, and cut down another of the guards; then they galloped through Mishani's tent and off into the dark again.

'*Put out that fire!*' Chien screamed. He kicked the blaze into burning clumps of wood and stamped on them. One of the other guards threw a pan of water across the embers, soaking Chien's boots in the process, while the remaining two had got their rifles up. Somewhere beyond their circle of vision, their attackers were repriming their weapons, ready to shoot again. The light dimmed suddenly as the fire was dispersed, and darkness took the camp.

'Mistress Mishani! Are you hurt?' the merchant cried, but Mishani did not reply. She had already clambered over the low rocks to the other side, keeping them between her and where she imagined the attackers to be, hiding her from the camp. Her heart was hammering in her chest with that same horrible nervous fear that had gripped her when the assassins came for her at Chien's townhouse. Were these more of the same? Was it her they wanted? She had to assume so.

'Mishani!' Chien called again, a tone of desperation in his voice; but she did not want them to find her. Right now, they were in the open, and they were the targets these new killers would go for. That gave her a chance.

She heard an anxious blast of breath, and suddenly remembered the horses. They had been tethered to a post on the near side of the camp. She could almost make them out if she squinted, ghostly blue shapes jostling in alarm. By Shintu's luck, they still wore their tack; the guards had been told by Chien to put up Mishani's tent each night before unsaddling their mounts. Her disdain for sleeping rough just might save her life.

'Mishani!' Chien cried again. Mishani was happy to let him carry on doing so. He was drawing attention to himself. Through a gap in the rocks, she could see that Chien and his remaining guards had adopted a defensive stance now, grabbing what cover they could, their guns pointed outwards. But the riders were not attacking yet. Dousing the fire had made the assassins' job of picking targets a lot harder. Mishani thanked the moon sisters for their decision to stay out of the sky tonight, and then crept to the horses.

The twenty feet that she had to cross felt like a mile, and she had the terrible intuition that at any moment she would feel the brutal smack of a rifle ball and know no more. And yet, to her mild disbelief, the moment never came. She slipped the tethers of her horse from the post and swung into the saddle with a stealthiness that surprised even herself.

That was when the second attack began.

They came in from three sides this time, in pairs. One of each pair had a rifle raised, the other a sword. They fired as they galloped in, and Chien's men fired back at the same time. By good fortune or poor aim, the defenders came off better: none of them were hit, but they managed to kill one of the horses as it bore down on them, striking it directly between its eyes so that it crashed to the ground and rolled over its rider with a cracking of bones.

And then there were swords, crashing against rifle barrels or the guards' own hastily drawn blades, and the cries of men as they fought desperately. Mishani, who had stayed motionless since the attack had begun for fear of drawing attention to herself, put heels to her mount. At her signal, it bolted, and the acceleration took her breath away. The cool wind caught her great length of hair and blew it out in a streamer behind her, and she plunged away into the concealing darkness.

Then, seemingly from nowhere – her eyes were still labouring to adjust to the night – there were other horses alongside her, blocking her in, and a hand grabbed the reins she was holding and pulled her horse to heel. All around, there was a percussion of hooves as they slowed hard and came to a halt, and guns were trained on her. Other men went racing away towards the camp, where Chien and his guards fought a losing battle.

A tall, broad-shouldered man – the one who had stopped her horse – studied her. She could not make out his face, but she glared at him defiantly.

'Mistress Mishani tu Koli,' he said, his voice a deep Newlands burr. Then he chuckled. 'Well, well, well.'

Seventeen

The town of Zila stood on the southern bank of the River Zan, grim and unwelcoming. It had been built at the estuary of the great flow, where the waters that had begun their six-hundred-mile journey in the Tchamil Mountains blended into the sea. It was not a picturesque place, for its original purpose had been military, as a bastion against the Ugati folk who had occupied this land before the Saramyr took it, guarding the bottleneck between the coast and the Forest of Xu while the early settlers raised the city of Barask to the north. It had been here for over a thousand years now, and though its walls had crumbled and been rebuilt, though there was scarcely a building or street left that had existed back then, it still exuded the same brooding presence that it had possessed in the beginning. Cold, and watchful.

It had been constructed to take advantage of a steep hill, which sloped upwards from the south and fell off in a sharp decline at the riverbank. A high wall of black stone surrounded it, which curved and bent to accommodate the contours of the land. Above the wall, the slanting rooftops of red tile and slate angled backwards and up towards the small keep at the centre. The keep was the hub of the town; in fact, the whole of Zila was constructed like a misshapen wheel, with concentric alleyways shot through by streets that radiated out from the keep like spokes. Everything was built from the dense, dour local rock, quite at odds with the usual Saramyr preference for light stone or wood. There were two gates in its wall, but they were both closed; and though there were pockets of activity on the hills outside the silent town, they were few and far between. Most people had drawn back within the protection of the perimeter, and made what preparations they could for the oncoming storm. Zila waited defiantly.

The Emperor's troops were coming.

It was early morning, and a soft, warm rain was falling, when Mishani and her captors arrived. They rode in along the river bank, down to the base of the sharp slope between the walls of Zila and the

Zan. Docks had been built there, and steep, zigzagging stairs to link them to the town itself. But no craft were moored; they had been scuttled or cast adrift and floated out into the sea, to prevent the enemy seizing them.

The riders dismounted, and a man broke away from the dozen or so who milled about and walked over to meet them.

'Bakkara!' said the man, making the gesture of greeting between adults of roughly equal social rank: a small dip of the head, tilted slightly to the side. 'I wondered if you'd be back in time. We're closing the last gate at noon.'

The man he had addressed – the man who had captured Mishani's horse, and the leader of the party – gave him a companionable blow on the shoulder. 'You think I'd let myself get locked out and miss the fun?' he cried. 'Besides, there's probably more food in there than in the rest of Saramyr, my friend. And a soldier fights on his stomach.'

'Might have known you'd be where the meal is,' replied the other, grinning. Then, catching sight of Mishani, he added: 'I see you brought back more than just supplies.' He glanced over at Chien, who was battered and bloodied in his saddle. 'That one has seen better days.'

'He wouldn't have seen any more of them if we hadn't arrived when we did,' Bakkara said, casting a look at the merchant. 'Bandits. These two were the only ones that got out alive.'

'Well, I hope they're suitably grateful,' replied the man; then he looked at Mishani meaningfully and winked at Bakkara. 'One of them, anyway.'

Mishani gazed at him icily until the humour faded from his face. Bakkara bellowed a laugh.

'She's a fearsome thing, isn't she?' he roared. 'It wouldn't do well to mock her. These are nobles we've got here.'

The man glared at Mishani sullenly. 'Get inside, then,' he said to the group in general. 'I'll take care of your horses.'

Mishani and Chien were forced to walk up the stone steps from the dock to the city. Chien was struggling because of his injuries, so their captors made allowances for him, and their progress was slow.

Mishani looked up at the towering walls above them. They were being brought into a city in revolt, and forced to weather it with them against the might of the armies of the empire. She did not know whether to thank the god of fortune or curse him.

The men who had attacked them had undoubtedly been her father's, though she had certainly not told Barakka that. She did not believe that bandits would choose a party of armed guards rather than any of the other dozens of unarmed travellers that had been scattered across the plains last night. Besides, they were too singleminded in purpose, and too few. Bandits would never attack an enemy which outnumbered them.

She had no idea how the men had tracked them this far, but it had shaken her that they had managed to get so close to her once again. What if she had been in her tent when they rode through it? It was plain now that her father did not care whether she came back to him alive or dead. She felt a slender knife of sadness slide into her gut at that. It was a terrible thing to admit to herself.

Then Bakkara and his riders had turned up. Perhaps she could have got away if not for their intervention, but the point was moot now. They had slaughtered Avun's killers by weight of numbers, in time to save Chien's life but not those of his guards. And then, instead of setting them free, they had asked Mishani and Chien to accompany them. It was phrased as a request, but they were in no doubt that they were captives. And besides, Chien needed medical attention, which they offered at Zila. Mishani acceded, to spare herself the humiliation of being tied and taken anyway.

Despite their purpose, they did not treat her like a prisoner. They were talkative enough, and she learned a lot from them during their journey, and the short camp they made on their way back. Most of them were townsfolk from Zila, peasants or artisans. They had been despatched to raid supplies from the travellers passing south down the bottleneck – without harming anyone, they took pains to emphasise – and bring them back to bolster the stocks in the city for the oncoming siege. Their scouts had reported several armies due to reach them the next evening to crush the revolt, and they were by turns fearful and excited at the prospect. Something had sparked an unusual zeal in them, but Mishani could not divine what. They seemed more like folk with a purpose than desperate men fighting for their right to feed.

But it was Bakkara that Mishani spent most of the journey with. An ingrained sense of political expedience dictated that she should not waste time with the foot-soldiers when she could forge relations with their leader; and he, apparently, was as happy to talk as his subordinates. He was a big man: swart, with small dark eyes, a stubbled lantern jaw and a squashed nose. His black hair was bound into ropes and tied through with coloured cord, swept back from his low forehead to hang down to his nape. Though he was nearing his fiftieth harvest, his bearish physique made him more than a match for most men half his age. In his voice and his eyes were a weary authority, a soldier who had seen it all many times before and had resigned himself to seeing it again.

It was through Bakkara that Mishani learned how they had known who she was, and why his men's reaction to their impending fate was so optimistic.

'It's not my habit to rescue noble ladies,' he had said with a rough grin, in response to her question. They had been riding through the early hours of the night, and the atmosphere had a surreal and disjointed quality, as if their group were alone in an empty world.

'Then what prompted you to break with tradition and kidnap me?' she asked.

'Hardly kidnapping, Mistress,' he said. He used the correct title, though the mode he spoke in was anything but subservient. 'Unless you want your man back there to ride the rest of the way to your destination in that state.'

Mishani angled her head, and the faint starlight caught the sharp, thin planes of her cheek. 'We both know that you would not let me ride away now,' she said. 'As for Chien, I care little for him. And he is certainly not my *man*.'

Bakkara chuckled. 'I'll be straight with you,' he said. 'Anyone else, we'd have let them go on their way. But not you. On the one hand, Ocha forbid harm should come to you; and I wouldn't like to let you go riding on your own any further south. Things are getting worse down there.' His face creased in a twinge of regret. 'On the other, you're an asset too valuable to pass up, and Xejen would kill me if I did. We may need you at Zila. So I'm afraid that's where you're going.'

Mishani had already worked out what her situation was before he mentioned Xejen's name and confirmed it.

'You're Ais Maraxa,' she said.

He grunted an affirmative. 'Aren't you lucky?' he said sarcastically.

Mishani laughed.

'You're something of a legend in the Ais Maraxa, Mistress, as I'm sure you know,' Bakkara continued with a wry tone. 'You were one of those who saved our little messiah from the jaws of death.'

'Forgive me, but you do not sound like the foaming zealot I would have expected of a man in your position,' Mishani said, provoking a bellow of mirth from the soldier.

'Wait till you meet Xejen,' he returned. 'He should match up to your standards much better than I.' His laughter diminished a little, and he gave Mishani a strange look. 'I believe in Lucia,' he said eventually. 'Just because I don't spout the dogma doesn't make my strength of conviction any the less.'

'But you understand it is rather harder for me to see the point of view your organisation espouses,' Mishani explained. 'For you, she may represent an ideal, and objects of worship I find are more effective when worshipped from a distance; but for me, she is like a younger sister.'

'*Worship* is a strong word,' said Bakkara uncomfortably. 'She is not a goddess.'

'That much I am certain of,' said Mishani. She found Bakkara curious. He did not seem entirely at ease with his professed allegiance, and that puzzled her.

'But she's something more than human,' the soldier continued. 'That much *I* am certain of.'

Mishani brought herself back to the present, and back to the frowning walls of Zila that rose above them as they climbed the steps, helping the wounded merchant. She was recalling all that she knew of the Ais Maraxa, remembering old conversations with Zaelis and Cailin, mining titbits of information from the past like diamonds from coal. It had been too long since she had paid attention to the Ais Maraxa; she had never given them as much credit as she should have. Now she had been away and out of contact for over two months, and in her absence the Ais Maraxa seemed to have showed themselves at last to the world at large. She would never have thought them capable. It was what everyone close to Lucia had feared.

They had begun as nothing more than a particularly radical and enthusiastic part of the fledgling Libera Dramach. Stories among the peasantry concerning a saviour from the blight were already rife long before the name of Lucia tu Erinima was heard. It was a natural reaction to something that they did not understand: the malaise in their soil that could not be checked. Though the Libera Dramach strove for secrecy, there were still those among them who talked, and stories spread. The tale of the imprisoned Heir-Empress became mingled with the already established webwork of vague prophecies, hope and superstition, and fitted in perfectly. In their eyes, the appearance of a hidden Heir-Empress who could talk to the spirits was a little too coincidental with the spread of the blight. It made sense that she had been put on Saramyr by the gods to engage the evil in the land. Certainly, there could be no other reason why Enyu, goddess of nature, would allow an Aberrant to be born into the Imperial family. Suddenly, the peasants talked not of a god or a hero who would save them, but a little girl.

Still, the organisation that would become the Ais Maraxa remained nothing more than a mildly over-enthusastic splinter of the Libera Dramach. Until the Heir-Empress was rescued.

The presence of their figurehead in the Fold was the incitement that they needed. Lucia's preternatural aura and her seemingly miraculous escape from death convinced them that the messiah they had dreamed of was here at last. They had become more vocal in their dissent, arguing that total secrecy was not the answer; they should spread the news that Lucia was alive throughout the land, to gather support for the day when she would lead them. Much of the peasantry had seen their faith crushed when the Imperial Keep fell, and telling them of the child's escape would only redouble their joy.

Zaelis had forbidden it outright, and eventually the dissenting faction had quieted. Several months later they had left without warning, taking with them some of the most eminent members of the Libera Dramach. It was not long after that reports began to filter back of an organisation calling itself the Ais Maraxa – literally 'followers of the pure child' in a reverent dialect of High Saramyrrhic – that was spreading uncannily accurate rumours far and wide.

Zaelis had fretted and cursed, and Cailin had sent her Sisters to divine the extent of the danger the Ais Maraxa posed; but it seemed at least that their worst fears had not been realised. Those few who had split from the Libera Dramach to form the Ais Maraxa had kept the location of the Heir-Empress a secret. Only a very select number knew where Lucia was. The rest of the organisation knew only that she was hidden, and passed that information on to others. It did little to reassure Zaelis, who thought them reckless and irresponsible; yet it had seemed for years that they were content to spread their message, and in the end Mishani had begun to discount them as virtually harmless.

Now the gates of Zila stood before her, and she walked at Bakkara's side into a town that was soon to close itself up for a siege. She wished she had paid more attention to Lucia's fanatical followers, for the oversight might yet cost her dearly.

The estate of Blood Koli lay on the western side of Mataxa Bay, on a cliff overlooking the wide blue water. Far beneath it were white beaches and coves, unspoilt stretches of sand that dazzled the eye. Several small wooden villages of huts, jetties and walkways built on stilts sprawled from the feet of the cliff out into the bay, and tiny boats and junks bobbed against their tethers. Several massive shapes bulked out of the sea in the distance, enormous limestone formations covered with moss and bushes, their bases worn away so that their tops were wider than their bottom ends, like inverted pinecones. The fishermen glided around them, stirring pole-paddles, and cast nets in their shadow.

The Koli family house was built close to the edge on the highest point of the promontory. It was a coral-coloured building, constructed around a circular central section with a flattened and ribbed dome atop it. The uniformity of its surface at ground level was broken by a square entrance hall that poked out like a blunt snout, facing away from the bay. Two slender wings encompassing stables and servants' quarters ran along the cliff edge. Cut in steps into the cliff itself was an enormous three-tiered garden, its lowest tier balconied and jutting out over the drop to the beach below. All kinds of trees and plants were cultivated there, and carved pillars of rock had been left in strategic places to maximise the aesthetic pleasure in the fusion of stone and greenery. On the highest tier was a small conservatory, a skeletal framework of tall arches and curved pillars, where Mishani's mother Muraki would sit to write.

She was there now, Barak Avun suspected, though he could not see from where he lounged on the lowest tier with Barak Grigi tu Kerestyn. No doubt concocting more of her stories, he thought with distaste. Sharing her family's problems with the empire. In all things she obeyed him, except in this. He had been furious when news of her latest book had reached him; it fuelled scandalmongers the breadth of the land. There was enough rumour about their missing daughter without her adding to it. But she would write what she would write, and she defied him to censor her.

Still, the damage could be minimised. If all went well, then soon he would have his daughter back, one way or another, and then they could concoct a cover story that would put all that dishonour to rest. If all went well . . .

'Gods, it's not so bad, is it?' said Grigi, who was lying on a couch and looking over the balcony to the bay. 'Up here, you can forget about the problems of the world, forget about the blight. Nuki's eye still shines on us, the sea still ebbs and flows. Our problems are small, when you look at them from this height.'

Avun regarded him with vague contempt. The obese Barak was drunk. Between them was a table scattered with the remnants of the food Grigi had devoured, and empty pitchers of wine. Avun was ascetic in his tastes, but Grigi was a glutton, and he had gorged himself all afternoon.

'They are not small to me,' Avun said coldly. 'The sea still ebbs and flows, but its fish are becoming twisted; and those fish paid for the food you have eaten. My fishermen have taken to holding back some of their catch for their own families. Preserving them against the famine. Stealing from me.' He turned his hooded eyes outward, to where the distant cliffs of the eastern side of the bay were a low, jagged line of deep blue. 'It is easy to pretend that nothing is wrong. It is also foolish.'

'No need to be so dour, Avun,' said Grigi, a little disappointed that his ally did not share his expansive mood. 'Heart's blood, you know how to bring a man down.'

'I see nothing to be cheerful about.'

'Then you don't see the opportunity that this famine brings us,' Grigi said. 'There is no stouter warrior than a man fighting for his life, and the lives of his family. All they need is someone to unite behind. That person will be me!' He raised his goblet clumsily, spilling a little wine onto the slabs of the balcony.

'There goes the Barakess,' said Avun, languidly indicating a brightly coloured junk that was slipping out of the harbour far below them, making its way through the clutter of fishing vessels.

Grigi shaded his eyes against the glare of the sun and looked down. 'Do you trust her?'

Avun nodded slowly. 'She will be there when the time comes.'

The afternoon's work had been satisfactory. Emira, a young Barakess of Blood Ziris, had visited them at her request. She had talked with them about many things: the threat of famine, the Blood Emperor, the plight of her own people. And, in her sly and roundabout way, she had wondered whether Blood Kerestyn intended to make a play for the throne, and whether they might need Blood Ziris's help when they did.

It was ever this way, in the game of the Imperial courts. Families backed each other in the hope that the one they supported would gain power, and in turn that family would elevate the ones that had helped them get there. As Mos's ineptitude became clearer, and with Blood Kerestyn the only realistic alternative, the high families were flocking to Grigi's banner without him even having to call them. With Blood Koli at his right hand, he was a powerful figurehead, and the strength of the empire was gathering itself to him.

But always there had been the problem of the Emperor's strength of numbers. With the Weavers at his side, and the Imperial Guards at his command, he was a near-invincible force. While Kerestyn forces had been smashed during the last coup, Blood Batik had walked unopposed into the city, and had grown since then. Even with overwhelming support from the other high families, Grigi knew it would be a close call. He had broken himself on the walls of Axekami once before; he would have to be very sure of himself before he would try it again.

Avun had brought him the solution to that problem this very day.

'I have a new friend,' he had said, as they walked through the chambers of the family house that morning. 'One very close to the Emperor. I was contacted not long ago.'

'A new friend?' Grigi had asked, raising an eyebrow.

'This person tells me that something is going to happen, very soon. We must be ready.'

'Ready?'

'We must assemble our support, so we can march on Axekami at a day's notice.'

'A day! Ridiculous! We would have to tell all the families well in advance, gather their forces here.'

'Then we shall do so, when the time is right. There will be a signal. And when it comes, we must act swiftly, and have our allies ready to do the same.'

Grigi had adjusted his purple skullcap on top of his head. 'That's a little too much to take on trust, Avun. Tell me just who this new friend of yours is.'

'Kakre. The Emperor's own Weaver.'

Eighteen

'It's time, Kaiku,' said Yugi.

Darkness was falling. The sky was a soft purple in the east, the harbinger of oncoming night. Iridima stood alone at half-moon amid a thick blanket of dim stars, pallid and ghostly in the dusk. The heat of the early autumn day was fading to a warm night, and a gentle breeze dispersed the muggy closeness of the previous hours.

They had found the Weavers' barrier, the edge of the secret that they had crossed the Fault to uncover. Nomoru had announced that they were nearing the point where she had lost her way on her previous visit, and an hour later they returned to the same spot, despite having headed steadily westward. If that was not enough, Kaiku's senses had begun to crackle; she was certain that she knew exactly where the barrier cut across the landscape, and when they had been turned around. She had been very careful to keep her *kana* reined tight as they passed into it. She did not want to try and tackle the barrier without the help of her father's Mask.

The four travellers sheltered in a dell for a few hours to wait for the cover of night. Kaiku spent them sat against a tree, holding the leering, red-and-black face before her, looking into its empty eyes. When Yugi spoke to her, she barely heard him. He had to shake her arm before she looked up at him sharply, annoyed; then she softened, and smiled in thanks. Yugi's eyes mirrored uncertainty for a moment, and he retreated.

Her mind flitted back, skipping over days of hard journeying, alighting eventually on the gloomy, doleful marsh where Yugi had lain dying. The battle to extract the demon poison was etched in Kaiku's memory; every probing fibre, every twist and knot were mapped onto her consciousness in shining lines. Despite herself, she felt a small grin of triumph touch her lips, and her spirits rose. But then her gaze fell on Yugi, who was shouldering his pack, and her grin faded a little.

Ever since he had awoken, Yugi had been *different* somehow. She had sensed something when she had been inside him, a faint wash from his mind that hinted at something dark and unspeakably ugly. She could not guess what it was, only that it lay deep and hidden, and unconsciousness had loosened it from where it was fettered. She watched him, and wondered.

Yugi tried not to notice, but he could feel her eyes on his back. His brush with the demons had sobered him, that much was certain. The proximity of death had reminded him of a previous life, before he had joined the Libera Dramach. Days of blood and blade and mayhem. He began to play with the dirty sash wrapped around his forehead; a totem of those times, times that he wanted desperately to forget but never could.

He pushed the thoughts away as the travellers got to their feet and made ready to breach the Weavers' barrier. The immediacy of the situation focused him. Their trip across the Fault had not been an easy one, but it would get worse from here on in.

'Is that going to work?' Nomoru asked doubtfully, motioning to the Mask in Kaiku's hand.

'We will know soon enough,' Kaiku said, and put it on.

Dreadfully, it felt like coming home. The Mask warmed to her skin, and she fancied that she felt it mould itself to the tiny changes in her face since the last time she had worn it. She felt a great contentment, a nostalgic warmth such as she felt as a little girl asleep in her father's lap. She could hear the comforting whisper of Ruito's voice, a phantom of his memory brushing against her, and tears sprang to her eyes.

She blinked them back. The Mask felt like her father because it had robbed him of some of his thoughts and personality when he had worn it. He had been killed for this piece of wood. The Masks were cruel masters, taking and taking in return for the power they gave, addicting their users until their victims could not live without them. Until they were Weavers. She would not let herself forget that.

Spirits, what would happen if a Sister of the Red Order became a Weaver?

'You look ridiculous,' said Nomoru, her voice devoid of humour. 'What's this going to achieve?'

Kaiku gave her a contemptuous glance. Strangely, she did not feel in the least bit ridiculous, wearing this Mask with its knowing leer. In fact, she felt that it suited her perfectly, and made her appear more impressive.

'What it will *achieve* is to get us through that barrier when you could not,' Kaiku replied airily. 'Let us be quick. I do not want to wear this thing a moment longer than necessary.'

She thought, as they departed, that those words felt curiously hollow. She had spoken them because she thought she was supposed to, rather than because she actually meant them.

The last light had fled the sky when they came up against the barrier. Topping a gentle rise in the land between two peaks of hulking stone, Kaiku felt the Mask become hot against her cheeks.

'It is here,' she said. 'Tie yourselves to me.'

Tsata produced a rope, and they did as she instructed. It was difficult to tell how much the Tkiurathi believed in the necessity of what they were doing, but he acceded to the will of the group without complaint.

Kaiku proceeded tentatively, holding her hand out before her. The Mask grew hotter still, rising in temperature until she thought it might burn her; and then her fingers brushed the barrier, and it was unveiled to her eyes.

She could not hold back a gasp. The glittering Weave-sewn tapestry swept away to either side of her, six metres high and six deep, curving up and over the steep contours of the Fault. It was a churn of golden spirals and whirls, spinning and writhing slowly, curling around each other and taking on new forms, stretching and flexing in a dance of impossible chaos. Like an eddy in the waters of reality, perception was turned around and thrown out on a new course in this place, and Kaiku marvelled anew at the complexity of the Weavers' creation.

'What is it?' asked Yugi. 'Is it the barrier?'

Kaiku realised by the tone of his voice that he was asking why she had stopped, not what the thing before them was. It was invisible to everyone but her. For a brief moment, she felt a smug and selfish glee at being the only one privy to this wonder; then, surprised at herself, she cast it aside.

'Hold hands,' she told them, and she gave her hand to Yugi. The others did the same.

She stepped into the barrier, and was consumed by the Weave. The first time it had happened, back on Fo, she had been tempted to let herself be swept away in the unutterable beauty of the golden world that surrounded her. This time she was ready for it, and her heart was hardened against its charms. In a few strides, she was through, pulling Yugi with her; but the sensation was a cruel wrench, and the return to reality made everything seem grey and bland by comparison.

Yugi came stumbling through backwards and tripped as he did, disoriented at finding himself turned around. He had let go of Nomoru, the next in line, and as he fell to the ground the rope around his waist tautened. She was tugging the other way. Kaiku could see her now: the barrier had faded from her sight as soon as she was past it.

Nomoru was trapped in the invisible zone of disorientation, blank-faced, labouring to drag herself back in the direction they had come and seemingly unable to understand why she could not get there. Tsata was in a similar state nearby, his face a picture of childlike confusion.

'Pull them through,' Kaiku told Yugi, and though he was still bewildered as to where he was, he did as he was told. Between them they dragged their companions across the barrier and onto the other side.

It took the better part of ten minutes for their thoughts to become coherent again, by which time Kaiku had removed the Mask and stashed it back in her pack. She studied them with fascination as they gazed glassy-eyed at each other like babies, or looked around at their surroundings as if completely unable to process where they were. No wonder that nobody could penetrate the barrier without a Mask. What a masterpiece of Weave-manipulation it was.

Once they had collected themselves, Nomoru was still unable to remember this area which she had once professed to know. So it was Kaiku who took the lead, as Nomoru's sense of direction seemed to be still suppressed, making her hopeless at navigation.

'We have to get away from this place,' Kaiku said. 'I am not convinced that it is safe to pass the barrier, even with the Mask. We may have alerted those who set it here.'

With that, they set off into the broken landscape to their right, skirting the inside of the barrier. Kaiku relied on her senses to let her know when they were brushing too close to the invisible perimeter, and using that as a guide, they lost themselves in the dark rills and juts of the Xarana Fault, and Iridima watched them go with half a face.

When they were far from the point where they had entered the domain of the Weavers, Nomoru called a halt.

'It's hopeless,' she said. 'Doing it this way. We'll never get there in the dark.'

The others wearily agreed. For a time, it had seemed like they were making progress; but then the night sky clouded, shutting out the glow of the stars and the single moon, and now they could barely see at all. They had been wandering amid a stretch of uneven gullies and scrub ground for some time now, scratching themselves on thorny bushes and probably going in circles. Their frustration was multiplied by the fact that they did not know exactly what they were looking for. Seeking out evidence of Weaver activity was a broad and vague objective, when they had no idea of the extent of their enemies' capabilities, nor what form such evidence might take. Now they were walking down a trench of baked mud, with steep sides rising up over their heads: an old ditch, long dry, and infested with weeds.

'We should rest,' said Yugi. 'We can go on when the sky clears, or when dawn comes.'

'I am not tired,' Kaiku said, who did indeed feel strangely energised. 'I will keep watch.'

'I will join you,' said Tsata, unexpectedly.

They threw their packs down at the base of the ditch; Nomoru and Yugi unrolled mats, and were asleep in minutes.

Kaiku sat with her back against the trench wall, her hands linked around her knees. Tsata sat opposite her, silently. It was eerily quiet; even the raucous drone of night insects was absent. Distantly, she heard the unpleasant cawing of some bird she could not identify.

'Should one of us go up to the top, to look out for . . .' she trailed off, realising that she had no idea what she expected might come for them.

'No,' said the Tkiurathi. 'We cannot see far, but there may be things that can see us in the deep darkness. It is better to be hidden.'

Kaiku nodded slightly. She had not wanted to go up there anyway, and it felt sheltered here.

'I wish to talk,' said Tsata suddenly. 'About Weavers.'

Kaiku brushed her fringe back from her face, tucked it behind one ear. 'Very well.'

'I have learned about them from Saran, but I still do not know how your people accept them,' he said.

The mention of Saran made Kaiku's eyes narrow. That was something that the encounter with the Omecha cultists and the ruku-shai had driven entirely out of her head.

'I am not sure I understand what you are asking,' said Kaiku.

'Let me say how I see it, and you may correct me afterward. Is that acceptable?'

Kaiku tilted her chin up, then realised with some embarrassment that she had used an Okhamban gesture rather than a Saramyr one.

'Once your civilisation was dedicated to great art and learning, to building wonderful architecture and long roads and incredible dwellings,' Tsata began. 'I have read your histories. And though I do not share your love for stone cities, or for the way you gather in such numbers that *pash* becomes meaningless, I am aware that all ways are not my ways, and I can accept that. I can even accept the terrible divide between the nobles and the peasant classes, and how knowledge is hoarded by one to keep the other in ignorant labour. That I find nothing less than evil, for it is so counter to the nature of my people;

yet if I began to talk about that, we would be here a lot longer, and it is the Weavers I wish to speak of.'

Kaiku was mildly taken aback, both by his bluntness – which verged on rude – and his eloquence. She had rarely heard Tsata say more than a few sentences at a time; but his evident passion for this subject seemed to have overrode his usual quiet reticence.

'When the Weavers came, your ancestors took them in,' he said at length, his pale green eyes steady in the darkness. 'They were dazzled by the power they might command with a Weaver at their side. Your nobles had so long been accustomed to treating lesser men like tools, that they thought they could use the Weavers in the same way, not knowing how dangerous a tool they were. For to accept the Weavers into your world was to make a pact; a pact that your ancestors made knowing full well the terms that they were agreeing to.' His head hung in sorrow. 'Greed ruined them. Perhaps they had noble causes at first; perhaps they thought that with the Weavers on their side, they could expand the empire and make it greater and more invincible. But sometimes the price is too high, no matter what the reward.'

Kaiku noticed that his hands were clenched in fists, the yellow skin taut around his knuckles.

'You invited the Weavers into your homes, and you fed them with your children.'

That shocked her. But though she drew breath to protest, she found that she could not. He was right, after all. It was a noble family's duty to supply their Weaver with whatever they wanted during their post-Weaving mania. She knew well enough some of the awful perversions that those creatures were capable of. As the backlash from using their Masks set in, like the withdrawal symptoms of a narcotic, they had no conscience in the face of their irrational, primal lusts and needs. Nothing was too depraved where the Weavers were concerned. Rape, murder, torture . . . these were only some of the desires that the Weavers demanded be satisfied. She knew of others. Blood Kerestyn's Weaver was reportedly a cannibal. Blood Nira had one who ate human and animal faeces. The current Weave-lord apparently had a penchant for skinning victims alive and making sculptures from them. Though not every Weaver's mania was harmful to others – some would do things as mundane as painting or merely hallucinate for hours – a lot of them were, and while they did not need to sate themselves every time they went Weaving, most Weavers still accounted for dozens of lives each. And as they become more insane and addicted and raddled with disease, the quantity increased.

She felt suddenly ashamed, remembering the simple joy she had felt in Hanzean at returning to her homeland from Okhamba. Saramyr was a place of beauty and harmony that she felt lucky to live in, and yet it was built on the bones of so many. Before the Weavers, there had been the systematic extermination of the native Ugati, a death toll that must have reached into millions. None of this was new to Kaiku – and still, it seemed so distant and so unconnected to her that she could not really identify with it – but hearing it put in such a straightforward way reminded her what a thin veneer civilisation was, a crust on which the dainty feet of the highborn walked, while beneath their soles a sea of disorder and violence seethed.

But Tsata was not finished. 'You are not to blame for the crimes of your ancestors,' he said, 'though often your society punishes sons for their fathers' mistakes, it seems. But now the Weavers despoil the very land you live on. That is the final joke. Your people have come to rely on them to the extent that you cannot bring yourselves to get rid of them, even though they will destroy all the beauty that you once loved. You have invested so much in making your empire bigger and better that you are destroying the very foundation that it is built on. You have built a tower so tall and so high that you have begun to take bricks from the bottom to put at the top.' He leaned closer to Kaiku. 'You are killing the earth with your selfishness.'

'I *know* that, Tsata,' Kaiku said. She was becoming angry; this seemed a little too much like a personal attack at her. Even though she was aware that Tsata did not subscribe to the evasions and politenesses of her society, she still found his manner of speaking too confrontational. 'What do you think we are doing here now? I am trying to *fight* them.'

'Yes,' he said. 'But are you fighting them for the right reasons? You fight for vengeance. Saran told me that much. Now the people of your land rise up, for their food is becoming short; but until then, they were content to let the blight creep, thinking that somebody else would deal with it. None of you fight for the good of the many. You only decide to struggle when it is in your personal interest.'

'That is the way people are,' Kaiku snapped.

'It is not the way *my* people are,' Tsata countered.

'Perhaps, then, that is why you still remain living in the jungle, and your children eaten by wild beasts,' she returned. 'Perhaps civilisation is built on selfishness.'

The Tkiurathi took the implied insult without offence. 'Perhaps,' he said. 'But I am not intending to compare my culture to yours, to judge the merits of one against the other.'

'That is what you seem to be doing,' Kaiki told him sullenly.

'I am telling you how your land looks through my eyes,' he said simply. 'Does honesty make you so uncomfortable?'

'I do not need to have you pointing out the failings of my people. Perhaps my reasons are not selfless enough to fit your taste, but the fact remains that I *am* doing something about the Weavers. I choose not to accept the way things are, for I know they are wrong. So do not lecture me on morality.'

Tsata watched her quietly. She calmed a little, and scuffed her heel in the dirt.

'I have nothing to teach you about the Weavers,' she admitted eventually. 'Your understanding of the situation is correct.'

'Is it a product of your culture, then?' Tsata asked. 'Because each of you strives for personal advancement rather than for that of the group, you will not act against a threat until it is in your interest to do so?'

'Possibly,' said Kaiku. 'I do not know. But I do know that much of our acceptance of the Weavers is born of ignorance. If the high families had proof that the Weavers were the ones responsible for despoiling the land, they would rise up and destroy them. That is what I believe.'

'But it's not true, Kaiku,' said Yugi. They looked over at him, and saw him sit up. He adjusted the rag around his brow and gave them an apologetic smile. 'Difficult to sleep with you two setting the world to rights,' he explained.

'What do you mean, it is not true?' Kaiku asked.

'I probably shouldn't tell you this, but I suppose it doesn't matter,' he said, getting to his feet and stretching. 'There's a lot of dealings high up in the Libera Dramach that we don't tell anyone else. One thing we made sure we did was to check your father's theory about the witchstones. When we were sure he was right, we . . . well, we made it known to some of the nobles. Subtly. Hints here and there, and when those didn't work, we actually presented them with proof and challenged them to check it themselves.' He scratched the back of his neck. 'Obviously, this was all through middlemen. The Libera Dramach was never really exposed.'

Kaiku waved a hand at him, indicating that he should get to the meat of the issue. 'How did it end, then?'

He wandered over to where they sat and looked down on them. 'They didn't do anything. Not one. Very few of them even bothered to verify the facts we gave them.' He laughed bitterly. 'All this time the Weavers have been kept in check by the fear of what might happen if the high familes rose up against them. Well, we tried to make that happen, and they ignored us.'

Kaiku was aghast. 'How can that be? When they can see what the Weavers are doing?'

Yugi put a hand on Tsata's bare shoulder. 'Our foreign friend here is right,' he said. 'It's not in their interest. If one or even a dozen high families acted on the information, they would lose their Weavers, and the other families who *did* have Weavers would crush them. There are too many enmities, too many old wounds. There'll always be someone trying to get the upper hand, thinking only about the short-term, seizing any chance they can get. Because people are selfish. The only way anything fundamental will change is if *everyone* decides to change *at the same time.*' He shrugged. 'And the only way that will happen is if there's a catastrophe.'

'It is true. You will have to wait until this land is so ruined that it can barely be lived on before it is in everyone's interest to act,' Tsata said. 'And by then, it may well be too late.'

'Is that the way of it, then?' Kaiku demanded, feeling unfairly outnumbered. 'That people have to die before anything changes?'

Yugi and Tsata merely looked at her, and that was answer enough.

The clouds cleared towards dawn, and they set off again to take advantage of Iridima's glow. By now Nomoru's sense of direction seemed to have returned, and by estimating the curvature of the barrier, she established a route inward that would take them towards the centre of the area that the Weavers had cut off from the world. It seemed reasonable to assume that whatever they were looking for lay there.

They had not travelled far before the land dropped steeply away before them, and they found themselves looking down a boulder-riven slope at the darkly glinting swathe of the River Zan. Its sibilant murmuring drifted up to them through the silence.

'Are we still upstream of the falls?' Yugi asked.

Nomoru made an affirmative noise. 'This way,' she said, turning them southward. Kaiku doubted if the scout had any more idea of where they were going than she did, but one way was as good as another when they were all lost.

The sky was beginning to lighten when Yugi stopped them suddenly. They had been on the alert for any signs of life, but nothing had appeared as yet. In fact, it was eerily empty. Even the animals seemed to have deserted this place.

'What is it?' Kaiku whispered.

'Look,' Yugi said. 'Look at the tree.'

They looked. Standing on a rocky rise above them in silhouette was a crooked tree, its branches bare and warped, its boughs twisted in a corkscrew and curling at strange angles. It hunched there like a foreboding signpost, a warning of things to come if they should proceed.

'It's blighted,' Yugi supplied redundantly.

'They have found another witchstone,' Kaiku said. 'And they have woken it up.'

'*Woken it up?*' Nomoru sneered. 'It's a *rock*, Kaiku.'

'Is that all it is?' Kaiku returned sarcastically. 'Then what are the Weavers hiding it for?'

Nomoru gave a snort of disgust and walked onward, heading downriver. The others went after her.

It was just past dawn when they found what they had been looking for; and it was far, far worse than they had imagined.

The ridge of land that they had been following began to curve away from the Zan below, and a great stretch of flat land opened up between the river's eastern bank and the high ground, a grassy and fertile flood plain. Their view of the plain was obscured, for they had been forced to retreat from the lip of the slope by a suddenly hostile terrain of broken rocks, but finally Nomoru picked them a route back to the edge so that they could command a good view of the land to the west, and that was when they saw what the Weavers had been hiding all this time.

The slope had steepened into an enormous black cliff overlooking the plain, and when Nomoru reached the precipice she ducked down suddenly and motioned that the others should do the same. The burgeoning daylight was flat and devoid of force, lacking yet the strength to imbue the world with colour. The sky overhead was a drab grey, and the solitary moon was heading towards obscurity behind the jagged teeth of the Fault. They scrambled on their bellies to where Nomoru lay, and looked over.

Kaiku swore under her breath.

On the far side of the flood plain, near the river bank, hulked a massive construction, a glabrous hump like the carapace of some monstrous beetle. It was a dull, rusty bronze in colour, formed of immense strips of banded metal. Around its base, smaller constructions clustered like newborn animals clamouring for their mother's teats. There, strange wheels of spiked metal rotated slowly, chains rattled as they slid on pulleys that emerged from narrow shafts in the earth, and stubby chimneys emitted an oily black smoke. From within came faint clattering and clanking sounds.

The observers gazed aghast at the edifice. It was like nothing they had ever seen before, something so alien to their experience that its very presence seemed out of kilter with the world. A dirty, seething horror, foul to the eye.

But that was not all. There was a more immediate and recognisable danger. The plain was awash with Aberrants.

The sheer number of the creatures that milled down there was impossible to estimate, for they were in no order or formation, and it was difficult to tell where one clot ended and another began. It was made worse by the variety of shapes and forms: a phantasmagoria of grotesqueries that seemed to have spilled whole from the imagination of a maniac. Thousands, perhaps; maybe tens of thousands. The horde carpeted the ground from the foot of the cliffs to the banks of the Zan, clustered in groups or imprisoned within enormous metal pens. Some stalked restlessly along the river, some slept on the ground, some squabbled and scratched.

Kaiku felt a pat on her shoulder, and she looked to see Nomoru proffering her a spyglass. It was a simple, portable affair – two glass lenses wrapped in a conical tube of stiffened leather – but it was effective enough. She took it with an uncertain smile of thanks. It was probably the first time Nomoru had ever volunteered any good will to any of them. Evidently the scale of what they had discovered had caused her to lay aside her petty surliness for the moment.

She put it to her eye, and the spectacle below sprang into noisome detail. Everywhere, the forms of nature had been twisted out of true. Dark, loping things like elongated jungle cats snarled as they prowled, their faces curious hybrids of canine and lizard; demonic creatures that might once have been small apes hung from the bars of their pens, lips skinning back along their gums to reveal vicious arrays of yellowed fangs; hunched, boarlike things with furious visages and great hooked tusks rooted in the dirt, compact barrels of tooth and muscle. Kaiku felt an uncomfortable thrill of recognition at the sight of a roosting-pen of enormous birds, with keratinous beaks and kinked, ragged wings with a span of six feet or more: gristle-crows, which she had last seen on the isle of Fo several years ago.

And yet there was a pattern in amid the chaos. The presence of the gristle-crows had alerted her to it, and now as she scanned the plain again she saw, in the bleak light of the dawn, that each Aberrant was not unique. There were perhaps a few dozen different types, but these types recurred over and over again. The same features cropped up, the same forms. These were not random offshoots of the witchstones' influence. These were discrete species. Though they were horrible to look at, there were no redundant features, no evolutionary characteristic that might hamper them. No deformities.

'Not there,' Nomoru said impatiently. She grabbed the end of the spyglass and turned it. 'There.'

Kaiku spared her an annoyed glance for her rudeness before she looked through it again. When she did, her blood ran cold.

There was a figure walking slowly through the horde, apparently heedless of the predators that surrounded it. At first, she thought it must be a Weaver; but if it was, it was like no Weaver she had ever seen. This one was tall, seven feet at least, and rake-thin. It walked with an erect spine instead of the hunch that Weavers seemed to adopt as their bodies became more riddled with foulness. Its robe was not patchwork like a Weaver's, but simple black, with a heavy hood; and though it wore a mask, it was a blank white oval, perfectly smooth except for two eye-holes.

'A new kind of Weaver?' she breathed.

'Don't know,' Nomoru replied.

Yugi took the spyglass and looked.

'What is it I'm seeing here?' he said, slowly panning across the horde. 'What are they doing?'

'Some kind of menagerie?' Kaiku suggested. 'A collection of Aberrant predator species?'

Nomoru laughed bitterly. 'That's what you think?'

Tsata's expression was grim. 'It is not a menagerie, Kaiku,' he told her. 'It is an army.'

Nineteen

At the same time that Kaiku and her companions were gazing down on the horde of Aberrants by the River Zan, Lucia and her retinue were arriving at Alskain Mar.

It lay almost one hundred and fifty miles away from Kaiku, east and a little south of her position, on the other side of the Xarana Fault near the River Rahn. Once, it had been a magnificent underground shrine, in the days before the cataclysm that rent the earth and swallowed Gobinda over a thousand years ago. Then its entrances had collapsed, and the roof had fallen in on it, and uncounted souls had been buried in the quake. Now it was a haunted place, the abode of something ancient and ageless, and even the most savage of the factions in the Fault stayed well away from there. A great spirit held sway in Alskain Mar, and the spirits guarded their territory resentfully.

But into that place Lucia was to go. Alone.

Her escort on the journey from the Fold was a small group of the most trusted warriors of the Libera Dramach, accompanied by Zaelis and Cailin. The leader of the Libera Dramach, the head of the Red Order, and the girl on which all their endeavours rested. It was risky for them to venture out of the Fold together, but Cailin insisted on coming and Zaelis could not let his adopted daughter face this trial without his support. Guilt lay heavy on his heart, and the least he could do was walk with her as far as he could.

Cailin had been furious when Zaelis had told her what he had done. Though he had implied to Lucia that he and Cailin were in agreement about asking her to go to Alskain Mar, it had in reality been his idea entirely. Cailin was in violent opposition, and not afraid to tell him so. She had faced him at his house, amid the quiet, cosy surroundings of his study.

'This is idiocy, Zaelis!' she had cried, a tower of black anger. 'You know what happened to her last time! Now you would send her up against a spirit unfathomably stronger! What possessed you?'

'Do you think I made my decision lightly?' Zaelis retorted. 'Do you think I enjoy the idea of sending my daughter into the lair of that *thing?* Necessity forces my hand, Cailin!'

'There is nothing so necessary as to risk the life of that girl. She is the lynchpin of everything we have striven for.'

'We will *lose* everything we have striven for if the Weavers find the Fold,' Zaelis said, stalking agitatedly around the room. The raised voices seemed to discomfit the still air. Lanterns cast warm shadows across the hardwood floor. 'It is easy for you to judge: you have the Red Order. You can disappear in a day, go into hiding, leave all of this behind. But I have a responsibility to what I have started! Every man and woman in this town is here because of what I created; even those who are not of the Libera Dramach have come because of the ideals that we represent.' He dropped his eyes. 'And they look to me as their leader.'

'The day will come when they look to *Lucia* as their leader, Zaelis,' Cailin said. 'Was that not the plan? How, then, can you dare risk her this way?' She paused, then added a final barb. 'Quite aside from the fact that she is, as you say, your own daughter.'

Zaelis's bearded jaw tightened in pain. 'I risk her because I have to,' he said quietly.

'Wait for the scouts to get back,' Cailin advised. 'You may be worrying needlessly.'

'It's not good enough,' he said. 'No matter what they find, the fact remains that the Weavers are in the Fault. They could have been there for *years*, don't you see? It is only because Nomoru is so good at what she does that she even noticed the Weavers' barrier. How many of our scouts have passed through that way and not even realised that they had been misdirected?' He looked up accusingly at Cailin. 'It was *you* that told me how those barriers worked.'

Cailin tilted her head. The raven feathers on her ruff stirred slightly. 'You are correct. The nature of the barriers are subtle enough so that most minds are fooled into thinking that they have got *themselves* lost.'

'Then what else might the Weavers have under our very noses?' Zaelis asked. 'We only found this one through blind luck.' He threw up his calloused hands in exasperation. 'I have been suddenly and shockingly faced with the fact that we are all but defenceless against the very enemy we have been fighting against. We have relied on hiding from them. But now I realise that they *will* find us, whether by accident or design, sooner or later. They may already have found us. We have to know what we are up against; and only the spirits can tell us that.'

'Are you sure, Zaelis?' Cailin asked. 'What do you know of spirits?'

'I know what Lucia tells me,' he said. 'And she believes it is worth trying.'

Cailin gave him a level gaze. 'Of course she does. She would do anything you asked of her. Even if it killed her.'

'Gods, Cailin, don't make this worse for me than it is!' he cried. 'I have made my choice. We are going to Alskain Mar.'

Cailin had not argued further, but as she was leaving she had paused at the threshold of the room and looked back at him.

'What was the purpose of all this in the beginning? What did you do this for? You created the Libera Dramach out of nothing. One man inspired all of that. But who inspired *you*?'

Zaelis did not reply. He knew it was a leading question, but he did not wish to be led.

'Which is more important to you now?' Cailin had asked softly. 'The girl, or the secret army you lead? Lucia, or the Libera Dramach?'

The memories echoed bitterly in Zaelis's thoughts as the company picked its way through the brightening dawn towards the ruined shrine. They had travelled overnight from the Fold for the sake of stealth. The going had been slow, as they had been forced to accommodate Zaelis's limp, and Lucia – who had never in her life had to walk on a journey of more than a few miles at a time – became exhausted quickly. The clouds that troubled Kaiku far away had not reached this far east, and they had the light of Iridima to guide them through the plunging terrain of the Fault.

As the first signs of day approached, they had come to a wide, circular depression in the land, a mile or more in diameter. It lay on a long, flat hilltop, thick with dewy grass and shrubs and small, thin trees. On the eastern side, the Fault began a disjointed but steady descent down to the banks of the Rahn. At the centre of the depression was a deep, uneven hole, a toothed shaft into the vast cavern beneath, where Alskain Mar lay.

They halted at the edge of the dip. Soul-eaters had been set in a rough circle around the perimeter, their surfaces weathered and their paint fading. They made a loud rattling as the wind brushed them, old knucklebone charms and stones of transparent resin tapping against the rock. Several of them were cracked, and moss had grown in the fissures. One had broken in half, and its upper section lay next to the stump.

Cailin cast a disparaging eye over the soul-eaters. They were superstitious artifacts cannibalised from the Ugati: slender, elliptical stones daubed in a combination of blessings and curses and hung with noisy and primitive jewellery. The stories went that when a spirit came near to a soul-eater, it would be terrified by the sound of the charms, and both repelled by the blessings and disgusted by the curses; then it would flee back to where it had come from and hide. They did not work, and had been dismissed as quaint bits of folklore by the Saramyr for hundreds of years; and yet these examples were recent, no more than fifty years old. Who could guess who had put them there, and what they had hoped to achieve? Maybe they had thought that an ancient method would work to pen an ancient spirit. In the Xarana Fault, the usual rules of civilisation did not apply.

They rested outside the depression as the sun climbed into the sky. Lucia curled up on a mat and slept. The overnight walk had been hard on her. She may have had plenty of energy, but for that she was still frail, having been sheltered all through her childhood. The guards ate cold food nervously, warily scanning the quiet hilltop. They were safe enough from any human danger here, for no settlements thrived this close to Alskain Mar; but the presence of the spirit could be felt by the least perceptive of men, and it made their skin crawl. Even the heat and light of the day did not dispel the chill. They kept catching flitting movements among the bushes out of the corner of their eyes; but whenever they investigated, there was nothing there.

Zaelis and Cailin sat together. Zaelis was regarding his sleeping daughter with concern; Cailin was silently studying the hole at the centre of the depression.

'There is still time to turn back, Zaelis,' the Sister said.

'Don't,' he said. 'The decision is made.'

'Decisions can be unmade,' Cailin told him.

Zaelis's brow was furrowed deeply, his eyes pained as he watched the rise and fall of Lucia's slender back. 'Not this one,' he said.

Cailin did not reply to that. If she had dared to stop him, she would have; but she could not jeopardise her own position or that of the Red Order by risking it. She found herself wishing that Kaiku or Mishani were with them. Perhaps they could have swayed Zaelis. A wild idea occurred to her, that she might use the Weave to manipulate him subtly; but Lucia would know, even if Zaelis did not, and the act would be a terrible betrayal of trust. She could not afford that.

So she had to watch as he sent all their hope into Alskain Mar, and wait to see if it came out again.

'What of Asara?' Zaelis said at length, starting a new subject suddenly. 'Have you heard from her? We may need her again very soon.'

'She is gone,' said Cailin. They both still referred to her as Asara, though they had known her as Saran in the brief time she had spent at the Fold. The identity of the spy they had sent away to scour the Near World for signs of the Weavers had always been known to them, but they had not known what guises she might take. 'She went just before Kaiku left. I suspect they had something of a disagreement.'

Zaelis raised an eyebrow.

'I do keep a very close eye on my most errant pupil,' she said. She looked east, to the autumn morning sky. 'I do not think we will be seeing Saran Ycthys Marul again, though. She is changing her identity.'

'Have you spoken to her, then? What do you know?'

Cailin's black and red lips curled in a faint smile. 'She is running a small errand for me. I managed to convince her that it was . . . in her interests.'

'An errand?' Zaelis repeated, his molten voice becoming suspicious. 'What errand, Cailin?'

Cailin looked at him sidelong. 'That is our business,' she said.

'Heart's blood! You just sent away my best spy and you won't even tell me why? What are you up to?'

'She is not *your* spy,' Cailin reminded him. 'If she is anyone's, she is mine. And she is abroad on matters of the Red Order now.'

'The Libera Dramach and the Red Order are supposed to be working together,' Zaelis said. 'What kind of co-operation is this?'

Cailin laughed quietly. 'If this were a *co-operative* effort, Zaelis, then we would certainly not be bringing Lucia anywhere near Alskain Mar. If I had the power, I would veto it. No, the Libera Dramach rule in the Fold, and well you know it. We owe you nothing. We may be helping you, but we are not beholden to you. And I have other interests to attend to before all this is over.'

Lucia woke in the afternoon, ate a little food, and made her preparations to do what had to be done. She did not speak to anyone.

After a time, she walked past the ring of soul-eaters to the edge of the hole that lay in the centre of the depression. The afternoon sun warmed her from behind, but on the nape of her neck and upper back – where the scarring was – her dead nerves felt nothing. Her gaze was distant, focused on the speckling of tiny clouds in the eastern sky, where the deep azure blended into shades of purple.

She let herself relax, and listened. The wind whispered sibilant nonsense at her, and the slow, stirring thoughts of the hilltop grumbled along so slowly as to be incomprehensible. There were no animals here: they had been driven away by an instinct that warned them of whatever lurked at the bottom of that hole in the earth. Lucia felt it too, all around her but concentrated mostly underground; it was like the distant soughing of some enormous animal, asleep but still aware of them. The air seemed taut, and tricked the vision with half-seen movements.

Zaelis appeared next to her with Cailin, and gave her an entirely unconvincing smile of reassurance. The Sister stroked the hair on the side of her head in a gesture of surprising tenderness.

'Remember, Lucia,' she said. 'Nobody is forcing you to do this.'

Lucia did not reply, and after a moment Cailin gave a slight nod of understanding and retreated.

'I am ready,' she told them, though she really wasn't.

Several of the guards who had travelled with them had brought the components for a cradle, which they had assembled as Lucia slept. It was little more than a lightweight chair made from interlocked pieces of kamako cane, and a system of ropes, both to secure Lucia into the chair and to provide a way of lowering it down into the cavern. They tied her into it awkwardly, for they regarded her with reverence and did not want to hurt her, yet they did not dare make their knots loose in case they should slip. When it was done, two of them picked her up while the remainder of the guards took up the slack of the long rope and secured it at its end to one of the more sturdy-looking soul-eaters. The two guards who carried her slid her gently out over the edge of the pit, allowing their companions to take her weight gradually. They did so without straining; she was slender enough that any of them could bear her without too much trouble. Finally, she was hanging over the shaft, the back of the chair resting against one wall.

Zaelis looked down on her, a final war of indecision going on behind his eyes. Then he crouched. 'Come back safely.'

She merely gazed at him with that strange, distracted look on her face, and said nothing.

'Let her down!' one of the guards called to his companions, and Lucia's descent began.

The first few metres were not easy. The men at the lip of the hole were forced to lean out as far as they dared to lower the rope, and Lucia had to fend off the black, wet rock of the shaft to stop her scraping against the sides. It took only a minute, but in that time Lucia's hands and legs were bruised and scratched all over.

Then the shaft opened out and she was hanging in a void above Alskain Mar, a tiny figure in a cradle dangling within the immensity of the subterranean cavern. The reality of her situation crowded in on her then, the terror of her predicament; and worse, the disbelief that her father had allowed it to happen. She realised only then that a part of her had been expecting Zaelis to change his mind, to tell her that she did not have to go, that he would not blame her if she backed away. Yet he had not. He had never even provided her an opportunity for second thoughts. How could he have done that to her? How *could* he?

The light of Nuki's eye was the only illumination here, a dazzling beam that drenched Lucia from above, limning her blonde hair and her back in unbearable brightness and casting her face into sharp shadow. Beneath her was water, a lake that glittered harshly where the sun struck it, so perfectly clear that it was possible to see the debris that cluttered its bottom. There were remnants of ancient stonework there, and hunks of broken rock eroded by time, grown over with lichens and aquatic plants. Islands were scattered about the lake, humps of pale cream rising above the waterline that had once been arches or the flanks of mighty pillars. She could see one wall of the cavern, but its rough curves faded into darkness on either side and left the rest of the chamber an unguessable abyss. Vines and greenery hung from the mouth of the shaft, straggling downward as if seeking the lake below. It was cold and dank here, and the only sound was the echoing drip of water and the occasional splash of a fish.

Most of the superstructure of the shrine was still standing, a thousand years after the earth had fallen in on it. It rose around Lucia in all its melancholy grandeur, colossal ribs of stone that thrust from the lake and arced up the curved sides of the cavern to broken tips. Huge pictograms were carved on the ribs in a language too old for Lucia to recognise, a dialect left behind in the evolution of society; their shapes suggested to her a grave and serious tone, resonant and wise.

Other sections of the shrine remained, too. Below her was the skeleton of a domed chamber, its floor raised enough so that the water lapped around its edges but did not swallow it. Fractured pieces of other rooms gave hints to the layout of the building before its destruction. On the wall before her, there was a massive section of stonework supported between two of the ribs, a piece of what had once been the original roof of the shrine. Angular patterns scrawled along its surface, a tiny glimpse of the majesty that this place had once possessed when it was intact. At the periphery of the light, she could see other structures, too dim to make out but evoking an impression of breathtaking size.

She felt suddenly, awfully small and alone. Alone, except for the presence that waited in Alskain Mar.

They lowered her towards the ruin of the domed chamber, and her creaking chair descended in steady increments, pausing between each gentle drop. Thankfully, she had no fear of heights, but she was dreadfully afraid of the chair or the rope giving way, even though she had been assured that they had taken every possible precaution and that the cradle was sturdy enough for someone six times her weight. She listened to her heart thumping, and tried to endure as she slowly neared the bottom of the cavern.

Then, finally, she was passing through the curled, broken fingers of the shattered dome, and her cradle bumped to the stone floor. She untied herself hurriedly, desperate to be out of it, as if they might haul her back up into the abyss again at any moment.

'Lucia?' Zaelis called from the shaft above, where the heads of the observers were dark blots against the blinding sunlight. 'Are you well?'

His voice rang like a blasphemy against the eerie peace of the cavern, and the air suddenly seemed to darken, to become thick with an overwhelming and angry disapproval so palpable that it made Lucia shy and whimper. The others felt it too, for she heard the guards exclaiming frightened oaths, and Cailin snapped something at Zaelis, after which he was quiet and did not shout any more.

The light swelled in the room again gradually, the tension easing. Lucia breathed again, but her hands trembled slightly. She looked back at the tiny, fragile cradle which was her only lifeline out of this place, and realised just how far from help she truly was. Standing on the edge of the slanting sunlight, she was just a willowy girl of fourteen harvests, wearing a scuffed and dirty pair of trousers and a white blouse.

Lucia, you are not somebody's sacrifice. Kaiku's words, spoken to her on the first day of Aestival Week. And yet here she was, in the lair of some unguessable entity, like a maiden offered to a mythical demon by her own father.

She willed herself to relax once again. The voices of the other spirits that she heard every day – the animals, the earth, the air – were silent here. It made her nervous. She had never been without them before, and it only intensified the loneliness and abandonment that she felt.

The occupant of the shrine was paying her little more attention now than it had been before. It was dormant and uninterested. If she would have to rouse it, she would have to do it *very* gently.

The time had come. She could not put it off any longer. She walked to the edge of the platform, facing the darkness, and knelt on the cool stone. She placed her hands flat on its surface and bowed her head. And she listened.

The process of actively communicating with a spirit was not as simple as language. Animals were easy enough for Lucia, but most spirits were largely ignorant of the world that humans saw and felt. There was no real lexicon through which humans and spirits were capable of understanding each other, since they did not share the same senses. Instead, they had to connect on a level far beneath reason, a primal melding which could only be achieved by becoming one with the nature of each other. A tentative, dim unity had to be formed, like that between a baby in a womb and its mother.

Now Lucia let herself become aware of the stone beneath her palms, and let the stone become aware of her. At first, the sensations were merely physical: the cold touch against her skin, the pressure of her flesh against the surface. They became sharpened and more acute as she slipped further into her trance, so that she became aware of the infinity of pores and creases in the skin of her hands, and could sense the microscopic cracks and seams in the stone that she knelt on.

By now she was entirely still, her breathing slowed to a languorous sigh, her heartbeat a dull and lazy thump.

Next, she let the sharing of sensation spread beyond the point of contact, expanding her awareness to include her whole body: the gush and pump of her blood, the net of follicles on her scalp, the snarled and dead tissue of her scars, the mesh of muscle in her back. She opened to the stone her knowledge of the steadily gathering potential of her ovaries and womb, which would soon become active; of the gradually lengthening bones in her limbs; all the processes of life and growth.

And with that, she let herself sink further into the essence of the stone, skimming its ancient, grinding memory. She felt its structure, its flaws; she sensed its origins, where it had grown and where it had been hewed from; she knew of its hard, senseless existence. There was no real life in a stone that had been separated from its mountain, cut from the greater entity of the land it was formed in; but there was still an imprint of things that had occurred here, an impression left by time on the character of the place.

Then, all at once, the shrine woke up around her. She almost lost her trance as her perception widened in one dramatic sweep, and she was feeling not just the stone but the entire structure of the shrine, a millennium of existence revealed to her at once. She sensed the pride and power of this place in its youth, felt its bitterness at its abandonment. This had been a site of great worship once, and it had not forgotten the days when men and women praised in its halls and burned sacrifices on its altars. Then she knew of a long emptiness, and of the coming of the new inhabitant, and the shrine was a place of power once again, though a wan and hollow shadow of its former self.

She began to tentatively probe, reaching toward this new inhabitant, to make it aware of her. Despite her trance, she was becoming fearful again. Even the oblique sensations she had received about the spirit that dwelt here had been massive and daunting, as if she were an insect brushing up against the flanks of some enormous beast.

Slowly, the spirit of Alskain Mar roused.

Lucia felt the change in the air around her with her finely attuned senses. The cavern was darkening, a blackness like smoky ink billowing into the light and defeating the glare of Nuki's eye. She could hear, distantly, Zaelis's exclamation of horror as the sight of her was obscured. The small heat that the beam of sun had provided faded away, and the temperature plummeted. She started to shiver; her breath came out in slow jets of vapour. The discomfort was causing her to slip back out of her trance again, and she retreated from the spirit to master herself, to relax.

But the spirit came after her. Her contact had stirred it, and it would not let her go without knowing something of the nature of the intruder in its lair. Lucia had a moment of terror at its sudden aggression before it engulfed her mind, melding forcefully with her in one cruel deluge.

There was the briefest instant where she was brutally faced with an immensity impossible to fathom with her human structures of thought. Then she died of shock.

And kept living.

Her eyes fluttered open. She lay face down on the floor of the ruined chamber. Her cheek and breasts hurt where she had fallen forward. There was light, pale blue and ethereal.

She raised herself up on her arms.

The illumination was coming from beneath the lake, underlighting her face eerily. The entire cavern was aglow. It was bigger even than her initial glimpses of it had suggested. The water cast shining ripples onto the walls and the remnants of the shrine. Overhead, the darkness was total, and no sight of the shaft through which she had entered Alskain Mar could be seen.

As her consciousness reassembled itself, she realised that the spirit of the shrine was still melded with her. She could feel it, tentative now. It sent a wash of knowledge, a recapitulation and something that she interpreted as an apology. The spirit had accidentally killed her, but only for moments. It had taken that long to absorb the nature of the girl, and to reactivate her biology, to repair the damage done to her sanity. Though she had died, she had not missed more than a couple of beats of her heart; her blood had barely time to slow.

Lucia realised with amazement that she was *communicating* with it. Or rather, it was communicating with her. She had known that it was hopelessly beyond her capabilities to make herself understood to a thing that was so alien, but she had never considered that the spirit might be able to simplify itself enough to descend to her level. Yet, in absorbing her nature, it had gained knowledge of her limitations and capabilities, and a rudimentary contact was achieved and held.

She crawled weakly to the edge of the platform, driven by a half-heard motivation, and knelt by the edge. Then she looked down into the water, and saw it.

There was no bottom to the lake any more. Though still as clear as crystal, it now plunged away to endless depths, from which the strange glow came. And down there, at some unguessable distance, the spirit looked back at her.

It had no form. It was like a dent in the water, hovering at the edge of Lucia's sight, more a suggestion of a shape than a physical entity. Somewhere within it two oval formations that approximated eyes watched her with a frightening intensity. It flickered with the invisible convection of the lake, sometimes jumping for a fraction of a second to another place before returning to its original location, flitting fitfully about while remaining perfectly still. It seemed at once small and looming to Lucia's eyes. She could not trust her perspective; it was as if she could reach into the water and touch it, though it appeared further away than the moons. Despite its best attempts at a manifestation she could comprehend, it still bent her senses just to look at it; yet look at it she did, for she knew that was what it wanted.

Awe and joy and raw terror clashed within her. She would never have believed she could ever achieve an understanding with a spirit such as this; but now that she had, she was committed to that contact, and there was no telling what kind of force she was dealing with. It could annihilate her mind in a fit of whimsy; it could keep her trapped here for an eternity as a companion; it could do something entirely beyond her imagination. She was still stunned and fragile from the mental impact of the spirit's first touch, from her momentary skip across the surface of death; she did not know if she was strong enough to deal with what was to follow.

But there was no other recourse now. She had questions to ask. Slowly, she spread her hands and laid them onto the cold surface of the lake. She exhaled a long, shivering breath, and a plume of vapour rose around her.

Then she began.

Twenty

'I will not go back!' Kaiku said, stalking around the rock-lined hollow where the travellers hid. 'Not yet. Not while we still know nothing about those creatures down there.'

'It's *because* we know nothing that we have to go back,' Yugi argued. He glanced up at Tsata, who was on lookout, crouched on the lip of a flat stone. 'We have no idea what kind of defences they can muster. And we're certainly not equipped to try and infiltrate them. What is it exactly you're planning to *do*, Kaiku?'

'It is not enough for us to return to the Fold with news of an Aberrant army hiding in the Fault,' Kaiku said. 'Why are they here? Who are they intended for? Is it the Libera Dramach, or somebody else? We need answers, not a report that will only breed more questions.'

'Keep your voices down,' Nomoru told them coldly.

They had observed the Aberrants and the strange Weaver-like newcomers for several hours before retreating from the edge of the cliff that overlooked the flood plain. Fearing the brightening day, they had pulled back to a less exposed spot where they could chew over their options. Nomoru had found them a pebbly dip between a cluster of tall rocks that leaned together, shutting out most of the sky. Despite the relative ease with which they had penetrated this far into the Weavers' protected area, they were all becoming increasingly nervous. The lack of any form of guards could be explained by the barrier they had passed through: as with the monastery on Fo that Kaiku had infiltrated in the past, the Weavers believed their barrier was infallible, and did not trouble themselves with security. But still, they had begun to feel that their luck was running thin, and something had to be done.

'If we stay and try to find out more, we run the risk that we are captured or killed,' said Yugi, running a hand through his hair before readjusting the rag around his forehead. He had dark circles under his eyes, and his stubbled cheeks made him look haggard and weary; but

192

he was the leader here, and he spoke with authority. 'Then nobody gets *any* answers, and no warning of what the Weavers are planning.'

'But what *are* they planning?' Kaiku said. She was unusually agitated. 'What do we know?'

'We know that they have a horde of several different species of Aberrant,' Yugi said. 'All predator species or specialised in some way. And they're all pure-bloods; no freaks.' Yugi shrugged. 'That means they've either selected them very carefully from their natural habitat, or bred them that way. This is what they have been moving in secret with their barges. This is what Lucia sensed on the river.'

'They're under control,' Nomoru said. She was sitting on the slope of the hollow, her face striped with the shadow of the rocks overhead, cleaning her exquisite rifle. 'Should have been fighting each other. They aren't. So they're under control.'

'Can they do that?' Yugi asked Kaiku. 'Can a Weaver influence that many creatures like that?'

'No,' Kaiku said. 'Not even a Sister could keep a constant check on all those minds at once. Not even a hundred Sisters, and they're a lot more . . . *efficient* with their use of the Weave than men are.'

'Maybe you're wrong,' said Nomoru. 'Maybe the Weavers *can* do it.'

'I am *not* wrong,' Kaiki returned. 'I would have sensed it, even if they could. Whatever was going on down there, it was too subtle to be Weavers controlling those creatures.'

'Then what about those black-robed people?' Yugi suggested. They had seen dozens of them, wandering between the scabrous masses of Aberrant beasts. 'Are they the keepers of the menagerie?'

'Perhaps,' said Kaiku. 'Perhaps not.'

'Could you find out?'

'Not by the method you mean. I do not know what I would be facing,' she said. 'If they caught me using my *kana*, the consequences could be disastrous. For all of us.'

'What about that building?' Nomoru said, squinting down the barrel of her rifle. 'Don't have any idea about that. Need to get closer.'

'It's a mine,' said Yugi. 'Surely that's obvious? The fact that the blight is present here means they've got a witchstone down there. It also means that it's been awake long enough to start corrupting the land.'

'I think the presence of the building is enough to indicate that they have been here a long time,' Kaiku pointed out. 'Yet they have not made any move to attack the Fold. So we can presume—'

'It's a flood plain,' Nomoru interrupted, continuing her original train of thought. 'How do you dig a mine on a flood plain? It would *flood*.'

Tsata had been listening to the conversation patiently. It had been obvious to him what to do since the start, but he knew that simple survival logic did not work on Saramyr; they insisted on complicating things. Now that they had argued their way around the subject enough to satisfy themselves, he decided the time was right to interject.

'I have a solution,' he said.

The others looked up at where he crouched, his pale green eyes flitting among the broken rocks that surrounded them.

'Two of us stay and investigate,' he said. 'Two of us go back.'

'Only Nomoru knows the way back,' Yugi pointed out.

'I know the way back,' Tsata said. After a lifetime of navigating his way through dense jungles, the relatively open terrain of the Fault was simple to remember. He could retrace their route easily, and avoid the dangers that they had passed through on their journey here.

'Nobody's staying,' said Yugi.

'*I* am,' Kaiku shot back.

'You're the only one who can get us out through that barrier,' Yugi reasoned.

'Then I will accompany you to the other side and then come back,' said Kaiku.

'I will stay with her,' Tsata put in. 'I would be more use here.'

'You're both in a real hurry to get killed,' Nomoru said with a nasty smile. 'I don't mind. I'll go with him.' She thumbed at Yugi. 'Safer.'

'We're all going back *together*,' Yugi said. 'We almost didn't make it here with four of us. With just two—'

Kaiku cut him off. '*You* almost did not make it here,' she said. 'Need I remind you to whom you owe the fact that you are here at all?'

Yugi sighed. 'Kaiku, I won't let you do this. And certainly not out of gratitude for saving my life.'

Kaiku brushed her fringe back from where it hung across her face. She had ever been a stubborn one, and now she had her heels firmly planted. 'It is not your choice,' she said. 'I am here as a representative of the Red Order; you do not have rank over me. And Tsata is under allegiance to no one.'

'You're not even *in* the Red Order! You're still an apprentice! Gods, Kaiku, don't you understand the *threat*?' Yugi cried. 'What happens if you're caught? You know how paranoid Cailin is about exposing any of her operatives; what do you think will happen if a Weaver gets hold of you? You'll jeopardise the whole of the Sisterhood! And besides,' he finished, his voice dropping to a hiss as Nomoru shushed him, 'you both know where the Fold is.'

Kaiku was unconvinced. 'Someone needs to stay and let everyone know if this army begins to move. Only I can do that; only I can get a warning to the Fold instantly if the Weavers start to march.'

'Correct me if I'm mistaken, but hasn't Cailin forbidden long-distance commounication between Sisters?' Yugi pointed out.

'She has not *forbidden* it,' Kaiku replied. 'She has merely made it clear that it is only to be used when absolutely no other option is available. As now.'

'And you think you are qualified to decide that? You think she would be happy for an apprentice to take that responsibility?'

'I do not care what makes her happy or otherwise,' Kaiku said dismissively. 'I am not her servant.' She paused for a moment, then continued. 'Why do you think she let me go to Okhamba with Mishani? She needed someone who could thread the Weave. In case we could not get the spy away, I was to send her the information he held. That was how important she considered it. This is how important *I* consider *this*. It is our only chance to find out what the Weavers are up to.' She swept her hand in a gesture of frustration. 'All this time, we've been too careful. *Cailin* has been too careful. And look at the result. The Weavers have an army under our noses! The Red Order should have been looking for this kind of thing, but Cailin is too afraid of any of them getting caught. If we do not find out *now* what is happening, it will be too late!' She met Yugi's eyes earnestly. '*We* are here and they are not, and if I return, Cailin will never let me get close enough again to make a difference.'

And there it was. That was the truth of it. If they retreated now, Cailin would not let her risk herself again, and they would have missed a potentially crucial opportunity to discover the Weavers' plans. She could not turn her back on this. Not with her oath to Ocha still smouldering in her mind, and her family's deaths unavenged.

Ocha looked after me once, she thought, recalling her frozen trek through the Lakmar Mountains many years ago. *He will do so again.*

'You'll make a difference, I've no doubt of that,' Yugi said, but he sounded defeated, and Kaiku knew that he would not argue any further. 'Whether it is a triumph or a catastrophe, time will tell.' He shrugged again. 'I can't stop you, Kaiku. Not by force or by reason. I just want you to know how many lives you're playing with.'

'For too long we have been too afraid of the Weavers,' Kaiku said. 'We have not dared to take a risk. We cannot hide forever.' She put a hand on his shoulder. 'I will be careful.'

'You'd better be,' said Yugi, then flashed an unexpected grin. 'I need you to come back safely to the Fold. So I can kill you for making me worry like this.'

The humour was forced, and nobody took it up.

'Are you finished?' Nomoru said drily. 'Can we go?'

Kaiku gave her a poisonous glance, then leaned close to Yugi's ear and breathed: 'I do not envy your company for the trip back.'

Yugi groaned.

Reki tu Tanatsua, younger brother of the Empress of Saramyr, had begun to regret ever visiting his sister at all.

He sat on the wide stone shelf of a window-arch in his chambers, curled up with the soles of his shoes resting against one end and his back against the other. He was looking out northward over the mighty walls of Axekami and the plains beyond, with the sparkling Jabaza curving in from the left side of the panorama, heading for the horizon and the mountains. It had been a hot and sultry day, and the very land seemed to laze in the burnished light as Nuki's eye sank to the west. Soft strips of cloud hung drowsily at the high altitudes, barely moving. Reki's head was resting against the arch, his arms crossed, a study in thoughtfulness lit in gentle fire and warm shadow.

When he had learned that his request to travel to the Imperial City had been granted, he had been ecstatic. Not only because it would be his first opportunity to travel there unaccompanied by family – he was seventeen harvests then; eighteen since the beginning of autumn – nor because he loved his sister dearly and had missed her since she had gone to live in Axekami. No, most of his happiness was because he could finally get away from his father, Barak Goren, whose constant disappointment at Reki was wearing more and more at the boy's nerves.

The age difference between Reki and Laranya, who was thirty-three harvests, was due to the fragility of their mother. Despite having a fierce strength of mind, she had a weak constitution. Giving birth to Laranya had nearly taken her life, and Goren, who cared for her deeply, would not ask her to try for another child. But though she saw how proud he was of his daughter, she knew that he wanted a son. Not as a matter of lineage, for Laranya was eminently suitable to become Barakess, and in Saramyr titles were passed down to the eldest regardless of gender, unless special dispensation were made to bestow it upon a different child. Rather, it was because he was the kind of man who needed to prove his virility through his offspring, and a strong son would make him proud in a way that even a firebrand like Laranya could not.

After many years, she could bear it no longer; she stopped drinking the herbal brew that prevented pregnancy, and she gave him Reki. And this one *did* take her life.

Goren was not so unfair as to blame Reki for the death of his wife;

but as Reki grew, it soon became clear that there were other reasons for Goren to be resentful. Whereas Laranya had the robust constitution of her father, Reki inherited his mother's frailty, and the rough-and-tumble of growing up always ended with him being hurt. He became shy and introverted, a lover of books and learning: safe things, that were not apt to turn on him. His father had little time for it.

The white streak in his hair and the scar running from the side of his left eye to the tip of his cheekbone were from childhood, a fall from some rocks where he hit his head and face. He knew even then not to go to his father about it, but simply huddled miserably until the pain and concussion went away.

His relationship with his father had never got any better, and Reki had long since ceased trying to please him. The opportunity to travel here from faraway Jospa was a relief to all concerned. But it was fast turning sour, and Reki began to wonder if he was not better off back at home in the desert. And whether Laranya might not be too.

The Blood Emperor's behaviour was becoming terribly unbalanced. It seemed that scarcely a day passed by without some terrible argument between Mos and Laranya. Arguments for them were nothing new, of course, but these had a surpassing savagery; and after witnessing that moment in the pavilion when Mos had almost struck his pregnant wife, Reki was afraid for her.

Reki was Laranya's confidant in these matters, and she passed on every detail. What he heard deepened his concern more and more. The Blood Emperor was suffering strange dreams that he talked about obsessively, even using them as accusations against his wife. Several times he had asked Laranya if she was being unfaithful to him. Once, he had asked her whose baby she carried; for they had tried for so long for a child, and it was no coincidence in Mos's eyes that she had become such close friends with Eszel around the time she had miraculously conceived.

What Laranya did not know, and Reki did, was that Mos had already drunkenly threatened Eszel when the poet was unfortunate enough to be present during one of his rages. Eszel had confessed his fears for his life to Reki; but Reki had not passed them on to Laranya. He knew his sister too well. She would use it as ammunition to confront Mos, and get Eszel into deeper trouble.

Reki had told Eszel that the best thing to do would be to make himself scarce for the time being, and Eszel had taken his advice. He had gone on a long trip to 'gather inspiration' for his poetry, and wisely left no address where he could be contacted. Reki was not sure whether Mos had heard about this yet or not, but Laranya certainly had, and was bitterly hurt by his desertion.

It was not only the Blood Emperor's personal life that was falling to pieces, however. His advisers hardly dared advise him, but they dared not act without his approval, either. Nothing was being done about the mounting crisis and the reports of famine in the far settlements of the empire. The high families' cries went unheard.

Reki wanted to leave, and he wanted Laranya to come with him. It was not safe here for her, and not good for her child. But she would not go; she would not forsake the man she loved. And she begged him to stay with her, for she had nobody else to turn to.

How could he refuse? She was his sister, the only person who had loved him unconditionally all his life. There was nobody more precious to him.

His dark thoughts were interrupted by a chime outside the curtained doorway. He cursed softly and looked around the room for the small bell he was supposed to ring to indicate permission to enter. It was not a custom in the desert, and he found it annoying. Eventually he decided that he would not bother with formality, nor with moving from the window-shelf where he lounged.

'Enter,' he called.

The young woman who brushed aside the curtain was breathtaking. She was utterly beautiful in every aspect: her features were small and flawless, her figure perfect, her grace total. Her dusky skin and her deep black hair – drawn back tightly across her scalp and passing through a complex junction of jewelled pins and ornaments before twisting down her back in three braids – marked her as being from Tchom Rin, like Reki. She wore soft green and blue cosmetics around her almond-shaped eyes, and a subtle gloss on her lips; a necklace of carved ivory rested against her collarbone. She was dressed desert-fashion, in an elegant white robe clasped at one shoulder with a round green brooch, leaving one of her shoulders bare.

'Am I interrupting?' she asked, in a voice like thick honey.

'No,' he said, suddenly very conscious of the insolent way he was lazing on the window-shelf. He slid clumsily down from his perch. 'Not at all.'

She slipped into the room and let the curtain fall behind her. 'What were you doing?' she asked.

He considered inventing something grand, but his courage failed him. 'Thinking,' he said, and blushed at the way it sounded.

'Yes, Eszel said you were a thinker,' she smiled, disarming him completely. 'I admire that. So few men seem that way these days.'

'You know Eszel?' Reki asked, unconsciously brushing back his hair with one hand. Then, remembering his manners, said: 'Would you like to sit? I can call for some refreshments.'

She looked over at the couches and the table he had indicated. There was a *lach* pitcher there on a silver tray, and several goblets of silver and glass, etched with swirling patterns. A selection of small cakes were arranged around the pitcher. 'You already have wine,' she said. 'Might we share it?'

Reki felt the heat rising in his face again. There were always refreshments at his table; it was a courtesy provided to him as an important guest. The servants periodically replaced the pitcher to keep it cool, even though he never touched it. He had found it vaguely irritating to begin with, but he felt it would be rude to ask them to stop bringing it. He had got so used to their unobtrusive visits by now that he had quite forgotten the wine was there.

'Of course,' he said.

She arranged herself on the couch, lying sideways with her legs folded and tucked underneath her. Reki sat on another, awkwardly. The simple presence of this woman was excruciating.

'Shall I pour?' she asked.

He made an indication that she should do so; he did not trust his tongue.

She gave another flicker of a smile and picked up the pitcher. Her eyes on the wine as she tipped it, she said: 'You seem nervous, Reki.'

'Does it show so much?' he managed.

'Oh yes,' she replied. She offered him a glass of the delicate amber liquid. 'But that is why Yoru gave us wine. To smooth the edges of a moment.'

'Perhaps you had better hand me the pitcher, then,' Reki said, and to his delight she laughed. The sound ignited a bloom of warmth in his chest.

'One glass at a time, I think,' she said, then sipped her drink, regarding him seductively.

For Reki, the momentary pause seemed an endless silence, and he struggled to fill it. 'You mentioned that you knew Eszel . . .' he prompted.

She relaxed back into the couch. 'A little. I know a lot of people.' She was not making this easy for him. She seemed, in fact, to be enjoying his discomfort. Just being this near her was making his groin stir, and he had to adjust himself so that it would not show.

'Why have you come to see me?' he asked, and then inwardly winced as he realised how blunt it sounded. He took a swallow of wine to cover it.

She did not appear to be offended. 'Ziazthan Ri. *The Pearl Of The Water God.*'

Reki was confused. 'I do not understand.'

'Eszel told me that you had read it, and that you gave him a very accomplished recitation of the story.' She leaned forward a little, her eyes bright. 'Is that true?'

'I memorised it,' Reki said. 'It is only short. The accomplishment was the author's, not mine.'

'Ah, but it is the passion of the speaker, the understanding of verse and melody, that can bring the heart from a story read aloud.' She looked at him with something like wonderment. 'Have you really memorised it? I suspect it is not as short as you pretend. You must have an exceptional recollection.'

'Only for words,' Reki said, feeling that he was coming uncomfortably close to bragging.

'I would be very interested to hear it,' she purred. 'If you would recite it to me, I would be *very* grateful.'

The tone in her voice forced Reki to shift position again to conceal his gathering ardour. He was blushing furiously now, and for a moment he could not think of anything to say.

'Let me explain,' she said. 'I subscribe to the philosophy of Huika: that everything should be experienced once in the interests of a completeness of being. I have spent fortunes for a glimpse of the rarest paintings; I have travelled long and far to see the wonders of the Near World; I have learned many arts unknown to the land at large.'

'But you are so young to have done so much . . .' Reki said. It was true; she could not have been more than twenty harvests, only a little older than him.

'Not so young,' she said, though she sounded pleased. 'As I was saying, I met Eszel before he left the Imperial Keep, and he told me about you.' She leaned over, reached out and stroked her hand lightly down his face, whispered: 'Ziazthan Ri's masterwork inside your head.' Then she let him go, and he realised he had been holding his breath. 'There are so few copies in existence, so few uncorrupted versions of the story. There is little I would not do to experience something so rare.'

'My father possesses a copy,' Reki said, feeling the need to say something, 'in his library.'

'Will you recite it to me?' she said, slipping off the couch and getting up.

'Of . . . of course,' he said, furiously trying to summon it to mind. His memory seemed to have become jumbled. 'Now?'

'Afterwards,' she said; and she put out her hands for him to take, and lifted him to his feet.

'Afterwards?' he repeated tremulously.

She pressed herself gently against him, one finger tracing the line of the scar on his eye. The softness of her breasts and body make his erection painful. He felt drunk, but it was nothing to do with the wine.

'I believe in a fair trade,' she said. Her lips were close enough to his so that he had to resist the almost magnetic pull of her. Her breath was scented, like oasis flowers. 'An experience for an experience.' Her hand slipped to the brooch at her shoulder, and she twisted it; her robe fell away like a veil. 'Unlike any you have ever had before.'

Reki's heart was pounding in his chest. A voice was warning him to caution, but it went unheeded. 'I do not even know your name,' he whispered.

She told him just before her mouth closed on his.

'Asara.'

The man screamed as the knife slipped under the warm skin of his cheek, slicing through the thin layer of subcutaneous fat to the wet red landscape of muscle beneath. Weave-lord Kakre rode the swell of the scream like an expert, angling the blade to account for the distortion in his victim's face. He sheared upward to the level of the eye socket, then cut towards the back of the skull, gliding through the soft tissue until a bloody triangular flap peeled away. At the sight, he felt a deep peace, a fulfilment that never seemed to wane no matter how many times he sated himself. The post-Weaving mania was upon him, and he was skinning again.

His skinning chamber was windowless, hot and gloomy, lit only by the coals of the fire-pit in the centre of the room. Underlit in the red glow were his other creations, arranged on the walls or hanging on chains in the heights: kites and sculptures of skin gazing at him from empty eyes, watching him at his craft. His latest victim was placed on the iron rack which was his canvas, tilted upright in a spread eagle. This particular piece he had been carving since dawn, and now it was a patchwork, a frame of muscle with jigsaw skin and half the pieces missing.

Kakre felt inspired today. He did not know if he would get a kite out of this one or if it would simply be therapeutic, but the joy of cutting rendered it immaterial. It had been too long since he had worked at his art, too long; but the rigours of his Weaving had lately increased, and his appetite had increased with it.

He realised that he had been standing admiring the flap of skin he had peeled for some time, and in that time the man had fainted again. Kakre felt a pang of annoyance. He was usually so good at keeping his victims awake, with herbs and poultices and infusions. His knifework was shoddy as well, he noticed suddenly. He glared at his withered,

white hand. His joints pained him constantly. Could that be a contributing factor? Was he losing his skill with a blade?

It was an idea too horrible to contemplate. Even though, distantly,
he knew that his Mask was eating him from the inside as it had eaten its
previous owners, the actual implications of that had never occurred to
him. How strange, that a mind as sharp as his might miss something as
obvious as that.

A moment later, he had forgotten about it again.

He put his bloodied blade listlessly on a platter with all his other
instruments, and wandered to the edge of the fire-pit before easing
himself into a sitting position. As always, he was planning.

Already the deceptions were being drawn. Blood Kerestyn and
Blood Koli were gathering a formidable army, but it was not formidable enough to challenge the might of Axekami yet. In a few more
years, maybe. But in those years, the source of the blight might be
discovered by the people at large. He had heard of rumours, extremely
accurate rumours, that were being repeated quietly in the courts of the
high families. They worried him. Soon the famine would bring the
country to the point of total desperation, and those rumours might be
enough to make the high families turn their wrath from Mos onto the
Weavers.

He did not have time to wait. Therefore, Kakre intended to tempt
Mos's enemies closer.

His overtures to Barak Avun tu Koli had been well received; but
Avun was a treacherous snake, as likely to bite the one who handled
him as the one he was set upon. Had Avun believed him? And could he
convince Grigi tu Kerestyn to believe him as well?

You must strike when I say! he thought. *Or this will all be for nothing.*

More distressing than that, though, was a message that had come
from the Imperial Keep itself, one sent by courier that he had failed to
intercept. He was not sure who had sent it, but he knew Avun had
received it, and he was anxious to know what it said. Another
doublecross? But who was making deals behind his back?

It worried at Kakre's mind even as he worried at the Blood
Emperor's.

At night, when Mos fell into a drunken sleep, Kakre wove dreams
for him. Dreams of infidelity and anger, dreams of impotence and
fury. Dreams calculated to tip him in the direction Kakre needed him
to go. It was a dreadful risk, for if Mos began to suspect him, all would
be lost. Even the best Weavers could be clumsy – he thought of his
aching joints, and wondered if his skill in the Weave had suffered also –
and they might leave traces of themselves behind that would fester,
until the victim eventually realised what had been done to them. If Mos

were not drinking too much and already beleaguered with stress, Kakre might not have dared it; but the Blood Emperor had become unbalanced long before the Weave-lord had begun to interfere with his mind.

Lies, deceit, treachery. And only the Weavers matter.

He sat in his ragged robes of badly-sewn hide and fur and little pieces of bone, rolling that phrase around in his head. Only the Weavers mattered. Only the continuation of their work. And it was Kakre's job – no, his *calling* – to manipulate this crisis to ensure their survival. There was only one way out of it that he could see, but it required a game to be played so skilfully, so subtly, that the slightest miscalculation could mean disaster.

The pieces were in place. But the board was anyone's yet.

Twenty-One

The besieged town of Zila sat grim and cold in the twilight, a crooked crown atop a lopsided hill. Hundreds of yellow lights burned in the narrow windows of its buildings, gathering up towards the keep at its tip. To the north, where the hill was viciously steep, the Zan was a black, restless torrent, dim fins of drab lime glinting on its surface. Neryn had taken early station high in the sky tonight, even before the stars had begun to show; she commanded the scene alone, bathing it in funereal green.

The soldiers ringed the town, just out of bowshot and fire-cannon range, which was some considerable distance. Seven thousand men, all told, representing four of the high families. Tents were being erected and mortars assembled. Campfires dotted the dark swathe of the siege-line like jewellery. Fire-cannons of their own had been set up on either side of the Zan where the ring cut across it, to prevent any attempt to escape by water either upstream or down. The absence of any visible boats at the docks did not concern them. They were taking no chances. Nobody was getting out.

Mishani looked out from a window in the keep, surveying the forces arrayed against the town, calculating.

'There are not so many as I would have expected,' she said at last. 'The muster is poor.'

'It's more than enough to take this town,' Chien said darkly.

'Still,' she said, turning away from the window. 'The high families have spared only a small fraction of their armies. They keep their true strength to guard their own assets against the coming conflict. And there are no Imperial Guards at all, nor Blood Batik troops. Where is the Blood Emperor when one of his own towns defies him?'

The room they shared was a little stark, with its bare stone walls and floor, but Mishani considered that she could have done much worse for a prison. There were two sleeping-mats, a coarse rug, and cheap, heavy wall-hangings emblazoned with simple designs. There was also a table, with smaller mats for sitting on, and the food they had been getting these last few days was bland but palatable. The heavy wooden door was locked, but there were a pair of guards outside who would escort them to the appropriate room when they needed to make toilet or get dressed. They were not treated badly by any means, but for the simple fact that they were confined to their room.

There were other excursions, beyond the necessities of privacy. Bakkara had visited several times, and twice had escorted Mishani around the keep. He was not subtle at disguising his motivation: he wanted to hear about Lucia, and Mishani suspected that beneath his tough exterior he was somewhat awed to be in the presence of someone who knew her personally. Mishani played up to the reflected glory. It got her out of that room, and besides, she had to admit to herself that she found Bakkara strangely attractive. The sheer, overwhelming *manliness* of him, which her cynical side found faintly amusing in a pitying kind of a way, was also what made him so appealing: his lack of social graces, his jaded air that suggested he was above bothering to please anyone, his brawny physicality. It was a contradiction that she did not even attempt to reconcile; she knew well enough that matters of intellect and matters of the heart were independent of each other.

Chien was not fit enough to leave the room for long periods. His injuries had been treated, but he had developed a bad fever, probably due to the overnight ride to Zila. He spent most of the day lying on his sleeping-mat, dosed into near-unconsciousness with analgesic tinc-tures and febrifuges, occasionally rousing himself to complain about the lack of information they were getting, or to protest on Mishani's behalf that a noble lady should be allowed her own room. Mishani wished it were so. Chien was beginning to annoy her. He did not take inactivity well.

The siege had been slow in coming. Troops arrived at different times, and co-ordinating them all efficiently took a long while. It had been three days since the first of the forces appeared, bearing the banner of Blood Vinaxis. They had been the first family ever to hold the Imperial throne, but they had diminished now, and were weak. Their holdings were directly in the midst of the blighted Southern Prefectures, and most of their money came from crops which passed through Zila on their way to Axekami. A lot of those crops were hoarded within the walls of the town. Small wonder, then, that Barak Moshito tu Vinaxis was first on the scene to get them back.

Mishani had learned from Bakkara that the Governor of Zila had been stockpiling a great deal of food against the coming famine, confiscating portions from the trade caravans that passed over nearby Pirika Bridge. He had been intending to keep enough only for the Town Guards and the administrative body, and to sell the surplus at extortionate rates to the high families when the starvation began to bite. The townsfolk would be left to get by as they could. It was the exposure of his plan by Xejen, leader of the Ais Maraxa, that had triggered the revolt; and now the townsfolk were sitting on a store of food that would last them through the winter and long beyond, with careful rationing. As long as their walls held and they kept the enemy out, they would be a tough nut to crack.

After Blood Vinaxis had come Blood Zechen, though Barakess Alita had sent generals in her stead; then a token force from Blood Lilira, who could afford many more, and whose Barakess Juun was similarly absent.

Last to arrive had been Barak Zahn, from his estates north of Lalyara, leading a thousand mounted Blood Ikati warriors and a thousand on foot, the green and grey standards of his family stirring limply in the faint wind as they approached. Mishani could appreciate the irony. It was Zahn whom she had been on her way to see, Zahn the reason that she had been captured; and now he came to her, and they found themselves on opposite sides of an uprising. The gods were nothing if not perverse.

There were a few quick thuds on the door, and Bakkara opened it without waiting for permission. Mishani could never get used to the doors in this keep; they seemed such an impediment. She supposed their purpose was defensive, but they stopped breezes getting through to lighten the humidity of the hot days. Luckily, the draughty stone walls compensated well enough.

Mishani was still standing by the window when the old soldier entered. Chien was sitting upright on his sleeping-mat, his face swollen from bruising and sheened with fever. He glared at Bakkara. The merchant seemed to have taken a strong dislike to the soldier, presumably because of the older man's rough tongue.

'You're wanted, Mistress Mishani,' he said.

'Am I?' she said dryly, an imperious tone in her voice that suggested she was not about to be ordered anywhere.

Bakkara rolled his eyes and sighed. 'Very well: I am here to request your presence at an audience with Xejen tu Imotu, leader of the Ais Maraxa, mastermind of the Zila revolt and maniacal foaming zealot. Is that better?'

Mishani could not help but laugh at the bathos. 'It will do,' she said.

'And how are you feeling?' he asked Chien.

'Well enough,' Chien replied rudely. 'Are you going to let us out of here now?'

'That's up to Xejen,' Bakkara said, scratching the back of his neck. 'Though I can't see your hurry. If we let you out of here, you'll still be stuck in Zila. Nobody's getting past that wall, one way or another, for a very long time yet.'

Chien cursed softly and looked away, breaking off the conversation.

'Are you coming?' Bakkara asked Mishani.

'Of course,' she said. 'I have been waiting to talk to Xejen for quite some time now.'

'He's been very busy,' Bakkara said. 'You may have noticed a little disturbance outside Zila that's causing us all some concern.'

They left Chien to his rest; he bade them a sullen farewell as they departed.

Bakkara took Mishani along a route that they had not walked before, but the surroundings were little different from any other part of the keep. It was dour and utilitarian, with narrow corridors of dark stone and little ornamentation or consideration for the natural flow of the elements.

Bakkara told her that it was built to the original plans, drawn up over a thousand years ago, which explained its miserable lack of soul. It was a military building constructed in a time when the recently-settled Saramyr folk were still using Quraal architectural ideas, where the weather was harsher and where ruthless practicality was far more important than the frivolity of aesthetics. As Saramyr evolved its own identity, the people began to explore the freedom of religion and thought and art that had been suppressed in Quraal by the rise of the Theocracy, and which had led them to choose exile. The blazing summers and warm winters made the stuffy and close Quraal dwellings uncomfortable to live in, and so they invented for themselves new types of housing, ones that accommodated their environment rather than shutting it out. Many old settlements still bore traces of the Quraal influence in some parts, but most remnants of that era had been torn down as they crumbled and replaced with more modern buildings. Saramyr folk had little love for ruins.

Xejen tu Imotu, leader of the Ais Maraxa, was pacing his chamber when they arrived. He was a bland-looking man of thirty-three harvests, thin and full of nervous energy. A mop of black hair topped his head, and he had sharp cheekbones and a long jawline that made his face seem narrower than it was. He was dressed in simple black clothes that hugged his wiry figure, and he scampered across the room to meet them as Bakkara knocked and entered.

'Mistress Mishani tu Koli,' he said, his speech rapid. 'An honour to have you here.'

'With such a gracious invitation, how could I refuse?' she said, glancing at Bakkara.

Xejen did not seem to quite know how to take that. 'I hope your confinement has not been too terrible. Please forgive me; I would have seen you earlier, but the task of organising Zila into a force capable of defending itself is taking up all of my time.'

He resumed his pacing around the room, picking up things and putting them back down, adjusting bits of paper on his desk that did not need adjusting. This room was as spartan as the rest in the keep: a few mats, a table, a desk and a small settee. Glowing lanterns depended from ceiling hooks, and outside the single window the twilight was deepening to darkness. If his headquarters were anything to go by, then Xejen could not be accused of the same abuse of power that the erstwhile Governor had.

Mishani decided to be blunt. 'Why was I brought here?' she asked.

'To my chambers?'

'To Zila.'

'Ah!' He snapped his fingers. 'Part charity, part misunderstanding. Bakkara, why don't you explain?'

Mishani turned to the soldier with a patient expression, as if to say: *Yes, why don't you?* It had been one of the few things he had refused to talk about; he had been waiting for Xejen's permission, it seemed.

'Well, first there was the matter of your friend Chien,' he said, scratching his stubbled jaw. 'Even if you hadn't been there, we couldn't leave him in the state he was in. Then—'

'That's the charity part,' Xejen broke in. 'And as for you, well, Bakkara made the entirely understandable mistake of assuming you were still well connected in the high families, and that you may prove very useful in attracting Blood Koli to come to our defence, to heighten the profile of our plight.'

Bakkara looked abashed and gave an apologetic shrug, but Mishani was not concerned with that. She did not take it personally.

'By the time you had come to my attention, the gates had been shut and we could not very well let you out,' Xejen chattered on. 'Of course, I realised immediately that you did not possess the worth that Bakkara imagined – excuse my plain speaking – because I knew that you and your father were very much at odds. And since you are, after all, something of a heroine to the Ais Maraxa, I would hardly use you as a bargaining chip and deliver you to him.'

'I am relieved to hear it,' Mishani said. 'Am I to take it, then, that my relationship with my father is known to the Ais Maraxa?'

'Only myself and a few others,' Xejen replied almost before she had finished her sentence. 'Many of us were part of the upper echelons of the Libera Dramach, don't forget; and we were there when you came to the Fold. But your secret is safe. I understand you have been a great help to the Libera Dramach by trading on the illusion that you are still a part of Blood Koli.'

'I still am, as far as I am aware,' Mishani said. 'Legally, at least. My father has not cut me off yet.' Though he *had* tried to kill her twice, she added mentally.

'Your mother's latest book has not helped matters in your case, I imagine,' Xejen commented.

'That remains to be seen,' Mishani said. Truthfully, she had not even begun to consider the implications that Muraki tu Koli's latest collection of Nida-jan tales might have.

Xejen cleared his throat, wandering restlessly to the other side of the room. Mishani found his constant motion dizzying.

'I'll not dance around the issue, Mistress Mishani,' he said. 'You'd be a great asset to our cause. One of Lucia's rescuers. Someone who knows her intimately.' He looked up at her sharply. 'You'd do wonders for the morale of these townsfolk, and lend the Ais Maraxa a good deal of credibility.'

'What are you asking me to do?' she prompted.

Xejen stopped for a brief instant. 'To support us. Publicly.'

Mishani considered for a moment.

'There are things I would learn first,' she said.

'Ah,' said Xejen. 'Then I will do the best I can to answer any questions you have.'

'What are you doing here in Zila?' Mishani asked, her keen eyes studying him from within the black mass of her hair. 'What purpose does it serve the Ais Maraxa?'

'Notoriety,' came the reply. 'It has been some years since we first learned of the sublimity of the Heir-Empress Lucia, some time since we broke away from the Libera Dramach whose more . . .' he waved his hand, searching for the word, '*secular* appreciation of her was blinkering them to the wider picture. In that time the Ais Maraxa have striven to spread the news that there exists one to deliver us from the evil of the Weavers, to end the oppression of the peasantry and to turn back the blight that ruins our land.'

Mishani watched him carefully as his rhetoric became more heated. She knew Bakkara had meant his comment about Xejen being a zealot as a joke, but she was conscious that there was a grain of truth in what the soldier had said, and now that she met him she suspected that Bakkara was not entirely at ease with his leader.

'But spreading the word is not enough,' Xejen continued, wagging a finger in the air. 'The Heir-Empress is a rumour, a whisper of hope, but the people need more than rumours to motivate them. We need to be a threat that is taken seriously. We need the high families talking about us, so that their servants see they are worried . . . so that they see that even the most noble and powerful are afraid of the followers of Lucia. Then they'll believe, and they'll come to her when she calls, when she returns in glory to take the throne.'

He was gazing out of the window into the night now. Mishani cast a glance up at Bakkara, who caught it. He looked skyward briefly in spurious exasperation, and the corner of his mouth curved into a faint smile.

'But even with our best efforts, we couldn't make the empire sit up and take notice,' Xejen went on. 'Until now. We've been working at Zila for a long time, and the onset of famine has given us just the climate we need to make our move. The fact that the Governor has stockpiled all our provisions for us . . . it's as if Ocha himself has given us his blessing. We can hold out for a year within these walls. By that time, there won't be anyone in the empire who hasn't heard of the Ais Maraxa and learned of our cause.'

'Are you not concerned about Lucia?' Mishani inquired. 'After all, if her name becomes so notorious, you can be sure the Weavers will be searching for her harder than ever. It is because she is presumed dead and her abilities are not generally known that we have managed to hide her so long.'

'The Weavers will still think she's dead,' said Xejen dismissively. 'They'll think we're just wasting time fostering rumours. Besides, they'll never find her. But what preparations are the Libera Dramach making for when she comes of age? None! We are building her an army, an army of common folk, and when she reveals herself they'll suddenly discover that their rumour of hope is real, and they'll come flocking to her banner.'

Mishani's inclination was to argue: what banner? If this was all about building Lucia an army, then he was making an extraordinary assumption in assuming that Lucia *wanted* one. She wondered if he would talk this way if he knew Lucia as she did. Not as some glorious general, nor as some beatific child assured of her own destiny. Just a young girl.

But she had no illusions about changing Xejen's mind, and she wanted to stay on his good side, so she held her tongue.

'But what of the siege?' she asked. 'How do you plan to deal with that? You will run out of food eventually.'

'You know what's going on in Axekami, Mistress Mishani,' he said, again clipping the end off her sentence in his rush to speak. 'The high families will have a lot more than us to worry about in this coming year. You can see yourself how little enthusiasm they have for a fight. Look at that army!' He made a sweeping gesture to the window. 'We have ways of communicating with our operatives outside Zila. They are already talking about our plight and what we represent. Word will spread. A lot may change in a year, but whatever comes, everyone will know the name of Lucia tu Erinima before we are done.'

Xejen crossed the room to face them, his thin features wan in the lantern light. There was an intensity in his eyes now, a fire ignited by his speech. Mishani had no doubt that he was a formidable orator when faced with a crowd. His conviction in his own words was indisputable.

'Will you help us, Mistress Mishani?'

'I will consider it,' she said. 'But I have a condition.'

'Yes, you wish to have your confinement ended,' Xejen finished for her. 'Done. A sign of good faith. It would have been sooner, but I had too many other things to worry about. I don't want you as a prisoner, I want you as an ally.'

'You have my thanks,' said Mishani. 'And I will think on your proposal.'

'I need not tell you, I suppose, that your freedom only extends to the walls of Zila,' Xejen added. 'If you try and leave the town, you will regrettably be shot. I am sure you will not attempt anything so foolish.'

'Your advice is noted,' Mishani said, and with that she made the requisite politenesses and left, telling Bakkara that she could find her own way back.

Chien was asleep when she returned, murmuring and stirring in the grip of a dream. She shut the door of their room quietly behind her and sat on a mat to think. A plan was forming in her mind. It was like the old days at court. The principal players had been introduced; now she just had to work out how best to exploit them.

But *this* man, she did not yet understand. There was a piece of the puzzle missing here, and had been since the start. Until she knew what it was, until she knew whether Chien was an enemy or a friend, she dared not act.

She studied him closely, trying to find an answer in the broad angles of his face. He muttered and turned away from her, rolling over on his mat and gathering the blankets around him tighter. He was shivering despite the warmth of the night.

'What *is* your secret, Chien?' she murmured. 'Why are you here?'

After a time, she got up and extinguished the lantern, undressed in the moonlight and slipped beneath her own covers. She was just drowsing when Chien began to sing.

She felt a smile touch the corner of her lips. He was dreaming, his voice a tuneless drone, too soft to vocalise the words properly. She listened, and listened, and then suddenly she sat up in bed, staring across the dark room at him.

He continued, oblivious, singing his fevered song.

Mishani's breath was a shudder. She felt her throat close up, and then she slowly sank down to her pillow and faced the wall, stifling her sobs with her blanket. Tears came and would not be held back, sliding over the bridge of her nose and dripping into the fabric.

She knew that song, and it all made sense now.

Twenty-Two

The Blood Emperor Mos tu Batik stormed through the marbled corridors of the Imperial Keep, his brow dark with fury. His beard, once close and tidy, had grown unkempt, the patches of grey more pronounced. His hair was a mess, hanging in draggles over his eyes and damp with sweat. Wine had spilled on his tunic, and his clothes were wrinkled and pungent.

There was madness in his eye.

Days and nights had blended into one, an endless half-consciousness swamped in alcohol. Sleep brought him no rest, only terrible dreams in which his wife rutted with faceless strangers. His waking hours were spent in a constant state of suspicion, punctuated by sporadic outbursts of rage, directed either at himself or at anyone else near him. He was spiralling slowly and inexorably into mania, and the only escape from the torture was intoxication, which provided a small surcease but only made him more bitter afterward.

He had taken enough. Now he meant to have it out, once and for all. He would not stand by while he was cuckolded.

There would be a reckoning.

It had started long ago, before Eszel the flamboyant poet. He had come to realise that, in the long nights he had spent alone while spite gnawed at his soul. He remembered other times, when Laranya had wanted to pursue her interests and he his, and how he had indulged her in whatever she wished. Times when he had been disappointed that she was not waiting for him when he returned from a particularly harrowing day in the council chamber. Times when she had laughed and joked with other men, who seem attracted like moths to a candle, drawn by the brightness and vivacity of her. He remembered the jealousy then, the seeds of resentment burrowing into a soil made moist by his natural inclination for domination. Among the delusions and venomous slanders that he had persuaded himself to believe in those lonely hours, he had found nuggets of truth.

He had come to realise that he wanted Laranya as two different people, and that she could not be both. On the one hand was the fiery, wilful and entirely insubordinate woman he had fallen in love with; on the other, the dutiful spouse, who would be there when he wanted her and be absent when he did not, who would make him feel like a man because a man should be able to control his wife. One of the reasons he had fallen in love with her – and stayed in love with her – was because she would not bend to his will, would never be meek and submissive; it was because she galled him that she challenged him and kept his interest. His first wife Ononi had been the model of how a woman should be, but he had not loved her. Laranya was impossible, would never be tamed no matter how he tried, and she had both captured his heart and poisoned it.

It was the child that had turned things bad. For years, Mos had forgotten those fleeting moments of mistrust and disappointment, the feelings erased as soon as he saw Laranya's face again. But now he brought them all back to pick over them like a vulture at a carcass. All that time, and no child; but now, suddenly, she was pregnant.

He remembered when she had told him, what his first reaction had been, an instant of doubt that he had swept away, feeling guilty for ever having thought it.

Just like Durun. Just like my son, and his scheming bitch wife, letting him raise a child that wasn't even his own.

History was repeating itself. But this time, Mos was ahead of the game.

It was late as he stalked towards the Imperial chambers. His sleep patterns were erratic and took no account of the sun or the moons, and he had begun to fear the nightmares so much that he would do anything to put them off. He had been awake for more than forty hours now, dosed up with herbal stimulants to counteract the soporific lull of the wine, thinking in tighter and tighter circles until there was nothing left but a white-hot ball of fury that demanded release.

Oh, she had come to him to plead, or to demand, or to shout. Different approaches to the same end: she wanted to know what had possessed him, why he was acting this way. As if she did not know.

There were others, too. Kakre loomed in and out of his memory, croaking reports and meaningless observations. Advisers came and went. In some dim fashion, he had been aware of the other affairs of state which he was supposed to be attending to, but everything had become transparent to him in contrast to the one overwhelming matter of Laranya. Until it was resolved, he could not care about anything else. Reason had failed. The spies he had set to watch his wife had failed.

But there was another way; the only resort he had left.

He threw aside the curtain and stamped into the Imperial bedchamber. The violence of his entrance startled Laranya out of sleep. She sat up with a cry, clutching the sheets to her chest in the warm dark of the autumn night. Something moved in the pale green moonlight, by the archway that led to the balcony beyond: a figure, blurred, gone in an instant. Mos blundered across the room in pursuit, roaring in anger.

'What is it? Mos, *what is it?*' Laranya cried.

The Blood Emperor's hands were clutched on the stone balustrade; he was glaring down the north-eastern side of the Imperial Keep where it sloped away in a clutter of interlocking sculptures and carvings. He cast about, looking up, then to his left and right, then leaning far out as if he might see underneath the balcony. It was no good. There were too many folds and creases in the ornamentation, too many looming effigies and archways where the intruder might have hidden himself. Gods, he was so quick! Mos had barely even seen him.

Laranya was at his elbow, in her nightdress, her touch fearful on his arm. 'What *is* it?' she asked again.

'I saw him, whore!' Mos bellowed, flinging her arm away. 'You can't pretend any more! I saw him with my own eyes!'

Laranya was backing away into the room. Some emotion midway between enragement and fear had taken her, and did not seem to know which way to resolve itself. There was a new edge to Mos tonight, and she was not at all sure what he might do.

'Who? Who did you see?'

'Shouldn't you know? Was it that effeminate poet? Or is there someone else I should know who enjoys my bed?'

'Mos, I have told you . . . I cannot prove it to you any more than I already have! There is no one!'

'*I saw him!*' Mos howled, stumbling after her, his face distorted and haggard. 'He was just here!'

'There was nobody here!' Laranya cried. Now she *was* afraid.

'Liar!' Mos accused, advancing, looming in the green-tinted shadows.

'No! Mos, you are drunk, you are tired! You need sleep! You are seeing phantoms!'

'*Liar!*'

She reached the dresser, knocking into it and tipping bottles of perfume and make-up brushes over. There was no further she could retreat.

'A man cannot rule an empire when he cannot rule his wife!' Mos snarled. 'I will teach you obedience!'

She saw in his eyes what he meant to do, even before he had raised his fist.

'Mos! No! Our baby!' she pleaded, her hand going defensively to her belly.

'*His* baby,' Mos breathed.

Laranya did not have time to ask who he meant before the first blows fell; nor did she find out afterward, when he left her alone on the floor of the bedchamber with her body aching and her face bruised and blood seeping from between her legs as their child died inside her.

Reki was woken by a servant calling his name outside the curtain of his room. Asara was already awake, watching him. She lay next to him in his bed, and as he saw her it seemed that the pallid green moonlight caught her at an odd angle, and her eyes were two saucers of reflected illumination, like a cat's. Then she looked to the curtain, and the moment passed.

His gaze lingered on her shadowed face for an instant, unable to draw away from the beauty there. She had indeed, as she had promised, given him an experience unlike any he had had before; but though he had repaid her with a flawless rendition of *The Pearl Of The Water God*, she had not gone away as he had feared, never to see him again. To his delight, she had barely left him since the moment they had met. A sweet recollection of lazy days and passionate nights flitted across his consciousness. And if it seemed too good to be true, then he was loth to shatter his fragile happiness by questioning it.

'What is it?' he called, his throat tight from sleep.

'The Empress!' the servant replied. 'The Empress!'

The tone in her voice made him sit up with a jolt of alarm. 'A moment,' he said, and slid naked out of bed to put on a robe. Asara did the same. He was too preoccupied to even glance at her sublime form. Though she had shared his bed for several nights now, and he already worshipped her like a goddess, it was all dashed away in that dreadful instant.

'Enter,' he called, and the servant hurried in, speaking as she came. It was one of Laranya's handmaidens, a servant of Blood Tanatsua rather than one of the Keep servants.

'The Empress is hurt,' she babbled. 'I heard her . . . we all heard them fighting. We went in after the Emperor had gone. We—'

'Where is she?' Reki demanded.

'The Imperial chambers,' the servant said, but she had barely finished before Reki swept past her and out of the room.

He ran barefoot through the corridors of the Keep, the *lach* floor chill on his soles, heedless of how ridiculous he looked sprinting in a bedrobe.

The Empress is hurt.

Imperial Guards in their blue and white armour stood aside for him; servants hurried out of his way.

'Laranya,' he was murmuring breathlessly to himself, his voice like a whimper. 'Suran, let her be all right. I will do anything.'

But if the desert goddess heard his plea, she did not answer.

His quarters were not far from his sister's bedchamber. The life of the Keep went on all around as if nothing had happened. Cleaners were polishing the *lach* and dusting the sculptures, night-time activities carried out unobtrusively when most people were asleep. By the time he reached the door to the Imperial chambers, he knew that all the servants here must have heard what the handmaiden heard; yet they pretended otherwise. Since Saramyr houses rarely ever had interior doors due to the need for breezes in the scorching summers, codes of privacy had arisen in which it was extremely rude to eavesdrop or to pass on anything that was inadvertently learned. That Laranya's handmaiden had broken that silence was an indication of how serious she felt it was.

He heard Laranya sobbing before he shoved the curtain aside, and though the sound made him feel as if his heart would break, he was desperately relieved that she was still capable of making it.

She was on the bed, on her hands and knees, in amid a tangle of golden sheets stained with thin smears of blood that looked black in the moonlight. She was weeping as she pawed through the sheets as if searching for something.

She looked up at him, framed between the curving ivory horns that were the bedposts, and her eyes were blackened and swollen.

'I cannot find him,' she whispered. 'I cannot find him.'

Reki's eyes welled. He rushed over to hold her, but she shrieked at him to stay back. He shuddered to a halt in uncomprehending misery.

'I cannot find him!' she howled again. Her battered face was made ugly by bruises and tears. He had never seen her this way before. Whenever she had cried in the past, it had been only a cloud across the sun; but suddenly she seemed like a shade of herself, all the vigour and spirit gone from her. She looked like someone he did not know.

'Who are you searching for?'

She grubbed around in the bloodied sheets again. 'I felt him come out, I felt him *leave* me!' she cried. 'But I cannot see him!' She picked up something tiny that looked like a dense clot of blood, holding it up to the light. Threads of sticky liquid ran through the gaps in her fingers. 'Is that him? Is that him?'

With a sickening wrench, Reki realised where all the blood had come from, and what she was looking for. He felt suddenly dislocated from

217

reality, one beat out of time with the world. He could barely breathe for the horror of seeing his sister this way.

'That is not him,' Reki said. The words seemed to come from elsewhere. 'He is gone. Omecha has him now.'

'No, no, no,' Laranya began to whine, rocking back and forth on her knees. She had discarded the clot. 'It is not him.' She looked up at Reki, her eyes imploring. 'If I find him, I can put him back.'

Reki began to cry, and the sight brought Laranya to new grief. She reached out for him with bloodied hands, and he slumped onto the bed and embraced her. She flinched as they hugged and he let her go reflexively, knowing that he had hurt her.

'What did he do to you?' Reki said, and Laranya wailed, clutching herself to him. He dared not hold her, but he let his hands rest lightly on her back, and tears of fury and grief angled down his thin cheeks.

After a time during which they did not speak, Reki said: 'He needs a name.'

Laranya nodded. Even the unborn needed names for Noctu to record them. It did not matter that they had no idea of the sex of the child. Laranya had wanted it to be a son, for Mos.

'Pehiku,' she muttered.

'Pehiku,' Reki repeated, and silently commended the nephew he would never see to the Fields of Omecha.

That was how Asara found them when she arrived. She had taken a little time to dress, though she wore no make-up and her black hair hung loose over one shoulder. She slipped inside the curtain without asking permission to enter, and stood in the green moonlight silently until Reki noticed her.

'I will kill him,' Reki promised, through gritted teeth. His eyes were red and his nose streaming, forcing him to sniff loudly every so often. Ordinarily he would have been mortified to be seen like this by a woman he found so attractive, but his grief was too clean, too justifiable.

'No, Reki,' Laranya said, and by the steadiness in her voice he knew that sense had returned to her. 'No, you will not.' She raised her head, and Reki saw a little of the old fire in her gaze. 'Father will.'

Reki did not understand for a moment, but Laranya did not wait for him to catch up. She looked to Asara.

'Look in that chest,' she said, motioning to a small, ornate box laced in gold, that lay against one wall. 'Bring me the knife.'

Asara obeyed. She found amid the folded silks a jewelled dagger, and brought it to the Empress.

Reki was faintly alarmed, unsure what his sister intended to do with the blade.

'You have a task, brother,' she said, her swollen lips making repulsive smacking noises as she spoke. 'It will be hard, and the road will be long; but for the honour of your family, you must not shirk it. No matter what may come. Do you hear?'

Reki was taken aback by the gravity in her voice. It seemed appallingly incongruous with the disfigured woman who knelt on the bed with him. He nodded, his eyes wide.

'Then do this for me,' she said, and with that she twisted her long hair into a bunch at the back of her head and put the knife to it.

'*Don't!*' Reki cried, but he was too slow; in three short jerks it was complete, and Laranya's hair fell forward again, cut roughly to the length of her jaw. The rest had come free in her hand.

He moaned as she held the severed hair up in front of him. She tied it into a knot and offered it.

'Take this to Father. Tell him what has happened.'

Reki dared not touch it. To take the hair would be to accept his sister's charge, to be bound by an oath to deliver it which was as sacred as the oath she had made by cutting it off. To the folk of Tchom Rin, the shearing of a woman's hair meant vengeance. It was done only when they were wronged in some terrible way, and it would take blood to redress the balance.

If he gave this to his father, Blood Tanatsua would be at war with the Emperor.

For the briefest of instants, he was dizzyingly aware of how many lives would be sacrificed because of this one act, how much agony and death would come of it. But an instant was all it was, for there were higher concerns here than men's lives. This was about honour. His sister had been brutally beaten, his nephew murdered in the womb. There was no question what had to happen next. And in some cowardly part of his soul, he was glad that the burden ultimately would not fall to him, that he was only a courier.

He took his sister's hair from her, and the oath was made.

'Now go,' she said.

'Now?'

'*Now!*' Laranya cried. 'Take two horses and ride. Switch between them; you'll go faster that way. If Mos finds out, if Kakre hears of this, they will try and stop you. They will try and cover this up with lies, they will play for every moment and use it to arm themselves against our family. Go!'

'Laranya . . .' he began.

'*Go!*' she howled, because she could not bear the parting. He scrambled off the bed, cast one last tearful look at her, then stuffed the hair into the pocket of his bedrobe and fled.

'Not you,' Laranya said quietly, even though Asara had shown no sign of leaving. 'I need your help. There is something that must be done.' Her tone was dull and flinty.

'I am at your command, Empress,' Asara replied.

'Then let me lean on you,' she said. 'And we will walk.'

So they did. Bruised and battered, her nightrobe bloodstained around her thighs, the Empress of Saramyr limped out of her bedchamber on Asara's arm, out through the Imperial chambers, and into the corridors of the Keep. The servants were too amazed to avert their eyes quickly enough. Even the Imperial Guards who stood station at the doorways stared in horror. Their Empress, well loved by all, reduced to a trembling wreck. It was not the done thing for a woman so abused to show herself in public, but Laranya did not shrink from it. Her pride was greater than her vanity; she would not play the game of the servants' silence, would not cower in secret and pretend that nothing had happened. She wore Mos's crimes on her body for all to see.

The Keep was asleep, and there were few people in the corridors and none that dared to detain her; but even so, the route to the Tower of the East Wind was a long and arduous ordeal. Laranya could barely support herself, and though Asara was uncommonly strong, it was a struggle. Her world was a mass of pain, yet still she was conscious of the eyes that regarded her with fear and disbelief as she staggered through their midst. Asara bore her stoically and in silence, and let Laranya direct her.

The Tower of the East Wind, like all the other towers, was connected to the Keep by long, slender bridges positioned at the vertices. It was a tall needle, reaching high above the Keep's flat roof, with a bulbous tip that tapered to a point. Small window-arches pocked its otherwise smooth surface. Far above, a balcony ringed the tower just below where it swelled outward.

The climb was hard on Laranya. The spiral stairs seemed endless, and she would not pause at any of the observation points where chairs were set by the window-arches to view the city. Only when they reached the balcony and stepped out into the warm night air did Laranya allow herself to rest.

Asara stood with her, looking out over the parapet. Close by, the city of Axekami fell away down the hill on which the Keep stood, a multitude of lights speckling the dark. Then the black band of the city walls, and beyond that the plains and the River Kerryn, flowing from the Tchamil Mountains which were too distant to see. The night was clear and the stars bright, and Neryn hung before them, the small green moon low in the eastern sky, an unflawed ball floating in the abyss.

'Such a beautiful night,' Laranya murmured. She sounded strangely peaceful. 'How can the gods be so careless? How can the world go on as normal? Does my loss mean so little to them?'

'Do not look to the gods for aid,' said Asara. 'If they cared in the least for human suffering, they would never have allowed me to be born.'

Laranya did not understand this, did not know what manner of creature she was talking to: an Aberrant whose form shifted like water, whose lack of identity made her a walking shell, loathsome to herself.

Asara turned to the Empress, her beautiful eyes cold. 'Do you mean to do it?'

Laranya leaned over the parapet and looked down to the courtyard far, far below, visibly only by pinpricks of lantern light. 'I have no choice,' she whispered. 'I will not live so . . . diminished. And you know Mos will not let me leave.'

'Reki would have stopped you,' Asara said quietly.

'He would have tried,' the Empress agreed. 'But he does not know what I feel. Mos has taken from me everything I am. But my spirit will strike at him from beyond this world.' She took Asara's arm. 'Help me up.'

The Empress of Saramyr clambered onto the parapet at the top of the Tower of the East Wind, and looked down on all of Axekami. With an effort, she stood straight. Her soiled nightrobe flapped about as the breeze caressed her. She breathed, slowly. So easy . . . it would be so easy to stop the pain.

Then, a gust, rippling the silk against her skin, blowing her newly shorn hair back from her face. It smelt of home, a dry desert wind from the east. She felt a terrible ache, a longing for the vast simplicity of Tchom Rin, when she had not been an Empress and where love had never touched her nor wounded her so cruelly. Where she had never felt her child die inside her.

And with that scent came a new resolve, a strengthening of her ruined core. It felt like the breath of the goddess Suran, revivifying her, imbuing new life. Why throw herself away like this? Why let Mos win? Perhaps she *could* endure the pain. Maybe she could survive the dishonour. She could revenge herself upon him in a thousand different ways, she could make him rue the tragedy he had brought upon himself. The worst he could do was kill her.

If her father declared war, he would be casting himself into a nearly hopeless battle for her sake. Dignity would demand it. All those lives. Yet, if she turned back now, she could send Asara to catch Reki, to stop him. She could seek retribution in ways far more subtle and effective.

'The wind has changed,' said Laranya, after standing there for some minutes, an inch from that terrible drop.

'Doubts?' Asara asked.

Laranya nodded, her eyes faraway.

'I think not,' said Asara, and pushed her.

There was an instant when the Empress of Saramyr teetered, a moment of raw and overwhelming disbelief in which the thousands of routes fate held for her collapsed down to one single dead-end thread; then she tipped out into the dark night and her scream lasted all the way until she hit the courtyard below.

Twenty-Three

One hundred and seventy five miles away from where the Empress was falling from the Tower of the East Wind, Kaiku and Tsata hunted by the green light of Neryn. The Tkiurathi slunk along the shadowed lee of a row of rocks, his gutting-hooks held lightly in his hands. Kaiku was some way behind him; she could not move at the speed he could and still remain quiet.

The cocktail of fear and excitement that Kaiku felt when on the hunt had become almost intoxicating now. For days they had been living on their wits and reactions, staying one step ahead of the beasts that wandered inside the Weavers' invisible barrier. The paralysing terror that she had experienced almost constantly at first had subsided as they had evaded or killed the Aberrant predators time and again. She had learned to be confident in Tsata's ability to keep them alive, and she trusted herself enough to know she was no burden to him.

The shrilling was somewhere to their right. She could hear it, warbling softly to itself, a cooing sound like a wood pigeon that was soft and reassuring and decidedly at odds with the powerhouse of muscle and teeth and sinew that made it. She and Tsata had begun to name the different breeds of Aberrant by now for the sake of mutual identification. They had five so far, and that still left an uncertain number of species that they had only glimpsed. Aside from the gristle-crows and the shrillings, there were the brutal furies, the insidious skrendel, and most dangerous of all, the giant ghauregs. Tsata had named the latter two in Okhamban. The sharp and guttural syllables seemed to suit them well.

On the other side of the row of rocks, a narrow trench cut through the stony earth, scattered with thorny, blight-twisted bushes and straggling weeds. The shrilling's paws crunched on loose gravel and shale as it walked. Its steady, casual gait disturbed Kaiku. As with the other creatures they had encountered, she could not get used to the eerie sensation that it was *patrolling*. Not looking for food or marking its territory or any other understandable animal instinct, but acting as a sentry. It went slow and alert, and if they followed it for long enough Kaiku was certain that it would come back to this spot, treading the same path over and over until it returned to the flood plain and another Aberrant would appear in its stead.

They were not acting like animals. It should have been carnage down on the plain, with that many violent predators in close proximity, but an uneasy peace existed as of enemies forced to be allies by necessity. Skirmishes and squabbles broke out, but never more than an angry snap or scratch before both parties retreated. And then there were the perfectly regular patterns of the gristle-crows' flight during the day, and the curiously organised patrols at night. No, there was something unnatural here.

Tonight, Kaiku meant to find out for sure what that was.

She kept her eyes on the stealthy Okhamban ahead of her. When he was like this, he seemed half-animal himself, a being of primal energy capable of shocking viciousness; it was a bizarre alter-ego to the quiet and contemplative man who had accompanied them across the sea, with his strange and alien mind-set.

A little way ahead of him, a hazy splash of pallid green moonlight spilled through a gap in the rocks. He looked back at her, making an up-and-over motion with one tattooed arm. She took his meaning. Adjusting her rifle on its strap across her back, she slipped up to the dark face of the barrier to their right. She listened: the gentle trill of the Aberrant drifted back to her, the scrape of its paws. With a deliberate tread, it passed the spot where she crouched.

In one quick motion, she pulled herself onto the top of the row and jammed her feet into the uneven folds to brace herself. She swung her rifle around and sighted down into the trench. Her ascent was not as quiet as she would have liked, but it made little difference. Shrillings navigated like bats, blatting a series of frequencies which were picked up and sorted by sense glands in their throat, building up a picture according to which frequencies returned to them and how long they took. It made them exceptional night hunters in their element, but it had the side-effect of limiting their field of perception to what was in front of them. Kaiku had her rifle trained on it squarely, but it kept steadily walking away from her down the trench, towards the gap in the rocks where Tsata waited.

She did not fire. Squatting in the light of Neryn and uncomfortably exposed, she held her nerve and her trigger finger. She was there as a back-up only, in case the worst should happen. The report of a rifle would alert everyone and everything within miles to their presence.

The shrillings were lithe and deadly beasts, an uncomfortable blending of mammal and reptile, preserving the most advantageous aspects of both. Their size, bone structure and movements were like a big cat, but their skin was covered with tough, overlapping scales of natural armour. Elongated skulls curved to a long, smooth crest. Their upper jaws were lipless, and rigid and beaklike, but from beneath them dark red gums sheathed killing teeth. They walked on all fours, though they could stand on two legs for a short time while balancing on their tails, and their forepaws each held a single outsized claw which could unzip flesh and separate muscle effortlessly. They were efficient carnivores who had climbed to the top of their rapidly shifting food chain in the blighted areas of the Tchamil Mountains, using their night-seeing capabilities to pinpoint animals that hid at the sound of their warbling. Fast, streamlined and deadly.

But so was Tsata.

He waited until the creature had just passed the gap in the rocks before he sprang. Movement so close to its body was picked up by some peripheral sense, and it curved its spine to meet him, its jaws gaping wide. But he had predicted it, and swung to one side, so that its teeth snapped shut on nothing but air. He rammed one end of his gutting-hook into its outstretched neck, behind its crest. It spasmed once, but in that time Tsata had swung onto its back, using the embedded gutting-hook as a lever, and buried his second blade into the other side of its throat. Its legs collapsed beneath it and it started to thrash before Tsata wrenched both blades upward, tearing them through the muscle of its neck and severing its vertebrae in a gout of blood and spinal fluid. The shrilling flopped. It was all over in an instant.

Kaiku scrambled down from her perch and slid into the trench. Tsata's gutting-hooks were laid aside, and he had turned the Aberrant's head so as to move its crest out of the way. Its black eye reflected his face as he felt amid the pulses of gore that ran down its neck.

'Have you found it?' Kaiku asked as she hurried up to him. His bare arms and hands were dripping with noxious blood, black in the green moonlight.

'Here,' he said. Kaiku met his glance. 'Can you do this?'

'I have to risk it,' she said. 'For the *pash*.'

He grinned. 'One day I will teach you how to use that word properly.'

The fleeting moment of camaraderie was too brief to enjoy. She put her hands where his were, and felt the repellent skin of the black, wormlike creature attached to the arch of the shrilling's neck, just above the point where Tsata's blades had cut. This was the fourth Aberrant they had killed between them, and every time they had found one of these nauseating things in the same place, deep in the flesh, dead.

This one was not dead yet, but it had only seconds left, its body failing as its host's systems ceased. Seconds were enough.

Kaiku touched it, and opened the Weave. Tsata watched her as her eyes fluttered closed. The dark gush of the Aberrant's blood over the wrists and hands became a trickle as the heart stopped pumping.

The link was easy to follow, once she was inside it. The slug-thing's fading consciousness was like an anchor in the body of the Aberrant beast. Small tendrils of influence were retreating as it died, the hooks it had buried into its deadly host; but the strongest link arced away across the Fault, connected to some far destination like an umbilical cord. She followed it, and it led her to a nexus where dozens of other similar links converged like ribbons around a maypole, wafting in the flow of the Weave.

She read the fibres, and the answers came to her.

The nexus was one of the tall, black-robed strangers. They were not Weavers; they could not shape and twist the Weave. Rather, they were the hands that held a multitude of leashes, and the leashes tethered the Aberrants through the vile entities embedded close to their spines. They were the handlers.

That was how the Aberrants were under control, she realised. Carefully, she probed further. She was not sure to what extent the link operated: did the handlers actively know what the Aberrants know? Did they see through the beasts' eyes? No, surely not, for if the handlers were linked mind-to-mind with the beasts then they would know of Tsata and Kaiku's incursions, and the Weavers would have reacted with much more alarm. She gave up trying to guess; it was useless to speculate at this point.

Her eyes flicked open, and the irises were deepest crimson. She stepped back.

'As we thought,' she murmured. Her gaze went to Tsata's. 'We should go. They will be coming.'

The two of them slipped up the trench, disappearing into the shadows. Tsata led with practiced ease; Kaiku followed, alert for danger. Distantly, a yammering and howling had begun, but by the time the other Aberrants arrived at the scene of the death, the perpetrators had long fled.

Kaiku's glance strayed to the Mask that lay on the ground beside her. Tsata, hunkered down next to her in the glade, intercepted the look.

'It is wearing you down,' he said softly. 'Is it not?'

Kaiku nodded slightly. She picked up her pack and threw it on top of the Mask, obscuring its mocking expression.

The night was warm, but a cooler breeze hinted at the promise of distant winter. Chikkikii cracked and snapped like branches in a fire from the darkness, a staccato percussion as they clicked their rigid wing-cases, underpinning the melodic cheeping of other nocturnal insects and the occasional hoot of some arboreal animal. Neryn's smooth face glowed through the gently swaying network of leaves overhead, dappling the small clearing in restful light, playing across the arches of tough roots that poked out of the ground and the colonies of weeds and foliage that had made their home here. A spray of moon-flowers nodded lazily, their petals open in drowsy grey stars, questing up toward the life-giving illumination.

The glade lay beyond the Weavers' barrier of misdirection, a mile east of the point where it began. They never rested inside the danger area, especially not now that the enemy was on the alert. Ever since the first Aberrant sentry had surprised them and they had been forced to kill it, the patrols had been more intense, and gristle-crows scoured the sky during daylight hours. They had only barely escaped that time, for they had wasted precious minutes examining the strange, slimy thing attached to the sentry's neck, and only Tsata's instincts had warned them in time to evade the dozen other Aberrants that came running. It had been just another part of the puzzle: how did the creatures know when one of their own had died?

Since then Kaiku had been forced to shield them more than once from the malevolent attention of a Weaver, hiding them as an unseen presence swept across the domain in search of the mysterious in-truders. The Weavers suspected that something was amiss, and the occasional death of one of their creatures must have caused con-sternation by evidence of the increased security; but they could not find the cause of the disturbance.

They were limited in their thinking. They imagined a rogue tribes-man from elsewhere in the Fault had somehow got inside and was now trapped and causing them minor inconvenience. They had not con-sidered the fact that someone was passing freely through their barrier, and so they never looked outside it. Nor, of course, did the Aberrants stray beyond those boundaries. Kaiku and Tsata took advantage of that, to sleep and plan in relative safety.

'I wish to apologise,' Tsata said, out of nowhere.

'Yes?' Kaiku said mildly.

'I was ungenerous in my judgement of you,' he said. He shifted position to a more comfortable cross-legged arrangement: it was one of the few mannerisms that Saramyr and Okhamba shared.

'I had forgotten about it,' Kaiku lied, but Tsata knew her people's ways well enough not to be fooled.

'Among the Tkiurathi it is necessary to say what we think,' he explained. 'Since we do not *own* things, since our community is based on sharing, it is not good to keep things inside us. If we resent someone for taking too much food at every meal, we will tell them so; we do not let it fester. Our equilibrium is maintained by approval or disapproval of the *pash*, and from that we determine the common good.'

Kaiku regarded him evenly with dark red eyes.

'I said that you took on this cause for selfish reasons, and it is still true,' he went on. 'But you are unselfish in your pursuit of that cause. You make many sacrifices, and you ask of nobody what you would not do yourself. I admire that. It runs counter to my experience of Saramyr folk.'

Kaiku could not decide whether to feel praised or insulted by that, for he had complimented her at the same time as deriding her countrymen. She chose to take it in a forgiving spirit.

'You *are* brutal in your honesty, and frank with your opinions,' she said with a weary smile. 'It takes a little time to get accustomed to it. But I did not hold myself offended by what you said.'

His reaction to that was impenetrable. She watched him for a short while. She had become quite used to him now, from the sap-stiffened orange-blond hair that swept back over his skull to the unusual pallor of his skin and the curves of the pale green tattoos over his face and down his bare arms to his fingertips. He no longer seemed foreign, only strange, in the way Lucia was strange. And he was certainly not hampered by the language barrier. He had improved since he had arrived on the shores of her homeland, and his Saramyrrhic was virtually flawless now. In fact, he was uncommonly articulate when he wanted to be.

'What do you think of us, Tsata?' she asked. 'Of Aberrants like me?'

Tsata considered that for a time. 'Nothing,' he replied.

'Nothing?'

'We cannot help the circumstances of our birth,' he said. 'A strong man may be born a strong child, may always outmatch his friends in wrestling or lifting. But if he only uses his strength, if he relies on it alone to make him acceptable, he will fail in other ways. We should only be seen by how we utilise or overcome what we have.'

Kaiku sighed. 'Your philosophies are so simple, and so clear,' she said. 'Yet ideals sometimes cannot weather reality. I wish that life were so uncomplicated.'

'You have complicated it yourself,' Tsata said. 'With money and property and laws. You strive for things you do not need, and it makes you jealous and resentful and greedy.'

'But with those things come medicines, art, philosophy,' Kaiku answered him. 'Do the wrongs in our society that we have to suffer outweigh the benefits of being able to cure plagues that would decimate less developed cultures like yours?' She knew he would not take this as a slight; in fact, she had picked up some of his indelicacy of speech, for only days ago she would have phrased her meaning much more cunningly.

'Your own scholar Jujanchi posited the theory that the survivors of such a plague would be the ones best able to carry on the race,' he argued. 'That your goddess Enyu weeds out the weaker elements.'

'But you would allow yourself to be culled by the whims of nature,' Kaiku put back. 'You live within the forest, and let it rule you like it rules the animals. We have dominated this land.'

'No, you have subjugated it,' he replied. 'More, you have annexed it from the Ugati, who by your own laws had the rights to be here. You did not like your own country, so you took another.'

'And on the way, we stopped at Okhamba, and the Tkiurathi came of that,' she reminded him. 'You cannot make me feel guilty for what my ancestors have done. You said yourself: I cannot help the circumstances of my birth.'

'I do not ask you to feel guilty,' he said. 'I am only showing you the price of your "developed" culture. Your people should not feel responsible for it; but it terrifies me that you ignore it and condone it. You forget the lessons of the past because they are unpalatable, like your noble families ignore the damage the Weavers are doing to your land.'

Kaiku was quiet, listening to the night noises, thinking. There was no heat in the argument. She had gone past the point of feeling defensive about Saramyr, especially since her culture had long ago ostracised her for being Aberrant. It was merely interesting to hear such a coldly analytical and unfavourable point of view on ways of life she had always taken for granted. His perspective intrigued her, and they had talked often over the last few days about their differences. Some aspects of the Tkiurathi way she found impossible to believe would work in practice, and others she found incomprehensible; but there were many valid and enviable facets to their mode of living as well, and she learned a lot from those conversations.

Now she turned matters to more immediate concerns. She brushed her fringe away from her face and adopted a more decisive tone.

'Matters are beyond doubt,' she said. 'The Weavers have a way to control the Aberrants. We do not know exactly how, but it is connected to the creatures that we have found on the back of the Aberrant's necks.' She rolled her shoulders tiredly. 'We can assume that every Aberrant down there has one.'

'And we know now that it is not the Weavers who control them,' Tsata added. 'But the *other* masked ones.'

'So we have that much, at least, to aid us,' she said, scratching at some mud on her boot. 'What is next?'

'We must fill in the gaps in our knowledge,' Tsata replied. 'We must kill one of the black-robed men.'

The next day dawned red, and stayed red until late morning. History would record that the Surananyi blew for three days in Tchom Rin after the Empress Laranya's death, striking unexpectedly and without warning. The hurricanes flensed the deserts in the east, sandstorms raged, and the dust rose like a cloud beyond the mountains to stain Nuki's eye the colour of blood. Later, when the news of Laranya's tragic suicide had spread across the empire, it would be said that the tempest was the fury of the goddess Suran at the death of one of her most beloved daughters, and that Mos was forever cursed in her eyes.

But Lucia knew nothing of this beyond a vague unease that settled in her marrow that morning, and did not abate until the Surananyi had ceased. She sat by a rocky brook on the northern side of the valley where the Fold lay, and looked to the east, and imagined she could hear a distant howling as of some unearthly voice in rage and torment.

Flen sat with her. He was tall for his age, gangly with sudden growth, possessed of a head of dark brown hair that flopped loosely over his eyes and a quick, ready smile. He had not smiled all that much this morning.

Lucia had changed.

She had not told him about the trip to Alskain Mar until after they had returned, and then only in the barest terms. Of course none of the adults thought he was important enough to know, but it was Lucia's decision to keep it a secret that hurt him. It was not entirely a surprise: nothing Lucia did was too unusual, for she had always seemed to operate on some level quite apart from everybody else, and it made her strange and fascinating. But it troubled him deeply that she was *different* now, and he was frightened that she was becoming more detached.

It was not something he could describe; only a feeling, in the instinctive way that adolescents navigated their way through the passage to adulthood. Like the sly, forbidden self-assuredness of a newly shed virginity that the inexperienced unconsciously deferred to; like the constantly switching hierarchy of friendships and leaders and scapegoats that was ingrained in pubescents without them knowing who gave them the rules or even that they were following rules at all.

There was a new distance in her pale blue eyes now. Something had been shed, and a new skin grown underneath; something lost, something gained. She had talked to a creature that was one step down from a god. She had *died*, however briefly, and it had shifted her perspective somewhere that Flen could not follow. She seemed to have aged, not outwardly but in the measure of her responses and her tone. And all Flen could think was that he was losing his best friend, and how unfair it was.

They sat together for a long time on the edge of that rocky brook, leaning against a boulder. Tall grasses rose all around them, tickling the backs of their knees. The brook trickled through a chicane of broken stone from the valley rim, and dragonflies droned about, moving in jerky little spurts to hover before their faces, studying them uncomprehendingly. The sky was pink, and the cascading tiers of houses to their right had a sinister and brooding quality in that light, no longer homely but a jumble of jagged edges and smoothly rounded blades.

Below them, on the flat valley floor, a herd of banathi was grazing, watched over by a dozen men and women on horseback. Flen watched them shamble idly about, cropping the grass with their wide, rubbery mouths. They were huge creatures but very docile, beasts seemingly destined to exist only to feed predators. Though the bulls possessed enormous curving horns, they only ever used them in the mating season when competing for females. In ancient times, they had roamed freely across the plains; now they were almost entirely bred for meat and milk.

It was while Flen was musing on the lot of the banathi that Lucia finally spoke, as he knew she would.

'Forgive me,' she said quietly.

Flen shrugged. 'I always do,' he said.

She took his arm and leaned her head on his shoulder. 'I know what you think. That things are different now.'

'Are they?'

'Not between us,' she replied.

Flen adjusted himself so that they were both more comfortable. He had bony shoulders.

'You understand, though,' she said. 'There are things I can't explain. Things there are no words for.'

'You live in a place different to me,' he said. 'It's like . . . you live beyond a door, and I can only see through the cracks around the edges.

You see what's inside the room, but I can only catch a glimpse. It's always been that way.' He put a hand on her thin forearm, her delicate wrist. 'You're alone, and everyone else is shut out.'

She smiled a little. How like Flen, to turn around her apology to make it seem as if it were she who deserved sympathy.

She drew herself upright again. 'I shouldn't tell you this . . .' she said, her voice dropping in volume.

'But you will,' he grinned.

'This is very important, Flen,' she told him. 'You can't let anybody else hear of it.'

'When have I ever?' he asked rhetorically.

Lucia regarded him for a moment. She had a way of seeing into people that was frankly uncanny; but she did not need to doubt him. She knew that Flen counted her the most important person alive, and not because of any expectations of healing the land or ruling the empire. It was simply because she was his best friend.

There was one thing that she had never quite been able to puzzle out about him, though: why did he *want* to be with her? Not that she thought herself unpopular: on the contrary, she had a wide circle of friends, who seemingly came to her without any effort on her part, attracted by some magnetism of personality that she did not really understand since she was by no means the most lively or social of people. But Flen had been virtually inseparable from her since the day they had met. He had always sought her out before any others, had always possessed a seemingly endless patience for her quirks and oddities. She had given virtually nothing back for a long time. She enjoyed his company, and allowed him to be with her, but she was in a world of her own and she had learned by then that it was useless inviting anyone to join her there.

Yet he had persisted. He was a popular boy himself, and she often wondered why he did not spend his time with someone whom he did not need to make such an effort for; but she was always his priority, and gradually, *gradually*, she became used to him. Of all the people she had ever known, he was the one closest to understanding her, and she loved him for it. She loved his guileless, unselfish heart and his honesty. Though they made a strange pair, they were friends, in the purity of that state that only exists before the complication of adulthood corrupts it.

'I'll tell you what I learned in Alskain Mar,' she said.

'Spirits, I thought you'd never get round to it,' Flen said mischievously. She did not laugh or smile, but she knew it was his way to joke when he was nervous or uncertain, and he was suddenly both. Lucia's expression was grave. She was remembering the horror on Zaelis's face as she passed on to him the things the spirit had showed her, the coldness in Cailin's eyes.

'Maybe *learn* is the wrong word,' she corrected herself. 'I didn't learn as if someone was teaching me. It was . . . as if I was remembering and prophesying at the same time; as if it was a memory and a prediction of a future that had already come to pass. At first it was hard to understand . . . it still *is* hard for me to think on it. The things I know now aren't clear.' She looked down at the ground and began to fiddle with a blade of grass. 'It was like hanging onto the fin of a whale, and having it plunge you down further than you can imagine to the wonders at the bottom of the sea. Except that your eyes can't focus underwater, so it's all a blur. You can't open your mouth to speak. And sooner or later you remember that the whale doesn't need to breathe as much as you do.'

'What did it show you?'

'It showed me the witchstones,' she said, and her gaze seemed suddenly haunted.

When she did not elaborate for a time, Flen prompted her: 'And what did you see?'

She shook her head slightly, as if in denial of what she was about to say. 'Flen, I am part of something much bigger than anyone thought,' she whispered. She clutched his hands and looked up to meet his stare. 'We all are. This isn't just about an empire; this isn't a matter of who sits on the throne, no matter how many thousand lives are at stake. The Golden Realm itself watches us with the keenest intent, and the gods themselves are playing their hand.'

'You're saying that the gods are controlling things?' Flen asked, unable to keep a hint of scepticism from his voice.

'No, no,' Lucia said. 'The gods don't *control*. They're more subtle than that. They use avatars and omens, to bend the will of their faithful to do their work. There's no predestination, no destiny. We all have our choices to make. It's *us* who have to fight our battles.'

'Then what . . .'

'Kaiku always said that the witchstones were alive, but she was only half right,' Lucia explained, uncharacteristically hurried. The words were trembling out of her and she could not stop them. 'They're not just alive, they're *aware*! Not like the spirits of the rocks in the earth; not like the simple thoughts of the trees. They're intelligent, and malevolent, and they are becoming more so with every passing day.'

Flen barely knew whether to credit this at all, but he did not have the chance to decide.

'The Weavers are not our true enemies, Flen!' Lucia cried, her face an unnatural red in the dust-veiled morning sun. 'They believe themselves the puppet masters, but they are only the puppets. Slaves to the witchstones.'

'This is—' Flen began, but Lucia interrupted him again.

'You have to hear me out!' she snapped, and Flen was shocked into silence. For the first time he began to appreciate the depth of Lucia's terror at what she had found out in Alskain Mar. 'The witchstones *use* the Weavers. They make them think that they are operating to their own agenda, but no Weaver really knows who sets that agenda; they believe it part of a collective consciousness. That consciousness is the will of the witchstones. The Weavers are only the foot-soldiers. They are *addicts*, trapped by their longing for the witchstone dust in their Masks, not even knowing that in gaining their powers they are sub-verting themselves to a higher master.'

She looked around, as if fearing someone was listening; and indeed it seemed that way, for the dragonflies had quieted and departed, and the wind had fallen. 'That first witchstone, the one beneath Adder-ach . . . it ensnared the miners who found it. It was weak then, starved for thousands of years, but they were weaker. They took the dust, driven by some compulsion they did not understand. They learned to give it blood in the same way. It grew, and as it grew its power grew, and it sent the Weavers out into the world to be its eyes and ears and hands. It sent them to find more witchstones.'

'But what *are* the witchstones?' Flen asked.

'The answers were in front of us, but nobody wanted to believe it,' Lucia whispered. '*I* would not have believed it, except that what the spirit of Alskain Mar showed me was more than truth or lies or fact or fiction. Even that spirit was not old enough to have witnessed what happened all that time ago, but it told me what it knew.'

She closed her eyes, squeezed them tightly shut, and when she spoke she was using a more formal mode of speech, used when referring directly to the gods.

'The gods fought, in an epoch when civilisation had barely left its cradle. In that time, the entity we call Aricarat, youngest of Assantua and Jurani, made war in the Golden Realm, for reasons lost to history. He almost overthrew Ocha himself, but in a last stand his own parents led an army that slew him, in a battle that tore the skies. At his death, his own aspect in the tapestry of the world – the fourth moon that bore his name – was destroyed, and pieces of the moon rained down onto the world in the cataclysm that Saran told us about.' She squeezed his hands harder. 'But he was not dead,' she whispered. 'Not while a part of him remained in the tapestry . . . in *our* world. The moon came down in pieces, and some of those pieces survived. In each of them, a tiny fragment of Aricarat's spirit remained. Dormant.'

'Fragments?'

Lucia nodded and released his hands, lifting her head. 'Fragments of a shattered god. They have lain there for thousands of years, until chance unearthed one again in the spot where Adderach now stands. Now it uses the Weavers to reach out to other fragments, unearthing them, awakening them with blood sacrifice. They are linked, as the Weavers are linked, like a web. Each one that they dig up makes the whole stronger; each one gives the Weavers more power. They are the fractured pieces of Aricarat; and each one they rescue is one step closer to his resurrection.' Her eyes filled with tears, and her voice became quiet and fearful. 'He's so angry, Flen. I felt his rage. Right now he is still weak, only a shadow of his former self, impotent; but his hate burns so brightly. He will dominate this land, and he will dominate all the lands. And when enough of the witchstones have been awoken, he will return, and wreak his vengeance.'

Flen did not have a response to that. The bloody light of Nuki's eye seemed infernal, bathing the valley in dread.

'Already his power works against Enyu and her children, the gods and goddesses of natural things,' Lucia continued. 'His very existence poisons the land, twists the animals and the people who eat of its crops. If he wins here, he will take the battle to the Golden Realm, against the gods themselves. That is why we have to stop him. For if the Weavers and the witchstones are not destroyed now, they will engulf the world like a shroud. And that will only be the beginning.'

A single tear slid from her eye and coursed down her cheek. 'It is a new war of the gods, played out here in Saramyr. And all of Creation is at stake.'

Twenty-Four

Over Zila, grey clouds blanketed the sky, turning midday into a muted, steely glower. A horseman in Blood Vinaxis livery rode from the massive south gate of the town, down the hill towards where the lines of troops waited, overlooked by tall siege engines. Behind him, the gate boomed shut.

Xejen watched him go from the window of his chamber at the top of the keep, hands clasped behind his back, drumming his fingertips nervously on his knuckles. When the rider was out of sight, he swung around to where Bakkara stood scratching his jaw. Mishani reclined on a settee against one wall, her hair spilling over her shoulder, her eyes revealing nothing.

'What do you think?' Xejen asked them.

Bakkara shrugged. 'What difference does it make? They're going to attack us anyway, whether we give them a "gesture of good faith" or not. They just don't want the embarrassment of dealing with a bunch of minor noble families who'll be angry if their sons and daughters get killed during the liberation.'

'Liberation?' Xejen said, with a high laugh. 'Spirits, you talk like you're on their side.'

'They'll call it a liberation if they win,' he said equably. 'Besides, what's the choice? We can hardly send them out any hostages. The mob had them when we took this town.'

'That news will not win you any friends,' Mishani pointed out.

'So we just refuse, then,' Xejen concluded, snapping his fingers at the air. 'Let them believe we have the hostages. As you say, they'll attack us anyway, sooner or later. But I have faith in Zila's walls, unlike you.' He finished with a sharp look at the grizzled soldier.

'I would not advise that,' Mishani said. 'A flat refusal will make them think you are stubborn and unwilling to parlay. Next time, they will not trouble themselves. And you may need to fall back on negotiation if things do not go according to your plan.'

Bakkara suppressed a smile. For such a small and dainty thing, she was remarkably self-assured. It was evidence of her skill at politics that she had, over the last few days, installed herself as Xejen's primary adviser while still never giving him a straight answer as to whether she would declare her support for the Ais Maraxa or not. Xejen was pathetically eager for her help, for Bakkara's help, for anyone who was more decisive than he was. In matters concerning Lucia, his mind was sharp and clear and inflexible; but now he had won himself a town, he appeared increasingly unsure of what to do with it. He may have been a powerful motivator, but he knew nothing of military matters, and left most of it to Bakkara, whom he had declared his second-in-command in Zila after the revolt.

'What would you do, then, Mistress Mishani?' Bakkara asked with exaggerated reverence. She ignored the tone.

'Send them Chien,' she said.

Bakkara barked a laugh in surprise, then shut his mouth. Xejen glared at him.

'Is there some joke I'm missing?' he asked.

'Apologies,' Bakkara said wryly. 'I'm merely touched by the noble sacrifice Mistress Mishani is making. She could have pleaded her own case, after all.'

Mishani gazed evenly at Xejen, disregarding the soldier's jibe. She had no intention of pleading her own case. If she went out there, news of her presence would be everywhere within a day, and she would be an easy target for her father's men. Besides, she knew perfectly well that Xejen would not allow her to leave. She was too precious an asset to him, and she remained so by making him believe that she shared the same goals and beliefs as he.

'Send them *one* hostage as a gesture of good faith,' she said. 'He does not know that the other nobles have died; for all he is aware, there could be many more imprisoned in the donjons of the keep. Chien is useless to you anyway, and what is more, he is very ill and your physician has been unable to do anything to help him.' She glanced at Bakkara. 'He is innocent, and does not deserve to be here.'

'He will tell them of the strength of our forces,' Xejen said, stalking around the room. 'He will name names.'

'He has barely been outside the room you put him in,' Mishani replied. 'He knows nothing of your forces.'

'And as to naming names,' Bakkara put in, 'isn't that what we *want* to happen?'

'Exactly,' Mishani agreed. 'Chien is a major player among merchants and maritime industries. If he starts talking, his ships will carry the word across the Near World.'

Xejen twiddled the fingers on one hand. He was obviously

persuaded, but he was making a great show of deliberation. Evidently he thought someone like Mishani might be fooled by that, and he would not seem quite so eager to agree with her.

'Yes, yes, it could work,' he muttered to himself. 'Will you talk to him, Mistress Mishani?'

'I will talk to him,' Mishani said.

As it turned out, it was not quite as easy as Mishani had thought.

'I will not leave you alone here!' Chien raged. 'You can't ask me to do this!'

Mishani was as impassive as always, but inside she was frankly shocked at the sudden fierceness of his emotion. He had been moved to more comfortable quarters after his confinement had ended. It was no different from the rest of the drab keep, comprising a few heavy wall hangings, rugs, a comfortable bed in consideration of his weak state and a few odds and ends like a table and a chest for clothes. She had not exaggerated the severity of his fever to Xejen; but he obviously felt well enough to get angry, even if he was still too weak to stand up.

'Calm yourself!' she snapped, and the sudden harshness in her voice quieted him. 'You are acting like a child. Do you think I would not rather come with you? I want you to go because you must do something for me that only you can do.'

His hair had grown out a little during his confinement, a black stubble across his broad scalp, and he had evidently not been inclined to put a razor to it yet. He gave her a reluctantly mollified look and said: 'What is it, then, that only I can do?'

'You can help save my life,' she said. It was calculated to stall the last of his indignation, and it worked.

'How?' he asked. Now he was ready to hear it.

'I need you to take a message for me,' she told him. 'To Barak Zahn tu Ikati.'

Chien watched her suspiciously. 'The Barak Zahn who is besieging this town?'

'The same,' she said.

'Go on,' Chien prompted.

'You must ask to meet him alone. You cannot let anyone else know I am here. If you do, my father's men will be waiting for me upon my release.'

'And what will I tell him?'

Mishani lowered her head, the thick, braided ropes of black hair swaying with the movement. 'Tell him I have news of his daughter. Tell him she is alive and well and that I know where she is.'

Chien's eyes narrowed. 'The Barak Zahn doesn't have a daughter.'

'Yes, he does,' Mishani said levelly.

Chien held her gaze for a moment, then sagged. 'How can I leave you here?' he asked, more to himself than her. 'There is an army outside, waiting to assault this place, and it is defended by peasants and tradesmen.'

'I know your honour demands that you stay, Chien,' Mishani said. 'But you will be doing me a service greater than all the protection you can offer if you leave Zila and take my message. That is all I ask of you. Barak Zahn will do the rest.'

'Mistress Mishani . . .' he groaned. 'I cannot.'

'It is my best chance at surviving this siege, Chien,' she told him. She walked over to his bedside and looked down. 'I know who sent you, Chien,' she said quietly. 'She swore you to secrecy, did she not? My mother.'

Chien tried to conceal his reaction, but against Mishani it was hopeless. The flicker in his eyes told her everything she needed to know.

'I will not ask you to break your oath,' Mishani said. She sat on the edge of his bed. 'She must have had word of me when I passed through Hanzean on my way out to Okhamba. I can only thank fortune that it was her people and not my father's who spotted me. During the month I was at sea, she contacted you; I imagine it was through a Weaver, but I doubt it was our family's. She asked you to safeguard me against my father.'

She felt tears threatening again, but she forced them down and they did not show. Her mother, her quiet, neglected mother, had been working behind the scenes all this time to protect her daughter. Gods, what if Avun had found out? What would have happened to Muraki then?

Chien was watching her silently, refusing to speak.

'She offered you release,' Mishani said. 'The bonds that tie you to Blood Koli have been all that have held your family back these long years, the marriage price of your mother, who was a fisherwoman in my father's fleet. If you were free of your debt, you would no longer need to offer my family the best price, the best ships to distribute their produce. You could rule the trade lane between Saramyr and the jungle continent.' She studied him closely for confirmation, although she was already certain that she was right. It all fitted at last. 'You would risk much for that, to free your family. My mother offered it to you. She is the only one other than Avun with the power to annul the contract. And she would do it, whatever the cost to herself, if you would keep me safe on my journey.'

Chien's eyes dropped, ashamed. He wanted to ask how she knew, but to do so would be to admit that she was right. Mishani did not wish to torture him. She understood now. All the time, she had been looking for his angle, trying to determine what he hoped to gain from her; but she had never considered *this*.

'There was one more thing,' Mishani said softly, pushing her hair back over one shoulder. 'My mother gave you a sign, in case there was no other way to persuade me. She knew how suspicious I would be. It was a lullaby, a song which she herself wrote. She used to sing it when I was young. It was about me. Only she and I knew the words.' She got up, her back to him. 'You sang it in your fever dream last night.'

Chien did not say anything for a long while; then finally, he spoke: 'If I do this for you, you will tell her that I fulfilled my oath?'

'I swear it,' Mishani said, not turning around. 'For you have acted with honour. Forgive me for mistrusting you.'

Chien lay back in his bed. 'I will do as you ask,' he said.

'My thanks,' Mishani said. 'For everything.' And with that, she left.

They did not see each other again before Chien was carried out of the gates and down to the waiting army. Mishani did not watch him go. She stood with her back to the window, alone.

Later, she offered herself to Bakkara, and they coupled urgently in his room.

She could not have said why she felt moved to do so then; it was entirely against her character. She should have waited, should have ensured that the moment was right. She found him appealing, and sensed that he felt the same towards her, but that was as far as it went; beyond that, there was only politics, and the fact that it made good sense to lie with him. She had ascertained by now that Xejen was not the leader his reputation made him out to be, and that Bakkara was eminently more suitable for the position. And she knew well the power a woman's art could have over a man, even one to whom she was merely an interesting and pleasurable diversion.

Yet, in the end, it had been something else that had driven her to him, to discard subtlety for immediate gratification. The episode with Chien had made her ache with a loneliness she had not imagined she could feel, a throbbing void that was too much for her to bear, and she wanted rid of it any way she could. The ethereal touch of her mother in her affairs had reminded her how adrift she was, how much she had given up to oppose her father. But she could not afford to grieve here. There was too much at stake.

She was not foolish enough to think that she could bury the pain permanently amid the throes of orgasm, but she could at least push it aside for a time.

Afterwards, when the treacherous glow had faded that sometimes made her say unguarded things, she lay alongside the soldier and ran her tiny hand over his scarred chest, curling her fingertips in the coarse hair between his pectoral bulges. His arm was around her, dwarfing her, and though she was bony and angular and thin she still felt soft against him. The warmth of a man's body was something she had almost forgotten that she missed.

'You do not think Xejen can do this, do you?' she said quietly. It was a statement.

'Hmm?' he murmured drowsily.

'You do not think he is capable of running this revolt and winning.'

He sighed irritably, his eyes still closed. 'I doubt it.'

'So why—'

'Are you going to keep asking questions all night?'

'Until I get some answers, yes,' she smiled.

He groaned and rolled over a little so that they were face to face. She gave him a little kiss on the lips.

'Every man's nightmare,' he said. 'A woman who won't shut up after she's been seen to.'

'I am merely interested in my chances of surviving the situation *you* put me in,' she said. 'Why are you here at all?'

He picked up a handful of her unbound hair that had fallen between them and rubbed it idly with his calloused fingertips.

'I come from the Newlands,' he said tangentially. 'There was a lot of conflict there when I was young. Land disputes, merchant wars. I was a boy, poor and hardworking and full and anger. Being a soldier was the best I could hope for, so I joined the Mark's militia, a tiny little village army. It turned out I was good at it. I got recruited into the army of a minor noble, we won a few battles . . . Gods, I'm even boring myself now.'

Mishani laughed. 'Do go on.'

'Let me skip all that. So many years – *many* years – later, I ended up a general in Blood Amacha's army, on the other side of the continent. I was something of a mercenary by then, not blood-bound to any master since my original Barak had managed to get himself killed and his family wiped out. I was there at the battle outside Axekami five years ago.'

Mishani stiffened fractionally.

'Don't worry,' he chuckled. 'I hardly blame you for what your father did. Especially after what Xejen told me about you and he.' His mirth faded, and he became serious. 'A lot of men I'd known died in that battle. I was lucky to get out alive.' He was silent for a moment, and when he continued his tone was resigned. 'But that's the way of it as a soldier. Friends die. Battles are won and lost. I do the best for myself and my men, but in the end, I'm just one part in thousands. A muscle. It's the brain that directs us all. It's those higher up who take the responsibility for a massacre like that. Sonmaga was a fool, and your father was treacherous. And many people were killed for both of them.'

Mishani was not sure what to say to that. She was suddenly terribly conscious of how strong he was. He could snap her bones like twigs if he just tightened the arm that he had around her shoulders.

'After that, I said I was done with soldiering,' he went on. 'But soldiering wasn't done with me, I suppose. Thirty years and more I've spent fighting other men's wars, sitting round fires with people and not knowing whether they'll be alive in the morning, living in tents and marching all over Saramyr. It may not sound like much, but it's hard to give up. There's a feeling between fighting men, a bond like you can't imagine that doesn't exist anywhere else. I tried to settle, but it's too late for me; I'm a soldier in the blood now.'

Mishani relaxed a little now that he had strayed off the more dangerous subject of her family's crimes. She began to idly trace lines on his arms as she listened.

'So I drifted. Couldn't find a purpose. I'd never needed one till then. I was drinking in a cathouse when I heard about the Ais Maraxa. Don't know why, but it caught my interest. So I started to investigate a little, and soon they heard about it and they found me.'

'You had something to believe in,' Mishani supplied for him.

His face scrunched as if in distaste. 'Let's just say it was a cause I thought was worthy. I'm a follower, Mistress Mishani, not a leader. I might command men, but I don't start wars, I don't change the world. That's not for people like me; that's for people like Xejen. He might not know a thing about war, but he's a leader. The Ais Maraxa would die for him.'

'Would you?'

'I'd die for Lucia,' he said. 'Seems much more sensible than any of the other causes I've been willing to die for in the past. Which were mostly to do with money.'

Neither of them spoke for a time. Bakkara was drowsing again when he felt Mishani's face crease into a smile.

'I know you're going to say something,' he said warningly. 'So have it over with.'

'You never answered my question.'

'Which one?'

'Why did you help take Zila if you thought that you couldn't hold it?'

'Xejen thought we could. He believes. That's enough.' He considered for a moment. 'Maybe the tide will turn yet.'

'So you don't take any of the responsibility? Even thought you think it's foolishness, you're following him.'

'I've followed greater fools,' he muttered. 'And responsibility is a matter for philosophers and politicians. I'm a soldier. Hard as it may be to imagine, I do what I do with no clearer motive than because I do it.'

'Or maybe you do not see your own motive.'

'Woman, if you don't shut up right now then I will be forced to do something to you to shut you up.'

'Oh?' Mishani said innocently. 'And what might that be?'

Bakkara showed her, and after that she let him sleep; but she was awake, and thinking.

She could not leave Zila: Xejen would not let her. And she certainly had no intention of remaining trapped in here for the next year. Instead, she had concocted a plan to invite Barak Zahn into the town in order to sound him out about Lucia, to make the negotiations she had wanted to make in Lalyara. To try and recruit him to the Libera Dramach with the news that they had his daughter. In Zila, she would bargain from a position of advantage, and Zahn would have to listen to her. But again, Xejen was the problem; he would stop her as soon as he knew what she was up to.

Xejen was an obstacle that had to be removed. Bakkara was not only the better leader, and the person most able to keep Zila in order and safe from their enemies, but he was also more malleable. Therefore, she would slowly work on both Bakkara and Xejen, undermining the one with the other to bring Bakkara – and hence herself – out on top. Once Bakkara had the primacy, she could manipulate him into her way of thinking, but Xejen was too intransigent, too rigid in his zeal.

This was her aim, then. She only needed time . . .

It was dark where Mos was.

The air stank of blood. Monstrous shapes loomed half-seen to either side and overhead. A quiet clanking came from above, the tapping of chains as they stirred in the heat. The only light was a sullen red glow from the embers of the fire-pit.

Into that light came a dead face, a corpse-mask of emaciated flesh in a ghastly yawn, hooded and shadowed. Mos looked at it across the fire-pit. His own features were haggard and drawn, his eyes swollen with weeping, his features slack.

Above them, Weave-lord Kakre's kites of skin gazed down emptily from the blackness.

'He is gone, then?' Kakre croaked.

'He is gone,' Mos replied.

'You have sent men to search for him?'

'He will not get far.'

'That remains to be seen.'

Mos looked down into the embers, as if there might be some solace there.

'What possessed me, Kakre?'

The Weave-lord did not reply. He knew well what had possessed Mos; but even he had not expected the Empress to commit suicide. It would have been enough for her to be beaten so that Laranya's father could learn of it and be incited to gather the armies of the desert in outrage. This was a better result than he could have hoped. And having Mos kidnap Reki in order to minimise the damage was just perfect; all it would take was a small leak of information, arranged by Kakre, and Tchom Rin's response would be assured.

Kakre had gone to Mos after the beating and found him weeping and pathetic, pleading for help – as if Kakre was someone he could confess to, who might offer succour. It had been made to look like coincidence, but very little that Kakre did was without forethought. While he was with the Emperor he could not Weave, for Weaving required all his concentration and Mos would know.

He had not been able to witness Laranya's last moments; but he had been provided with a perfect alibi that exonerated him from any suspicion of a hand in the Empress's death. Even Mos – poor, poor Mos – had never even thought of the possibility that the dreams that sent him mad had been coming from Kakre. Kakre had been too sly; he had cut away that line of reasoning from Mos's mind, so that it never got to flower.

'Barak Goren tu Tanatsua will hear of his daughter's death long before Reki reaches him,' Kakre rasped at last. 'And he will know the circumstances. Laranya was not discreet about her condition.' He stirred, his hood throwing his face into shadow. 'Her hair was cut, Mos. You know what that means.'

'Perhaps if we have Reki, his father may pause and listen to reason.' Mos's words were empty of feeling. He did not really care either way. He was merely going through the motions of being Emperor, because he had nothing else left now.

'Nevertheless,' Kakre said, 'preparations must be made. With your marriage to Laranya, the desert Baraks were pacified for a long time; but now that link is severed, they will react badly. They have ever been the troublesome ones. Too autonomous for their own good, within their trackless realm of sand.'

Mos gazed blankly at Kakre for a time, sweat creeping from his brow in the heat of the skinning-chamber.

'If they come to Axekami, they will encourage the other discontented Baraks,' Kakre told him. 'Imagine a desert army marching through Tchamaska and up the East Way, intent on demanding satisfaction for Laranya's death. Imagine how powerless that will make you seem.'

Mos could not really picture it.

'You should send men to Maxachta,' the Weave-lord advised. 'Many men. If you must meet them, meet them in the mountains at the Juwacha Pass. Contain them there. Prevent them from coming into the west.'

'I need all my men here,' Mos replied, but there was no strength in his voice.

'For what? For Blood Kerestyn? They have made only noises and taken no action. It will take them years to become strong enough to challenge you. Axekami is unassailable by any force in Saramyr at the moment; unless the desert Baraks join with those in the west, that is.'

Mos thought on that for a little while.

'I will send men,' he said, as Kakre had known he would. Mos had not been listening to his advisers, and Kakre had carefully underestimated the size of the forces that were being ranged against the Emperor in the wake of the gathering starvation. The signal would be sent tonight to Barak Avun tu Koli, advising him to begin the muster of the armies. The Imperial forces were dividing, and many thousands would be marching far from Axekami to meet the potential desert threat, leaving the capital weaker for their absence.

The game begins, Kakre thought, and behind his mask his ruined face twisted into a smile.

Twenty-Five

Kaiku slid recklessly down the shale slope, her boots pluming dust in the sharp white moonlight. Tsata had already reached the bottom and was levelling his rifle back up it, to where the undulating rim was framed against Aurus's huge, blotched face. At any instant, he expected to see the silhouette of their pursuer blocking out the light, for it to come raging down after Kaiku.

The ghaureg roared, a sound that was a cross between a bear and a wolf cry. It was closing on them fast.

Kaiku fled headlong past him as he covered the point where he guessed the Aberrant monster would emerge. The land around her was virtually devoid of vegetation, just a broken tangle of rocks and hard, stony soil. She made for a spot where the land slipped lower and a ridge rose up on the left. Maybe cover could be found there. Or maybe the ghaureg would just use it to jump down on top of them.

Then Tsata was with her, taking the lead. They ran at a crouch down the decline, the ledge screening them from view. The ghaureg bellowed again, terrifyingly close. Over the thump of her heart and the scuff of their footsteps she heard the creature loping nearer, its heavy tread reminding her of the sheer mass that their pursuer possessed. If they got within reach of those arms, those rending hands, they would be ripped to pieces.

The apparent disappearance of its prey gave the Aberrant pause. Tsata and Kaiku took advantage of that to put distance between them and it. The decline became shallow and fractured, depositing them into a wide, flat-bottomed trench scattered with rocks. On the far side, a natural wall rose to higher ground, pale and grim in the combined light of Aurus and Iridima, whose orbits had lately begun to glide closer, threatening the prospect of a moonstorm if the third sister joined them in the nights to come.

Kaiku struck out for a cluster of rocks. They were too exposed here. If they could get out of its sight for long enough, she was sure it would give up the chase. Though the ghauregs were brutal and dangerous, they were not the most intelligent of the predator species that the Weavers had collected.

But Shintu was not on her side that night. They had almost gained the shadow of the rocks when the Aberrant appeared on the ridge. Kaiku caught a frightened glance of its shape, its head low between its hunched shoulders as it surveyed the trench. Then it saw them, its eyes meeting Kaiku's and sending a shiver down her back. With a howl, it leaped from the ridge down to the floor of the trench, a clear twenty feet; Kaiku felt the impact of its landing through the soles of her boots.

Ghauregs. They were the largest of the Aberrants that Kaiku and Tsata had yet encountered in the Fault, and by far the most vicious. But they were also the most disturbingly akin to humans, and that struck Kaiku worst of all. When she had first heard their roars and seen their shaggy outlines in the night, she had found them unsettlingly familiar; it was only days later when she realised that she had hidden from those very creatures in the Lakmar Mountains on Fo, huddling and shivering in the snow during her lone trek to trace her father's footsteps back to the Weaver monastery. Then, they had been ghostly, half-seen things, glimpsed against white horizons; now they were brought into relief, and she found that they were worse than she had imagined.

They stood eight feet high, though their habitual slouching posture meant that they would be even taller if fully upright. They were some-what apelike in appearance and though they could run on all fours, their back legs were thick and large enough to allow them to stand on two legs, and they tended to walk that way, contributing to their grotesquely human-like appearance. Their skulls were huge, domi-nated by enormous jaws that were heavy enough to account for their slouch. The jaws were like steel traps, bearded with shaggy fur and full of omnivore teeth, blunt at the sides and sharp at the front. Small, yellow eyes and a snub snout were little more than mechanisms for locating what to eat next.

Their bodies were covered in a thick grey pelt, but their hands and chests and feet were bare, and the skin beneath was a wrinkled black. Though they did not have the natural weaponry of some of the other predator species, they made up for it in sheer size and power: their strength was truly appalling. And they were not slow, either.

Kaiku froze for the shortest of seconds as it landed in the trench and began to pound towards them on all fours, paralysed by the sheer size of the beast. Then Tsata was pulling her again, and she fled.

Her *kana* boiled inside her, fighting for release, as they raced across the trench. She dared not let it go. She had only been able to get away with using it before, on the dead shrilling, because she had employed it in an extremely subtle way. If she did something as violent as attacking the Aberrant, the Weavers here would detect it and spare no effort to find her.

Yet they were fast running out of other options.

'Here!' Tsata cried suddenly. 'This way!'

Tsata sprinted past her in a burst of speed and changed direction, heading up the trench to where a section of the far side had split and cracked, making a shallow fissure in the rock. Tsata reached it at a run and clambered up. Kaiku reached the sheer wall a moment later, her rifle clattering painfully against her back as she threw herself up at the fissure. She was no stranger to rock-climbing – it had been one of the challenges she and her brother Machim had competed at when they were children – but she could afford no purchase on her first try. Fear made her waste a second looking over her shoulder. The ghaureg was racing towards her, galloping on its knuckles, its matted hair flapping against its massive body.

'Climb!' Tsata shouted, and she did so. This time she found something to grip on to, wedging her fingers inside the fissure, and she pulled herself high enough to get a foothold. Tsata's hand was reaching down to her. Too far away. She found another purchase, took the strain on that and scrabbled for another, higher spot to put her free boot.

'Kaiku, *now!*'

The toe of her boot dug in, and she propelled herself with it, her hand reaching for his. He caught her with a grip like a clamp and wrenched her upward, the veins standing out on his tattooed arm. She was pulled over the lip and into his arms an instant before the ghaureg reached her, and its hand missed her ascending ankle by inches.

There was no time for relief. Kaiku extricated herself from her companion's grip and they ran again. The ghaureg could jump, but it was too heavy to get much height. The top of the trench wall was out of its reach, but it would not be long before it found an alternative way up.

Things had become too dangerous. Whatever the truth about the relationship between the Aberrants and the strange, masked handlers – which Kaiku had dubbed Nexuses – it was obvious that the Weavers knew something was amiss inside their protected enclosure, and had determined to remedy it. Kaiku and Tsata's forays through the barrier had become progressively more risky. The blighted, bleak land that surrounded the flood plain where the Aberrant army was stationed now swarmed with sentries. Time and again they had been forced to retreat without getting anywhere near the plain, let alone managing to find one of the Nexuses. Tsata's suggestion that they should kill one of the black-robed figures so that Kaiku could try and divine their nature was looking increasingly impossible; and it was becoming apparent to both of them that they could not keep on trying with things the way they were. Sooner or later they would be caught or killed.

The ghaureg was just bad luck. Normally they were easy enough to avoid, for they were hardly silent creatures and not particularly skilled hunters, relying on brute strength to dominate the food chain in the snowy wastes they had been gathered from. But Kaiku and Tsata had been avoiding a furie that had picked up their trail, and in their haste to get out of that Aberrant's path they had accidentally ran into another. It was the kind of slip that Kaiku had begun to think Tsata incapable of making, but it appeared that even the Tkiurathi was fallible.

She just hoped that discovery would not cost them their lives.

'Which way is it?' she panted, as they raced over the uneven ground.

'Ahead,' he replied. 'Not far.'

Not far turned out to be a lot further than Kaiku imagined, and by that time the ghaureg was on them again.

It spotted them from a rise in the land as they headed across a slice of flat terrain, and howled as it gave chase. Kaiku observed that it seemed to be the way of the ghauregs to go to high ground when trying to spot prey, for they were without natural predators and hence unafraid of revealing themselves out in the open. She noted it in case they ever had the misfortune to deal with one again. Staying low and close to obscuring walls was the best policy when trying to avoid this species.

But it was too late now. The beast was thundering down after them. They scrambled up a shallow slope, dislodging rocks and soil in little tumbles as the ground shifted beneath their feet. At the top was a withered clump of blighted trees, stark in the moonlight, which Kaiku recognised. They were at the edge of the Weaver's territory.

'The Mask, Kaiku!' Tsata urged, glancing back along the flat ground that they had just crossed. The ghaureg burst into sight, galloping relentlessly after them.

They ran again as Kaiku pulled the Mask out from where it was secured to her belt. But she had secured it too well, and in her haste the lip snagged on her clothing and the Mask spun from her hand, clattering to the stone, its mischievous face leering emptily.

She swore in disbelief. Tsata had his rifle out in a moment, tracking the approaching Aberrant as Kaiku ran over to where her Mask had fallen. The ghaureg had covered the distance between them fast, and Kaiku was not exactly sure how far the barrier was from here, and whether they would get to it in time.

It was the last, fleeting thought that crossed her mind before she scooped the Mask up and put it to her face.

The warm, sinking sensation of mild euphoria was stronger this time, more noticeable than it had ever been before. The intimation of her father's presence was stronger too; the smell of him seemed to emanate from the grain of the wood, gentling her as if she were a child in his arms again. The Mask was a perfect fit for her face, resting against her skin like a lover's hand on her cheek.

'*Run!*'

Tsata's voice shattered the timeless instant, and she was back to the present. The Mask was hot against her: the barrier had to be close. She fled, and Tsata dropped his arm and fled with her. The ghaureg bellowed as it raced up the treacherous incline, unhindered by the sliding soil, its hands and feet digging deep into the earth and throwing out stony divots behind it.

'Give me your hand!' Kaiku cried, reaching back for Tsata. The barrier was upon them, suddenly, and she realised it was *too* close, for if Tsata was not with her then he would not get through.

He reacted almost before she had finished her sentence, springing toward her and clamping his hand tight around hers. The ghaureg was mere feet away from them now, blocking out the moons with its bulk, its teeth dripping with saliva as it roared in anticipation of the kill.

The Weave bloomed around Kaiku, the world turning to a golden chaos of light as she plunged headlong into the barrier. She felt Tsata loose his grip instantly, felt him tug to the right as his senses skewed and he tried to change direction; but she had his hand, and she would not let it go. She pulled him as hard as she could, felt him trip and stumble sideways as his body went in a direction that all his instincts told him not to. His balance held for several steps before the two of them fell out of the other side of the barrier, and the Weave slipped into invisibility behind them.

Tsata was on his hands and knees, the familiar listlessness and disorientation in his eyes. Kaiku ignored him, her attention on the ghaureg. The creature had turned around and was racing away from them at an angle, pounding back into the heart of the Weaver's territory as if unaware that its prey was no longer in front of it. She kept her gaze on it until it had disappeared from sight behind a fold in the grey land.

Tsata recovered quickly, by which time Kaiku had reluctantly taken off the Mask. She had begun to feel guilty about doing so of late, as if it were some sort of betrayal, that by doing so she was disappointing her father's spirit somehow.

The Tkiurathi's brow cleared; he sat down on the rock and looked at Kaiku.

'That was an extremely lucky escape,' he said.

Kaiku brushed her fringe aside. 'We were careless,' she said. 'That is all.'

'I think,' said Tsata, 'the time has come to give up. We cannot get close to the Weavers or the Nexuses. We have to return to the Fold.'

Kaiku shook her head. 'Not yet. Not until we find out more.' She met his gaze. 'You go.'

'You know I cannot.'

She got to her feet, offered her hand to him. He took it, and she helped him up.

'Then it seems that you are stuck with me.'

He regarded her for a long moment, his tattooed face unreadable in the moonlight.

'It appears so,' he said, but his tone was warm, and made her smile.

Chien os Mumaka lay on a bed in the infirmary tent outside Zila, hazing in and out of consciousness. Sleep would not come to him, though his body ached and it felt as if the ends of his bones were rubbing against each other. The tent was empty apart from him. Several rows of beds lay waiting to be filled when the conflict began. It was cool and shadowy, and he was surrounded by the muted sounds of a military camp: subdued voices rising and falling as they passed near, the snort of horses, the crackle of fires, unidentifiable creaks and taps and groans. Out here near the coast, on the plain south of the fortified town, the night insects were not so numerous or noisy, and the dark seemed peaceful.

He had been taken into the care of a physician as soon as he had arrived at the camp, who had given him an infusion to drink, in order to bring down his fever. Chien had demanded weakly that he see the Barak Zahn. The physician had dismissed him at first, but Chien was insistent, declaring that he had a message of the gravest importance and that Zahn would be very unhappy with whoever delayed him. That gave the other man pause for thought. Chien knew well enough from his time as a merchant that people were more likely to do what they were told if they believed that they would be held responsible for the consequences of inaction. Yet the physician did not like to be ordered about within his own infirmary, and Chien was very ill, and Zahn was already abed by that point.

'In the morning,' the physician said, snappishly. 'By then you will be well enough to have visitors. And I will *ask* if the Barak wishes to see you.'

Chien was forced to be content with that.

Once alone, Chien was left to think about the events of the day. Gods, that Mishani was a sharp one. He did not know whether to feel ashamed or philosophical about how she had outguessed him in the end. It was not as if he could help what he said in dreams. In fact, he was inclined to think it was the will of the gods, or more specifically of Myen, the goddess of sleep, who had more than a little of her younger brother Shintu's trickster blood in her. In which case, who was he to feel bad about it?

And she was right: he had to grudgingly admit that. Leaving her was the best way he could help her. He had failed to protect her twice; it was only by the narrowest margin that she had survived the attentions of her father's assassins. He did not know what kind of game she was playing with Zahn, but he was glad that he would be out of it once his message was done. His obligation would be fulfilled then. As long as Mishani survived, Muraki would be honour-bound to release Blood Mumaka from their ties to her family.

He managed a small smile around the pain of the fever. His whole life, he had been fighting an uphill war, overcoming the prejudice of being an adopted child. It had not helped that his parents had subsequently managed natural children, though physicians had given them no hope of it. Every day he had been forced to prove himself against his siblings. But though he might not be elegant or subtle or educated, as his younger brothers were, he could hold his head with pride. As if it were not enough that he had been instrumental in raising up his family from the disgrace his parents had put them in, he was now going to free them from the debt they had incurred by choosing love over politics.

Unconsciousness slipped towards him, bringing respite from the fever; but he came awake again suddenly as something moved at the tent flap. He raised his head with some effort, peering into the darkness. His eyes refused to focus properly.

He could not see anyone, but that did not lessen his certainty. There was someone in here with him. The sensation of a presence crawled across his skin. He got himself up on his elbows, cast around again, trying to find the elusive shadow he had glimpsed. His head went light. A hallucination? The physician had warned him that the infusion might have side-effects.

'Is someone there?' he said at last, unable to bear the silence any longer.

'I'm here,' said a voice at Chien's bedside, and the surprise made him start violently. A black shape, made fuzzy by the drug in his system, standing next to him.

'You've caused my employer a great deal of trouble,' the man hissed, and as he did so Chien felt a gloved hand smothering him, holding his nose, and a wooden phial shoved between his lips before he could close them. He thrashed, tried to cry out and gagged on the liquid in his mouth a moment before another hand clamped over his face, preventing him from spitting it up. He swallowed reflexively to clear his airway; and only then did he realise what he had done.

'Good boy,' the shadow said. 'Drink it down.'

He stopped thrashing, his eyes wide in mute terror. A new drowsiness was spreading through him, turning his muscles to lead. His limbs become too heavy to lift; his head lolled back onto the pillow. A dreadful sleep descended on him, too fast for him to resist.

In seconds, he was still, his eyes open, pupils saucers of black staring at the roof of the darkened infirmary tent. The intruder took his hands away from Chien's face, watched as his breathing became shallow gasps and finally stopped altogether.

'I commend you to Omecha and Noctu, Chien os Mumaka,' the assassin murmured, closing the merchant's eyes with his fingers. 'May you have more luck in the Golden Realm.'

With that, the shadow was gone, slipping out into the camp to resume his guise as a soldier in Barak Moshito's army. Barak Avun tu Koli may have been far to the north, but his reach was long.

Chien lay cooling in the darkness, a death that would be attributed to fever in the morning, and his message remained undelivered at the last.

Reki tu Tanatsua, brother-by-marriage to the Emperor of Saramyr, huddled in the corner of an abandoned shack and wept into his sister's hair.

He had crossed the Rahn at sunset, having ridden headlong from Axekami all through the previous night. The bridge on the East Way had been far too dangerous, but he had found a ferryman without any trouble: a small mercy, for which he should have been grateful, if he had been capable of feeling so. But there was no room in him for anything but grief, and so he sobbed in the shadows of the old field-worker's hut that he had found to shelter in, amid the smell of mouldy hay from the pallet bed and rusted sickles leaning against the thin plank wall. The horses whickered nearby, uncomfortable at being kept in such close quarters; but he had not dared leave them outside, and they were too exhausted to be restless. They munched oats from their feed-bags, and ignored him.

He had ridden all day and most of the night, but sleep could not have been further from his mind. He did not care if he never slept again. He did not believe that this overwhelming sorrow and bitterness and pain would ever go away. How cruel the world could be, that just when he had found a searing happiness in Asara, it was all torn away and he was flung into the night, forced to abandon his sister and charged with a terrible responsibility. He could not bring himself to recall the pitiful state Laranya had been in when he had found her. It was a blasphemy against the person she had been, had *always* been until Mos had beaten her like that. The agony seemed too great to allow him to draw breath; the physical ache in his chest and stomach doubled him over.

Then, he had no idea that his sister was already dead.

They would be looking for him, she had said. They would try and stop him. Mos had crossed a line, and there was no telling what he might do now. Reki did not really understand: he had not known what his sister intended to do, how she had exposed her humiliation to the servants of the Keep so that rumour would be unquenchable, how she had meant to take her own life to ensure that vengeance would come from the desert. He did not think Mos would dare capture him and keep him against his will. As abhorrent as his actions were, kidnap was another order of magnitude.

None of that mattered though. He had his sister's black hair twisted around his fist. She had charged him with delivering it to their father. Honour bound him, as it would bind Blood Tanatsua. And Blood Tanatsua, one of the most powerful of the Tchom Rin families, would call on the other families in the name of Suran to aid them. Reki had no doubt his father could and would raise a great army to his banner.

The desert folk were traditionally insular, dealing with affairs within their own territories and not involving themselves in the politics of the west. The Emperors and Empresses were happy to let them do so. Even with Weavers at their command, the desert was a difficult place to administer, and those who lived in the fertile lands on this side of the Tchamil Mountains had little knowledge of the complex ways of the Suran-worshippers. Though they were all part of the Empire, in a land as vast as Saramyr it was possible for neighbouring cultures to be as foreigners to each other.

Reki held war in his hand. It was a responsibility he did not want. And yet to shirk it would be to betray his sister, who had suffered terribly at the hands of the man she loved. His own grief was nothing compared to hers, but that was no comfort to him. It seemed the crying would never stop, a racking spasm like vomiting, bringing up a bottomless void of shame and guilt and hate and woe.

He was so consumed by his own misery that he did not hear the door to the shack open and close, nor the newcomer walk over to him. It was only when he felt a touch on his shoulder that he suddenly scrambled away, pressing himself up against the corner of the shack, cringing from the shadow who stood over him.

'Oh, Reki,' said Asara.

He whimpered at the sound of her voice and threw his arms around her legs, his weeping beginning afresh. She knelt down next to him, allowing him to hold her and she him. There in the darkness he clung to her as if she were the mother he had never known, and she soothed him. For a long time, they stayed like that. The horses murmured to themselves, and the autumn wind rattled the shack door against its latch.

'Why are you here?' he managed at last, touching her face with beatific wonder as if she were some deity of mercy come to rescue him.

'Do you suppose you can do this alone?' she asked. 'I followed your trail as easily as if you had left me a map. If I did, so can others. Without me, you will be caught by next moonrise.'

'You came after me,' he sobbed, and embraced her again.

She pushed him away gently. 'Calm yourself,' she said. 'You are not a child any longer.'

That stung him, and his tear-blotched face showed how wounded he was.

'We must go now,' she told him, her voice firm. She was a sleek outline in the shadows, but her eyes glittered strangely. 'This place is too dangerous. I will take you by roads quicker and less travelled. I will see you discharge your sister's oath.'

Reki clambered to his feet, and Asara rose with him. His eyes burned and his nose ran. He wiped the back of his hand across his face, ashamed.

'You could be executed if you are caught,' he whispered.

'I know,' she replied. 'I will ensure we are not caught.'

He sniffed loudly. 'You should not be here.'

'But I am.'

'Why?' he asked again, because she had never really answered him the first time.

She kissed him swiftly on the lips. 'That, you will have to work out for yourself.'

They led the tired horses out to where Asara's own horses were, and headed away into the night. Later, she would tell him of his sister's suicide. But for now, it was enough to get him to safety, and to guard him on his long trek south-east to his father's lands. She would ensure he delivered Laranya's hair into the hands of Barak Green. She would make certain that he started the civil war that had to come.

As they travelled across fields and fens, Asara's eyes were flat. She was thinking on the murder of the Empress.

She had not originally intended to assassinate Laranya. In truth, she had been sent by Cailin only to keep an eye on developments within the Imperial family, for word of Mos's growing insanity was leaking out and Cailin believed that something would happen soon. She wanted Asara there to deal with it when it did. Asara had infiltrated the Imperial Keep only days before Mos's little disagreement with his wife.

As a spy she was peerless, and getting into the Keep – and into a shy young man's bed – was easy for a creature such as her. She was old, despite her appearance, and she had seen much and studied much. It was simple to charm her way into the company of the poets and playwrights and musicians that Laranya surrounded herself with. She had a greater wealth of knowledge than most of them, which was remarkable in a woman of such apparent youth. From there, gossip about Eszel and Laranya had led to Reki, and so she had formed her introduction. It had not been difficult. He was still a boy, still inexperienced in the way of women. It was simple to seduce him.

Then, the Empress. Reki had told her about the dreams Mos had been having. Asara had put the piece together with the massing armies of Blood Kerestyn, the approaching famine and what she had learned of the Weavers in her guise as Saran Ycthys Marul, and come to only one conclusion. The one she would have suspected anyway. The Weavers were driving Mos mad with jealousy. They meant him to harm his wife.

They *wanted* to draw the desert families into the conflict. And therefore, so did Asara. When opportunity came her way, she did not hesitate.

If there was one thing that Asara knew for certain, it was this: the Libera Dramach could not beat the Weavers as things stood. Not now, not in ten years' time, and probably not ever. The instant that Lucia revealed herself and made her claim to the throne, she would be killed, the Libera Dramach annihilated by the full force of the Weavers. Lucia could not win the Empire.

But with a little help from Asara, the Weavers could.

Twenty-Six

The assault on Zila came in the dead of night.

The clouds that had been stroking Saramyr's western coast had consolidated into a dour blanket by sunset, and when the darkness came it was almost total. No stars shone, Aurus was entirely invisible, and Iridima was reduced to a hazy smear of white in the sky, her radiance choked before it could reach the earth. Then the rain began: a few warning patters, insidious wet taps on the stone of the town before the deluge came. Suddenly the night was swarming, droplets battering down from the sky, hissing on torches and smacking off sword blades.

It was a painful, aggressive downpour, forcing its way through the clothes of the men who stood armed and on watch, their eyes narrowed as they watched the distant campfires of the besieging armies. They flickered in a ring around the hill upon which Zila sat, beacons of light in otherwise total darkness, illuminating nothing. Eventually, they went out, doused by the rain.

The onslaught kept up for hours. Zila waited, a crown of glowing windows and lanterns hanging suspended in rainswept blackness.

The man who first noticed that something was amiss was a calligrapher, an educated man who, like many others, had found himself swept up in the events that had overtaken his town and did not really have any clear idea how to swim against the tide. He had been assigned to the watch by some structure of authority he did not understand, and had unquestioningly obeyed. Now he was soaked and miserable, holding a rifle he did not know how to use and expecting at any moment to be struck in the forehead by an arrow from the abyss beyond the walls of the town.

It was, perhaps, this fearful expectation that made him more attentive than the others on the watch that night. They had settled themselves in, after several nights of inactivity, for a long period of negotiation and preparation before any actual combat would occur. The heat of the revolt had cooled in them now, and most had resigned themselves to a long autumn and a long winter trapped inside Zila. What choice did they have? They did not like the idea of throwing themselves on the mercy of the armies, even if they could leave. Some were wondering whether it might not have been better just to let the Governor keep hoarding his food, and take their chances with the famine; but their companions reminded them that they were thinking from the luxury of a full belly, and if they had been starving now, they would not be so complacent. There was food in Zila, more than they would have outside.

Like the calligrapher, many wondered now how they had got into this mess, and what they could possibly do to get out of it with their skins.

It was while chewing over these very thoughts that the calligrapher began to hear noises over the constant tumult of the rain. The wind was switching back and forth in fitful gusts, spraying him with warm droplets, and when it came his way he thought he heard an occasional creaking sound, or the squeak of a wheel. Being a timid man, he was reluctant to embarrass himself by pointing these out to any of the others on the watch, so he chose to do nothing for a long while. And yet time and again he heard the sounds – very faint, blown on the breeze – and gradually a certainty grew in his breast that something was wrong. The sounds were fleeting enough to be imagination, except that he had none. He was level-headed, practical, and had never been prone to phantoms of the mind.

Eventually, he shared his concerns with the next man on the wall. That man listened, and after a time he reported to his officer, and so it came to the commander of the watch. The commander demanded the calligrapher's account of what he had heard. Other men joined in: they had heard it too. They stared hard into the darkness, but the shrouded night was impenetrable.

'Send up a rocket,' the commander said eventually. He did not like to do it: he thought he might unduly alarm the troops and the enemy both. But he liked less the crawling trepidation that was ascending his spine.

A few minutes later, the night was torn by a piercing shriek, and the firework arced into the sky, trailing a thin stream of smoke. Its whistle faded to silence, and then blossomed into a furious ball of light, a burning phosphorescence that lit the whole hillside.

What they saw terrified them.

The base of the hill was aswarm with troops, frozen in the false sun like a bas-relief. They were draped in tarpaulins of black over their leather armour, disguising their colours, and under that camouflage they had advanced from the campfires, crossing in secret a potential killing field where the folk of Zila might have been able to shred them with bowshot and fire-cannon. Beneath the tarpaulins, they looked like a slick-backed horde of grotesque and outsize beetles, creeping insidiously up to the walls of the town, dragging with them mortars and ladders and fire-cannons of their own. The very suddenness of the image was horrifying, like pulling back a bandage to find a wound swarming with maggots.

Perhaps three thousand men were climbing the muddy hill towards Zila.

There was a great clamour as the firework died, both from the town and from the troops below. They cast off their tarpaulins in the last light of the rocket, and tugged them away from the sculpted barrels of the fire-cannons, which were shaped like snarling dogs or screaming demons. Then blackness returned, and they were hidden once again; but Zila was speckled in light, and could not hide.

Alarm bells clanged. Voices cried out orders and warnings. Men scattered dice or bowls of stew as they scrambled to the weapons that they had left carelessly leaning against walls.

Then the fire-cannons opened up.

The darkness at the base of the hill was lit anew with flashes of flame gouting from iron mouths, briefly illuminating the troops as they broke into a charge. Shellshot looped lazily up and over the walls, black orbs leaking chemical fire from cracks in their surfaces as they spun. They crashed through the roofs of houses, shattered in the streets, tore chunks out of buildings. Where they impacted hard enough, they burst and sprayed a jelly which ignited on contact with air. Blazing slicks raced along the cobbled roads of Zila, and the rain was powerless to extinguish them; dark dwellings suddenly brightened from within as their interiors turned to bonfires; howling figures, men and women and children, staggered and flailed as their skin crisped.

The first salvo was devastating. The second was not long in following.

Bakkara was out of his bed before the first screech of the rocket had died, and was strapping on his leather armour when the shellshot hit. Mishani had woken at the same time, but she had not understood what the firework might mean. At the sound of the explosions, however, she was in motion herself. While Bakkara was at the window, throwing open the shutters, she was slipping into her robe and winding her hair in a single massive plait which she knotted at the bottom.

Bakkara cursed foully as he looked down onto the rooftops of Zila, saw the flames already rising.

'I *knew* they'd do it like this,' he grated. 'Gods damn them! I knew it!'

He turned away from the window to find Mishani putting her sandals on. Ordinarily it took her a long while to make herself ready, but when elegance was not an issue she could do it inside of a minute.

'Where do you think you're going?' he demanded.

'With you,' she said.

'Woman, this is not a time to be a burden, I warn you.'

The room shook suddenly to a deafening impact, a tremor that made Bakkara stumble and catch hold of a dresser to steady himself. The keep had been struck. A fire-cannon's artillery would not penetrate walls this thick, but there was a flaming rill left on the keep's flank that dripped down into the courtyard below.

'I am not staying here; it is the most prominent target in Zila,' she said. 'Go. Do not concern yourself with me. I will keep up.'

She could not have said why she felt the need to accompany him, only that to be wakened in this way had frightened her, and she did not want to be left alone to wonder at what fate might befall the town.

'No, you're right,' Bakkara said, sobering for a moment. 'I have a safer place to put you.'

Mishani was about to ask what he meant by that, but she did not have the chance. Xejen burst into the room, jabbering frantically. He had evidently been awake, for he was not sleep-mussed and his hair was neat; in her time observing the leader of the Ais Maraxa, Mishani had established that he was a chronic insomniac.

'What are they doing, what are they *doing*?' he cried. He registered Mishani's presence in the room, then looked at Bakkara with obvious surprise on his face. He had evidently not known that they were sleeping together. 'Bakkara, what are they—'

'They're *attacking* us, you fool, as I *told* you they would!' he shouted. He pushed past Xejen and out of the door. Xejen and Mishani followed him as he hurried through the keep, adjusting his scabbard as he went. Outside, the staccato crack of rifles had begun as the men on the walls organised themselves enough to mount a defence.

'We were negotiating!' Xejen blustered, running to keep up with Bakkara's strides. 'Don't they care about the hostages? Are they intending to burn an Imperial town to the ground?'

'If that's what it takes,' Bakkara replied grimly.

As a soldier, he was used to the frustration of suffering for a leader's incompetence, and accepted it. In a chain of command, even if one man thought he knew better than the one above him, he still had to accept his superior's orders. Bakkara had not, in his heart, thought that the Baraks Zahn tu Ikati and Moshito tu Vinaxis would dare a ploy like this, but he had warned Xejen of the possibility.

Xejen had not heeded him. He believed, as he had always believed, that troops of the Empire would try and wait them out. They would waste time with diplomacy, letting the people become bored and complacent and dispirited, hanging on until the rebels' morale slipped. Then they would make offers to the people themselves, to try and incite a coup from within. At the very worst, they would assault the walls, and Xejen believed that they could be held back easily from the advantage of high ground. The Empire's hands were tied to some extent: they would not want to cause any more damage to the town itself than they had to, and the Emperor would not want to kill thousands of Saramyr peasant townsfolk, especially when things were so volatile.

If Xejen knew anything, he knew how to play people, how to inspire them or make them doubt. And he had intended to use the time spent in negotiation to spread the doctrine of the Ais Maraxa, to give the people of Zila something to believe in, a purpose that would keep them unshakable. He had banked on the generals being unenthusiastic about the fight, seeking to preserve their strength for the civil war that was brewing.

Xejen thought only in his own terms, and he assumed – fatally – that everyone else of education thought that way too. After all, sense was sense; surely anyone with a mind could tell that? He had thought it would come to a battle of wills. He was wrong.

They burst out of the keep into a tumult of rain and screams and flame, then ducked reflexively as shellshot came rushing over their heads to explode across the far side of Zila, spewing burning jelly onto the rooftops. Bakkara cursed roundly and raced down the stone steps towards street level, his hair sodden in an instant. The streets were alive with people running and calling to each other, seeking any kind of shelter in their panic, frightened faces sidelit by fire.

The steps of the keep folded back on themselves twice before they reached the surrounding plaza. Several guards stood at the bottom, professional soldiers who knew better than to desert their posts even under an assault like this. Bakkara clapped one of them on the shoulder.

'Get more men!' he said urgently. 'Sooner or later these people are going to end up thinking the only safe place in Zila is the keep, and they'll want in. You need to hold them back. We don't want them taking sanctuary; we want them out there fighting!'

The guard snapped a salute across his chest and began giving orders. Bakkara did not wait. He was heading for the southern wall, where the sounds of battle were beginning already.

Those with military training in the Ais Maraxa had known it would be a tall order to co-ordinate peasantry and artisans into an effective defence force, but even they had not expected quite such spectacular disorganisation. The Baraks' battle plan had been perfectly pitched to sow confusion, sending Zila into a panic by its sheer callous brutality. Fire-cannons rained shellshot indiscriminately upon the town, taking no care to aim. Mortars pitched bombs through the air, destroying chunks of masonry and doing real damage to the walls of the keep. The men of Zila had been ready for a fight, but this was no fight; this was a massacre.

Or so it seemed. Actually, as men like Bakkara knew, there were far fewer casualties than the level of destruction would suggest. The intent was to make the damage look worse than it was. The rain was stopping many of the fires spreading too far, and the outer wall of the town was as strong as it always had been. But the townsfolk saw only that their houses were being burned and their families were fleeing in terror, and many of them ran from their posts to try and save their loved ones from whatever danger they imagined them to be in.

It took a long time, too long, for Zila's own fire-cannons to open up, blasting flaming rents in the lines of the attackers, sending them scattering. Fireworks whistled into the sky and turned into blazing white torches, lighting a scene of labouring ghosts at the foot of Zila's wall as the soldiers clambered through mud and bowshot and rifle fire, shields locked above their heads. Shields were rarely used in Saramyr combat except for such purposes as this, and so they were fashioned from thick metal to make them heavy enough to deflect rifle balls. Men fell at the flanks of the formations, but the core remained strong as ladders were passed under the canopy of shields. Distantly, the sinister creaking of the siege engines could be heard approaching through the night, and reinforcements who had not been part of the first assault were arriving.

But the worst consequence of the disorganisation was this: all eyes were on the south, and nobody was looking north, to the river.

The darkness and rain and cloud that had concealed the Baraks' armies so effectively had done the same for the soldiers that had crossed the Zan and ascended the steep side of the hill, filing up the stairs from the docks to the small gate at the top and then fanning out along the wall.

The men on the north side had not lessened in their vigilance, but under the conditions it was impossible to see anything, and the chaos of the bombardment had put the more nervous men into a panic. The watch commander's request to have fireworks sent up on the north side of the town got lost somewhere in the muddle, and while he was waiting for a reply that never came, disaster struck.

★

Four soldiers guarded the small northern gate on the inside. It was massively thick, studded with rivets and banded with metal, practically unbreachable due to its width and compact size. The angle of the slope beyond, which plunged down to the south bank of the Zan, made foolish any attempt to assault it. Men would have to use the stairs – for the grassy sides were just too sharp an incline, especially in this rain – and they would be easy targets for anything the defenders cared to drop on them from above. Any attackers would be forced to huddle close to the tiny margin of level ground by the walls, where burning pitch could be poured on them, while a few soldiers fruitlessly battered at the gate. There was not even enough clearance between the gate and the edge of the slope to manoeuvre a ram effectively.

Giri stood in the lantern-lit antechamber with his three companions on duty, listening to the destruction of Zila going on outside. He was a soldier by trade, but he did not have the temperament for it. He did not enjoy fighting, nor did he revel in the camaraderie that other soldiers thrived on. Most of his time was spent trying to get himself posted in the place where there was least likely to be any danger of him losing his life. He believed himself lucky this time. This was probably the safest place in the town.

He only began to suspect that something was wrong when his head began to throb. At first it was nothing alarming, just a slight, dull pain which he expected to pass momentarily. But it increased rather than diminishing. He squinted, blinking his right eye rapidly as it started to get worse.

'Are you unwell?' one of the other guards asked him.

But Giri was very far from well. The agony was becoming unbearable. He pawed at his right eye with his fingertips, wanting by some perverse instinct to touch the area that hurt; but it was inside his head, like a small animal scrabbling within his skull. He could see another guard frowning now, not at Giri but at something else, as if a sudden thought had occurred to him that was too important to dismiss.

They had all taken on that expression now, a curious attentiveness as if listening to something. Then the guard who had spoken turned back to him, his sword sliding free from its sheath.

'You're not co-operating, Giri,' he said.

Giri's eyes widened in realisation. 'No, stop! Gods! It's a Weaver! They've got a Weaver out there!'

The blade plunged into his chest before he could get any further.

One of the three remaining guards, those who had not had such an adverse reaction to the Weaver's influence, doused the lanterns and unbarred the gate. They drew it open to the rain and darkness outside. Barely visible was a Mask of precious metal cut into angles, a splintered, jagged visage of gold and silver and bronze. Behind the hunched figure, soldiers in black tarpaulins waited with swords drawn. They rushed past and slew the unfortunate puppets, then crowded into the antechamber.

Stealthily, they crept onward into Zila.

'Report!' Bakkara roared over the crashing of burning timbers and the shattering din of the explosives.

'They're all over us!' the watch commander cried. He was a man of middle age with a drooping moustache, now lank with moisture. 'They've got to the walls and they're putting up ladders. A third of the men have left their posts already; they're running around like idiots inside the town.'

'You didn't stop them?' Bakkara was incredulous.

'How? By killing them? Who would kill them? The townsfolk won't, and if the Ais Maraxa get sword-happy, what pitiful defence we have left will collapse.' The commander looked resigned. 'Men won't fight if they aren't willing. We started a revolt; we didn't create an army.'

'But they'll be killed if they *don't* fight!' Xejen blurted.

He, like the others, was sheltering beneath the wooden awning of an empty bar near the southern wall. People ran by on the street, intermittently lit by flashes. Mishani listened to the exchange with half her attention elsewhere. She was scared rigid beneath her dispassionate exterior. The pummelling tumult all around her, the knowledge that they could be incinerated at any moment, was shredding her nerves. She wanted desperately to turn back to the keep; she wished she had never left it. Looking up through the rain, she saw it rising in the centre of the town. Though its sides were scored and scorched, and chunks had fallen free, it still seemed many times safer than where she was now. Fear had driven her towards where the action was, for she had no wish then to remain in a tower that was being bombarded. But she knew nothing of war, and was shocked by its ferocity. Twice they had almost been hit by shellshot; several times they had passed by burnt and blasted corpses. Mishani had seen atrocities like this before, when she had been a victim of subversive bombing in the Market District of Axekami; but that had been one terrible moment of danger, and then the horrifying aftermath. Here, the bombs kept coming, and sooner or later one of them had to hit her.

The commander was looking at Xejen gravely. 'They're saying the men will be spared if they surrender. We can hear Barak Moshito down there somewhere.'

'Impossible!' Xejen cried.

'Weavers,' Bakkara said. 'They can make a man's voice carry. They used to do it when generals were addressing troops, back when I fought in the Newlands. There would be two thousand men there, but every one could hear as if the general was right in front of them.'

'Weavers?' Xejen repeated nervously.

'What did you expect?' he grunted.

'We need you on the wall, Bakkara,' the commander said. 'It's a shambles up there. They don't know how to deal with an all-out attack.'

'Nobody is surrendering!' Xejen snapped suddenly. 'Tell the men that! Whatever Moshito says!' He snorted. 'I'll go to the wall and tell them myself.'

The commander looked uncertainly at Bakkara. 'You mean to lead the men?' he asked Xejen.

'Since I must, yes,' he replied.

'Xejen . . .' Bakkara began, then subsided. But Mishani would not let him defer to Xejen, not here. Even amid her fear, she saw that they were at the fulcrum of the balance of power; and the time had come to throw her own weight into the fray.

'Gods, Xejen, let him do his job!' she snapped, imbuing her voice with a crisp and disparaging tone. 'He is the man to lead the battle, not you!'

Bakkara's brows raised in surprise. His eyes flicked from Mishani to Xejen. 'Go to the safehouse. There's nothing you can do here.'

'I have to be here!' Xejen protested immediately.

But now it was a matter of pride; as much as he would not have admitted it to himself, Bakkara would not be overridden in front of his woman, however inaccurate that term might be. Mishani had judged him aright.

'You will do Lucia no good if you get killed!' Bakkara barked. 'And you, Mistress Mishani, this is not your fight. If you're caught up in the fray, they'll kill you, noble or not.'

'Ladders!' someone cried in the distance. 'More ladders coming!'

The commander glared at Bakkara urgently. 'We *need* you!' he repeated. 'They're trying to scale the wall!'

'*Go!*' Bakkara shouted at Xejen, and then he turned and ran, following the other soldier.

Xejen and Mishani stood together under the awning, the rain splattering off it and onto the cobbles. Bakkara did not look back. Xejen seemed momentarily bereft of direction. Mishani, noting his expression, guessed that things would be different if they managed to weather this battle. Bakkara, without even intending to, had taken a great step towards becoming the head of the Ais Maraxa, and Xejen had been diminished. It would serve Mishani well.

'We should do as he says,' Mishani suggested. She surprised herself by how calm she sounded, when all she wanted to do was flee towards what little sanctuary she could find. Bakkara had mentioned the safehouse once before: a small, underground complex of chambers that the Ais Maraxa had discovered while rooting through the usurped Governor's notes. A retreat where they would be protected from the bombs and shellshot.

Xejen spat on the ground in frustration and stalked away in the direction they had come. 'Follow me!' he said, his long jaw set.

They hurried through the grim, steep streets of Zila. The tall buildings crowded in on them threateningly as they slipped off the main thoroughfares and through the narrow lanes that ran between the spoke-roads. Flaming rubble had blocked many routes, and some buildings had fire licking from their windows, burning from the inside out. People pushed past them in the other direction. Some of them recognised Xejen. A few pleaded with him, as if he had the power to stop this. He told them to get up on the wall and fight, if they had any pride in their town. They looked at him in confusion and ran on. As far as they were concerned, things were hopeless.

The analytical part of Mishani's mind was studying Xejen even through the fear. He was enraged by the turn of events, betrayed by the weakness of the townsfolk and by Bakkara; and yet she saw by his manner that he still had supreme faith in his plan, that no matter how bad it looked the walls of Zila *would* hold. He cursed as he went, muttering in fury at the sight of men shepherding their families away from the blazing buildings, genuinely unable to believe that they did not see the best way to keep them safe was to fight for their town.

That was when she realised unequivocally that his belief in his cause had blinded him, and that was why they would be defeated. The Ais Maraxa were dangerous, not only to the Empire but to the Libera Dramach as well. Zaelis had known that from the start. They were a liability, driven by their fervour to act without caution and to stretch themselves beyond their abilities. Fortune had put them in this town at a time when it was ripe to overthrow its inept ruler, but it had not given them the resources or experience to govern it, and certainly not to face two very competent Baraks and a multitude of war-tested generals.

She had been working towards a way to resolve this mess in her favour, a route to safety; but events had turned on her too quickly. Where was Zahn? Had he chosen to ignore her message? Gods, did he not realise how important she was to him? If she survived the night, she told herself, she might still have a chance of getting out of Zila alive. If she survived the night.

She was thinking just that when the mortar bomb struck the building next to her with a deafening roar, and the whole frontage came slumping down into the street.

It was only Xejen's perpetually keyed-up reactions that saved her. He had seen the projectile an instant before it hit, and he darted into the open doorway of the building opposite, grabbing the cuff of Mishani's robe as he went. At the instant she was stunned by the noise and light and the blast of concussion that physically pushed her backwards, she was also pulled hard through the doorway, and she fell over the step as the street where she had just been turned into an avalanche of stone and timber.

A billow of dust blew into the room, forcing itself into Mishani's lungs and making her choke. Through tearing eyes she could vaguely make out the shape of Xejen. Then she heard the sound of splitting wood and the terrible, ominous groan of the house all around them. She had barely realised that she had evaded death by a hair's breadth before she heard something crack overhead, and knew that she had not evaded it at all. Her stomach knotted sickeningly as she heard the last of the beams give, and then the ceiling came in on top of her.

Bakkara's blade swept in a high arc, shattering the soldier's collarbone and almost removing his head. His victim's grip went loose on the ladder and he fell, crashing onto the men beneath him and dislodging several, who went screaming towards the upturned shields of their companions below. Bakkara and another man got the end of the ladder and pushed away; it swung back, teetered, and then pivoted in a quarter-circle and tipped over, shedding the last of the men on its back as it crashed onto the heads of the troops that assaulted Zila's southern wall.

'Where *is* everyone?' he cried in exasperation, racing to where another ladder was already clattering ominously against the parapet. They could have held this position with a tenth of the men attacking it, but there was barely even that. It was all the defenders could do to keep the troops from getting over the wall. In the back of his mind, he noted that Zila's fire-cannons had gone silent, and the Baraks' troops attacked fearlessly now.

It was an Ais Maraxa man who answered him, a soldier as weathered and weary as he. 'They fled the wall, the cowards,' he grated. 'Some to their families, some because they want to surrender. They'll hide 'til this is through, gods rot them.'

Bakkara swore. This was a disaster. The townsfolk had all but given up, demoralised utterly by the sight of their homes burning and the apparently overwhelming odds. They could have held out, if they had stayed together. But that required unity and discipline, and Xejen's ragtag army of peasants had neither.

He had no time to think further, for he was already at the new ladder, where two Blood Vinaxis men had spilled onto the stone walkway and were running at him. His sword swung up to meet the ill-advised overhead strike of the first, then he stamped on the side of the man's foot, feeling the joint give under his heel. His enemy shrieked and clutched his ankle reflexively, and Bakkara beheaded him while his guard was down. He slumped to the ground, blood gushing from his severed neck to be washed away by the pouring rain.

The Ais Maraxa soldier, whose name was Hruji, had despatched his opponent with similar efficiency, and the two of them tipped the ladder back before any others could get to the top.

Bakkara glanced grimly up and down the wall. There were too few men here, too few. Almost all of them were Ais Maraxa. The peasants had left them to it. In the lantern-light, he saw small clots of soldiers rushing back and forth, desperately engaging the encroaching troops. But the troops were endless, and his men were flagging.

There were not enough to keep the enemy at bay over such a perimeter.

'Bakkara!' someone cried, and he turned to see a dishevelled man come racing along the walkway towards him. He knew the face, but memory failed at the name.

'Give me some good news,' Bakkara warned, but at the man's expression he knew what news he had to give would certainly not be good.

'They've got in through the north gate! They've taken the north wall. The peasants are surrendering . . . some are even *helping* them in the streets up there. Our men are fleeing south, towards the centre.'

That was it. There was no more time for procrastination.

'We fall back to the keep,' Bakkara said, the words like ashes in his mouth. 'The town is lost. Meet at the rally point. We go from there.'

Hruji and the messenger both saluted and ran to spread the order. Bakkara turned flat eyes to the scorched and damaged building that rose above the burning streets of Zila, and wondered if his decision would do them any good at all, or if he was merely delaying the inevitable. He suspected the latter.

A moment later, a horn sounded a shrill, clear note that echoed into the battle-tainted night: the signal to give up the wall.

The retreat was as disorganised as the rest of the defence had been. The Ais Maraxa had been the last to give up their posts, but not all of them were soldiers, and the withdrawal turned into a rout as enemy troops began pouring over the vacated wall and into the town. Booted feet splashed through streets that had turned into shallow rivers of murky water, fearful glances were cast over shoulders at the tide of swords and rifles and armour cresting Zila's parapets. The Ais Maraxa ran headlong through the glow cast by the street lanterns, flicking from shadow to light and back again, fleeing to gather in a dour square that stood at the crossing of a spoke-road and a side street.

Bakkara stood at the square's north end as the ragged fighters poured in from all sides, surveying them bleakly. Their expressions were disbelieving, their faith in their cause tattered. For so long they had worked in secret, and they had thought themselves invincible, righteous crusaders for a cause blessed by the gods. But the moment they had stepped into the light they had been smashed by the power of the Empire. It was a cruel lesson, and Bakkara considered what would become of the Ais Maraxa if they managed to get themselves out of this.

Now sufficient numbers had crammed into the square for him to call the order to head for the keep. Through the fires of the shellshot that were still bursting all around them, he led the crowd at a run up the steep, cobbled spoke-road that headed towards the looming structure at Zila's hub. Maybe there they could at least give the enemy pause. New strategies could be mooted, new plans made.

But who would make them?

He dashed the rain from his eyes, casting his doubts away as he did so. Regroup and defend. That was the next thing he had to do, and he did not think beyond that. He had never thought beyond his next objective. That was his nature.

They came to the end of the spoke-road, and it opened out into the great circular plaza that surrounded the keep. Bakkara slowed to a halt, and so did the men who ran with him. The stillness spread backwards, until even those at the rear of the crowd who could not see had ceased jostling, subdued by a dreadful trepidation.

Ranked before them, at the foot of the keep, were more than a thousand men; double the amount that Bakkara had mustered.

Bakkara took a breath and assessed the amount of trouble they were in. The space between the Ais Maraxa and the enemy troops was all but empty, a dark, slick expanse of crescent-shaped flagstones. A pair of large fires to their left – where shellshot jelly still burned against the downpour – cast multiple yellow glints across the divide. The troops were a mixture of all the Bloods who had arrayed themselves against the revolt; but he also saw peasants there, townsfolk of Zila, eager to buy their own lives by abetting the invaders. He tried to feel disgust, but he could not. It seemed petty now.

There above them, on the steps leading to the keep, he picked out the dimly shining Mask of a Weaver. The face of precious metals was an obscenity against the ragged robes that he wore. Bakkara did not need to look up any further to know that the keep had already been breached.

Men were murmuring in fear behind him. The very thought of facing a Weaver was enough to make them balk. Yet the enemy forces that had scaled the southern wall were catching up to them with every wasted moment. Bakkara sensed that he had to act now, or he would lose them.

Their lives were forfeit if they were captured. He knew that, with the certainty of a man who had seen war over and over. He also knew that there were worse things than dying.

'Ais Maraxa!' he roared, his voice carrying over the crowd. It sounded like someone else's voice, someone else's words. 'For Lucia! *For Lucia!*'

With that he raised his sword high and cried wordlessly, and as one the men that followed him did the same, their instant of weakness passing at the sound of Lucia's name, reminded of the faith that had brought them here in the first place. Bakkara's chest swelled with an emotion so glorious that he could not put a name to it, and he swung his sword forward to point at the enemy who waited to receive them with better weapons, better guns, and greater numbers.

'*Attack!*' he bellowed.

Rifles cracked and swords rang free of their scabbards as the last of the Ais Maraxa surged forward to the death that awaited them, and in his final moments Bakkara knew what it was like to be a leader at last.

Twenty-Seven

When Nuki's eye rose over the eastern horizon, it looked down on a very different Zila.

The Surananyi in Tchom Rin, the rage of the pestilent goddess of the desert at the murder of the Empress, had blown itself out by now, and left the successive mornings with a brittle and crystalline quality. It was such a light that fell across the broken crown of Zila, its rooftops blackened and timbers open to the sky, trailing dozens of streamers of thick smoke into the air where the gentle wind blew them northward. No longer grim and defiant, it was a carcass of its former pride, and those townsfolk that walked its streets went shamefaced and terrified of the consequences of their insurrection.

Everywhere was the slow, lazy movement of an aftermath, like tired revellers cleaning up after a festival. As the sun climbed to its zenith, camps were being broken and repitched closer to the hill. Some troops were departing altogether, their presence urgently needed elsewhere. Corpses of the shot, impaled or incinerated were cleared away from the foot of the town wall, and a steady stream of carts rolled from the south gate carrying the dead from within.

The process of restoring order and meting out punishment would not be short. Zila had defied the Empire, and an example had to be made. That was Xejen's downfall, in the end. He had not accounted for the Baraks' ruthless determination to keep the status quo in these times. A famine was coming, was already biting at the edges of Saramyr and gnawing its way inward. Society teetered on the brink of chaos. In such a climate, any dissent had to be stamped on as hard as possible. Only with rigid order could the Empire make its way through the hard times ahead. The peasants had to learn that revolution was impossible. And so the high families had assaulted Zila with force far beyond anything Xejen or the townsfolk had expected, caring nothing for the sanctity of non-combatants or the structural damage to one of Saramyr's most important settlements. If they had not been able to breach the wall, they would have burned Zila to embers or smashed it flat with explosives.

Rebellion was unacceptable. The people of Zila had learned that now, and they would learn it again and again over the next few weeks. The message would carry. The Empire was inviolable.

But to the Barak Zahn tu Ikati, it felt like trying to blow life into a cadaver. The Empire, to him, had died long ago. He had been instrumental in the planning of last night's attack, but his contribution had been emotionless. He did not burn with zeal for the preservation of their way of life like Barak Moshito tu Vinaxis did, or the generals sent by the other high families.

Yet he had felt that way once. Before Mos usurped the throne, before Anais tu Erinima was killed. Before his daughter died.

It was midday when he walked from the doors of the scorched keep, down into the plaza where the last of the Ais Maraxa dead were being cleared away, their slack limbs and gaping faces sundered by scabbed wounds. The congealed blood on the crescent flagstones was cooking in the fierce heat, a sticky and sickly-sweet odour that cloyed in the back of the throat. The grey and shattered streets of Zila had dried already, and now they were dusty and quiet, a maze of bright sunlight and harsh black shadow in which cowed men and women skulked and would not meet his eye.

He was a lean, rangy man, with spare features and pox-pitted cheeks that had become lately gaunt and hollow. His trim, prematurely white beard hid most of it, but not around his eyes, where the toll of his long suffering was easy to see. Over fifty harvests had passed him by, but none had been as hard as the last few. Not since Lucia was lost.

The moment of their meeting was engraved upon his memory as if it had happened yesterday. He had lived it every day since, recalling over and over the fundamental shift that he had experienced when he first laid eyes on the Aberrant child. Suddenly he had been aware of a level of feeling that he had not known existed, something deeply primal and irresistible in force, and he knew then what a man must know when he watches his wife give birth: an overwhelming introduction into the mysteries of the wonderful and terrible bond between parent and child. He saw her, and he *knew*. Every instinct blared at him at once: *she is yours*.

She knew, too. It was in the way she threw her arms around him, and he saw it in those pale eyes, and in the gaze of pure betrayal she gave him as tears welled in them.

Where were you? they asked, and they tore his heart into pieces.

The fact that he had not known he had a daughter did not make it any easier for him. Of course, her age and the time of her birth corresponded with the short, tempestuous affair he had conducted with the Blood Empress all those years ago, but then he had known that Anais had still been sleeping with her husband during that period, and when it was announced that she had become pregnant it had simply seemed impossible that it might be his. The idea had occurred to him only briefly, and then been dismissed. If she suspected it was Zahn's issue, he was certain that she would have either told him, or poisoned it in the womb without ever letting anyone but her physician find out that she was with child. They were the only politically expedient courses of action. When she did neither, Zahn reasoned that it was nothing to do with him: he had already surmounted the bitterness that he had felt when she had broken off their dangerous relationship, and was happy to be out of it now that an heir had become involved. Children were simply something that Zahn had no interest in. Or so he thought.

But in that instant when they had met, the grief and loss and regret crushed him. He felt like he had abandoned her at birth.

He had retreated from the Imperial Keep, stunned by what had happened, but he had not intended to retreat for long. He would have confronted Anais, even amid all the civil unrest that was going on at the time, even though he had no proof beyond the simple certainty that he was right. He would have demanded to know why she kept Lucia from him. He would have done all sorts of reckless things, like a hot-headed youth, if Anais and their daughter had not been killed first.

Something had withered inside him at the news, and had never grown back. Some crucial part of his soul had shrivelled and black-ened, and robbed the colour from the world. He tried to tell himself that it was ridiculous for him to be so affected by this. After all, he had been content in ignorance for years, and he had only known his true connection to Lucia for a very short time. How could he feel loss for something he had had so briefly?

But the words were hollow, and their echoes mocked him, and he stopped trying to apply sense to senselessness.

Misery spread like a cancer, killing other parts of him. Food no longer gave him joy. His companions found him saturnine and melan-choly. He took little interest in the affairs of his family and his estates, delegating many tasks that should have been his to younger brothers and sisters. He was no less competent as a Barak, but he was dis-interested, stripped of ambition. He maintained his family's holdings well enough, but he had no passion for the political games and the jostling for status that were an integral part of Saramyr high society. He was merely treading water.

But something was to happen this morning that would ignite a flicker of something long forgotten in his breast, something so foreign to him now that he struggled to recall its name.

Hope. Foolish hope.

A woman had been detained by Blood Ikati troops after she had been found unconscious in the ruins of a building, having been struck on the head by a falling beam as the ceiling above her came down. That same beam had saved her life, for it had collapsed at an angle and sheltered her from the bricks raining around her. She had been uncovered by peasants who had begun to dig for survivors, and turned over to Zahn's men along with a much greater prize: Xejen tu Imotu, whom the peasants eagerly denounced as the leader of the Ais Maraxa.

Though nobody knew who she was, her noble attire and hair were enough to mark her as not being of Zila, and her proximity to Xejen when she was found was damning. She was kept under guard and nursed until she awoke, at which point she demanded to see Barak Zahn tu Ikati, claiming that she was Mishani tu Koli.

'I will see her,' he had told the messenger who brought him the news. Then, remembering himself, he added: 'Have my servants bathe and dress her first, if needs be. She is high-born. Treat her as such.'

And so he strode through the newly hushed streets of Zila, to where Mishani waited for him.

Mishani met him by her sickbed, but not in it. She was weak from breathing dust and badly bruised all over, and she had suffered a terrible blow to the back of her head that was causing her eyes not to focus properly. The physicians would not let her leave her room; indeed, they hovered about in case she should faint from the exertion of getting out of bed. The knowledge that she was noble and important to their Barak had turned them from imperious and haughty men into fawning servants. When Zahn chimed and entered, he dismissed them with a flick of his hand.

The physicians had commandeered a row of undamaged houses for their base of operations, and filled the beds with injured soldiers and townsfolk. Mishani, whether by chance or by virtue of her dress, had been put in the master bedroom of some wealthy merchant's abode. The bed was plainly expensive, and the walls were decorated with charcoal sketches and elegant watercolours. In an ornate bone cradle there was a pattern-board depicting a seascape, the washes of colour suspended within a three-dimensional oblong of hardened transparent gel. Zahn idly wondered if the person who possessed all of this had been killed at the hands of the townsfolk during the revolt, in last night's bombardment, or if they were still alive now and simply thrown out on the street. Revolution was an unpleasant business.

Mishani tu Koli was standing by her bed, dressed in borrowed robes with her voluminous hair combed and loose. She appeared to be entirely unhurt, but Zahn knew well enough that she was simply not letting it show. There were clues: she was wearing her hair in a style that covered her cheeks, to hide scratches on her ear; there was a faint patch of blue on the back of her wrist where the cuff of her robe did not hide it; then there was the telling fact that she had not strayed far from the edge of her bed, in case her strength failed her. He had met her several times before in the Imperial Court when she was younger, and her poise had always been remarkable.

'Mistress Mishani tu Koli,' he said, performing the correct bow for their relative social rank. 'It grieves me to hear that you have been injured in this calamity.'

She returned the female form of the same bow. 'By Ocha's grace, I have not suffered as much as I might have,' she said. None of the weakness of her condition bled into her voice.

'Would you like to sit?' Zahn offered, gesturing at a chair. But Mishani was not about to take any concessions.

'I prefer to stand,' she said levelly, knowing that there was only one chair and no mats in the room. He was well over a foot taller than her; if she sat then he would be looking down on her at a steeper angle than he already was.

'My servants have told me that you wished to see me,' he said.

'Indeed,' came the reply. 'I have been wanting to see you ever since I was detained in Zila by the Ais Maraxa. Though in the end you had a somewhat violent way of bringing our meeting about.'

Zahn gave her a hint of a smile.

'May I ask you a question?' she said.

'Of course.'

'What has become of Xejen tu Imotu?'

Zahn considered that for a moment. 'He lives, barely.'

'Might I know where he is?'

'Are you concerned for him?'

'I am concerned, but not for the reasons you imagine,' she told him.

Zahn studied her for a moment. She was a sculpture in ice.

'I let Barak Moshito deal with him,' Zahn said. He linked his hands behind his back and walked over to the pattern-board, studying it. 'Moshito will undoubtedly turn him over to his Weaver. I cannot say I feel sympathy. I have little love for the Ais Maraxa.'

'Because they remind you of your daughter,' Mishani finished. 'They make you believe in the possibility that she is still alive, and that is a raw wound indeed.'

Zahn's head snapped around, his eyes flashing angrily.

'Forgive my bluntness,' she said. 'I was heading to Lalyara to find you with the intention of divining your feelings towards her. Now I cannot afford the time to be delicate.' She fixed him with a steady gaze. 'Her life hangs in the balance. Xejen tu Imotu knows where she is.'

Zahn made the connection immediately. If Xejen knew, then the Weaver would get it out of him. And if the Weavers knew . . .

This was too fast, too much to believe. If he accepted that, then he accepted his daughter was still alive. He shook his head, running his fingers down his bearded chin.

'No, no,' he murmured. 'What is your agenda, Mishani tu Koli? Why were you here, in Zila?'

'Did Chien not tell you this?' she asked.

'Chien? Ah, the hostage. I am sorry to say he died the night he was brought out of Zila.'

Mishani's face showed nothing. She felt no grief for him: he was merely a casualty. What did concern her was that it meant her father's men were aware she was in Zila, and they would be very close indeed. She had to win Zahn's trust now, in any way she could. It was imperative that she got out of the town in secret, and the only way she would do that would be under Zahn's protection.

'So, will you answer my question?' he prompted. 'Why were you in Zila?'

'Misfortune,' she said. 'I was waylaid as I travelled to find you. Although it seems the gods have brought us together anyway.'

'That is too convenient,' he said. His tone had become a lot less polite now. 'You know that your being here is enough to have you beheaded. And you certainly were not a prisoner; you were found with the leader of the Ais Maraxa.'

Mishani had feared this. If she had been able to meet him at Lalyara, then his suspicions would not have been aroused; but circumstances had forced her into a position in which any play she made would seem like bargaining for her life.

'You are correct,' she said. 'I was brought here against my will, but they did not keep me as a prisoner. I am something of a heroine to their cause because I helped to save your daughter. It does not mean I endorse it.'

'Stop these *lies!*' Zahn cried suddenly, grabbing the pattern-board and tipping the cradle. It hit the floor and smashed into coloured shards. 'Lucia tu Erinima died five years ago and more. Her father was Durun tu Batik. I do not know what leverage you think you have over me, Mistress Mishani, but you are sorely misguided if you believe you will win your freedom by trying to resurrect a ghost.'

Mishani's triumph did not show on her face, but she knew she had the advantage now. A man such as Zahn did not abandon his dignity easily; his skills at negotiation had kept Blood Ikati a major player in the courts, and his display of rage showed how sensitive the subject of Lucia was to him.

'You could have me executed,' Mishani said, her voice cold. 'But then you will only learn that I was telling the truth when the Weavers kill your daughter. Could you live with that, Zahn? You have not been living with it well these past years.'

'Heart's blood, you do not know when to stop!' Zahn cried. 'I will not hear any more of this!'

He was heading for the curtained doorway when Mishani spoke again.

'Zaelis tu Unterlyn was there on the day you met your daughter,' she snapped, her voice rising. 'It was he who organised the kidnapping of Lucia. On the very day that Blood Batik overthrew Blood Erinima, we stole the child and hid her. No corpse was ever found because there *was* no corpse, Zahn! Lucia is alive!'

Zahn's shoulders were hunched, his hand on the curtain. She had not wanted to bring the leader of the Libera Dramach's name into this, but matters were too critical. She could not let him leave.

He turned back to her, and his face was suddenly haggard again.

'You *know* you believe me,' she said. A sudden rush of light-headedness took her, but she fought against it. It was stiflingly hot; she did not know how much longer she could go without sitting down.

'I cannot believe you,' Zahn croaked. 'Do you understand?' He knew how clever Mishani could be, he knew the ways of the court, and though he wanted more than anything to think that Lucia could be alive, he would not be manipulated. He was no friend to Blood Koli, and he had no reason to trust one of them. He would not lose his daughter again, by allowing himself to think he might regain her and then to discover it was a bluff. He could not go through that. He had been numb so long that it had become a shield against the world, and when it came to the moment, he found that he was afraid to discard it.

He turned to go again. This kind of torment could not be borne.

'Wait,' Mishani said. 'I can prove it.'

Zahn had almost dreaded to hear those words.

'How?' he said, his head bowed.

'Xejen will be interrogated,' she said. 'You must attend.'

'What good will that do?'

'He knows where she is, as I do. Sooner or later, we will talk. The Weaver will try to keep it secret; he will try to obtain the information for his kind alone. He will scour Xejen's mind and then decide what to tell you. You must not let him. *Make* him share what he learns *as he learns it*. Have him make Xejen speak only the truth, and ask Xejen yourself. The Weaver cannot refuse you if you order him.'

Zahn was silent, his back to her. Mishani knew that this was a desperate play, but it was all she had. The lives of thousands depended on her. If she was unable to prevent the Weavers finding the Fold, then at least with Zahn on her side she might be able to get them a warning in time to do something about it. It was a slim chance, but better than none at all.

'You will learn the truth at the same time as you condemn her to death,' Mishani said. 'But if I cannot persuade you to stop this, then that must be the price we all pay. If you will not believe what your heart knows, then you will hear your daughter's name on the lips of a Weaver.'

'Pray that I do,' Zahn replied. 'For if not, I will be back, and I will have you killed.'

'I pray that you do not,' Mishani said. 'For I would give my life in exchange for all those who will die to convince you.'

Xejen tu Imotu thought that his story was over when the ceiling came down on him, but he regained consciousness to find that there was an epilogue, and it was full of agony.

He woke on a bed in the donjon of the keep, and woke screaming. The pain from his shattered legs propelled him out of oblivion, an idiot, senseless roar of breathtaking brutality. His trousers had been cut away above the knee. His legs were massive and blue-purple, obese with swelling and the terrible bruising of drastic trauma. Both of them kinked unnaturally in several places. No attempt had been made to set them, and the snapped ends of bone made bulges against the blotched skin.

He screamed again, and screamed until his throat was raw. At some point, he blacked out.

When he awoke again, it was to a new horror.

He felt himself pulled into awareness, his mind hooked like a fish and dragged out of the protective cocoon where it sheltered from the inconceivable pain. His eyes flickered open. Afternoon light misted in through the dusty air from a barred window high on one wall, scattering across his ruined legs and the bare stone cell. Figures surrounded him, but one leaned closer than the others. A Mask of angles, sharp cheeks and jutting ridges of chin and forehead, some of gold and some of silver and others of bronze; a mountainous metal landscape, crafted by a master Edgefather, surrounding the dark, black pits of the eyes.

A Weaver.

He sucked in a breath to shriek, but a pale, withered hand passed over him, and his throat locked.

'Be silent,' hissed the voice behind the Mask.

There were two others here. He recognised the Baraks: Zahn, tall and rangy and gaunt; Moshito, stocky and bald and grim-faced. They looked down on him pitilessly.

'You are Xejen tu Imoto?' Moshito asked. Xejen nodded mutely, his eyes tearing. 'Leader of the Ais Maraxa?' He nodded again.

Zahn shifted his gaze to the Weaver. This one was in the employ of Blood Vinaxis, a particularly vicious and sadistic monster if Moshito's accounts were to be believed. His name was Fahrekh. Zahn's own Weaver he had left back at his estates at the disposal of his family; he detested Weavers, especially since he suspected that the last Weave-lord, Vyrrch, had been responsible for the coup in which Lucia had disappeared.

He caught himself. Already he was amending his beliefs to suit Mishani. In which Lucia had *died*, he forced himself to think. Blood Koli was an enemy, Mishani was an enemy, and however they might have learned of his weakness, he would not let her exploit it.

But gods, what if she *was* telling the truth? If Xejen talked, then neither the Weavers nor the Emperor would rest until Lucia was hunted down. Was there any way to stop this? Was there?

He bit down on his lip. Idiocy. Foolishness.

Lucia was dead.

'Are you sure he will do as you told him?' Zahn asked Moshito, motioning at the bent and hooded figure crouching over the bed.

'I have heard my Barak's command,' Fahrekh said, with a curl of disdain in his voice. 'Nothing will be hidden. You will ask him your questions. I will ensure he answers and speaks true.'

Xejen's eyes roved from one to the other in alarm.

'It is as he says, Zahn,' Moshito replied. 'What's got you so suspicious?'

'Weavers always make me suspicious,' Zahn replied, trying to keep the uncertainty and indecision out of his voice. Yet he wondered whether the Weaver might not simply scour Xejen's mind in secret and take what he wanted, and whether there was any way they could tell. Heart's blood, how had it fallen this way: that the only method he had to prove Mishani right would also put that same knowledge in the hands of those who would desire Lucia's death?

It came down to a matter of faith. Could he believe Mishani? Could he believe his daughter was alive? Once, perhaps. But his faith had died along with the other parts of his soul, and he had to know. Belief was not enough. He had to *know*.

'Begin,' said Moshito.

Fahrekh turned his gleaming face slowly toward the broken figure on the bed, the afternoon light skipping from plane to plane in triangles of brightness.

'Yes, my Barak,' he muttered.

As the Weaver bored into his thoughts and will like a weevil into the bole of a tree, Xejen found his throat free to scream again. Fahrekh found that he worked better when his victims were responsive.

Twenty-Eight

The science of predicting the orbits of the three moons was ancient. Though moonstorms came at apparently random intervals, over hundreds of years it was possible to see a pattern of unwavering regularity. Astronomers could now tell almost exactly when the three moons would be in close enough proximity to spark a moonstorm. Navigators relied heavily on their ability to plot the course of the moons so that they could assess what effect each would have on the world's tides. Though it was only the learned who knew just when a moonstorm would hit, usually rumours carried far enough among the peasantry to make almost everyone aware of it.

None of which was any help to Kaiku and Tsata, who were out in the open when the moonstorm struck.

There had been developments since the night when they had narrowly escaped the ghaureg, and all thoughts of turning back for home had been cast aside. Though they had previously abandoned any hope of catching or killing one of the Nexuses, they had resolved to observe the flood plain and see if any more information could be gained about the foul, seething building that crouched near the banks of the Zan. They kept themselves at a distance, where the sentries were sparse enough to avoid. Getting close to the plain was impossible now, for it was too well guarded.

Kaiku's determination to stay was rewarded sooner than she thought. The very next night, the barges began to arrive.

She had theorised that the river must have been the method for getting all these Aberrants here in the first place, and that they must be transporting food from the north which they had stockpiled in the strange building for their army of predators. Kaiku and Tsata had witnessed several mass feedings, in which great piles of meat were brought out on carts driven by the same docile midget-folk that had served the Weavers at the monastery on Fo. She called them *golneri*, meaning 'small people' in a Saramyrrhic mode usually applied to children. She should have expected that they would be here: the

Weavers were notoriously incapable of looking after themselves, afflicted as they were by a gradually increasing insanity as a result of using their Masks.

Still, for all that, they had never seen any evidence of river travel until now; but when the barges arrived, it was in a multitude.

They had appeared during the day, so when Kaiku and Tsata breached the barrier that night they found them already waiting. They crowded the banks of the river on either side, a clutter of more than three dozen massive craft along the edge of the flood plain. For two nights a steady stream of carts went back and forth in the moonlight and the golneri swarmed to unload great bales and boxes. Suddenly the Weavers' apparently random barge-buying enterprises over the last five years made sense: they had been moving the Aberrant predators along the rivers, gathering them together, assembling their forces. Kaiku wondered what kind of influence the Weavers had over the barge-masters that walked the decks, to trust them with the knowledge of this secret army. It had to be something more than money.

On the third night, the boarding began.

The initial shock at finding the flood plain half-empty when they arrived just after dusk was quickly surmounted by what was happening on the river. The Aberrants were being herded up wide gangplanks into the holds of the fat-bellied barges, a steady stream of muscle and tooth parading meekly onto the cargo decks under the watchful eyes of the Nexuses. There were so many barges that they could not all berth along the bank at once, and they queued northward to receive their allocation of the monstrosities, and headed upstream when they were done. It seemed that the barrier of misdirection did not cover the river; but then, nobody came this far down the Zan anyway, for the great falls were just to the south and no river traffic could pass that. Kaiku and Tsata watched in amazement at the sheer scale of the logistical maneouvring.

'They are on the move,' Tsata said, his pale green eyes shining in the moonlight.

'But where are they moving to?' Kaiku asked herself.

As dawn broke, and the last of the barges departed, Kaiku and Tsata retreated beyond the barrier to rest; but sleep would not come easily that day, and they spent their time restlessly chewing over the implications, and whether they should risk warning Cailin via the Weave. This was what they had remained behind for: to raise the alarm if the Weavers should make a move towards the Fold. But the barges were not heading that way. They were going towards Axekami, and from there they could travel to any point along the Jabaza, the Kerryn or the Rahn.

Tsata pointed out that it was possible they could re-enter the Xarana Fault via the latter river. The Fold was only a dozen miles or so to the west of the Rahn. But Kaiku did not dare to send word unless it was absolutely necessary, and they did not know enough of where those barges were going.

Eventually, they agreed that they would stay two more nights. If no other information had come to light by then, they would head east for a day to get as far from the Weavers as they might, and Kaiku would send her message. What perils that would bring, she had no idea. Perhaps the Weavers would not notice her at all, and Cailin's edict against distance communication was simply her being overcautious. Or perhaps it would be like a waterfowl trying to sneak through a roomful of foxes.

The next night brought the moonstorm.

It was because they had been out of contact with the world for so long, existing in their own little society of two, that they did not expect it. They had crossed the Zan and were watching from a bluff on the western side, where the sentries were much fewer. There, the high ground reached like fingers towards the edge of the river, cutting off suddenly in sheer cliffs as it came to the water. Wide open-ended valleys lay between the cliffs, nuzzling gently against the banks. Kaiku and Tsata had hidden themselves in a brake of blighted undergrowth that fringed a tall promontory, and were lying on their bellies watching the inactivity below through Nomoru's spyglass. She had reluctantly consented to leave it with them in amid sullen threats as to what would happen if they did not bring it back intact.

The moons had risen from different horizons – Aurus in the north, Iridima in the west, and Neryn from the south-west – so that there was no warning until they had almost converged, directly overhead.

Kaiku felt the sharpening in the air first, the strange plucking sensation as if they were being gently lifted. She looked at Tsata, and the golden-skinned man with his green tattoos looked corpselike and unearthly in the moonlight. The rustling of the tough bushes in which they sheltered seemed a rasping whisper. Her senses tautened, picking up a sensation of unseen movement like rats in the walls of a house.

She looked up, and felt a thrill of alarm as she saw the three orbs, all half-shadowed at a diagonal angle across their faces, crowding towards each other in the sky. Clouds were boiling out of nowhere, churning and writhing under the influence of the muddled gravities.

'Spirits,' she muttered, glaring down at the plain. 'We need to get to shelter.'

★

They barely made it.

The moonstorm began with a calamitous shriek just as they found the shelter they were searching for. It was a deep and wide shelf in a hulking accretion of limestone, with a broad overhang for a ceiling, as if some enormous beast had taken a bite out of the smooth side of the rock. The bottom sloped up towards the top so that it narrowed as it went further in, but even at the back there was enough space for Kaiku and Tsata to huddle under, he cross-legged, she with her arms around her knees.

The rain followed that first unearthly cry, coming down all at once, and suddenly the previously quiet night was a wet roar of pummelling rain, bowing the gnarled stalks of the blighted foliage and spattering furiously against unyielding stone. Kaiku and Tsata found that they were quite dry in their little haven. Though the lip of the shelf became quickly soaked, they were well clear of the storm's reach.

Tsata broke out some cold smoked meat and split it with Kaiku, as he always did, and for a time they sat in silence, watching the rain and listening to the saw and scrape of the sky tearing itself to pieces. The desolate scene flickered purple in the backwash of the eerie lightning that attended the phenomenon.

Kaiku felt uneasy. Moonstorms had always frightened her, even as a child; but events in her past had rendered them heavy with bad memories. Her family had died in a moonstorm, poisoned by her own father to save them from what the Weavers would do to them. And both that moonstorm and the subsequent one had seen her fleeing for her life from the shin-shin, the demons of shadow that the Weavers had sent to claim first her and then Lucia.

There was concern in Tsata's eyes as he regarded her.

'It will be brief,' he said reassuringly. 'The moons are only passing each other; they have not matched orbits.'

Kaiku brushed her hair away from where it hung across one side of her face and nodded. She felt a little awkward as the recipient of his sympathy. Why had she told him about her family, anyway? Why had she talked of her past to him? It was strange, that one as guarded as she was should have done so: and yet, somehow, to speak of such things with him did not seem as hard as it did with anyone else. With anyone Saramyr.

Kaiku had lost track of the time that had passed since she had left the Fold. A month? Had it been that long? The beginning of Aestival Week and her betrayal by Asara in the guise of Saran seemed distant memories now; she had been too busy to dwell on it. The land was beginning to feel autumnal, the mugginess of summer dispersed by cooler breezes even if the heat of the daytime had not diminished by much. The food they had brought with them had been eaten long ago, so they hunted animals outside the Weavers' barrier when they were not sleeping, or gathered roots and plants to make stews. There was a kind of cleanness to the way they had been living since Nomoru and Yugi had departed. The diet was rough and had far too much red meat in it for Kaiku's liking, but she felt oddly close to the land, and that made her happy.

By night, they braved the Aberrant sentries, and Kaiku was becoming very good at the lessons Tsata taught her. He no longer had to worry about keeping an eye on her when they were sneaking through the rucks and pleats of broken land. Rather, he had begun to rely on her, making her more of a partner and less of a pupil. She had become stealthy and adept at hiding, more observant and competent than she had been a few short weeks ago. And in those weeks they had come to know one another very well, in a way that they never had on the confinement of the ship from Okhamba to Saramyr.

Kaiku had disliked him for a long time after he had risked her life as bait for the maghkriin back in the jungles of his home continent; but now she understood him better, and it made perfect sense through his eyes. She knew it was probably a transient thing, like her friendships with the travellers who had accompanied them on the junk the first time she had crossed the ocean; but for the moment, she felt closer to him than anyone she could remember in recent years. The constant companionship, the weeks of doing everything as a pair, reminded her of the relationship she had shared with her brother Machim, back in a time before she had ever known true loss.

But for all that, there were still barriers; it was just that they were in different places to the usual ones. She had surprised herself by telling him about her family, yet he had never spoken of his own. She knew why well enough: because she had not asked. He would not refuse her if she wanted to talk about him – Okhambans, she had learned, were notoriously co-operative – but it was that very knowledge that prevented her. She felt that by asking him she might be forcing him to speak of something he did not want to, and that he would be bound by his nature to suffer that for her. She still did not wholly comprehend his mentality, and was wary of being as rude to him as he unwittingly was to her at times.

Perhaps it was the strange, faintly unreal atmosphere of the moon-storm, or the sudden feeling that she had been cheated out of her secrets while he still kept his, but she decided then to risk it.

'Why are you here, Tsata?' she asked. Then, once the first step was taken, she said with more conviction: 'Why did you come to Saramyr? Gods, Tsata, I have been with you practically every moment for weeks now and I still know nothing about you. Your people seem to share everything; why not this?'

Tsata was laughing by the time she had finished. 'You are truly an amazing people, your kind,' he said. 'I have been tormenting you all this time and you have resisted your curiosity so.' He smiled. 'I was interested to see how long you would hold out.'

Kaiku blushed.

'Forgive me,' he said. 'You are so obsessed with manners and formality that you have not dared ask me about any information I did not volunteer first. With all you have learned about me and the Tkiurathi, have you not guessed the value of openness yet?'

'It is *because* you are so open that I did not want to ask you about things you had not mentioned,' she replied, feeling embarrassed and relieved at the same time.

He laughed again. 'I had not expected that. I suppose it makes a kind of sense.' He gave her a wry glance. 'It seems that I am not as familiar with your ways yet as I thought.'

The skies screamed overhead, and a jagged shaft of vermilion lightning split the distant horizon, making Kaiku cringe unconsciously.

'Saran was the same,' Tsata said. 'He never asked me my motives, was content in ignorance. He believed that it was my business, I suppose, and not his.'

'Hers,' Kaiku corrected bitterly. Kaiku had told him about Asara, though not about how she had almost coupled with her. Tsata had not been in the least taken aback by the deception, or by the idea of an Aberrant that could take on other forms and other genders. There were frogs in Okhamba that could change sex, he had told her, and insects that could rebuild their bodies in cocoons. She was not without precedent in nature, only in humanity.

Tsata became thoughtful for a moment. 'The answer to your question is simple,' he said at length. 'Saran told me of his – or her – mission, and of the danger the Weavers posed to Saramyr. He also spoke of what he believed might happen if they won this continent. They would invade others.'

Kaiku nodded at that: it ran concurrent with what she had already guessed.

'I went with him to the heart of Okhamba to see if his theories bore weight. I returned convinced.' He rubbed absently at his bare upper arm, fingers tracing the green swirls of the tattoo that covered him. 'I have a responsibility to the greater *pash*, that of all my people. So I determined to come to Saramyr and see the threat for myself, to observe what your people's reaction would be and to carry the news back home if I could. I will need to tell my people as Saran told yours. That is why I came here, and that is why I will have to leave.'

Kaiku felt abruptly saddened. It was no more than she had expected, but she was surprised at her own reaction. Their time in this isolated existence was limited, and his words were a reminder that it would have to end soon. The return to the real world, with all its attendant complications, was inevitable.

'That is what I had surmised,' Kaiku said, her voice not much louder than the hiss of the rain. 'It seems I am learning to predict you also.'

Tsata gave her an odd look. 'Perhaps you are,' he mused. He looked out over the bleak, rain-lashed landscape for a short time, listening to the horrible racket of the moonstorm.

Kaiku stiffened suddenly. She scrambled to the edge of the rock shelf and looked about.

'Did you hear something?' he asked, appearing next to her in a crouch.

'The barrier is down,' she said.

Tsata did not understand her for a moment.

'*The barrier is down!*' she said, more urgently. 'The shield of misdirection. It is gone. I can sense its absence.'

'We should get back to the flood plain,' Tsata said.

Kaiku nodded, her expression grim. The barrier had come down. The Weavers were not hiding any more.

She dreaded to think what that might mean.

Cailin tu Moritat's eyes flicked open, and her irises were red as blood.

'Kaiku,' she breathed, aghast.

There were two other Sisters in the conference chamber with her. It was one of the upper rooms of the house of the Red Order, its walls painted black and hung with pennants and symbols of crimson. They had been sitting on mats around the table in the centre of the room, talking softly over the maelstrom that howled and battered at the shutters like some hungry and thwarted beast. The glow of the lanterns and the sinuous path of the scented smoke from the brazier that sat between them had taken on a malevolent quality under the warping influence of the moonstorm, and their identically painted faces seemed narrow and shrewd with conspiracy.

The other two looked at Cailin. They did not need to see her red eyes to know that something had happened; they had felt it stroking past them, a whisper in the Weave that could only have been one of their own.

Cailin stood up suddenly, rising to her full height.

'Gather our Sisters,' she said. 'I want every one of us that resides in the Fold to be here in this house in an hour's time.'

She left the room before the others could rise to obey, stalking away and down the stairs, out onto the muddy, makeshift streets. It was barely midnight. Zaelis would still be awake. Not that she would have hesitated to rouse him anyway; this was far too important.

She passed along the deserted ways of the Fold, a tall and thin shadow slipping through the rain, seeming to slide *between* the droplets, for as heavy as the downpour was it only dampened her slightly. She was furious and afraid all at once, and her thoughts were dark as she went.

Kaiku. Gods, how could she be so reckless? Cailin did not know whether to applaud her or curse her. She had been in an almost constant state of worry since Yugi and Nomoru had returned with news of the Aberrant army massed on the banks of the Zan, and of Kaiku's refusal to return. If Kaiku had been captured during that time, the Weavers would have flensed her mind and gleaned everything they would need to know about the Red Order. Now, Kaiku had used the Weave to send a message more than a hundred miles, spooling a thread across all that distance. It only took one Weaver to sense it, to catch that thread and piggyback to its destination or track it to its source, and all the Red Order's years of secrecy would be undone. Bad enough that the Weavers knew there was *one* Aberrant woman who could beat them at their own game – the previous Weave-lord Vyrrch had warned them of that just before she killed him – but one was only a freak occurrence, a lone misfire of nature like Asara was. Two of them communicating hinted at much greater things, at collaboration, at organisation. If the Weavers caught even the slightest indication of the Red Order's existence, they would dedicate all their efforts to wiping them out.

The Red Order were the single biggest threat to the Weavers, maybe even greater than Lucia herself, because against them the Weavers did not have the superiority afforded them by their Masks. The Red Order could Weave too, but their power was inherent and natural to them, and that made them better at it than men, who needed clumsy devices to penetrate the realm beyond the senses.

But the Sisters were few, too few. And Cailin dared not expose them unless it was absolutely necessary.

Now, perhaps, that time had come. For as angry as she was with Kaiku for taking such a risk, Cailin was equally disturbed by the message. Matters had taken a very grave turn. Action was needed, and soon; but it might not be in the way that Zaelis imagined. Cailin's overwhelming priority was the survival of the Red Order. Beyond that, very little mattered.

Though the journey between her house and Zaelis's was a short one, the rain had stopped and the skies quieted by the time she got there. The moons were gliding apart again, and the raging clouds now drifted listlessly, thinning and dispersing. The storm had been quick and savage, and its ending was as abrupt as its beginning.

The dwelling that Zaelis shared with his adopted daughter Lucia was an unremarkable one, nestling on one of the Fold's upper tiers amid several other houses that had been built to the same design. It was a simple, two-storey building of polished wood and plaster, with a balcony on the eastern side to look out over the valley, and a small shrine by its door with carved icons of Ocha and Isisya surrounded by burnt incense sticks and crushed flowers and smooth white pebbles. A single paper lantern burned outside, illuminating from within the pictograms of welcome and blessing it offered to visitors. Next to it hung a chime, which Cailin struck with the small hammer that hung alongside it.

Zaelis was at the door almost immediately, inviting her inside. It was a humble room, with a few mats and tables, potted plants nodding drowsily on stands, some ornamental weapons on the wall and an oil-paint landscape from a Fold artist whose work Zaelis seemed to admire, though the appeal had always escaped Cailin. A single lamp hung from the ceiling, putting the epicentre of illumination overhead and casting flattering shadows on everyone within. Lucia sat cross-legged on a mat in her nightgown, drinking a herbal infusion from a ceramic mug. She looked up as Cailin came in, her eyes blandly curious.

'She couldn't sleep,' Zaelis explained. He noted absently that Cailin's twin ponytails should have been dripping with water, the raven feathers of her ruff lank with moisture, her make-up smudged; yet none of these things were true. 'The moonstorm.'

Cailin did not have time for niceties. 'Kaiku has contacted me across the Weave,' she said. Zaelis's face fell at her tone. Lucia, unperturbed, continued to regard the Sister over the rim of her mug, as if she was merely relating something that the girl had known all along.

'Is it bad?'

'It is very bad,' she replied. 'The Aberrants are most certainly under the Weavers' control, through the medium of those beings that Yugi reported, which she calls Nexuses. Several nights ago most of them departed northward by barge up the Zan, but thousands were still left. Now all but a few of those have departed as well. The Weavers have dropped their barrier, and the Aberrants are on the move.'

'Where?' Zaelis demanded.

'East. Across the Fault. Towards us.'

Zaelis felt a pit open in the bottom of his stomach. 'How long?'

'They travel fast,' Cailin said. 'Very fast. She estimates we have four days and nights before they are upon us.'

'Four days and nights . . .' Zaelis repeated. He looked dazed. 'Heart's blood.'

'I have matters to attend to in the wake of this news,' Cailin said. 'I imagine you do too. I will return in a few hours.' She gave Lucia a peremptory tilt of her head. 'I doubt any of us will sleep tonight.'

With that, she was gone as fast as she had come, walking back towards the house of the Red Order, where she would prepare for the arrival of her brethren. Around her, the first gently glittering flakes of starfall had begun, tiny crystals of fused ice drifting down in the green-tinted light of the triple moons. It would fall sporadically for the next day or so. She ignored it, for her mind was on other things. She did indeed have matters to attend to, and a decision that might well be the most important she ever had to make.

The Fold had been compromised, and the Weavers were coming. She knew as well as Zaelis that four days and nights was not enough time to try and evacuate the population of the Fold across the hostile Fault, and even if he did, they would be caught on the run and killed. Where would they go? What would they do? He would not abandon all he had worked for, all his weapons and supplies and fortifications; nor would he abandon the townsfolk. He would be forced to make a stand here, at least until an alternative could be made feasible.

Her choice was simple. Zaelis and the Libera Dramach were bound to this place, but she was not. Should the Red Order stand with them against the Weavers, or should they leave them to their fate?

Yugi arrived at Zaelis's house shortly afterward. Lucia had dressed, and returned to her spot on the mat. She should have been asleep by now, but she did not appear to be tired in the slightest.

Zaelis had been too preoccupied to disapprove. His mind was full of dark musings in the wake of Cailin's news. He was thinking of Weavers, and gods, and Alskain Mar. Did the Libera Dramach even stand a chance, if what the spirit had shown Lucia was true? If this was indeed some conflict of the gods, what hope did they have of resisting the tides? Were they like some cork bobbing on a stormy ocean, powerless to act, merely staying afloat? He had a depressing sense that his life's work had been merely an illusion, an old man's folly, creating a resistance that could not, in the end, resist anything. He blamed Cailin, bitterly, for bringing them to this: for holding them back, for advising secrecy when action was needed. And now, finally, their cover had been somehow torn away, and they were exposed. They were not strong enough to fight the Weavers head-on, Zaelis knew that. Yet the alternative was to give up, and that he could never do.

He realised immediately that Yugi had been smoking amaxa root. It was in the sheen of his eyes and his dilated pupils, and the pungent smell still clung to his clothes.

'Gods, Yugi, I need you clearheaded!' he snapped in lieu of a greeting.

'Then you should have called for me in the morning,' Yugi retorted cheerily. 'As it is, I'm here. So what do you want?' He saw Lucia and gave her a little bow. Lucia returned it amiably with a dip of her head.

Zaelis sighed. 'Come inside and sit down,' he said. 'Lucia, would you brew something strong for Yugi?'

'Yes, Father,' she replied, and obediently went to the kitchen.

Zaelis sat opposite Yugi on the floor mat and studied him, gauging how far gone he was and whether he would take in anything that was said. Yugi's recreational use of amaxa root had always been a source of worry, but he had been doing it ever since Zaelis first knew him, and despite the dangers it had never bloomed into addiction. Yugi seemed to possess an unusual resistance to its withdrawal symptoms, and he insisted that he was able to take it or leave it as he chose. Zaelis had been sceptical for a long time, but he had been forced to accept after a while that Yugi was right. He was able to go without for weeks and months at a stretch, and it had never affected his reliability. He said that he used it to 'cope with the bad nights'. Zaelis was unsure what this meant, and Yugi would never talk about it.

It was simply an unfortunate moment that Zaelis had caught him at, and despite his annoyance he could not expect Yugi to be ready for action every moment of every day. Eventually, Zaelis decided that he was only mildly intoxicated, and that he would still be sharp-witted enough to understand what was being said to him. He had become adept at judging his friend's state over the years. And so he began to explain to Yugi what had occurred.

Shortly afterward, Lucia came back with a brew of lathamri, a bitter black infusion that promoted awareness and stimulated the body. She paused at the threshold of the room, looking at the two men sitting locked in conversation. Her father, white-bearded and rangy beneath his robe, his swept-back hair seeming thinner than she remembered and the lines of his face etched a little deeper. Yugi, scruffy as ever in a shirt and trousers and boots, with the omnipresent rag tied around his forehead, penning the unruly spikes of his brown-blond hair. She was assailed suddenly by a terrible sense of the gravity of the situation, that these two men were discussing life and death for hundreds or even thousands of people, and it was all down to her.

They are coming for me, she thought. *Everyone that dies here will die because of me.*

Then Yugi noticed her, and smiled, and ushered her over. He took the mug from her with a grateful nod and then said to Zaelis: 'She should hear this. It concerns her.'

Zaelis grunted and motioned for her to sit down.

'We need to get you to a safe place, Lucia,' he said, his voice a rumble in the back of his throat. 'There's no way we can get the people out of the Fault in any number at short notice, and they would be too many to hide. But a few, a dozen or so . . . an escort . . . we could send you north-east. To Tchamaska. There are Libera Dramach there who can hide you.'

Lucia barely reacted. 'And you will stay here and fight,' she said.

Zaelis looked pained. 'I have to,' he said. 'The Libera Dramach practically built this place. After we took it over all that time ago . . . well, the stockpiles alone are worth defending. If we can hold off this attack, we can buy time to move them out, to start again.' He laid his hand on her arm. 'People came here because *we* drew them here, even the ones who aren't a part of the organisation. I'm responsible.'

'You're responsible for me too,' Lucia said. Yugi looked at her in surprise. He had never heard Lucia use such an accusatory mode with her father.

Zaelis was plainly hurt. He drew his hand back from her. 'That's why I'm sending you out of harm's way,' he said. 'It will only be for a short time. I will come and find you afterward.'

'No,' said Lucia, quite firmly. 'I will stay.'

'You can't stay,' Zaelis told her.

'Why not? Because I might be killed?' She leaned forward, and her voice was a furious hiss that shocked him. 'You'll abandon me, but you won't abandon them! Well, neither will I! All these people, all my friends and my friend's families, all of them are going to die here! Because the Weavers want *me*! Most of them will never even know why. And you want me to leave them, to go and hide again until the Weavers hunt me down and *more* people die?' She was shouting now. '*I'm* responsible for these people as much as you are. You made me responsible when you promised them a saviour from the Weavers. You tied all their lives to me and you never once asked me if I *wanted* that!'

Her last words rang into silence. In all her life, they had never heard her raise her voice in anger. The force of it, coming after fourteen years of placid calm, stunned them.

'I will not go,' she said, her voice dropping again but losing none of its steel. 'I will stay here and live or die with you, and with the people to whom you bound me.'

Yugi looked from Lucia to Zaelis and back again. Suddenly, she no longer looked like a child, and he caught a glimpse of her mother's fire in her glare. Zaelis was dumbstruck. Finally, he swallowed, and he dropped his eyes from the fierce and unfamiliar girl who had taken the place of his daughter.

'So be it,' he said, his mode formal and distant. 'Do as you will.'

Yugi felt the moment become excruciating, even softened as it was by the pleasant fuzz of the amaxa root.

'Remember that army of Aberrants coming our way?' he said with forced flippancy. 'If anybody's interested, I have a plan.'

Asara sat with her arms around one knee and the other leg tucked beneath her, and watched the starfall drifting down over Lake Sazazu. The grass was sodden, and the moisture soaked through her clothes to dampen her skin. The water still rocked with the memory of the storm, flashing fitful arcs of moonlight from shore to distant shore. Night-birds swooped back and forth, plucking at fish that were attracted to the surface to nibble at the tiny ice-flakes, thinking them to be food of some kind. The sensation of unreality was fading now, returning the world to normal.

Alone, she gazed out over the lake, deep in thought.

Reki slumbered back in the shelter they had made. He was so exhausted he had slept through the chaos. The thought brought a twitch of a smile. Poor boy. His grief and misery had destroyed him, but she still found herself with a strange affection for the bookish young Heir-Barak. Where she would have been disgusted at the weakness of someone else for wallowing so in their agony, for him she made an exception. It was, after all, her fault.

The last few days had been curious. She had expected pursuit, but Mos's men were either criminally inept or were not searching for them at all, and she found that very odd. It worried her more than if they had been hot on Reki's trail. Surely they knew what he carried, and what it meant for the Empire? And yet Asara had stayed effortlessly ahead of the game. Such good fortune was frankly suspicious.

Reki had not taken the news of his sister's death at all well, and they had been forced to rest a while here, for he was in no state to go on. His lamentations would draw attention to them. Even when he was silent, he bore such a shattering sorrow in his eyes that people would remember him. In retrospect, Asara thought that she should probably have kept Laranya's suicide quiet until they were in a safer place; but what was done, was done. He would have felt betrayed if she had kept it from him any longer, and she wanted him smitten.

She left him to sleep, to heal himself of tragedy. Asara had watched many dramas like this over the course of her long life, and they bored her in the main; but she was curious to see how Reki would fare under this test of his mettle. Though he was as easy to manipulate as any man, he had innocence and inexperience as his excuse, and she found those qualities appealing enough so that she did not have to entirely fake her interest in him.

But she herself could not sleep. She was thinking of an argument, weeks ago, and of Kaiku.

After her deception had been revealed, after she had fled from Kaiku in shame, she had gone to Cailin. It was ever her way: to run from what hurt her, to change herself and hide again. Cailin would provide her with an excuse to leave, something that she could tell herself was the *real* reason she was going, and not Kaiku at all.

But somehow it had descended into an argument. Cailin was just that little bit too haughty, taking her for granted, *telling* her that she had to go to the Imperial Keep.

'I am not your servant, Cailin!' Asara had spat, whirling around the black-and-red conference chamber of the house of the Red Order. 'You would do well to remember that.'

'Spare me these half-hearted attempts at independence,' the Sister had replied coldly. 'You know you can leave at any time. But you will not leave, will you? Because I can grant what you desire most in the world.'

Asara had glared at her furiously. 'We had a deal. I did not agree to be your subordinate!'

'Then we are equals, if you prefer,' Cailin said. 'It changes nothing. You will do as I ask, or you may break the deal. But until then, you will help me get what I want. And then, I will give you what *you* want.'

'*Can* you?' Asara had accused. 'Can you do it?'

'You know I can, Asara, and you know I will. You have my promise.'

'And you have *my* promise,' she returned savagely, 'that if you trick me I will be avenged. You would not want me as an enemy, Cailin.'

'Stop these threats!' Cailin had snapped. 'The deal stands. It requires a certain measure of trust on both our parts, but you knew that from the beginning.'

Trust. Asara could have laughed. Trust was an overrated commodity. But Cailin knew what it was that Asara longed for, what she would risk almost anything to get. And so Asara worked for the Red Order, partly because they had the same goals, mostly because it was the only way she could imagine her wish might be granted.

An end to the loneliness, to the emptiness, to the void inside her. It was almost too precious to imagine.

Twenty-Nine

The sun was setting on the Xarana Fault, igniting the western horizon in clouded bands of red and silver and purple. In the golden light of the day's end, Yugi and Nomoru crouched on a bluff overlooking a land riven with ghylls and canyons, from which flat-topped plateaux, rocky hills and buttes thrust upward unevenly.

Below them, hidden within the creases of the Fault, men and women were dying. The sounds of gunfire and occasional detonations echoed into the calm sky. Wisps of smoke seeped like fumes from the cracks. Fleeting glimpses of movement caught their eyes from time to time: swiftly retreating figures, pursued by dark and terrible shapes. At several points over the last few hours, the battle had spilled up out of the shadow and into the open, skirmishes across hillsides or areas of scrubland. Yugi did not recognise half of the factions that he saw, but he was sure they were not Libera Dramach or folk of the Fold.

'Getting close,' Nomoru said, her tone suggesting that she did not care one way or the other about it.

'We're not slowing them by much,' Yugi observed distractedly.

'What did you expect?'

Yugi shrugged at that. He did not want to deal with Nomoru's surly pessimism now. He had more pressing concerns.

Kaiku's estimation of the Aberrant army's speed had been accurate. Three days had passed since the night of the moonstorm, and their rate of advance had been steady and rapid. A force of thousands were swarming through the Fault at roughly twice the speed that Yugi and his band of three companions had traversed it in the other direction. In a place like the Fault, that was a recklessness verging on insanity. He wondered if their strength of numbers had been enough to overcome the dangers that they would have faced: the clan armies, the canyons bristling with traps and deadfalls, the swamps that belched poison miasma, the haunted places. For a force so big, there was no safe route. How many had they lost? And would it matter, in the end?

The Libera Dramach scouts – Nomoru included – had brought back

296

scattered reports, but the army were simply moving too fast. They learned most of what they knew from other friendly clans, driven before the invaders, and the intelligence they had gleaned had come too recently to really do anything about it. The army had smashed through any settlements that had got in their way, overwhelming them in a tide and then ploughing onward. The clans and factions in or near the path of the Aberrants were in turmoil. Some were fleeing eastward, towards the Fold; word had been spread that it would be a last stronghold against the enemy, and it would welcome any clans who would unite with them there. A frankly dangerous gamble, to invite any of the other people of the Fault inside their fortifications, but Yugi knew that Zaelis had no other choice now.

Other communities – the vengeful remnants of those that the army had passed through, or simply those who recognised the threat – were harrying the flanks and tail of the horde. The Xarana Fault was made for hit-and-run manoeuvres, and these people had lived there the better part of their lives and knew every trick. But the Aberrants ignored the attacks nibbling at their fringes, forging onward unstoppably towards the Fold with no consideration for casualties.

Yugi's mood was dark. How did they know? How did they find out where Lucia was? He cursed the Weavers and their ungodly methods. Heart's blood, it could only have been a matter of time, but why *now*? In a few more years Lucia would have been of an age to take the throne, and they could have begun to gather real armies to support her, could have come out of hiding and challenged Mos and the Weavers.

He caught himself, remembering her shocking tirade on the night of the moonstorm. They had so long been used to Lucia being dreamy and passive, like a veil drifting on the winds, that they had not considered what she wanted at all. They had assumed that she would have objected by now if she had any objections to make. Her detachment went so deep that they had ceased to think that opinions were something that applied to her. Yugi felt a solemn guilt at how they had taken her for granted. Whatever else she was, she was also a fourteen-harvest girl, with all the associated complications, and her patience and tolerance were not endless.

He dared not think what it might mean if she developed a stubborn streak like Kaiku had. So much relied on her.

A particularly loud explosion, near at hand, brought his mind back to the present. Nomoru rubbed a hand through her thatch of hair and scowled.

'You're cutting it fine,' she warned.

'Let's go,' he said.

They headed away from the bluff, down a narrow slope bulwarked on either side by root-split walls of earth. There was a man there at the bottom, tensed to run, looking at them expectantly.

'They're coming!' he called. 'Be ready!'

The man sketched a salute and fled, scrambling up another slope that looped off to their right. Yugi and Nomoru carried on down without pause, their rifles clattering against their backs. They passed two more runners on the way, despatching them to their respective destinations with orders. Yugi found himself thinking how much easier, how much faster this might be if they had the women of the Red Order as relays; but Cailin had refused to commit them to the advance forces, insisting that the element of surprise was vital in their deployment. She would keep them at the Fold. Privately, Yugi wondered if she would deploy them at all.

They sprinted out into the open, running low, and the wall to their left fell away to spit them out onto a colossal shelf overlooking a barren, dead-end canyon. Sheer walls of sandy rock, banded with the striations of countless epochs, plunged down hundreds of feet to a dusty floor of churned earth. Birds rode the thermals below them in the slowly reddening light. Yugi felt a vertiginous moment at the sudden exposure to the chasm; the hot wind of the failing day blustered around him. Then they were hunkering down amid dozens of riflemen who hid behind a heap of stone further along the shelf, and he was grateful that the drop was hidden from sight.

'Any activity down there?' he asked.

'Nothing,' said a scarred young man named Kihu, whom Yugi had left in charge. 'Can't expect it yet though. Sun's still out.'

'No, you're right,' Yugi mused. 'You, you, and you,' he picked out two men and a middle-aged woman, all Libera Dramach. 'Stay here and watch; I want to know if anything moves in this canyon before we get back. Everyone else, into position. They're on their way.'

His orders were obeyed immediately and without question. It was what they had been waiting for. With a grim eagerness, they broke cover and headed further along the enormous rock shelf. It slanted down for some way, finally joining a greater outthrust mass that jutted out away from the cliffs they had been hugging to their right.

The vista broadened dramatically. The canyon they had been watching over was only one branch of a fork, the southernmost arm of a great junction. To the west, there was a breathtaking trench that crooked out of sight amid a clutter of buttes. East, the trench continued on, narrowing slightly. Yugi and the riflemen were running along the divider between the southern canyon and the eastern one, a steadily tapering promontory that collapsed at its tip into a series of ledges fringed with tough bushes and wretched trees.

As they ran, Yugi caught sight of one of the runners signalling across the canyon, catching the last rays of Nuki's eye with a hand-mirror. A moment later, flashes returned in acknowledgement from concealed positions along the opposite ridge. The junction was crawling on all sides with Libera Dramach, hidden among the broken landscape.

Yugi felt a surge of fierce pride. Nothing had stopped the relentless onslaught of the Aberrants so far, but then nobody had been given a chance to prepare until now. He remembered how he had doubted the wisdom of Kaiku's decision to stay with the army. Now he had cause to be thankful for it. It was only because of the risk Kaiku took that they had been given enough warning to organise. The Weavers had charged heedlessly through the Fault, oblivious to their casualties; but Yugi planned to give them pause for thought here.

'Gristle-crows!' someone called, and Yugi looked up to see the first of the huge black Aberrant birds soaring overhead. They scrambled down the sloping tip of the divider, concealing themselves among the ledges and the dry foliage that clung there. Nomoru slid down next to him in a billow of dust, her exquisite rifle clenched in her thin hands, and the two of them crouched together amidst a brake of bushes. The walls of the eastern and western canyon were not so high as the southern arm, and the floor rose up too, so that they were perhaps seventy feet above it by the time they had dug in. They waited motionless, listening to the harsh caws of the gristle-crows as they circled, scouting ahead of the main mass of Aberrants that were pouring towards them.

'Is this going to work?' Nomoru whispered.

'If it doesn't, at least there'll be nobody left alive to tell how we failed,' he replied.

Nomoru cackled quietly and primed her rifle. She motioned up at the birds with her eyes. 'Want me to bring them down?'

Yugi shook his head. 'You've got your targets. Until then, you don't fire a shot.'

He settled himself, watching the mouth of the western canyon, from which the Aberrants would come. The enemy army had spread out somewhat but the Fault bottlenecked here, several routes converging into this one canyon, and it would be driving a good portion of the Aberrants this way. The alternative was to clamber up to the open high ground, but Yugi was sure they would not take that route. The reckless speed of the army meant only one thing: they wanted to surprise the Fold, so that the Libera Dramach would not have a chance to spirit Lucia away. Equally, that was why they went along the Xarana Fault rather than travelling the smooth plains on its outskirts. They would not expose themselves if they could help it, either to their intended victims or to the world at large.

Yugi wondered suddenly why they were using such a bludgeoning force instead of sending assassins, or Weavers, to quietly pick off the dispossessed Heir-Empress. Perhaps, he thought, they simply did not have time. He thought of the *other* army, that had departed northward in barges. The Weavers' eyes were elsewhere, it seemed. They had matters even more important than Lucia to attend to.

The sun had almost disappeared, and the last of the red was fading from the sky, when the first sounds of the army were heard. The gristle-crows had departed now, as Yugi had expected. Kaiku had informed them about the various types of Aberrants she had encountered, and what strengths and weaknesses she had been able to learn. Gristle-crows never flew at night; she guessed that their vision in the dark was very poor.

The steadily growing noise prompted a trickle of dread in Yugi's chest. It was a distant cacophony to begin with, but it swelled with alarming speed, a clash of gibbering and yammering, of bellows and snarls, becoming an overwhelming blanket of chaos and madness. Gunfire from the Libera Dramach and other clanfolk that were picking at their sides provided sporadic punctuation.

Yugi gripped the stock of his rifle tight, and felt the first inklings of real doubt. It was like waiting at the breakwater for a tsunami.

The horde came thundering into sight, turning into the western canyon, and he paled as he saw them spread like oil to flow between the buttes and around the rocks, a fluid mass of corruption that took his breath away. He was not prey to the prejudice against Aberrants that all Saramyr had been brought up with – indeed, it was almost possible to forget that such a thing existed in the liberal world of the Fold – but he was unable to suppress his disgust and fear at the sight of the monstrosities that now came towards him. Nature twisted out of true, a collision of species and traits, changes accelerated by the Weavers' blight and making a mockery of Enyu's plan.

How can these things and Kaiku be the same? he asked himself.

They were travelling at a pace akin to a jog, a speed at which they were tireless and could travel day and night with very little rest. There was no organisation in their formation, and yet somehow they managed not to trample each other as they went. Massive ghauregs towered over galloping, boarlike furies, lumbering along as the smaller Aberrants pushed past them and clamoured onward. Spidery-limbed skrendel scuttled at the fringes, monkeylike things with long fingers that kept out of the way of the larger beasts by leaping nimbly up the sides of buttes, where they hissed at each other. Shrillings slid between their clumsy allies with sinuous grace. In amongst them were others, too hard to identify at such a distance, shrieking and growling as they plunged down the canyon.

'Gods,' murmured Nomoru. 'If they get to the Fold, we're all dead.'

'So many dogs, but who's got the leash?' Yugi said, peering through the bushes. 'Where are the Nexuses? Where are the Weavers?'

The army poured out of the western canyon, into the junction where their route forked. There was no indecision: they headed east. The gristle-crows' advance reconnaissance had already determined that the southern fork was a dead end, and they communicated that knowledge to the Nexuses by the strange link they shared through the nexus-worms. Yugi and the other riflemen who hid amid the ledges at the tip of the promontory hardly dared to breathe as the horde swept by beneath them and to their right, the rumble of thousands of feet, paws and claws shaking the earth.

'There they are,' whispered Nomoru, more to herself than to Yugi. She was gazing down the canyon with a calm and intense focus, and he followed her eyes to where the first of the Nexuses had come into view.

They were some way back, hidden amidst the mass, riding on beasts that looked like manxthwa except that they were hairless, and much faster. The sight of a Nexus, even so far away, brought a dreadful nausea to Yugi's gut. They were too much like Weavers in their cloaks and their blank masks. As another came into view, he noticed that they were surrounded by a retinue of ghauregs that never strayed far from them, shielding the Nexuses with their massive bodies.

'They're protecting the Nexuses,' Yugi said, raising his voice over the din of the Aberrants passing them by. 'Can you do it?'

Nomoru gave him a disparaging look, but if she had been about to offer some snide reply, she missed her chance. At that moment, the air was shattered by a tremendous explosion, making the ground shudder violently. Yugi and Nomoru ducked instinctively as a scatter of pebbles and loose earth sloughed down on them from the ledge above.

The detonation was incredible, echoing the breadth of the Fault, destroying enormous sections of rock in a billowing cloud of dust that blasted up and down the canyon and plumed high into the sky. The Libera Dramach had placed explosives all along both sides of the eastern canyon, just beyond the junction. The initial concussion rained stones and rocks and boulders on the front line of the Aberrant army, bringing them stumbling to a sudden halt as they were battered by falling debris. But that was only the start, for a moment later came the grinding roar of collapsing rock, a monolithic rumbling that pounded the ears, and the canyon sides came down.

The Aberrants squealed and howled and stamped each other

underfoot as they dissolved in confusion, but it was too late to avoid the avalanche of stone that slumped upon them. It smashed into their disordered ranks with unstoppable force, pulverising bone and rending bodies, crushing them to mangled dolls or ripping them limb from limb. Those who were not caught directly beneath the incomprehensible weight of rock were driven into it by the ranks behind, and the life squeezed from them. The dust that filled the canyon reduced visibility to almost nothing, only a yellow and stinging world filled with animal shrieks. Still the Aberrants pushed onwards, swept up in their own tide, unwittingly propelling more of their kind into the rock barrier where they bent and snapped like twigs.

Yugi raised his head and gave Nomoru a grin. 'Now let's show them what kind of fight they have on their hands,' he said.

The riflemen opened fire.

There were almost a hundred of them positioned all around the junction, high above the invaders. Though the seething dust stung their eyes and made it impossible to see down to the canyon floor, the Aberrants were packed so closely that it was harder to miss than to hit. They shot indiscriminately, pulling back the sliding bolt on their weapons after each report, pausing only when their ignition powder burnt out or when they needed to reload. A murderous and inescapable crossfire turned the air into a hail of rifle balls, shredding the Aberrants that were caught within it. It punched through chitinous armour and ripped through skin and fur and flesh, fountaining blood in its wake. The canyon resounded with the agonised cries of the beasts as they flailed under the assault, seeking enemies and finding none.

Yugi, closer to the ground than the men and women on the canyon rims, was firing with the rest of them. Kihu and the other riflemen who were hidden among the ledges kept up an uneven staccato of weapon reports above and below. Occasionally, one of the agile skrendel rose out of the dusty murk, trying to climb the sides of the canyon to escape the bloodbath, but Yugi had two men down there whose job was to shoot them if they tried, and they never got close to the Libera Dramach position.

Amid all of that, Nomoru was as still as a statue, her hand around the barrel of her black-lacquered rifle, tracing the silver intaglio there. The dust was steadily clearing, blown down the canyon by the evening breeze as the land cooled. The writhing, panicked shapes of the Aberrants were becoming visible again, dim shadows in the faint glow of the recently departed sun. The sky overhead was a deep blue, so dark that it was almost black now.

'They're turning!' someone cried. 'They're turning!'

It was true. The Aberrants, desperate to escape the killing zone and realising that their way east was blocked, had begun to flood down into the southern canyon. Yugi felt a surge of bitter triumph, wondering whether the Nexuses had lost control of their troops or if they themselves had instigated it. Either way, the result would be the same.

'Hold this position!' Yugi cried. They were beginning to run out of ammunition and ignition powder now, but he did not want them to let up yet. Not until Nomoru had her chance.

As if responding to his thought, she lifted her rifle to her shoulder, sighting through the bushes. The dust was settling, and the scene on the canyon floor was unveiling itself to the eyes of the ambushers. The ground was littered with shattered bodies, but it was barely possible to see them beneath the stampede of grotesqueries that trampled them.

Yet even as they saw the disorder they had sown, they noticed the Aberrants beginning to slow. The rifle fire from overhead was petering out now as guns overheated and powder punches emptied. The panic seemed to be diminishing with uncanny speed, decelerating the head-long rush into the southern canyon.

'Nomoru,' Yugi warned, realising now that he had an answer to his own question. 'They're getting control back.'

Nomoru ignored him. She had her eye to the sight, her body poised with a grace entirely at odds with her appearance or her character.

Down in the canyon, the Nexuses were gathered together, surrounded by their bodyguard of ghauregs. No expression could be seen behind their masks, but Yugi could almost feel their intent, their *will*, dominating the animals that they commanded.

She fired; the ball missed the shoulder of a ghaureg by an inch and hit one of the Nexuses in the face, smashing the blank white mask inward in a bloody spidercrack. The Nexus lurched, swayed and fell from its saddle.

The reaction among the Aberrants was immediate. A small section of them flew into a rage, different breeds attacking one another, and the hysteria spread swiftly. The riflemen concentrated their assault on the surrounding beasts.

Nomoru fired again. Another Nexus was pitched backward and fell from his mount.

Then someone from one of the canyon rims tipped an explosive package down into the fray, a bomb on a sizzling fuse, and when it went off pandemonium ensued. The stalled rush of the Aberrants became a charge down the only exit left to them: the southern canyon. Nomoru, unperturbed, took down a third Nexus. The ghaureg body-guards were in disarray now. Two of them were tearing apart one of the Nexuses' mounts. Chaos spread as the Nexuses' guiding minds

303

winked out like candles. The other Nexuses were retreating, forging back through the crush as best they could. As the last of the light drained from the sky, Nomoru put up her rifle and said: 'Out of range now.'

Yugi clapped her on the shoulder in congratulation. She scowled at him.

'Time to go,' he said. 'It's not over yet.'

Accompanied by the rest of the riflemen in their group, they climbed back up to the top of the promontory and retraced their steps as swiftly as they could, heading along the lofty ledge that overlooked the southern canyon. Gunfire was still pocking the air behind them, sharp raps resonating emptily. As they got higher, they could see the vista across the Fault had turned a secretive blue-black in the twilight, and that the edge of Aurus was just rising in the north. It was cooling fast by the time they reached a vantage point and crouched at the lip of the ledge.

Below them, the Aberrants had swarmed in, and the vanguard had almost reached the end of the canyon and were slowing hard, realising that there was nowhere for them to go. But with no guiding force behind them they had no way to communicate to the hundreds who were coming after, and those that slowed were forced underfoot by the ones who had not yet seen the danger. The Aberrants piled up against the end of the canyon, the broken bodies of their kind forming a brake like earth before a plough. Still more crammed in behind them, seeking to escape the gunfire at the junction. Finally, when the immutability of their situation became apparent, they slowed and stopped, having packed the canyon with the dead and living.

The remaining explosives detonated at that point.

The Aberrants howled in fear as the mouth of the canyon collapsed, tons of rock hammering down, forming a wall with crushed corpses as its mortar. Sealing off their only escape, trapping hundreds of them there.

There was a pregnant pause, an expectancy that even the twisted animals felt. They prowled and paced, snapping at each other, clawing at the unyielding rock. Snarling struggles broke out. The rifles had fallen silent across the Fault.

It was difficult for those above to see in the fading light, but some of them had spyglasses, and they looked down and waited.

Whether the ghaureg was the first one to go or merely the first one they noticed, nobody could be sure. But as they watched, suddenly and without warning, the enormous beast disappeared into the earth.

The Aberrants were milling uneasily now, sensing that something was amiss here. Another one, this time a furie, was swallowed up by the ground. It had time to let out a distressed squeal and then it was gone.

'Gods,' murmured Kihu, who was hunkered next to Yugi. 'This is going to be a slaughter.'

And then it was happening all over the canyon. Aberrants were disappearing, simply dropping into the earth as if the ground beneath their feet were suddenly gone. At first it was one at a time, and then several began to vanish at once, and moments later there were dozens being sucked under. The animals began to panic afresh, rearing and shrieking and roaring, attacking each other in their confusion. The skrendel, by far the most intelligent of the predator species, were trying to climb the canyon walls; but while they could get themselves off the deadly ground that way, the stone was too smooth for them to escape the trap. The canyon was emptying fast, as living and dead alike were swallowed by the churned earth of the canyon floor.

Those with spyglasses began to see the swift wakes of things speeding just below the surface, shallow humps that arrowed towards their targets. Even in the darkness, it was possible to spot the insidious swatches of blood that soaked upward from the earth, the ground too glutted to hold it all in. The Aberrants ran and scuttled on soil made damp with the fluids of their own kind, attempting a hopeless evasion as the things that hunted them swarmed about in a multitude. The skrendel were snatched from the walls by sudden profusions of thin tendrils that burst from the ground and enwrapped them, pulling them under in the blink of an eye, like a chameleon's tongue picking off a fly.

By the time true dark had fallen, and Aurus was some way into her ascent, the canyon was quiet again. The only sign that the Aberrants had ever been there was the glistening of the moonlight on the canyon floor, where the blood of the dead creatures gradually soaked back into the earth.

Yugi let out a low whistle. There had been stories told about this place ever since he had arrived in the Fault, and several people who had not listened to those stories had provided more concrete proof of their veracity by dying here. But he had never imagined the sheer voraciousness of the *liha-kiri* – the burrowing demons.

A woman came racing down from further up the ledge to stand before them. 'They're heading back, Yugi,' she said breathlessly. 'They're retreating.'

There was a cheer from those assembled, and Yugi was pounded by companionable slaps on his shoulder and back. He grinned roguishly.

'They'll not be in quite such a hurry to get to the Fold now,' he said. 'Well done, all of you.'

He would allow them a few moments of self-congratulation before he would urge them to withdraw. They deserved that much, at least. They had struck the Weaver army a terrible blow today, but the Weavers would not be so reckless a second time. Despite the hundreds they had killed, they had not done more than dent the enemy's numbers. The Weavers, whatever else they were, were not tacticians, and they had fallen into a trap that any experienced general would have avoided; but their insanity also made them unpredictable, and that was dangerous.

He caught Nomoru's eye, the only person not celebrating, and knew that she was thinking the same as he was. They had won a small respite, but the real battle would be at the Fold. And it might very well be a battle they could not win.

Thirty

Nuki's eye had risen and set since the massacre of the Aberrants, and Iridima held court in the cloudy sky far to the west of the Fold. Kaiku and Tsata stood on the western bank of the Zan in the moon-shade of a thicket of tumisi trees that had somehow resisted the blight emanating from the nearby witchstone. The warm night was silent, but for a cool autumn breeze that stirred the leaves restlessly.

Across the river sat the bizarre building that dominated the flood plain, the strange grublike hump of banded metal that they had wondered about for weeks now. It seethed a foul-smelling, oily miasma, and it groaned and squeaked with the rotation of the massive spiked wheels that turned slowly at its sides. Smaller constructions were clustered around it, as indeterminate of purpose as the central edifice. Slats of metal in their sides sometimes lit up brightly from within, accompanied by a bellow as of the sudden roar of a furnace; chains would unexpectedly clank into life, rattling along enormous pulleys and cogs that strung like sinews between the buildings; mechanisms would jitter fitfully and then fall silent. From this side, it was possible to see the mouths of the twin pipes that ran underground the short distance to the riverbank, half-submerged grilles peeping over the gently flowing surface of the Zan.

Kaiku watched the building closely, her eyes hard. She hated it. Hated its incomprehensibility, hated its alienness, its unnatural noise and its stench. It was like the blight made manifest, a thing of corruption that belched poison. And more, she hated it because it was keeping her here while her friends and her home were in desperate peril back in the Fold, and even though she could not be with them, would never have got there in time, it clawed at her heart that she had not at least tried.

But it seemed as if that gods-cursed Okhamban way of thinking had rubbed off on her in the time she had spent with Tsata, that curious selflessness of surrendering themselves to the common need over personal desires. On that night under the moonstorm when the barrier had gone down, when they had watched the predator horde swarming away from the flood plain and heading east towards the Fold, she had wanted nothing more than to go after them. No matter that they moved far too fast to catch up with, and that she would be only one among thousands even if she *could* get to the Fold in time. The old Kaiku would have gone anyway, because that was her nature.

But she had not gone. She knew what Tsata was thinking, and she was surprised to find that she was thinking the same. The flood plains were all but empty now, only a skeleton guard remaining to supervise the Weavers' base here in the Fault. And they were the only ones in a position to take advantage of such an oversight.

The only ones who could get to the witchstone.

Tsata did not even need to talk her round. A chance like this might never come again. Whatever the outcome of the battle to the east, they owed it to their companions to make use of the opportunity that had unwittingly been provided. They were going into the Weavers' mine.

'There,' muttered Kaiku, as a deep growl came from within the bowels of the building. There were a series of loud clanks, and a moment later the pipes in the riverbank spewed forth a torrent of brackish water, blasting the hinged upper and lower halves of the grilles open. The torrent continued for several minutes, carrying with it chunks of rock and organic debris and other things impossible to identify in the moonlight, depositing it all for the Zan to sweep away southward towards the falls. Finally, the roar of the water subsided to a trickle, and the grilles swung closed, no longer forced apart by the pressure. There were a few more heavy thumps from within the brooding building, and then the only noise was the steady rush of the river.

Kaiku and Tsata emerged from the thicket and crawled through the long grass to the water's edge. The banks of the Zan were not as barren as the surrounding high ground, being provided with a plentiful supply of fresh water, and the foliage was welcome cover. The two of them went on their knees and elbows to where a log lay some distance upstream, a warped thing that corkscrewed midway along its length. They had rolled it there the previous night in readiness. The tree had been weak enough to topple when they wrapped rope around its top and pulled it down. After that they had been able to tear the branches off by hand, and fashion a very good float with which to cross the river.

They watched the flood plain for some time. There were shapes there in the dark, perhaps a hundred spread over the whole expanse. Some were wandering idly, but most were asleep. The patrols, what few there were now, were largely on the eastern side of the river; the intruders had little fear of the occasional sentry they had encountered on the western side. The cliffs rose behind the plain, a frowning black wall. Kaiku remembered when they had first lain on that edge and looked down at the enormous army the Aberrants had assembled, terrified of the sheer power that had been gathered here. Now the plain seemed so deserted that it was almost ghostly.

Once satisfied that nothing was paying attention to the river, they waited for Iridima to hide her face behind a cloud. Kaiku was thankful that they had not had to delay any longer than this for the right conditions in which to attempt their infiltration of the mine; the inactivity, combined with her fears for her friends, had frayed her nerves. But the season was with them: though the weather throughout the year in Saramyr did not vary all that much, due to its position close to the equator of the planet, autumn and spring were generally cloudier and rainier than winter or summer. The habit of dividing the year into seasons was something they had brought with them from temperate Quraal and never really shaken off.

A feathery blanket of cloud slid across the face of the moon. Kaiku and Tsata glanced at each other once for confirmation and then rolled the log quietly into the river and dropped in after it.

The water was surprisingly warm, heated over and over by the sun during the many hundreds of miles it had run from the freezing depths of the Tchamil Mountains. Kaiku felt its sodden embrace swamp through her clothes and over her skin. She gauged the tug of the current. The river was sluggish here, gathering itself before the rush towards the falls to the south. She got the log under her armpits and waited for Tsata to do the same; then, when they were balanced, they kicked out into the river.

The crossing was completed in silence and darkness, with only the plangent lap of the water against the log as they glided towards the eastern bank. They had struck out at an angle upstream, trusting the current to carry them down to where the hulking carapace of the mine brooded sullenly. Their estimation was good, and their luck held, for Iridima stayed hidden and the night remained impenetrable. They bumped against the far side a few dozen feet from the mouths of the pipes, and there they grabbed hold of the bars of the grille and let the log drift away. It was too dangerous to tether their float here; it might be seen when the sun rose.

The weeks they had spent observing the flood plain had borne fruit in the end. Though Kaiku had been frustrated by their inability to get close to a Nexus or the mysterious Weaver building, they had gleaned much about the comings and goings that went on here, and made many theoretical plans. But the one that had obsessed Kaiku the most involved the rhythmic evacuation of water through those pipes. She was unable to gauge exactly how long it was between each deluge, for she had no means accurate enough, but both she and Tsata agreed that it was more or less regular, and that there were several hours at least separating one from the next. The water was coming from somewhere, she reasoned. As long as they timed their entry right, they would be able to crawl up one of the pipes and investigate. Presumably the grilles were there to stop debris or animals from the river getting in; and that meant that there would be somewhere for them to get *to*.

It was only now that she looked into the mouth of one of the pipes, sheltered from the sight of the plain by the rise of the riverbank, that the reality of her plan hit home. Once in there, she would be trammelled, hemmed in by the cold sides of the pipe, with nowhere to go but forward or back. She felt a fluttering panic in her belly.

Tsata put his hand on her wet shoulder and squeezed, sensing her hesitation. She looked back at him, his tattooed face almost invisible in the dark. She could feel the determination in his gaze and took a little of that for her own.

Between them, they pulled down the lower half of the grille. There was some kind of spring mechanism on it to help it close against the push of the river, but it was weak and rusted from lack of maintenance. Kaiku went first, taking a breath and ducking under the upper grille to emerge on the other side, looking back through the bars at Tsata with her hair plastered across one side of her face. The pipe was big enough to stand in if she hunched over; the river water came up to her waist. Tsata followed her through, letting the grille close behind him after checking that there was no apparent locking mechanism.

'If it comes to that,' Kaiku said, reading his thoughts, 'I'll blow them apart.'

Tsata knew what she implied. It had been enough of a risk to send the warning to Cailin; even though the Weavers had not caught her, they might well be more alert now if they had detected it. To use her *kana* in here would be a virtual death sentence; but for all that, she would use it if she had to. She was merely making that clear to him, and to herself. Whatever Cailin advised, her power was her own, to use as she would.

Tsata found himself smiling. If ever she took the robes of the Red Order, Cailin would have a fight on her hands to keep this one in line.

They made their way into the pipe, the gentle splashes as they forged the water aside echoing amid the sussurance. Other sounds came to them, distant grindings and irregular clumps and scrapes, made eerie by reverberation. Darkness closed about, utter blackness, with only the faint slitted circle of the pipe mouth providing any kind of touchstone to their location. Once they had gone inward for some way, they stopped. Tsata began unwrapping the candle that he had tied in a waterproof bag on his belt.

'Wait,' Kaiku whispered.

'You need the light,' he said. He did not need to point out that he did not, at least not yet. He had vision like an owl's, an inheritance from the purestrain Okhambans that had bred with the refugees from Quraal all that time ago and produced the Tkiurathi.

'Wait,' she said again. 'Give me time.'

Her eyes were adjusting to the darkness fast enough that she could actually see shapes appearing out of the blackness: the blank curve the pipe, the shifting contours of the water.

'I can see,' she said.

'Are you sure?' Tsata asked, surprise in his voice.

'Of course I am sure,' she said, amused. 'Put the candle away.'

He did so, and they went onward. They had guessed that the pipe would not be very long, since the buildings they fed from were set close to the riverbank, and Kaiku found it was not so much of a trial as she had expected. The claustrophobia of her situation did not bother her as she had thought it might, as long as she did not dwell on the possibility of all those tons of water smashing into them. But she was confident enough in the unwavering regularity of the evacuation, and confident enough in herself that she was not plagued with her usual doubts and fears.

With a faint hint of wonder, she realised how much she had grown since Aestival Week: since she had been tricked by Asara and out-matched demons in the Weave; since she had healed a dying friend by instinct alone and spent weeks living on her wits, killing Aberrants, relying only on herself and this foreigner with his barely comprehensible ways. She was fundamentally the same as she always had been, but her attitude had changed, matured, bringing with it a self-assuredness that she never knew she had.

She found that she liked herself that way.

Presently, the sporadic clanks and groans became louder, enveloping them, and chinks of what seemed like firelight began to appear in the pipe, minute rust-fractures hinting at what lay beyond. Then, as they rounded a bend so slight that they had barely noticed it, they came in sight of the end.

Kaiku blinked at the brightness. The pipe appeared to widen as it neared its termination, joining with the second pipe that ran alongside it to make one huge oblong corridor. Its floor sloped upward so that it was above the level of the river water that they had been wading through. Beyond it she could only see what looked like a wall of dull, bronze-coloured metal.

She glanced at Tsata. He murmured something in Okhamban, his eyes on what lay ahead.

'What does that mean?' she whispered.

Tsata seemed faintly taken aback that she had heard him. He had not meant to say it aloud. 'It is like you might say a prayer for protection,' he replied.

'But you have no gods in Okhamba,' Kaiku said. 'And you do not believe in your ancestors living on in anything but memory.'

'It is addressed to the *pash*,' he said. For the first time, she saw him embarrassed. 'I was asking for your protection, and offering you mine. It is merely a custom.'

Kaiku wiped the sodden hair back from her face. 'And how am I supposed to respond?'

'*Hthre*,' he said. Kaiku repeated it, unsure of her pronunciation. 'It means you accept the pledge and offer your own.'

She smiled. '*Hthre*,' she said, with more conviction this time.

He looked away from her. 'It is merely a custom,' he repeated.

They crept out of the water and along the widening pipe. After so long in night and darkness, the warm, fiery glow at the end made them feel uneasy. Their progress was wary, hugging the walls as they flattened out, their fingers running over rusting panels fused together by some craft that neither Kaiku nor Tsata knew. As they neared the light, they saw that it was not a wall at the end but a steep slope, like a chute, which they were at the bottom of. They peeked out of the end of the pipe, but there was nobody there. Above them, they could see only darkness, and around them were the walls of the chute that fed into the pipe where they emerged. The source of the glow was similarly obscured.

But there was a ladder, made of metal, fixed against one side of the chute.

Kaiku climbed. There was nothing else to do, and no other, more subtle way up. Tsata remained at the bottom, his hide clothes dripping and forming a puddle around his shoes. She wished suddenly that there had been some way to waterproof her rifle and bring it along. It would have comforted her, even if she knew it would be little help in the event that they were discovered.

She reached the top of the ladder, and her stomach fell away as she saw the true immensity of the Weavers' mine.

The humped roof of the building was not, as she had expected, the ceiling of some kind of dwelling; rather, it was the cap of a colossal shaft that plunged down into abyssal depths. The shaft was not a straight drop; the blackness at its bottom was obscured by stone bulges where the sides narrowed and jags of rock that projected into the centre. Vast ledges scarred it, and pillars rose up like blunt needles, made small by comparison to their surroundings.

The chute that Kaiku had clambered out of was set on the edge of a great semicircular sill. Its lower lip continued up above her to an enormous dump-tank which sat upright in a cradle of curled iron. A pair of spiked wheels rotated slowly behind it, huge cogs dragging up scoops affixed to rattling chains which tipped water into the dump-tank and then headed monotonously downward again to collect more.

Kaiku, peripherally aware that the immediate vicinity appeared to be deserted, clambered out of the chute and stood there gawking, awed by the sheer size and strangeness of the place.

The illumination that she had seen from the bottom of the chute was provided by metal torches and pillars which burned with flame; but it was not like any normal flame, being more similar to combusting vapour. They billowed clouds of smoky fire that trailed upward and then dissipated, turning to noisome black fumes which floated away to collect at the top of the shaft. She realised that the darkness above her was not through lack of light, but that it was a churning pall of smoke which slowly vented itself into the clean air outside through pores in the cap.

The multitude of ledges and pillars were linked with a network of precarious walkways, rope bridges and stairways that hung like spiderwebs across the shaft. Walls were scabbed with props and joists of wood and metal, delineating pathways for mine carts to travel, and caves opened all over the shaft, glowing from within. Paternosters groaned and steamed in the depths, furnaces blazing at their heart as they rotated in idiot procession. Iron cranes jabbed out into nowhere, still carrying loads, abandoned. Thin waterfalls plunged endlessly, issuing from cave mouths to fall into nothingness, or to strike a rock ledge further down in a mist of spray before running off and down again. Kaiku saw small, ramshackle wooden huts clustered together, sometimes built on the tip of a pillar and linked only by a single bridge to the rest of the mine. It was hot in the shaft, and reeked; there was an unpleasant tinny taste that caught at the back of the throat.

Kaiku stared in wonder and terror at the thing the Weavers had created. She had never seen so much metal in her life, nor seen it wrought in such quantity. What kind of forges must the Weavers have? What had been going on for over two hundred years in the heart of their monasteries where the Edgefathers crafted their Masks? What kind of art had created those strange torches, or those hissing and steaming contraptions that moved without anything apparent to power them?

She felt a touch on her upper arm and jumped, but it was only Tsata.

'We are too exposed,' he said, his eyes flickering over the scene with a glint in them that might have been disgust, might have been anger.

She was glad to tear herself away from it.

They retreated along the sill to the sides of the shaft, where the enfolding darkness lurked. The huge metal torches were only sparsely placed about the mine, and though the area they illuminated was much greater than a normal torch or lantern would be, it still left areas of deep shadow. From here, Kaiku and Tsata carried out a more thorough observation of their surroundings, looking for movement. There was none. The shaft appeared to be deserted.

'Your eyes,' Tsata said after a time, motioning at her.

Kaiku frowned, making a querying noise.

'They have changed. Your irises have more red in them than before.'

She gave him a puzzled look. 'Before?'

'Before we entered the pipe.'

Kaiku thought on that for a moment, remembering the surprise in Tsata's voice when she had refused the illumination he had offered.

'How dark was it in there?' she asked.

'Too dark for you to see,' he replied.

Kaiku felt a thrill of unease. Had she . . . *adapted* herself? Had she been using her *kana* without even knowing it, the tiniest increase in her senses to compensate for her lack of vision? She did not even know how she would go about doing that, but her subconscious certainly seemed to. Just like with Yugi, cleaning him of the raku-shai's poison. The more she used her *kana*, the more it seemed to use her, making her a conduit rather than a mistress. Was that what it was like for all the Sisters? She would have to discuss it with Cailin when she returned.

If there was anything left to return to.

She strangled that thought as soon as it arrived. There was no time for doubts now. The Aberrant horde would almost be upon the Fold, and there was nothing in the world she could do about it. She could only hope that her warning had given them enough time to prepare or to get away from there.

They headed along the sill and onto a walkway that hugged the sides of the shaft, curving round to the entrance of a tunnel. The walkway was made of iron, supported by joists driven into the rock and hanging over an unfathomable drop. Kaiku did not want to touch the railing with her bare skin. Railings in Saramyr were made of carved wood, or occasionally polished stone; never a metal like this, rusting and flaking in the updrafts of steam, spotted with brown decay.

It was a relief when they came to the end of the walkway. Stone she could trust.

The tunnel led inward and down, and they took it warily. It was scattered with debris – rocks and pebbles, mouldering bits of food and broken hafts and chips of wood – but it was as empty as the rest of the place appeared to be, and there was little evidence here of any actual mining being done. The walls were uneven and ancient.

'This is natural,' Tsata said quietly, with a short indicative sweep of his hand. 'Like the shaft. There is no artificial framework here, nor any shoring up of the sides. What they have built, they have built on top of what was already there.'

'Then they did not mine all of this out?' Kaiku asked. Her clothes had dried in the heat now, and rubbed her uncomfortably.

'No,' he agreed. 'This place had stood for a long time before the Weavers came to it and built their devices.'

Kaiku found some comfort in that. Initially she had been stunned by the thought that the Weavers could have carved out something so massive in only a few years. Tsata's observation made the Weavers seem a fraction more mortal.

But still, as they descended, and the tunnel branched and led them through chambers that were makeshift kitchens and storerooms piled with food in barrels and sacks, they found the place eerily, utterly deserted.

'Do you think they have gone?' Kaiku whispered. 'All of them?'

'What about the small men?' Tsata asked. 'Would they have left?'

The small men: it took Kaiku a moment to realise that Tsata was talking about the diminutive servants of the Weavers. He had taken the name she had given them – golneri – and mistranslated it with the incorrect gender. His Saramyrrhic was excellent, but he was not beyond making mistakes now and then. It was not his mother tongue, after all.

The golneri. That was another mystery, to go with the Nexuses, the Edgefathers and the imprisoned, intelligent Aberrants that she had witnessed in the monastery on Fo. Heart's blood, this was all connected somehow. For so long, the Weavers had been such a dreadful and inextricable part of the people of Saramyr, and yet so little was known about them. How many more surprises had they been keeping in the depths of their monasteries these past centuries, stewing in their own black insanity while they hatched their plots?

What had the people of Saramyr allowed to happen, right under their noses?

Kaiku shook her head, as much to dismiss the enormity of her own question as to reply to Tsata's. 'The golneri will still be here.' A thought struck her. 'I think it is so empty because the Weavers did not expect the army to have to leave,' she said. 'That would explain the stockpiled food also. Most of the army went north, and the rest remained to guard this place. But the Weavers here found out about the Fold somehow, after the main mass had left. Whatever the barges are doing is too important to turn back from; instead, the Weavers sent all that they had left here to the Fold. There are still enough Aberrants outside to deter casual attackers, and remember: nobody knows this place is here. The Weavers believe it is an acceptable risk. The second army will be gone for two weeks at the most – time to get to the Fold, decimate it, and come back – and when it returns the barrier will be up again and this place will be impregnable once more.'

'Kaiku, they may not take the Fold,' Tsata muttered. 'Do not give up yet.'

'I am simply guessing what they are thinking,' Kaiku told him, but there was a tightness to her voice that told him he had struck a nerve. She closed herself off to the visions of what might be happening even now in her adopted home.

'Their forces are stretched,' Tsata said. 'That gives us hope. If they had to leave themselves all but defenceless to get at Lucia, then they must have their attention elsewhere, on something more important.'

Kaiku nodded grimly. It was small comfort. She could venture a guess where those barges were headed: to Axekami, to the aid of Mos's troops. The Weavers were going to use Aberrants to secure Mos's throne, and to keep themselves in power throughout the oncoming famine. Shock troops that would make men's hearts quail and their knees buckle just before they were ripped to pieces. A show of force to bring the nobles and peasantry of Axekami back into line.

The Weavers were making their move in the game for control of Saramyr, and Kaiku could not imagine anything that could stand against them. The coup that had been brewing ever since Mos had allowed the Weavers to hold rank and land like one of the high families was destined to fail. Gods, it was as if everything had been set up just to make it harder for the Libera Dramach. If the Weavers consolidated themselves around the throne they would become immovable.

Kaiku found herself becoming angry. If only Cailin had not been so cursedly paranoid, keeping the Red Order reined and secret, not allowing them to challenge the Weavers. Because of that, the Weavers had spread unchecked, and the secrets they held remained secret, so that nobody could plan against them.

Cailin. So in love with her precious organisation, like Zaelis was with his. So afraid to endanger herself, to fight for her cause. She would not commit the Red Order against the Weavers; she was selfish, like Zaelis was, like *everyone* was, hoarding her power, biding her time, waiting until it was too late. Why had she held back so long? Why had a woman so shrewd, so commanding, allowed matters to get so out of hand?

Kaiku caught herself. Where was all this coming from?

But the answer had presented itself almost as soon as she posed the question. She *suspected* Cailin. She had suspected her from the beginning, from their very first meeting, when she had mistrusted her Sister's apparently altruistic invitation to join the Red Order. So much time had passed, and she had almost forgotten, almost become used to Cailin's ways; but nothing had changed, not really.

It was her encounter with Asara that had reminded her, the deep and fundamental deception that she had been subjected to. Cailin *knew* who Saran really was, and yet she had kept the secret, even though she must have suspected Kaiku's feelings for him. It had been Asara that had watched her for two years in the guise of her handmaiden, waiting for Kaiku to manifest her *kana*. Asara who had brought her to Cailin. Now Asara who had given five years of her life to glean clues buried by thousands of years of history all over the Near World.

Yet no matter what Tsata thought, Asara was not working for the greater good; she was selfishness personified. Whatever she was up to, it was for her good and hers alone. She and Cailin, locked in a conspiracy of two, hidden behind veils of misdirection and always, always working towards *something*. Something that Kaiku had not been let in on.

Machinations, wheels turning within wheels. She was not like Mishani. She sickened of deceit.

They were forced to cross the shaft again as they descended, for the tunnel branches that they chose looped around and spat them back out into the open. They endured a passage across an immeasurable void on a thin metal bridge anchored by spidery struts to the surrounding rock. On the way, they came so close to one of the curiously beautiful waterfalls that Kaiku might have reached out and touched it if she were not unreasonably afraid that her interference in the flow might trigger some sort of alarm.

When they regained the safety of the tunnels, and the massive weight of the stone closed in around them once more, they began to come across the long-expected signs of life. This tunnel had been adapted from its original form, which was probably too uneven or obstructive to be viable as a corridor, and it was braced with a metal framework. The torches that burned here were of the usual kind, not the strange contraptions belching inflammable gas that were present in the enormous dark of the shaft.

It was the golneri. The smell of cooking meat and the sound of muttering voices alerted the intruders. They instinctively drew back into shadow, listening to the jabber of the golneri's incomprehensible dialect. Kaiku wondered where they had come from, how they had come to be so enslaved by the Weavers. A pygmy tribe, hidden in the depths of the Tchamil Mountains, subjugated all those years ago when the first Weavers' baptism of slaughter was over and they disappeared into the uncharted peaks of Saramyr? Certainly, it was not beyond possibility. Between her home in the Forest of Yuna and the Newlands to the east, the mountain range was three hundred miles wide. From Riri on the southern edge to the northern coast which abutted them, they stretched for over eight hundred miles, dividing Saramyr into west and east with only two major passes along that whole length. There were unexplored areas of the Tchamil Mountains so vast that an entire civilisation could have thrived there and nobody in Saramyr would be the wiser. Even after more than a thousand years of settlement, the land was simply bigger than they could swell to fill it; and in those empty places the spirits still held sway, and resented the encroachment of humankind.

She would probably never know. Whatever the golneri were or had been, now they were merely appendages to the Weavers, to feed them and care of them when their masters' insanity took hold. Kaiku tried to pity them, but she had precious little pity left, and she saved it for her own kind.

They crept onward until the tunnel became a small cavern, hot and smoky and redolent with the scent of crisping flesh. The tunnels were by no means smooth and straight, their sides a mass of folds and natural alcoves, and the haphazard placement of torch brackets throughout the mine left enough gaps between the light for them to conceal themselves to some extent. They crouched near the mouth of the cavern and looked in.

Animals turned on spits; vegetables boiled in vats. Strips of red meat hung on hooks over smoking embers, and elsewhere great fires blazed. Fish were being decapitated and eviscerated, their guts tossed aside to slither in the accumulated filth that carpeted the floor. Dozen of the tiny beings were here, their faces screwed up into wrinkled clutters, eyes vacuous and expressions strangely immobile. They were swarthy and skinny, looking like resentful children, their features set in permanent scowls as they rapped orders at one another in their unfamiliar language. Kaiku watched them with a fascination, mesmerised by their ugliness, until with a start she noticed that several of them were looking back at her. The shock of being discovered made her heart leap in fright.

'Tsata . . .' she murmured.

'I know,' he said quietly. 'They have sharp eyes.'

They kept very still. Now the first ones who had spotted them were returning to their work, and others were noticing them. Their presence did not seem to excite any kind of alarm. After a time, they were entirely ignored. Kaiku breathed again. She had half-expected that reaction from her experiences with them when she had penetrated the Weavers' monastery on Fo, but her relief was still profound.

'They do not seem concerned,' Tsata observed, wary of a trick.

Kaiku swallowed against a dry throat. 'Then that is our good fortune,' she said. 'The Weavers have never had much need for guards. Their barriers have kept everything and everyone out for hundreds of years. They have not needed to fear for so long, they have forgotten how to.'

She stood up, and walked out of hiding. The golneri paid her no attention. Slowly, Tsata joined her, and they crossed the underground kitchen together, expecting at any moment for a clamour to be raised. But the golneri's indifference was total.

'I would not rely on that, Kaiku,' Tsata said. 'I think they will be guarding their witchstone very closely, and they will not entrust these small men or Aberrants with the task.'

Indeed, Kaiku thought, and his words reminded her of something that she had been trying to push to the back of her mind since they had taken on this task. There were still likely to be Weavers here. She might have beaten a demon with her *kana*, but they were lesser things. She dared not match herself against even a single Weaver. The stakes were too high, even for her.

Yet they had to know. Had to know whether the stories Asara had brought back from the other continents were true. Had to know if the Weavers had any vulnerabilities at all. For her oath to Ocha, for her dead family, for her friends who might even now be dying at the other end of the Fault, they had to strike a blow.

Somehow, they had to destroy the witchstone.

Thirty-One

For the second time in his life, Barak Grigi tu Kerestyn sat on horseback in the midst of an army and looked upon the city of Axekami.

It was beautiful in the light of the early morning. Nuki's eye was rising directly behind it in the east, the brilliance carved into rays by the spires and minarets of the capital, casting a long shadow like reaching fingers towards the throng of thousands who came to possess it. The air had a hazy, beatific quality, a fragile shimmer that made promises of the winter to come, where the days would be warm and still, and the night skies clear as crystal.

Axekami. Grigi could feel the desire kindling in his heart just by shaping the word in his mind. Those towering beige walls that had thwarted him once before; the jumble of streets and temples, libraries and bath-houses, docks and plazas. A chaotic profusion of life and industry.

His eyes travelled up the hill to where the Imperial Quarter lay, serene and ordered beneath the bluff that the Keep sat on, its far side aflame with sunlight and its western face in shadow. His gaze lingered on it, drinking in the sight of its magnificence, roaming over the temple to Ocha that crowned it and the Towers of the Winds that rose needle-thin at its corners. The Jabaza, distantly visible, wound in from the north, and the Zan headed away to the south, junks and barges waiting idly near the banks. Axekami had been sealed tight since the night before, as it always was in times of threat, and no river traffic was getting in or out.

How he wanted that city, craved it as if it were a mistress long denied him. The throne had slipped from Blood Kerestyn before, but now he was here to restore his family to the glory they deserved. He felt an elation, a certainty of the righteousness of his cause. The revolt in Zila had showed just how weak Mos's hold was on his empire. The fact that he had left the matter to local Baraks and sent none of his own troops only made things look worse for him. How the people of

320

Axekami would welcome Grigi this time, instead of uniting to fight against him as they had before.

And the only thing standing against him was the twenty thousand men camped between him and his prize.

'History repeats itself,' he grinned, flushed with the proximity of his dream. 'Except that five years ago in summer, you were on *that* side.'

'Briefly,' Barak Avun said, the reins of his mount gripped in one bony fist. 'Let us hope that history is kinder to us this time.'

'After today, we will *write* history,' Grigi said expansively, and pulled his horse into a canter.

The two of them rode together along the rear of the battle lines, one huge and obese, the other gaunt and ascetic. Their Weavers were not far away, keeping pace, hunched ghoulishly in their saddles. They were on hand to co-ordinate instructions between the multitude of Baraks and Barakesses whose forces stood as allies.

The high families had flocked to Kerestyn's banner as the alternative to the ineptitude of Mos. If there had been any doubt, it had been dashed when the Empress Laranya fell from the Tower of the East Wind. Rumours of Mos's state of mind had reached them long before, but his wife's apparent suicide in response to the beating he delivered her was the final evidence that the Blood Emperor was insane. Grigi trusted that they would stand firm simply because there was no other option. None of the other high families, including Blood Koli, had the support or the power to make a play for the throne. Even if one or all of them betrayed him now, the families would simply fracture into an evenly-matched and self-destructive squabble, and they knew that. It was Grigi, or Mos.

The armies stood on the yellow-green grass of the plains to the west of Axekami, where so much blood had been spilt before. The sheer numbers present defeated the eye, thousands upon thousands, an accretion of humanity too vast to take in. Each man a different face, a different past, a different dream; yet here they were anonymous, defined only by the colours dyed on the leather of their armour or the hue of the sashes that some wore tied around their heads. Great swathes of warriors, sworn by blood to the families that ruled them. Each one a weapon for their nobles to wield, and in their hands a weapon of their own. Divisions of riflemen, swordsmen, riders of horses and manxthwa, men to operate fire-cannons and mortars; they stood in formations according to their allegiance or their speciality, their discipline utter, their dedication total. For these were soldiers of Saramyr: their lives were subordinate to the will of their masters and mistresses, and disobedience or cowardice was worse than death in their eyes.

The defenders were predominantly attired in red and silver, the colours of Blood Batik. Those wearing other colours were the few whose dogged loyalty to the Imperial throne had blinded them to Mos's faults, or whose hatred of Blood Kerestyn had led them to join against him. The Imperial Guards he had kept within the city, but Mos had sent the remainder of his forces out onto the battlefield. Mos knew that if he allowed the usurpers to lay siege to the city, with the onset of famine and his unpopularity among the people he ruled, then it would only be a matter of time before the end.

Mos would not let himself be cornered. Instead, he chose to meet his enemy head on. Even weakened by splitting his forces, he possessed an army not much smaller than the combined might that Kerestyn had brought against him.

But Grigi had a trick up his sleeve. He had the Weave-lord.

Gods, the treachery was spectacular. Grigi could not even begin to imagine how Kakre had arranged the Empress's death, but it had weakened Mos just enough. All the time Kakre had been conspiring with Grigi and Avun tu Koli, spinning secret deals, plotting to get rid of the unpopular Mos and install a new, powerful ruler in the shape of Grigi. Like a rat leaving a sinking ship, and swimming to a new one.

Of course, such untrustworthiness made them dangerous. And Weavers were not the only ones who could be sly. Once he was firmly in his rightful place, Grigi would use Kakre's betrayal of Mos as an excuse to get rid of the Weavers once and for all. The people would demand it. Grigi had no wish to have his own ship sunk under the weight of the rats that clambered aboard.

He looked at Avun, his small eyes agleam amid the folds of his face. Avun returned the gaze unblinkingly. As if summoned, the two Weavers rode up alongside, one with the visage of a grimacing demon, one with an insectile face of gemstone, a Mask of incalculable wealth.

Avun nodded imperceptibly at Grigi. Grigi's voice was trembling with excitement as he turned to the Weavers and spoke.

'Begin.'

The rising roar of the armies as they closed on each other floated high into the sky, reaching to where Mos stood on a balcony of the Imperial Keep and looked down over the distant battle. His eyes were hollow and his beard thin and lank; a soft breath of air from the city below stirred his hair where it hung limply against his forehead. His flesh seemed to hang off his broad, stocky frame now, and he held a goblet of dark wine in one hand, nursing it as tenderly as if it were the child he had killed. But his gaze was clear, and despite the grief written so plainly on him, he seemed more his old self than in recent days.

How ridiculous it seemed, he thought. The plains surrounding Axekami were so flat that there was no real terrain advantage to be had, so Kerestyn had simply marched up to the city, Mos had sent his men out, and they had stood there waiting to kill each other. An idiotic civility. If there had been any passion involved, the enemy forces would have torn into each other on sight; but war was passionless, at least from where he stood. So they lined up their pieces in preparation for a charge, and only commenced when everyone was ready. It was enough to make him laugh, if he had any laughter in him.

The charge looked strangely surreal, like homing birds released from their cages. The front ranks simply dissolved into a mad dash as the signal to attack was given, and were matched by their counterparts on the other side. The distant report of fire-cannons preceded flashes of flame as sections of the charging troops were immolated. Riflemen were firing, reloading, firing, switching guns when their powder burned out. Horsemen swung out to the flanks. Manxthwa-riders powered through the foot-soldiers, their mounts turned from docile beasts of burden to angry mountains of shaggy muscle in the heat of combat, kicking out with their spatulate front hooves, their sad and misleadingly wise-looking faces turned to snarls. Up here, it was possible to see the formations moving in a slow dance, arranging themselves around the great central mass where the foot-soldiers hacked each other into bloody slabs in a dance of exquisite bladework.

'You do not seem at all concerned, my Emperor,' Kakre said, stepping out onto the balcony. Mos's nose wrinkled slightly at the sick-dog smell of him.

'Perhaps I simply don't care,' Mos replied. 'Win, lose, what does it matter? The land is still blighted. Perhaps Kerestyn will kill me, perhaps I will kill him. I don't envy him the task he takes on with my mantle.'

Kakre regarded him strangely. He disliked the tone in Mos's voice. It was entirely too light. Since the death of Laranya, Kakre had ceased twisting the Emperor's dreams, trusting his own despondency to make him pliable without the risk of manipulating his mind directly. For a time, it had worked: he had barely questioned Kakre when he had advised that an army should be sent to forestall the desert Baraks, had not even checked the size of Kerestyn's army for himself. And yet now, despite his words, that despondency seemed to have fallen from him. Perhaps he was simply being fatalistic, Kakre reasoned. He had good reason to be, oh indeed.

Kakre's mind went elsewhere, to another battle, where at the very same moment the last remaining thorn in the Weavers' side was about to be removed. How things had shifted in their favour, that the Ais Maraxa should be foolish enough to expose themselves by inciting a revolt in Zila. Kakre had promised Mos that he would deal with the cause of that revolt and he had meant it. He had contacted Fahrekh, Blood Vinaxis' Weaver, and all the others in the vicinity and given them one simple instruction: take one of the leaders alive, and strip their mind raw. Chance had delivered them Xejen tu Imotu, but it could as easily have been one of a half-dozen others. The Ais Maraxa had been troublesome for so long: they were too well hidden, and Kakre did not have the time to ferret them out, especially as their connection with the Heir-Empress might have been a false lead. But their zeal had been the end of them, and now it would be the end of their divine saviour. For Lucia *was* alive, and furthermore, Fahrekh had found out where she was.

The timing was fractionally inconvenient. Kakre would have liked to send an even greater number of Aberrants to the Fold than they had mustered, but the bulk of their force had been needed elsewhere. Even so, there were more than enough; enough to weather the occasional mistakes and setbacks, such as the massacre of the Aberrants in the canyons west of the Fold.

Kakre did not want to take the risk of simply killing the Heir-Empress and then have the Libera Dramach use her as a martyr. He wanted the Libera Dramach too, to smash that last resistance, to capture their leaders and force them to give up their co-conspirators until all sedition was stamped out. And if he was fortunate, more fortunate than he dared hope, he might even find that Weaving bitch that had killed his predecessor.

Today, in the span between sunrise and sunset, all the Weavers' troubles would be removed.

He had all but forgotten about his suspicious mood when he felt the mental approach of another of his kind. Fast as the flicker of a synapse, he dived into the Weave to meet him, flashing along the currents of the void until the two minds joined in a tangle of threads, knotting and mingling, passing information, then pulling away into retreat. Kakre was back into himself in moments, rage bursting into life inside him. He turned his attention to the battle again, looking hard at the tiny figures that fought and died down there.

A mile north-west of the combat, a vast clot of red and silver had appeared, moving fast towards the rear of the Blood Kerestyn forces. Eight thousand Blood Batik troops, as if from nowhere. From the Imperial Keep, they could see fifteen miles to the horizon, and there had been no sign of the troops until now.

'Mos!' he croaked. 'What is this?'

Mos gave him a dry look. 'This is how I beat Grigi tu Kerestyn,' he said.

'*How?*' Kakre cried, his fingers turned to claws on the parapet of the balcony.

'Kakre, you seem discomfited,' Mos observed, mockingly polite. 'I'd advise you not to take out your aggressions on me as you did before. I may be Emperor for a very long time yet, despite your best efforts to the contrary, and it would be well not to make me angry.' He smiled suddenly, a mirthless rictus. 'Do we understand each other?'

Kakre had been listening in disbelief, but now he found his voice again. 'What have you done, Mos?' he demanded hoarsely.

'Eight thousand cloaks, matched to the colour of the grass on the plains,' he said. He sounded nothing like the broken man that he had seemed to be only a few short hours ago. Now his voice was flat and cold. 'I didn't send my men to meet the desert Baraks. And I didn't send them after Reki either. I had them all double back. I had something of an intuition that Kerestyn might hear of this opportunity, and that he might come in greater numbers than I expected. Before dawn, I sent them out and had them hide under their cloaks and wait. You'd never see them unless you were close.'

Kakre's eyes blazed within the black pits of his Mask. 'And what about the desert Baraks?' he hissed.

'Let them come,' Mos shrugged. 'They'll find Kerestyn shattered and me ruling in Axekami with nobody to challenge me. And of course, my loyal Weavers by my side.' This last was delivered in an insultingly sardonic tone. 'Sometimes it's best not to let anyone know everything, Kakre. A good ruler realises that. And don't forget I helped make Blood Batik great long before I met you.'

'I am your Weave-lord!' Kakre barked. 'I *need* to know everything!'

'So you can turn it against me? I think not,' Mos said, his voice quiet and deadly. He was a man who had nothing left to lose, and even the terror of the Weavers had no hold on him now. The Imperial Keep had cast them both in shadow, but Mos's rage made him seem darker still. 'I'm no fool. I know what you're doing. You treat with Koli and Kerestyn to get rid of me.' His eyes filled with tears of sheer hatred. 'You should never have let go, Kakre. You should never have stopped the dreams.' He leaned closer, breathing in the stench of corrupted flesh, showing his enemy that he was not afraid.

'*I know it was you,*' he whispered.

The gaping death-mask of Kakre looked back at him emptily.

'I can kill you in a moment,' the Weave-lord said, the words issuing from the cavernous black mouth dripping with venom.

'But you daren't,' Mos said, leaning back and away from him. 'Because you don't know who will be Emperor by nightfall now. And you won't use your cursed mind-bending power on me, because you can't be sure it will work. You slipped up once, Kakre. You didn't cover your tracks when you left.' He was almost shaking with disgust. 'I *remember*. I remember your filthy fingers inside my head. The memories came back; you didn't bury them deep enough.'

He turned away, back to the battle, the tears still standing in his eyes. 'But I still need you, Kakre. Gods save me, I need the Weavers. Without you, there's no way to get in touch with Okhamba and the Merchant Consortium fast enough to avert this famine. There's no way to keep this land together when people begin to starve. It will be chaos, and riots, and slaughter.' He took a shuddering breath, and the tears spilled at last, twin tracks losing themselves in the bristles of his beard. 'To expose you, to call the noble houses to rise up and throw you out, would cause the death of millions.'

Kakre's reaction was unreadable. He faced the Emperor for a long while, but the Emperor would only look at the battle below. Eventually, Kakre turned his attention back that way also.

'Watch closely, Kakre,' Mos said through gritted teeth. 'I still have one trick left to play.'

The noise of the battle was immense, a thuggish, constant bellow underpinned by the boom of artillery and counterpointed by the scrape of steel on steel, the screams of the dead and the dying, the bone-snap reports of rifles. In the killing ground at its centre, men struggled and fought in amidst a crowd of allies and enemies, a world of disorder where every angle could bring a new attack, the survivors owing their continued life to luck as much as skill. Arrows smacked into shoulders and thighs like diving birds plunging after fish. Swords carved through flesh, causing death in ways far more brutal than fiction or history would present. The neat beheadings and swift killing strokes were few; blows glanced, slicing meat from the forearm or hacking halfway through a man's knee, splitting someone's face from left cheek to right ear in a spray of shattered bone or chopping into an artery to leave the wounded man bleeding white on the grass of the plains. Flame sprang up in slicks as shellshot burst, burning jelly sticking to skin and cooking it, men flailing and shrieking as their tongues blackened and their eyeballs popped and ran sizzling down their faces. The air was smoke and blood and the sick-sweet smell of charred bodies, and the battle raged on.

'I need the Bloods Nabichi and Gor back here *now!*' Grigi was demanding of his Weaver. His high, girlish voice made him sound panicky, but he was far from that. Grigi was very hard to rattle, and the seemingly inexplicable appearance of eight thousand Blood Batik troops behind them was merely a clever move to be countered. Already he had a force moving up to delay them while he could get his fire-cannons turned around and aimed. It was going to make this fight more costly, but he could still win it with shrewd leadership.

'That fool Kakre is going to pay for this,' he promised, reining his horse around. He did not care that other Weavers were within earshot, both Blood Kerestyn's and the gemstone-Masked Weaver of Blood Koli. 'Why didn't he warn me about the extra troops? And where's this *intervention* he promised?' He glared at Barak Avun, blaming him for Kakre's mistakes; after all, it was through Avun that Kakre had contacted him.

Avun, who had been watching the battle with his hooded, drowsy eyes, turned and gave Grigi a bland stare.

'There will be an intervention,' Avun said. 'Just not as you imagine.' He flicked a gesture at his Weaver.

The stabbing pain in Grigi's chest took his breath away. His multitudinous chins bunched up as he gaped, clutching at his leather breastplate. A sparkling agony was spreading along his collarbone to his left arm, numbing his hand. His eyes were wide with disbelief. They flicked to his own Weaver, desperate supplication in their gaze, but the grimacing demon looked at him pitilessly. Grigi gasped half a curse as the strength drained from his limbs.

'History does repeat itself, Grigi,' Avun said. 'But it appears that you do not learn from it. You had me betray Blood Amacha last time we were here; you should have known that I cannot be trusted.'

Grigi's face had reddened, his eyes bulging as he fought for air that would not seem to come. His heart was a bright star of agony in his chest, sending ribbons of fire through his veins. The sounds of the battle had dimmed, and Avun's voice was thin in his ear as if from far away. He clutched at his saddle as realisation struck like a hammer: he was dying here, now, surrounded by these three impassive figures on horseback. Gods, no, he wasn't ready! He hadn't done what he needed to do! He was within sight of his prize, and it was being snatched from him, and he could not even make a sound to voice his defiance at his tormentor.

His Weaver. His Weaver was supposed to defend him. They were always loyal, *always*. The very fabric of their society depended on it. If a Weaver did not serve his master in all things, then the Weavers were too dangerous to exist. They even killed each other in the service of the family that supported them. But this one was letting him die.

How had Avun won round his Weaver? *How?*

'You will find that the orders you sent did not get through to their intended recipients,' Avun was saying languidly. 'And they will most likely be quite surprised when my troops turn on them, and they are sandwiched between Koli and Batik men to the west and Mos's main force to the east. It will be quite a slaughter.' He raised an eyebrow. 'You, of course, will not live to see it. Your heart gave out in the heat of battle. Small wonder, for one so fat.'

The pain in Grigi's body was nothing compared to the pain in his soul, the raw and searing frustration and anger and terror all mixing and mingling to scald him. His vision was dimming now, turning to black, and no matter how he fought against it, no matter how he struggled to cry out and make a sound, he was mute. Men of Blood Kerestyn were only metres away, and yet none of them marked him, none of them saw what the Weavers were doing, reaching an invisible hand inside him to squeeze his heart. To them, he was merely in conference with his aides, and if his expression was distressed and gawping, something like a landed fish, then they were not close enough to notice.

He looked to Axekami, and it was dark now, the shadowed fingers of its spires reaching out across the carnage to enfold him. Twice he had sought it; twice been denied. Unconsciousness was a mercy. He did not feel himself slump forward and then slide from his saddle, his mountainous body crashing to the earth; did not hear the cries of alarm from Avun, false words to Grigi's men as they gathered; did not see him and his Weaver slip away from the crowd, to turn the battle with perfidy. There was only the growing golden light, and the threads that seemed to sew through everything, wafting him like fallopian cilia towards what lay beyond oblivion.

Kakre's hood flapped about his Masked face in a flurry of wind as he watched the battle unfold. Nuki's eye had risen overhead now. It was hot in the direct sun, and Kakre's sweltering robe was entirely inappropriate, but he did not retreat. Neither did Mos. Reports came to them both: to Mos through his runners; to Kakre through the Weave. The morning had passed, and the forces led by Blood Kerestyn were decimated. The armies of some of the most prominent high families in the land had been cut to pieces. Kerestyn themselves, who had dedicated almost all their troops to this venture, would not be able to rise again for decades, if ever. Weakened, they would be unable to continue fighting in the vicious internecine dealings of the nobles, and would be torn apart.

Avun tu Koli had been clever. Whatever deals he had made, he had managed to execute them without Grigi finding out. It was not only

Blood Koli that turned on Kerestyn, but several other families as well, tipping the balance far enough in the Emperor's favour to make it virtually impossible for Blood Kerestyn to turn the tide back. Ragged armies were fleeing in retreat now, Grigi's allies deserting him as their cause became hopeless. Kakre noted that Blood Koli troops were almost entirely intact; Avun tu Koli had drawn them out of the conflict, letting the others take care of the battle, content to watch from the sidelines and preserve his men.

'It was you,' Kakre said at last. 'I remember now. I had learned of a message to Avun tu Koli, sent from the Keep, but I failed to intercept it.' He felt a pang of concern that he had forgotten about it until this point.

'Avun tu Koli has always been an honourless dog,' Mos replied. 'And that makes him reliable. He'll always choose the winning side, no matter what his previous loyalties. I just had to convince him that I would win. Look at him, holding his men back. Blood Koli will be the most powerful family behind Batik after this, and he knows it.' He scratched at his beard, which had gone scraggy and heavily scattered with white as if withered by his grief. 'You tried, Kakre, and it was a cursed good try. But you are stuck with me, and I'm stuck with you. No matter what you've done, we need each other.'

The words almost caught in his throat: *no matter what you've done*. As if he could dismiss the murder of the woman he loved so easily. As if he could ever love again, or feel anything but sorrow and hatred and shame. Locked with the Weavers in a symbiosis of mutual loathing, he saw nothing but evil in his future; but evil must be endured, for the sake of power. He had lost a son, a wife, and an unborn child now. Such things could drive better men than him to ruin. But he had nephews, and other relations that could take the reins of the Empire when he was gone; and he had a duty to his family, to Blood Batik. He would not give up the throne while he still breathed.

'You are mistaken,' said Kakre, his voice a dry rasp. 'And your runners come now to tell you why.'

An urgent chime outside the door of the chamber behind them made Mos whirl. He stepped into the room, out of the sun to where the coloured *lach* of the walls and floor and pillars kept the air cool. He stopped halfway to the curtained doorway, and looked back at where Kakre was coming through the archway after him.

'What is this, Kakre?' he demanded. Suddenly, he was afraid. 'What is this?'

The bell chimed again. Kakre's scrawny white hand emerged from the folds of his robe and gestured towards the doorway.

'Tell me!' Mos roared at the Weave-lord.

The runner thought that this was an invitation to enter, and he drew the curtain aside and hurried in, blanching as Mos swung a furious glare on him and he realised his mistake. But he was terrified already, and he blurted out his message recklessly as if by delivering it he could expel its meaning from him and purge the horror that his words carried.

'Aberrants!' he cried. 'There are Aberrants all over the docks. Thousands! They're killing anything that moves!'

'*Aberrants?*' Mos howled, swinging back to Kakre.

'Aberrants,' Kakre said, quite calmly. 'We sailed bargeloads of them into Axekami last night, and then you shut the gates and locked them in. You'll find that many more are deploying on the west bank of the Zan now and heading towards the soldiers outside Axekami. They will slaughter anyone not wearing the colours of Blood Koli.'

'Koli?' Mos was choking on the sheer enormity of what Kakre was saying. Aberrants? In Axekami? The most dreadful enemy of civilisation at the very heart of the empire? And the Weavers had *brought them here*?

'Yes, Koli,' Kakre replied. 'Quite the treacherous one. Ever ready to step over the corpses of his allies to victory, like a true Saramyr. He has been on my side all along.'

Mos had the terrible impression that Kakre was grinning behind his Mask.

'Let us not delude ourselves, Mos,' he croaked. 'The Weavers see the way that Saramyr is turning. Soon, you would try to get rid of us. The people would demand it. Grigi tu Kerestyn was plotting to do the same. That cannot happen.'

The runner was rooted to the spot, trembling, a young man of eighteen harvests witnessing an event of an importance far beyond anything he could ever imagine being privy to.

'At this time, Aberrants are pouring from the mountains, from our mines, from dozens of locations where we have collected them and hidden them from your sight. You were kind enough to be part of the process of demolishing the standing armies of the nobles with this charade being played out beyond Axekami's walls. Our Aberrants will take care of the rest.'

For an instant, Mos was too stunned to take in what the Weave-lord was telling him. Then, with a strangled cry of rage, he lunged, a blade sliding free of the sheath where it had been hidden at his belt. Kakre put up a hand, and Mos's charge turned into a stumbling collapse as his muscles spasmed and locked. He went crashing to the ground in a foetal position, his face contorted, jaw thrust to one side, his fingers jutting out at all angles, his wrists bent inwards and his neck twisted, as if he were a piece of paper screwed up and discarded. His eyes rolled madly, but he could only make a hoarse gargle emit from his mouth.

The Weave-lord stood over the Emperor, small and hunched and infinitely lethal. 'The time of the high families is over,' he said. 'Your day is done. The Weavers have served you for centuries, but we will serve you no longer. The Empire ends today.'

He waved his hand, and Mos burst. Blood splattered explosively from his eyes, ears, nose and mouth, from his genitals, from his anus. His belly split and his sundered intestines coiled out in a gory slither; his vertebrae shattered from skull to coccyx.

In an instant, it was over. The ruined corpse of the Emperor lay amid a blast-pattern of his own fluids on the green *lach* floor of the room.

Kakre raised his head, the corpse-Mask fixing on the messenger. The shock and disbelief on the young man's face was comical. He dropped to his knees, haemorrhaging massively.

There was silence in the room; but outside, in the streets of the city, rifle fire could be heard. Bells were tolling. An alarm was being raised.

The brightness of the sunlight on the balcony made the room seem dim in comparison. Kakre studied the bodies of the men he had killed. An Emperor and a servant, both just husks in the end.

The Aberrant predators in Axekami would rampage through the city, crush all resistance, bring the populace savagely to heel. All over northern Saramyr, huge armies of beasts were sallying forth from the Tchamil Mountains and along the rivers, an accumulation of decades of planning and five short years of unrestricted movement within the empire. Monstrous hordes, blossoming out from within like spreading cancers under the auspices of the Weavers and the Nexuses.

Messages begging for help would not get to where they were sent. Weavers would disappear, their masters murdered. So long had the nobles of Saramyr relied on the power of the Weavers to communicate that they would not know what to do. So long had they accepted the Weavers' servitude that they could not imagine rebellion. Suddenly, they would be alone, isolated in the midst of a massive country, separated by huge expanses from anyone who could help them. By the time they adapted it would be too late. The high families would be overthrown.

The game was done, and the Weavers had won.

Kakre walked slowly from the room. When Mos's corpse was discovered, the Imperial Guards would draw the obvious conclusion. But by that time he would be back in his chambers, and the door was thick enough to withstand the Imperial Guards long enough for the Keep to fall, if they should hunt him down.

Besides, he had a celebratory titbit waiting there, brought to him last night for just this occasion. A young woman, smooth as silk, lithe and beautiful and perfect. And such skin she had, such skin.

The Juwacha Pass lay between Maxachta and Xaxai, bridging the Tchamil Mountains where they narrowed, reaching from the fertile west to the desert of Tchom Rin in the east. Apart from the Riri Gap on the south coast, it was the only major crossing-point between the two halves of the divided land. Legend had that Ocha himself had parted the mountains with one stamp of his foot, to open Tchom Rin and the Newlands to his chosen people and give them licence to drive the aboriginal Ugati out. More likely it was some cataclysmic shifting of the earth that had carved the sinuous route between the peaks, one hundred and fifty miles long, as if the upper and lower parts of the range were simply drawn apart and the ground between had stretched flat.

At its widest point it was two miles across, though it narrowed to half a mile at the western end, where its mouth was guarded by the sprawling city of Maxachta. What obstacles had been strewn across it on its discovery – boulder formations, glassy hulks of volcanic rock, massive jags of black stone: imperfections thrown up in the violence of its creation – had been destroyed with explosives and levelled long ago. The mountains had many passes for the agile, but for an army the Juwacha Pass was the only feasible way across without heading five hundred miles south to Riri.

Reki tu Tanatsua reached the summit of the mountain ridge at mid-morning, with the sun low and clear and sharp, shining directly in his eyes. Reki's thin face was bearded now, the hair growing surprisingly thick for such a young man. His black hair had become shaggy, the streak of white dyed to make it invisible. His finery had gone, traded away for sturdy peasant travelling-clothes, and his gaze was flintier and wiser, less that of a child and more that of a man. He laboured up the last few yards to the top, crunching through autumn snows that dusted the ground lightly at this altitude, and there he stopped and looked back.

Asara came up behind him, clad in a fur cloak, her clothes as simple and hardwearing as his. She wore her hair down, and her face was unadorned, but even without effort she was strikingly beautiful. The exertion of the climb had not even tired her. Beyond her, over the peaks, Maxachta spread across the yellow-green plains, tiny domes and spires shining as they came out of the frowning shadow of the mountains. They had passed it the day before yesterday and given it a wide berth, shunning habitation, just as they now chose a mountainous trail to the south of the Juwacha Pass rather than risk meeting anyone on it. It was a harder road, but a safer one, for all ways had become dangerous now.

Reki offered a hand to her, and she took it with a smile. He helped her the last few steps to the tip of the ridge, and there they walked to the far side and looked down.

The mountain ridge that they had climbed lay ten miles in from the western end of the pass, at the point where it curved slightly north-ward. From its heights, it was possible to see a long way in either direction. Asara had judged it a prudent point to take stock of where they were and anticipate any dangers ahead; Reki had submitted without argument. He had long learned to trust her in these matters. She had kept him alive thus far, and she was astonishingly capable for a woman her age. He desired her and was in awe of her at the same time.

But there was another motive behind their ascent. Asara had a suspicion which she was unwilling to share with Reki, and she wanted to be certain of it before she continued. Her Aberrant eyes were ex-ceptionally sharp, and the tiny wheeling dots that she had spied from afar had set her to thinking. Now she saw her suspicion confirmed.

The mountains shouldered together to the east, forming a narrow, grey valley. It was carpeted in dead men and Aberrant beasts. Carrion birds plucked and pulled flesh so fresh that it had hardly even begun to decompose, or circled silently overhead, as if spoilt for choice and unable to decide where next to feast. From where they stood, the corpses were one incoherent jumble, bodies upon bodies in their thousands.

Thousands of desert folk. Men and women in the garb of Tchom Rin.

Asara shaded her eyes and scanned the pass, picking out broken standards and faded colours. She saw the emblems of the cities of Xaxai and Muio, in among those of other high families. It took her only moments to find the one she was looking for.

Blood Tanatsua, tattered and torn, lying across several bodies like a shroud. The emblem of Reki's family. And she knew enough of desert lore to realise that the standard was only raised above an army when the Barak himself was present.

The desert families had marched quickly at the news of Laranya's suicide. Had Kakre's Weavers been setting things up here too, playing the families as Kakre was doing in Axekami? Certainly, it seemed that this army had moved with uncanny speed, even assuming that news of the Empress's death had been communicated instantly by Kakre to his foul brethren in the desert. A vanguard, perhaps? A show of might?

The desert cities would not declare war on the strength of what they had heard. It would take the token that Reki carried to make them do that. But now, it seemed, his errand was redundant.

She glanced at him. His vision was not as good as hers, but he saw enough. He stared down on the scene for a long time in silence, his face still but tears welling in his eyes.

'Is my father down there?' Reki asked.

'Who can say?' Asara replied, but she knew that he was, and Reki caught it in her tone. She could only imagine what had happened: how these men had been ambushed by Aberrants, how even this massive force had been outnumbered by the tide of monstrosities pouring from the mountains. Yet how could the Aberrants be so organised, so numerous, so purposeful? Could this, too, be some dark result of the Weavers' ambitions? It seemed impossible, yet the alternatives were even more impossible yet.

Reki wiped his eyes with the back of his hand. He did not grieve for his father, to whom he had been a source of endless disappointment; he had enough residual bitterness to pretend that he did not care. He wept instead for the death of his people. He wept at his first sight of the cost of war.

They made a fire on the summit of the ridge, careless of the consequences, and there Reki took out the sheaf of hair that had been his sister's, and burned it. The acrid stink carried up on the thin trail of smoke into the morning sky, the ends of the hair glowing, curling and blackening. Reki knelt over it, gazing into the heart of the blaze at the last part of his sister he had as it smouldered into ash. Asara stood at his shoulder, watching, wondering how he would feel if he ever knew that his sister's murderer was the woman by his side. Wondering what would happen if she was ever on the receiving end of his promised vengeance.

'The responsibility passes to me,' he said, eventually. 'What was to be my father's cause is now mine.'

Asara studied him. He stood up, and met her eyes. His gaze was steady, and there was a determination there that she had never seen before.

'You are a Barak now,' she said quietly.

His gaze did not flinch or flicker. Finally, he turned it eastward, looking over the peaks, as if he could see past them to the vast desert beyond where his home lay. Without a word, he set off that way, heading down the far slope of the ridge. Asara watched him go, noted the new set to his shoulders and the grim line of his jaw; then, with one final look to the west as if in farewell, she followed him.

Thirty-Two

Yugi sprinted along the barricade, the air a pall of acrid smoke and his face blackened and grimed with sweat. The sharp clatter of rifle fire punctured the cries of men and women. Aberrants roared and squealed as they were mown down in their dozens, and still they kept coming.

Yugi slung his rifle over his shoulder and drew his sword, leaping over the corpse of someone whose face had been ruined by shrapnel – they had let their weapon overheat and it had exploded – and racing towards where a skrendel had slipped over the barricade and was struggling with Nomoru. She was holding her lacquered rifle between them to fend off its scorpion-like tail-lashes, her head ducking back as the creature bared long, yellowed fangs and snapped at her. It sensed Yugi's approach and scampered off in a flail of spindly limbs, realising it was outnumbered; but Nomoru was faster, and she caught it by its ankle, tripping it so that it sprawled in the dust. It was all the time Yugi needed to plunge his sword into its ribs. It screamed, spasming wildly, raking claws at the two of them; but Yugi put his weight on the sword and pinned the creature to the ground, and Nomoru got to her feet, aimed calmly and blew its head to fragments.

'Are you hurt?' Yugi asked breathlessly.

Nomoru gazed at him for a long moment, her eyes unreadable. 'No,' she said eventually.

Yugi was about to say something else, but he changed his mind. He raced back to the barricade, sheathing his sword and priming his rifle, and joined the rest of the defenders as they shredded the creatures surging up the pass towards them. A moment later, Nomoru appeared alongside him, and did the same.

But the Aberrants were endless.

The fighting had begun at dawn. The efforts of Yugi and several other Libera Dramach traps and ambushes had slowed the advance of the Weavers' army, but only enough to buy them an extra night of preparation. Still, that night had given several clans, factions and

335

survivors of previous Aberrant attacks time to get to the Fold and join the Libera Dramach in their stand. Since sunrise, Yugi had fought alongside some of the very Omecha death-cultists who had tried to kill them several weeks ago. He had also battled next to warrior monks, frightened scholars, crippled and deformed Aberrants from the nearby village in which non-Aberrant folk were not allowed, spirit-worshippers, bandits, narcotics smugglers, and any of three dozen other types of person that had either been cast out from society or had chosen to separate themselves from it.

The Xarana Fault, for all its diversity and constant infighting and struggles for territorial power, was united in one thing: they all lived in the Fault, and that made them different. And now the factions had put aside their differences to struggle against an enemy that threatened them all, and the Fold was where they would turn back the tide or die trying.

They had engaged the Aberrants in the Knot, the labyrinth of killing alleys that guarded the Fold to the west. There, the creatures could not get through more than a few at a time, and the spots where the way opened up enough to get more than two or three abreast had been trapped with explosives or slicewires or incendiaries. More defenders were positioned on top of the Knot, to pick off the cumbersome gristle-crows that acted as lookouts for the Nexuses and to cover the horseshoe of flat stone that abutted the western side of the valley, in case the Aberrants chose to forsake the narrow defiles and come over the top. In the Fault, it was necessary to think three-dimensionally in battle.

By mid-morning, the paths of the Knot were choked with Aberrant dead, but the defenders had been driven back steadily. Reports had come to Yugi of the fight to the north and south of the Fold, where the enemy were trying to circumvent the Knot entirely to attack the valley from the eastern side. It was the first tactical move that they had made. Yugi took a little heart from that. The Weavers did not know the first thing about how to fight a war; they had simply thought to sweep aside everyone in their way, caring nothing for the casualties they sustained. Thousands of Aberrant predators lay as testament to their ineptitude.

And yet it still seemed that in the end, they would be proved right in their assumption that they could simply trample down the opposition by weight of numbers. Ammunition was running very low now, and it was not getting to some of the places that needed it. The defenders' death toll had been light thus far, but when they lost the advantage of ranged weapons and had to close in hand-to-hand, the Aberrants would even the balance.

In all this, there was no sign of the Nexuses, nor of the Weavers.

Nor, Yugi noted, the Red Order. Where in the Golden Realm was the help Cailin and her painted kind were meant to provide? Just to have them on hand to facilitate communication between groups of fighters would have been a huge help; but they were nowhere to be found.

Heart's blood, if she's run out on us, I'll kill that woman myself, he thought.

They had held this pass for over two hours now. There were only a limited number of ways out of the Knot, and each one had been fortified with one or more fire-cannons, as well as hastily constructed stone walls and earth banks. The sides of the defile rose sheer on either side, and the Aberrants were being forced to crowd uphill along an uneven surface of blood-slick stone to get to the barricade at the top. The sun had been slanting down into the enemy's eyes all morning, dazzling them, though it had now risen overhead and would soon begin to do the same to the defenders.

Rifles were fired dry, then swapped with loaders who refilled the chambers of the weapons and then swapped back when the next one was done. A small stack of guns steamed in a shadowed alcove, cooling so that the heat of repeated shooting would not make the ignition powder explode all at once. Three men attended to the fire-cannon behind the barricade, which was fashioned in the shape of a demon of the air, its body streamlined and mouth agape to spit flame. Half of the defile was ablaze from shellshot, sending thick black clouds of smoke up towards the defenders and making them squint. Yugi had been forced to limit use of the fire-cannon for fear of unwittingly providing the Aberrants with too much cover. The hot reek of bubbling fat and blackening flesh had resulted in vomiting behind the barricade, and in the midday heat the stench of warming stomach acids was appalling.

'They're trying again,' Nomoru said, setting her rifle stock under her armpit and sighting. She took her eye away to glance at Yugi. 'Wish I'd stayed with Kaiku now,' she deadpanned. Yugi laughed explosively, but it came out with a manic and desperate edge to it.

Despite the fact that the Nexuses had not been seen yet, their presence was still much in evidence in the way the Aberrants acted. They would attack in number, return and regroup in a very military fashion, and their strikes became more careful and organised as the day progressed. Yugi suspected that the Nexuses were hanging back after snipers like Nomoru had taught them that it was dangerous to show themselves, but their influence could still be observed.

There had been a short pause in the attacks after the skrendel had managed to slip over the barricade. That had been a lucky run, a product of too many people swapping weapons at once, combined with the speed and agility of the creature. Now the Aberrants were coming again, dark shapes running around the flames and through the swirling smoke. Rifles cracked once more, pummelling iron balls into the attackers at high velocity, smacking through flesh and shattering bone.

But this time, the Aberrants did not fall.

It took the defenders too long to realise that the creatures were still coming. The riflemen and women had paused, expecting the Aberrants to collapse and provide a clearer shot at the ones behind. By the time Yugi had yelled at the fire-cannon crew, and another salvo of bullets had failed to stop the rush, Nomoru had realised what was going on.

They were using their dead as shields.

Out of the smoke came a half-dozen ghauregs, each with another one of their number propelled before them: limp bags of muscle that jerked like dolls as they absorbed the hail of rifle balls. The monstrous, shaggy humanoids were powering over the heaped corpses of their companions, forming a line across the defile behind which a horde of other Aberrants pressed forward. Nomoru picked off two of them by dint of her skill with the rifle, and another one had its legs shot out from under it by some quick-thinking defenders, but they had no sooner stumbled than they were borne up again by another ghaureg, lifted and presented as targets so that the creatures behind could push on. The fire-cannon roared, but it was fired in haste before the operators could decline the elevation enough; it blasted the middle of the horde to flaming ruin and prevented any more from getting through, but that still left too many, who discarded their burdens as they reached the barricade and began to clamber over.

Guns were thrown aside and swords drawn as the defenders crowded to counter the assault. Yugi saw a ghaureg pick up an Aberrant woman by her leg and fling her into the side of the defile; he heard the breaking of her bones as she hit. Then he was in close, ducking a swipe from the creature's enormous arm, his blade lashing out to sever the hand at the wrist. The beast roared in pain, then jerked as two men came from behind it and buried their weapons in its back. Its huge jaw went slack and the light went out in its eyes, and it slumped to the ground with a bubbling sigh.

He cast about for Nomoru, but the wiry scout was nowhere to be seen. The warble of a shrilling warned him an instant before it leaped from the top of the barricade towards him. He dodged the first pounce, but it reared up on its hind legs and slashed a sickle-claw, which cut a furrow through his shirt and missed his skin by the width of a hair. His counterstrike was pre-empted by a rifle shot from his left, which smashed through the creature's skull armour and dropped it to the dusty ground. He glanced at his saviour, already knowing who it would be. Nomoru had retreated to a nook further up the pass and was crouching there, picking off Aberrants one by one. She was no hand-to-hand fighter; she was much more deadly from a distance.

Reassured now that he knew where she was, he swung back to the fray. The barricade had collapsed under the weight of the ghauregs that lumbered over it. Already the ground was cluttered with the fallen, attacker and defender alike. The Aberrants were heavily outnumbered, and their reinforcements were cut off by a wall of flame further down the defile, but they took three for every one of them that died. Yugi vaulted a man whose throat had been torn out and ran to the rescue of another who was facing a furie alone. He recognised it from Kaiku's description: like some demonic boar, its multiple tusks huge and hooked, its trotters like blades, its back tufted with spines and its face warped into a snarl. His attempt at intervention was foiled as something appeared as if from nowhere in front of him, an awful, shrieking creature with tentacles whirling around a circular maw and a body black, hairless and glistening. It was already wounded, maddened with pain; he finished it off in moments, but by the time he returned to his original objective, the man had been stamped underfoot by the furie and lay bloodied and dead in a rising haze of dust.

He was about to chase after the beast, motivated by some illogical sense of responsibility at allowing the man to be killed, when he heard the rising wail of the wind-alarms from behind him, an eerie, mournful howl coming from the east. More of them joined in, the Libera Dramach lookouts spinning tubes of hollow wood on long ropes around their heads to create a noise that could be heard for miles. It was an idea stolen from the Speakers at the Imperial councils, who used smaller versions to call for order among the assembly. Yugi had been dreading to hear it ever since that morning.

Somewhere along the defensive line, the enemy had broken through. They were at the Fold, and behind the Libera Dramach positions. The retreat had been sounded.

He went for the furie anyway. The fight was not yet over here, though the Aberrants were few in number and were being whittled down at great cost to the defenders. If there were going to be any folk left to retreat at all, there would need to be more Aberrant blood spilt. Thinking of the streets of his home being trampled under the feet of these predators, he let his anger and frustration fuel him, and with a cry Yugi threw himself into the battle.

The rim of the Fold was a mass of fortifications, and no more so than on the western side. Enemies coming down from the north, south or east slopes could be engaged on the valley floor, where the defenders would have the advantage of height, being able to attack from the plateaux and rain death down on any invaders. But anyone surmounting the western end would be above the town, critically negating the Libera Dramach's ability to use artillery for fear of hitting their own buildings. The invaders could spill over the cave-riddled cliffs like a river over a waterfall, flooding down through the steps and levels of the town. Because of this, the western edge was guarded most fiercely of all; and since it was directly in their way, that was where the Aberrant army struck hardest.

The primary defence was a stockade wall, a triple layer of tree trunks driven into holes bored into the stone. The effort it had taken to dig out the foundations had been enormous, but in the Xarana Fault security was the most important priority. Kamako cane scaffolding had been built up behind the wall, supporting walkways and small pulleys, a jumble of ladders and ropes. Now it was aswarm with men and women, vibrating beneath the weight of running feet. Fire-cannons bellowed from their positions atop the wall; ballistae threw rocks and explosives, lobbing them in languid and deadly arcs against the clear blue sky. The sound of rifles was a deafening and constant rattle, interspersed with the sinister hum of bowstrings, and the air stank of burnt ignition powder and sweat.

Zaelis tu Unterlyn clambered up the last ladder to the top of the wall, his lame leg making the climb awkward. His heart was racing: the chaos all around him terrified him. He was no general. He knew little of the arts of combat and had never been this close to conflict before. The defence of the Fold he had left in the hands of men like Yugi, who knew what they were doing. For his own part, he felt suddenly demoted and useless. It was a hard thing for him to surrender the reins of an organisation he had built from the ground up, even temporarily. Between that and his daughter's sudden and entirely unexpected rebellion against his will, he felt more like an old man than he ever had before. He feared he was not taking it well.

The last few days he had been either interfering in the battle plans of men who clearly knew their business better than he did, or clashing with Lucia. Having never had to discipline her before, he had no idea what to do. She was not like other children he had tutored in years past. To some extent, he dared not punish her at all because he relied so much on her as the uniting force behind his organisation, and to estrange her would be divisive to the Libera Dramach.

Were they right, Lucia and Cailin? Did Zaelis truly care for the Libera Dramach more than he cared for his own daughter? Had he adopted her simply to keep his most important asset under his control?

Gods, he did not even want to think what that said about him, but he could not wholly dismiss the idea either.

Alskain Mar. It had all started at Alskain Mar, when he had pushed Lucia into using her powers again, had lowered her into the lair of a creature of unimaginable power and unguessable intent. Because he was afraid of what might happen to the people of the Fold, he had risked her. Heart's blood, what had possessed him? Even when he had been agonising over his choice, had it been because he had been weighing the danger to his most precious figurehead, not to his *daughter* as he should have been? She had been so passive and pliable for so long that he had almost forgotten there was a person behind those distant eyes. No wonder she felt betrayed. No wonder she turned on him.

He could see her drifting closer to Cailin day by day. Since Alskain Mar. But he could not allow the Red Order to have Lucia's heart; they were too influential by half as it was, and they shared little of the Libera Dramach's dedication of purpose. They were looking to their own advantage, their own survival. And they were secretive. Cailin had not shared her plans concerning the invasion with Zaelis, and had refused to participate in collaborative strategies. Now she had disappeared entirely when he needed her most.

One thing he feared more than losing Lucia was losing her to Cailin. But once again, the question scratched at him: *whom do you love, your daughter or the people you gathered to follow her?*

He was still thinking it as he climbed onto the walkway and looked out over the stockade wall and to the west, but the sight there chased it from his mind as the blood drained from his cheeks.

The Aberrants were everywhere, a vast black swathe pressed up against the stockade wall, a terrible horde of tooth and muscle and armoured skin that gnashed and raged with bloodlust. They had poured out of the labyrinth of thin defiles and ravines that led down into the Knot and thrown themselves against the stockade walls to be massacred. Black columns of smoke billowed upward, where shellshot had made flaming ruin of the attackers. Explosions scorched the stone and sent broken bodies flying as ballistae found their mark.

At the base of the wall, hundreds lay crushed and dead, and still more piled on top to add their corpses, forming a steadily growing slope of blood and gristle. They were concentrating their efforts in several spots, seeking to make a mound big enough to get over the wall. Their suicidal singularity of purpose was horrifying; but worse, it was unstoppable.

Next to Zaelis, four men took a cauldron of molten metal that had been winched up from the ground and tipped it onto those creatures that were clamouring beneath them, but their animal screams only signified new additions to the slippery heap that was already halfway up the stockade.

'Burn them!' someone was shouting. 'Bring oil and burn them! *Keep* them burning!'

Zaelis looked along the wall at the man who was striding along the walkway towards him. Yugi. He was dirtied and gore-smeared, his hair in its usual disarray behind the rag around his forehead, but he broke into a grin as he saw Zaelis, and greeted him warmly. He sent a runner down the line of the stockade to spread the order, which had come from the general in command of the western defences, and then looked Zaelis over.

'Heart's blood, you look terrible,' he said.

'No more than you,' Zaelis countered. He scratched his bearded neck, which was itching with sweat. 'I'm glad to see you got back behind the wall in one piece.'

'Zaelis, what's happening? Where are the Red Order? We *need* them to organise ourselves. It's taking too long for word to get from one place to another.'

'I know, Yugi, I know,' Zaelis said helplessly, moving aside as someone jostled past them with a murmured apology. 'But you've dealt with their kind.'

Yugi nodded grimly. 'Where's Lucia?' he asked.

'Hidden,' Zaelis said. 'Guarded. She would not leave. That was all I could do.'

'She's your *daughter*!' Yugi was aghast.

'I could hardly force her,' Zaelis replied. 'She is not like a normal child.'

'That's *exactly* what she's like,' Yugi said. 'She's fourteen harvests of age, and every one of those things out there is baying for her blood! Don't you think she's scared? You need to be with her, not out here.'

Zaelis was about to protest, but Yugi overrode him. 'Show me where she is,' he said, grabbing the older man's arm.

'You have to stay!' Zaelis said.

'If she's going to be guarded, *I'll* guard her.' He was propelling them both towards a ladder now. 'There are Weavers about, Zaelis. If I've learned one lesson from this whole mess, it's that you can't keep *anything* hidden from them for long.'

The cellar of Flen's house was hot and dark. What light there was came from imperfections in the fit of the floorboards overhead, thin lines of warm daylight spilling through to stripe the faces of the two adolescents that were concealed there.

As with most Saramyr cellars, the air was too dry for mildew or damp, and though plain it was kept neat and presentable with the same fastidiousness as the rest of the house. The wooden floor and walls were sanded and varnished. Barrels and boxes were neatly stacked and secured with hemp webbing. Bottles of wine lay in racks, half-seen outlines in the gloom.

A set of steps ran up to a hatch in the ceiling, which had been closed on them an hour ago. Since then, they had sat on floor-mats down here, whispering to each other, taking occasional sips from the jug of berry juice that they had been provided with and ignoring the parcel of food wrapped in wax paper that came with it. Overhead, the creaking footsteps of the guards went to and fro, sometimes blocking the light so that it seemed as if a great shadow crossed the cellar.

They hid, and waited, and listened to the reverberations of the fire-cannons in the distance.

'I hope he'll not be hurt,' Flen said, for the dozenth time. His train of thought had been returning to the same subject over and over again, whenever enough silence had passed.

Lucia betrayed no sign of impatience, but she did not respond. She had feared he might bring it up again. A few minutes ago Lucia had experienced an unpleasant intuition that Flen's father – the object of his musing – had been killed. She could not say for sure, but it would be far from the first time her instincts had informed her of something she could not possibly have known otherwise. Perhaps she had unconsciously picked it up from the indecipherable sussurus of the spirit-voices that surrounded her, some half-gleaned shred of intention or meaning that hinted at revelation. She had, after all, been giving Flen's father a lot of thought on her friend's behalf.

Flen looked up at her, expecting her to reassure him; but she could not. Hurt flickered in his eyes. She hesitated a moment, then slid nearer to him and hugged him gently. He hugged her back, looking over her shoulder into the darkness that surrounded them, and the two of them embraced in the dim island of illumination for a time, the lines of sunlight from above moulding to the contours of their shoulders and faces.

'They're all being killed,' she whispered. 'And it's my fault.'

'No,' Flen hissed before she had even finished. 'It's not your fault. What the Weavers did isn't your fault. It's *their* fault you were born with the abilities you have; it's *their* fault. You didn't do anything.'

'I started this all,' she said. 'I let Purloch take that lock of my hair. I let him go back to the Weavers with proof I was an Aberrant. If I hadn't done that . . . Mother might still be alive . . . nobody would be dying . . .'

Flen clutched her harder, his own troubles forgotten in the need to reassure her. He stroked her hair, his fingers running onto the burned and puckered skin at the nape of her neck, gliding over its nerveless surface.

'It's not your fault,' he repeated. 'You can't help what you are.'

'What am I?' she said, drawing back from him. Had it been any other girl, he would have expected tears in her eyes, but her gaze was fey and strange. Did she feel remorse or guilt as other people did? Did it make her truly sad? Or had what he had taken as self-recrimination simply been a statement of fact? So long he had known her, and he would never understand her properly.

'You said it yourself. You're an avatar.'

Lucia studied him carefully, and did not reply, which prompted him to explain himself.

'It's like you told me,' he said. 'The gods don't want Aricarat back, but they won't interfere directly. So they put people like you here instead. People who can change things. Remember how the Children of the Moons saved your life when the shin-shin were after you? Remember how Tane gave his life up for you, even though he was a priest of Enyu and he was supposed to hate Aberrants?' He wrung his hands, not sure that he was articulating himself properly. He imagined that Lucia did not like to be reminded of Tane's sacrifice, though he told himself that she did not always react as he thought she should. 'He must have known that his goddess wanted you alive, even though you stood against everything he believed in. Because Aricarat is killing the land, and the Weavers serve Aricarat, and even though you're an Aberrant – *because* you're an Aberrant – you're a threat to the Weavers. Just like the moon-sisters wanted you alive, so you could help fight against their brother.'

He took her hands earnestly, trying to make her see what seemed so clear to him. 'If you hadn't been born the way you are, there'd be no Libera Dramach. There'd have been no Saran, and we'd have never known about Aricarat at all until it was too late. The gods might have been fighting this war ever since the Weavers first appeared, but it's only now that we know what we're fighting *about*.'

'Maybe,' she conceded. She smiled faintly, but there was no amusement in it. 'I am no saviour, Flen.'

'I didn't say you were a saviour,' he replied. 'I just said you were put here for a reason. Even if we don't know what that reason is yet.'

She seemed about to reply, her lips forming a response for her friend, when her expression changed. She snapped him the curved-finger gesture for quiet, her eyes wide; at the same moment, there was a sigh and a slump from overhead. Flen looked up, then blinked and flinched as something dripped onto his cheek through the gaps in the floorboards. He wiped it automatically from his face, and gave a tiny noise of terror as he saw blood on his fingertips.

'*Weavers*,' Lucia whispered.

There was another slump from above, then several more. The sound of the guards falling. Flen could only imagine how the Weavers had got here, what dreadful arts they had used to slip into the heart of the Fold while the Aberrants pounded at the perimeter. Had they twisted the minds of the soldiers to make their appearance different? Had they been able to walk with impunity through the streets of the Fold, cloaked in illusion? Who knew what the Weavers could really do, what they had practised for centuries in secret, what particles of knowledge their reawakening god had taught them?

But speculation was useless. They were here now, and here for Lucia.

'Don't be scared,' he said to her, though he was far more frightened than she was. They huddled against the wall opposite the stairs, trapped there in the grille of light with hot darkness crowding all around.

Something was shifted from above the hatch. A rug was rolled back. Concealment was pointless; they knew exactly where she was.

A rectangle of light opened at the top of the stairs, silhouetting three figures against the blinding brightness of the day. Motes drifted in the sunbeams that pushed past them, but they were ragged heaps of shadow.

'Lucia . . .' whispered a hoarse voice.

She got to her feet. Flen got up with her. His attempt at a defiant posture was laughable; he could barely stand for fear.

The Weavers came down the steps, moving slowly, their arthritic and cancer-ridden bodies making them ungainly and weak. Gradually she saw them as they moved from the dazzle into the gloom: three Masks, one of coloured feathers, one of bark chips, one of beaten gold.

'I am Lucia tu Erinima,' she said, her voice low and steady. 'I am the one you have come for.'

'We know,' said one of the Weavers; it was impossible to tell which. They had reached the bottom of the stairs now. Flen's eyes flickered around the cellar, probing the darkness as if searching for escape. He was almost sobbing with fright now. Lucia was a statue.

The feather-Mask Weaver raised one white and sore-pocked hand, unfolded a long fingernail towards Lucia.

'Your time is done, Aberrant,' he whispered.

But the threat was never carried out. As one, the Weavers shrieked and recoiled, whirling away from Lucia and Flen. The children backed off as the creatures writhed and spasmed, wailing in sudden torment, their limbs seizing spastically. There was a nauseating crack as a Weaver's arm broke, the bone pushing a lump through his patchwork robe; a moment later, his legs snapped, the knees inverting with appalling violence and sending him screaming to the floor. One of the others was lying on his side and bending backward, pushed as if by some invisible force, howling as his vertebrae clicked, one by one, until finally his spine gave way. The Weavers jerked and twisted as their bones fractured and broke again and again, over and over in hideous torture. Blood seeped from beneath their Masks and they soiled themselves, but still they screeched, still they lived. It was many minutes before it ended, by which time they were not even recognisable as humanoid, merely bloodied, jagged pulps like piles of sticks beneath their mercifully concealing robes and Masks.

Flen had turned away in horror, crouching in the corner, his hands over his ears; Lucia had watched the scene dispassionately.

Cailin tu Moritat stepped into the light from the hatchway, her irises a deep crimson in amid her painted face. From their positions of concealment, the other Sisters emerged: ten of them in total, all with the red-and-black triangles on their lips, the red crescents across their eyes and down their cheeks. All wearing variations of the black dress of the Order.

Cailin looked down on Lucia, her face half-hidden by shadow, limned in the light from outside. Her expression could not be seen.

'You did well, Lucia,' she said.

Lucia did not reply.

The Weavers had walked into a trap, following Lucia's Weave-signature. Had they known what the late Weave-lord Vyrrch had known, they would have realised that Lucia was usually undetectable, that her power was too subtle to pick up on their trawls across the infinity of golden threads. But with the Sisters' help, she had made herself visible to them. It was too tempting for them to resist.

The Sisters were elated now, casting glances at each other in mutual congratulation. Among them, only Cailin had ever faced a Weaver before. Now they were blooded. The instant of conflict that had ended in them taking control of the Weaver's bodies and cracking their bones like sticks had been a long and arduous struggle in Weave-time. What had seemed less than a second to Flen and Lucia had been an eternity to them. Even though they greatly outnumbered their foes, it had been by no means an easy match. Yet they had won through unhurt, and the shattered corpses at their feet bore testament to their abilities to face these creatures and win.

Lucia was listening to the harsh and agitated thoughts of the distant ravens. They had been sent away so that their presence would not reveal Lucia's position or deter the Weavers, and were going frantic at what might have happened. She had been forced to command them in this instance, something she rarely did. She sent them a wash of reassurance, and their turmoil eased like water taken off the boil.

'You *all* did well,' Cailin said, raising her voice to include the Sisters. 'But this was not your true test. We kept them from alerting their kind; that means we still have the element of surprise, at least for a short time. Let us not waste it. Now the real battle begins!'

The Sisters murmured in approval and headed up the stairs, through the hatch. They heard running feet overhead, and voices.

'Zaelis and Yugi are here,' Cailin said. She glanced at Flen, who was still cowering in the corner, the horror of the Weavers' death too much for him.

'You have my deepest gratitude, Cailin,' Lucia said, sounding older than her fourteen harvests. 'You did not have to stay and fight for the Libera Dramach.'

Cailin shook her head slowly, then bent down to Lucia's level, which was not so far now. 'I fight for you, child,' she said; and with that, she kissed Lucia on the cheek in a gesture of tenderness utterly at odds with her character. Then she straightened and swept up the stairs and away.

There were a few words exchanged, out of sight, and Yugi and Zaelis appeared, slowing as they descended the steps, aghast at the ruin of the Weavers below them.

'You're late, Father,' Lucia said coldly.

He had no chance to reply to that, for at that moment the mournful howl of the wind-alarms began for the second time that day. The breath he had drawn to respond was exhaled as an oath.

The wall had been breached. The Aberrants were inside the Fold.

Thirty-Three

Kaiku and Tsata had been lost for hours by the time they came across the worm-farm.

The mine beneath the flood plain was bigger than they had imagined, a maze of tunnels and caverns running off the vast central shaft that looped and split and joined with no rhyme or reason in its structure. Some parts were entirely abandoned, or appeared to have never been inhabited or used at all; other parts were cluttered with stores and tools and all manner of mining equipment, yet they were nowhere near anything that was being mined. They had stolen explosives from these stockpiles, of which there were plenty, piled dangerously high and kept without care, left to sweat volatile chemicals. They had expected to find explosives eventually – indeed, they had relied on it, for it was the only way they had to destroy a witchstone as far as they knew – but not in this state. It would only take a spark in one of those rooms to bring half the mine down. Kaiku did not want to think about that happening while they were inside. They gingerly wrapped what they needed in rags and stowed it in a sack which Tsata carried.

They saw golneri from time to time, but the diminutive folk always ignored them and went about whatever business they had. They found several dead ones as well, horribly mutilated, victims of the Weavers' appetites. Other evidence of the Weavers appeared as they descended further and further into the groaning, steaming darkness of the mine. There were strange sculptures chiselled out of the rock, depictions of some inner madness that Kaiku could not guess at. Tunnels were scrawled with pictograms in all kinds of languages and some that appeared to be entirely made up, swirls of gibberish in which sometimes a horrible moment of sense could be made out, hinting at dark and twisted musings. One particularly disturbing cave was hung with dozens of female golneri, swinging by their ankles from a system of pulleys and ropes and eyelets, their throats cut and blood staining the ground below in a flaky brown patina. Kaiku found herself thinking that not only were the golneri forced to see this slaughter every time they passed through the cavern, but that it must have been them who assembled the complex system of ropes in the first place. Like making prisoners tie their own nooses. She wondered what the golneri had once been, and how their pride had been so destroyed that they could suffer atrocities like this and apparently not care.

They had come across a Weaver not long afterward.

Kaiku sensed him before they saw him. He was Weaving, though not in any structured way that she could recognise. Instead, his consciousness was streaming like a flag tied to a railing, anchored at one end while the other was tattering and rippling in the flow of the Weave. Later, they heard him mumbling and shrieking, a thin, reedy sound that floated down the tunnels to their ears. Though Kaiku was not sure there was any need, they backtracked to avoid him. She had seen that kind of Weaver at the Lakmar monastery. Their minds had been lost, eroded by their Masks, and they spent their time wandering, their thoughts flapping free in the bliss of the Weave, tethered by one last cruel thread of sanity to their bodies.

Kaiku was sure it was daylight outside, but they were far underground now, and there was no way to tell. As they descended, they found more mysteries. Great chambers of fuming contraptions that clanked and pistoned. Massive black furnaces that filled the caverns with red light. Golneri scuttled to and fro, feeding the flames with coal, their faces grimed and streaked with sweat. The noise was deafening, abhorrent, and made Tsata and Kaiku cover their ears and flee. They passed immense paternosters leading up into the darkness, splashing water as it tipped over the edge of the bucket-scoops and fell endlessly into the abyss below. The inflammable-gas torches rumbled menacingly at them from the walls of the larger caverns, or from metal posts, belching gouts of smoky flame from their tips. Occasionally they came across mining operations, where golneri stood on metal scaffolds, chipping and chiselling. Chains rattled and pulleys shrieked as the loads were moved around the scaffolding, lowered to the ground or dumped slithering down chutes. Coal to feed the furnaces. But what were the furnaces for?

Kaiku had wondered why a place so massive should be so empty, but then she reasoned that this place was not a monastery or a stronghold. The Weavers only wanted one thing out of this mine: the witchstone. And that was buried deep, deep under the earth. There were simply not enough uses for all the multitude of caverns and miles of natural tunnels in between. They needed to stockpile the vast amounts of food required to supply their standing army, to house the golneri and the Weavers and the Nexuses, to mine the fuel for the furnaces and to accommodate all the machinery and contraptions; but even that only accounted for a fraction of the total size of the subterranean network. And on top of that, the place appeared to have been virtually deserted when the army headed off north and east.

But there was one thing she had not accounted for: where had the nexus-worms come from? She found her answer in the worm-farm.

They came into the cavern on a shadowed metal gallery, little more than a rusting walkway bolted against one wall to form a bridge between two apertures in the stone. The roof of the cavern was low and wide. Illumination came from gas-torch poles linked by strange metal ropelike things that snaked between them. The intruders hunkered down and looked upon the scene below them, the curve of their cheeks and the lines of their forearms and knees lit a soft amber.

The cavern was carpeted in squirming black, a constant and nauseating movement accompanied by a sound like the wringing of wet and soapy hands. Nexus-worms: uncountable thousands of them. Raised earthen banks cut through the mass with a typically Weaveresque lack of order or pattern, and along these travelled dozens of golneri, who occasionally plunged into the crush of slimy bodies to sow some kind of powdery food among the worms, or throw buckets of water across them. But the golneri were not the only ones who walked along the banks; there were Nexuses there too, accompanied by loping shrillings, who trilled and warbled softly as they followed their masters at heel like dogs. The flaming poles cast flickering glints on the moist backs of the worms, thousands of reflected crescents like an oily sea at sunset.

'Gods . . .' Kaiku breathed, mesmerised.

As they stared, it became apparent that there were not only nexus-worms in amid the crush. From their observations of the Aberrants they had killed, Tsata and Kaiku had determined that the worms were smooth and almost featureless, except for a round, toothless mouth for ingestion – fringed with little bumps – and an opening for excretion at the other end. The creatures secreted some kind of acid spittle which allowed them to burrow into the skin of their victims, where they affixed themselves with hundreds of hair-thin filaments extruded from the bumps around the mouth. Tsata had discovered that when he tried to pull a dead one free from its host and found it inextricably attached by a thick mass of these fine threads. Saramyr lore was nowhere near advanced enough to understand what they did next; but the result was obvious enough. They subverted the host's will to their own, which was in turn under the command of something else – the Nexuses.

Yet now they saw other types of creature. There were several flat, narrow things with short tails. Tiny tendrils waved in the air above them like a cloud, occasionally descending to stroke the worms that clustered around them. They were about the length and width of a man's forearm, and the worms behaved as piglets to a sow, writhing over one another in an attempt to get close.

There was a third type, too, much bigger than the other two: sluglike creatures, two or three feet high, with blotchy stripes of venomous orange against the glittering black. These things appeared to be little more than enormous rubbery maws surrounded by a sphincter of muscle, so that they resembled bags with drawstring necks. Some were obesely large while others looked starved and withered. Tsata spotted the flat, narrow creatures oozing into and out of the mouths of the fat ones, though never the thinner variety. They went right *inside*, deep into whatever passed for its innards, and were later vomited out on a slick of steaming bile. Kaiku witnessed another phenomenon too: one of the thinnest of the sluglike things belched out a thrashing heap of minuscule worms, like black maggots, which immediately began to squirm around in their own fluids and then headed off in search of the powdery food the golneri were sowing.

They spent some time on that walkway in the shadows, observing, before Tsata spoke quietly.

'I have it,' he said. 'Three sexes.'

Kaiku looked at him quizzically.

'We have something similar in Okhamba,' he told her. 'Watch what happens. The nexus-worms are the males. They clamour to insemi-nate the females, which are those longer ones. The third sex is essentially a womb. The females crawl into its mouth and deposit the fertilised eggs. The eggs hatch inside and feed off whatever sustenance the thing provides; the fat ones have great stores of it inside them, and they get thinner as the pregnancy advances and their reserves are depleted. Then they give birth by vomiting up the larvae, each of which grows into one of the three sexes, and the cycle continues.'

Kaiku blinked. She had never heard of a three-sex system on Saramyr. Although, she reminded herself, these things were probably *from* Saramyr. Some kind of unrecorded creature, warped by the witchstones' influence into this new configuration? Or had they always been there, hidden within the vast tracts of unexplored land in the mountains, found and exploited by the Weavers decades or centuries ago?

'I would guess that the females share a link with the males,' Tsata theorised. 'A kind of hive-mind with many queens. The males are like the drones.'

Kaiku did not need any more. She could imagine how these things worked: the males crept up on sleeping animals or Aberrants in the wild, affixing themselves, taking them over, making them slaves. The males and the womb-things appeared to be mindless enough, but the females moved with purpose. The males were merely there to create the link to the females, through which the *females* controlled the subjugated animal. What better kind of defence for a creature's nest than to use relatively massive and expendable proxies as guards? Or what better hunter-gatherers, since the nexus-worms themselves were physically helpless? She found herself marvelling at the sinister ingenuity of these parasites.

But the Nexuses controlled the males now. How was that possible? Certainly not through the Weave. It was vital that they knew, if they were to have any hope of disrupting them.

Kaiku's thoughts fled as a warbling shriek sounded from the floor of the cavern, ascending in pitch until it hurt the ears. An instant later, it was joined by another, and another. The shrillings were all looking at the spot where Kaiku and Tsata crouched; and now the Nexuses had turned their blank white faces that way too.

'They have seen us!' Kaiku hissed, remembering too late that the shrillings did not need to *see* at all, that darkness was no obstacle for their sonic navigation system.

'Time to be elsewhere,' Tsata muttered, and they ran.

It was a measure of their determination, perhaps, that they both chose to run onward rather than back, picking unfamiliar territories over caverns they had already passed through. They raced along the walkway, their feet clanging on the metal, and burst into the tunnel on the far side. The wailing of the shrillings was echoing from all directions now. The alarm was spreading.

'Hold this,' Tsata said, shoving the small sack of explosives into Kaiku's arms. She whimpered at the rough treatment it was suffering.

They headed down a bare and featureless tunnel, lit by occasional torches in wall brackets, most of which had gone out. The gas-flames were only generally present in the larger caverns and in areas where normal torches would not provide enough illumination. Shadows flickered by against the rough angles of the rounded walls, some ancient lava tube from an ancient cataclysm. Tsata ran ahead of Kaiku, and she saw that he had his gutting-hooks drawn, one in each hand. Gods, she wished she had her rifle now. She only possessed a sword which she was pitifully ineffective at using. That, and her *kana*, which would bring every Weaver in the mine down on top of her.

The shrilling leaped out of nowhere, reaching Tsata as the tunnel kinked right and obscured their vision any further. But Tsata's reactions were honed by generations of life in a jungle where a man would get less warning than *that* before he died. He dropped and rolled under the shrilling's pounce, his blades scything across its unarmoured belly and unzipping it from throat to tailbone. It hit the ground at Kaiku's feet in a slick of its own guts, pawing the ground helplessly in its death throes.

But the shrilling had not been alone. Two more of its kind ran into view, accompanied by a Nexus. Kaiku felt a slow chill as she looked upon the thing, seven feet tall and rake-thin, robed and cowled in black with its featureless mask hiding it completely. She put down the stack of explosives and drew her sword.

'Stay back,' Tsata said, without taking his eyes off the enemy. He was in a fighting crouch now. 'You would do no good here.'

He was right; and yet she felt terrible having him face three enemies alone without her, a deep and wrenching fear and guilt that surprised her in its intensity. Subconsciously, she was already preparing her *kana*. Whatever the cost, she would not let him die at the hands of these creatures.

The two shrillings came at him at once, moving with the fluidity of jaguars. One of them reared up on its hind legs to strike with the sickle-claws on its forepaws; Tsata used that moment to dart out of its reach and engage the second shrilling, which snapped at his belly with its fanged jaws. He barely evaded the bite, and the smooth bony crest of the creature butted him in the thigh, knocking his counterstrike awry and causing his blade to glance off the scales on its back instead of finding the soft spot where the throat joined the long skull. The first shrilling lashed out with its other claw, overreaching itself in the attempt; Tsata grunted as it tore into his arm, but he turned inside the strike and drove his gutting-hook into the rearing beast's chest. Its ululating death-cry was deafening, and it appeared to confuse the other shrilling, which suddenly went still as its frequency-sensitive glands were overloaded. The first shrilling had barely hit the floor before Tsata was on the second one, driving both his gutting-hooks into the back of the creature's neck, slicing through the nexus-worm affixed there. The Aberrant shivered and went boneless, collapsing in a heap, borne down by Tsata's weight.

Kaiku had seen the Tkiurathi fight enough times during the last few weeks, but his deadly grace never ceased to amaze her. He faced the Nexus now over the corpses of its shrillings, his bare left arm pumping blood over his golden, tattooed skin to run down the lower edge of his forearm and drip from his wrist.

There was a moment of hesitation. The Nexus was an unknown quantity. They had no idea of its capabilities.

Tsata's good arm snapped out and sent his gutting-hook spinning through the air. The Nexus was either not fast enough to get out of the way or simply chose not to; either way, the blade buried in its body with a sickening impact, and its knees buckled. It fell silently to the floor.

The Tkiurathi did not waste any time. The cries of the other shrillings were getting nearer. He pulled the gutting-hook out of the Nexus as Kaiku ran up to him.

'You're bleeding,' she said.

Tsata gave her one of his unexpected smiles. 'I had noticed,' he replied. Then he reached down and tore off the mask of the Nexus, and Kaiku caught her breath at what was uncovered.

Its face was dead white, cracked with thin purple capillaries, its expression as blank as the mask Tsata had thrown aside. The mouth was a thin slash, hanging open and toothless. Its eyes were large and pure black, reflecting Kaiku as she peered into them with an expression of horror.

But for all that, it was the face of a child.

Beneath the veined skin, a multitude of thin tendrils sewed over the forehead and across the sunken cheeks, terminating at the lips and ears and eyes and throat, dozens of tiny bumped lines radiating along the contours of the skull.

Tsata raised the Nexus's head and pulled back its hood. Buried in the flesh of the scalp, sunken into the skin, was one of the nexus-worm females, a glistening black diamond shape. Its tail ran down the nape of the neck and disappeared between the shoulder blades, diving into the spine.

'Now we know,' Tsata said.

Kaiku sheathed her sword and squatted by the fallen thing, appalled to the point of disbelief. The Nexuses were human symbiotes, their will joined with the nexus-worm females who shared their body. The females in turn controlled the males, who controlled the Aberrants. The Weavers must have been capturing predators for years in the mountains, perhaps subduing them with their Masks before implanting them with worms, building the superstructure of their army. No civilised humans would fight for the Weavers, so they had built a force of killing beasts, monsters spawned by the blight that the Weavers themselves had created. And they controlled them with the Nexuses.

But *children*? They affixed the female worms to children? Was that the only way to achieve the necessary integration, to implant them early? Did that explain the freakish way they had developed?

Kaiku gritted her teeth in rage, feeling tears come to her eyes.

It had no tongue. The stump was still there.

They did this to children.

Tsata grabbed her arm. 'There is no time to grieve for them, Kaiku,' he said, bringing her to her feet and handing her the sack of explosives.

Then they were running again. The shrillings' cries were coming from before and behind now. The tunnel ended in a three-way junction, cluttered with discarded metal components of some kind of half-built contraption. Tsata did not hesitate, choosing a tunnel and heading into it, apparently oblivious to the wound that was streaking blood down his arm. There was not so much noise from that direction, and the tunnel was uneven and rough. It bore the signs of a passage rarely used, and that meant it was less likely that anything would be coming down it. Torches became infrequent, so Tsata snatched one and carried it with him. Kaiku hung back, conscious of letting the flame near the dangerous burden she was carrying.

The sensation of Weaving crackled over her in a wave, a dark and malevolent interest sweeping the mine. Someone was looking for them. Kaiku carefully made them invisible to the seeker, blending their signatures into the Weave. It was one of the first things Cailin had taught her to do after she had got her power under control, and as bad a pupil as she had been, after five years of practice it was a discipline she was very good at. The Weaver's attention prickled across them and away, searching the tunnels and caverns. Kaiku did not drop her guard. Now she knew that there was at least one Weaver here sane enough to be a danger.

She looked back. The sounds of pursuit were echoing up the tunnel from the junction now. She did not think the shrillings were good trackers, but there were few places to hide in these tunnels, and Tsata needed to stop so he could tend to his wound. It was pumping out a worrying amount of blood and leaving a very obvious trail.

She began to be afraid. Beating the demons in the marsh, healing Yugi, hunting for weeks with Tsata: all these had combined to make her feel somewhat invulnerable of late, more mistress of her abilities and herself, more confident in her choices. But now she became suddenly aware of their situation, and it hit her that they were in the midst of a Weaver lair, surrounded by enemies, and that they might very well not get out again. Her *kana* was next to useless since she did not dare take on a Weaver; and despite Tsata's martial skill he tended to rely on surprise to win his battles. He might have killed three shrillings and a Nexus, but it had been a near thing, and despite his uncomplaining nature he was hurt badly.

Ocha, what have I got myself into? Should I have gone back to Cailin when I had the chance?

But that thought only reminded her of what might be happening at the Fold now, images of slaughter and terror.

She pushed her indecision aside. It was too late for regrets or second-guessing.

Tsata came to a sudden halt. Kaiku caught him up, her gradually reddening eyes flickering nervously over the torch in his hand.

'Down there,' he said, pointing. There was a gash in the rock at ground level, through which something was moving, throwing back his torchlight in rapid firefly glimmers. It took Kaiku a moment to realise that it was water.

The tightness of the cleft made her hesitate, a moment of claustrophobia assailing her; but then the trilling of their pursuers sounded again, closer than ever, and her mind was made up. Leaving the sack of explosives, she slid feet-first into the gap. It was too dark to see what was below, but the water hinted at where the ground would be. She slipped as far into the cleft as she could, until her legs were dangling through, and then dropped.

There was a blaze of pain as something ripped up her lower back, and then a moment of falling. She hit the ground with a jarring impact that buckled her knees. The water was only an inch deep.

'Kaiku?' Tsata's voice came through from above.

She put her hand to her back, and it came away wet.

'It is safe,' she said. 'Put out the torch. And watch the rocks; they are sharp.'

Tsata carefully handed the sack of explosives to her and then slipped through. Once there, he doused the torch in the water, plunging them into darkness. The sound of the shrillings and hurrying feet seemed suddenly louder.

'Can you see?' Tsata whispered.

'No,' Kaiku said, wondering if her eyes would adjust as they had last time. 'Lead me.'

She felt his hand in hers, the clasp wet and warm. Blood trickled over his wrist and into their grip, across the gullies of her palm, welling between her slender fingers. He was using his good arm to carry the explosives; this was his wounded one. The sensation did not repulse her. Instead it seemed a strange intimacy, cementing their link with his life fluids. She felt an entirely inappropriate rush of pleasure at the sensation.

Then they were moving. He led her into the blackness, splashing softly as he went. The air was cold and dank down here, the breath of the deep earth, and it took Kaiku a moment to realise that there was a breeze, and that Tsata was heading into it. She was surprised to find that her lack of vision did not perturb her. She was not alone here, and she trusted Tsata absolutely. Once, she would not have even entertained the idea of putting her faith in this man, this foreigner with his foreign ideas, who had once used her as bait for a murderous hunter without a second thought. She wondered if he would do the same thing now. Would the closeness that had grown between them make him loth to risk her life so casually again? She could not say. But she understood his ways better now, his subordination of the individual to the greater good, and she knew that as things stood he would never abandon her down here, would give his own life for hers if it was better for the both of them. There was something touching in the raw simplicity of that.

She began to make out the edges of the tunnel, and the rippling of the water that ran past their feet. At first it was so gradual that she could not tell whether her mind was tricking her, but then it became too pronounced to discount. The world took shape steadily in a flat monochrome, until she could see as well as if Aurus were in the sky above them.

After a time, when the sounds of pursuit had faded behind them and it seemed as if they were all alone in the mine again, Tsata drew to a halt at a spot where the tunnel wall pulled away from the stream and the floor rose above the level of the water. Kaiku could feel the Weaver still searching for them, but his probing was far away.

'There is a dry section here,' he said.

'I can see it,' Kaiku replied.

Tsata looked back at her, then for an instant glanced at their linked hands. Kaiku belatedly realised that for some while he had been leading her when she had been perfectly capable of leading herself. She had simply not wanted to surrender that reassuring touch.

'I need to treat this wound,' he said. 'It is not closing.'

The next few minutes, more than any other, taught Kaiku how different the stock of their two continents were, how the Okhamban environment had bred tough and resilient folk while in Saramyr luxury had made the nobles soft. She watched him perform surgery on himself in the darkness, biting her lip as he used the tip of his gutting-hook to scrape out a shard of claw that had broken in the wound, cringing as he used a thin needle of smooth wood and some kind of fibrous thread to stitch the edges together. He refused her help – though she had made the offer with no idea how she *could* help – and efficiently sewed himself up, with no indication of the pain beyond an occasional hiss of breath across his teeth.

When he was done, he took a tiny jar of paste from a pouch at his waist and applied it to the still-bleeding slash. His body tensed violently, making Kaiku jump. His features screwed up in an expression of intense pain; the veins of his arm and throat stood out starkly against his skin. A faint wisp of evil-smelling smoke was rising from the wound.

Kaiku was suddenly reminded of Asara's words, coming from the lips of Saran Ycthys Marul: *in Okhamba there is very little medicine that is gentle*. The paste seemed to be literally scorching the wound shut.

She watched helplessly, listening to Tsata gasp at the shocking agony of the healing process, but finally his breathing steadied. He washed off the paste with water from the stream. His wound no longer bled, instead there was an ugly, puckered scar.

Kaiku was about to offer some words of comfort when they heard the warbling cry of a shrilling echo down the tunnel. The Nexuses had not given up the pursuit. They had found their quarry again.

Kaiku hauled Tsata to his feet, hefted the sack of explosives, and they ran once more.

The tunnel curved downward, and the water gathered pace on its descent, making the floor slippery. The noise of the shrillings had multiplied now. Evidently they had followed Tsata's trail of blood to the gash where she and the Tkiurathi had slipped through, and surmised where the intruders were. Suddenly, the Weaver's attention roved over them again, like a cruel and terrible glare; she was almost caught unawares, and she concealed them only just in time. It was because she was so intent on keeping them hidden that she barely noticed the new light at the end of the tunnel, and it was only when the Weaver's mind was elsewhere that she came back to herself and realised that Tsata was slowing.

The tunnel ended in a grille, bronzed with rust, an impassable line of thick square columns through which the water sluiced away to the cavern beyond. A foul, uneasy glow bled through from the other side, bathing them in strange light. They could hear the clanking of the Weavers' contraptions. On either side of the tunnel there were several vertical cracks and openings, all of them barred and dark.

Tsata had stopped, casting a look back up the tunnel, where the clamour of the chase continued to grow. Kaiku ran past him to the grille. She knew that appalling, unnatural illumination. It was branded on her memory, a nightmare that refused to fade.

She looked through the grille, and there was the witchstone.

They had been brought at last to the bottom of the shaft, the hub of the network of subterranean corridors which the Weavers had taken for their own. The tunnel mouth opened high in the shaft wall, over a massive underground lake, its surface still and black. Two narrow waterfalls plunged from above, throwing up low clouds of mist that hazed the scene. Bare, rocky islands hunched sullenly there, and tapering skewers of limestone thrust upward towards the dizzying heights, where distant fires burned at the tips of the metal gas-torches.

The noise of the machinery was all about, and everywhere was movement. Huge cogs, half-submerged, drove scoops which rotated steadily, drawing the water from the lake to dump it in catch-tanks somewhere above. Pipes were set vertically in the shaft walls, rising from beneath the surface to disappear into boxy buildings of black iron which steamed and roared, blazing an infernal red from slats in their sides. From there, further pipes went upward, into the darkness. Sluice-gates had been built into the sides of the shaft. Small huts sat on the flatter islands. Everywhere there were walkways of metal, a precarious three-dimensional web that connected the islands and the machines, and the golneri scuttled around between them on incomprehensible errands.

In the centre, on an island of rock all its own, the witchstone lay. It was vaguely spherical, perhaps twenty feet in diameter, heavily scarred with deep pits and pocks and lined with thousands of tiny gullies. But like the one she had seen before, this one appeared to have *sprouted* in a way that no rock could have done. Dozens of thin, crooked arcs of stone reached from its side into the water, or drove like roots into the surrounding earth; they branched out towards the distant walls of the shaft, questing, or formed bridges to the nearby islands. It looked grotesquely like a rearing spider, and its luminescence made Kaiku queasy and cast disturbing shadows onto the walls.

She understood now. The great scoops descending and ascending, the pipes that evacuated into the river, the machinery and the furnaces and the horrible, oily smoke. Nomoru had unwittingly struck on the answer long ago, but it was only now that Kaiku looked upon the lake that she realised it.

How do you dig a mine on a flood plain? It would *flood*.

This mine was not about mining, it was about water. The Zan was constantly leaking into the shaft through the thin wall that separated it from the river; when it flooded, the leakage was even worse. This whole place had probably been underwater for thousands of years, ever since it was formed. These machines were a massive drainage system, a way to move the water up the shaft and back out into the river so the Weavers could get to the witchstone that had been down here all this time. It was a constant battle to pump the river out of the shaft faster than it could leak through or flood over, to keep the witchstone above water where they could feed it blood sacrifices. Those furnaces and clanking contraptions had to be what gave power to the process, through some evil art that Kaiku did not understand.

Gods, the sheer *scale* of their determination staggered her.

'Kaiku . . .' Tsata murmured.

She looked back at him, and followed his gaze.

In the side-tunnels, behind the bars, figures were moving. Distant howls and moans had begun, and strange cackling and gurgling noises. From the direction in which they had come, the shrillings were calling louder than ever, nearly upon them now. And at their backs was the grille.

'Kaiku,' he said softly. 'We are trapped.'

Thirty-Four

The defenders were losing the battle for the Fold.

Though the western end still barely held out, the fortifications on the northern side of the valley had been overwhelmed. What little chance they had of keeping back the Aberrant army was lost when the Weavers appeared on the battlefield. They spread their insidious fingers of influence among the men and women of the Fault, twisting their perceptions so that they saw enemies wherever they looked. The defenders began to fight among themselves. Brothers slew one another; members of different clans and factions fractured and became embroiled in bloody internecine squabbles. Some fled in fear, thinking that the Aberrants had already breached the fortifications. It was not long before their mistaken assumption became fact.

With the defenders in disarray, the nimble skrendel swarmed over the stockade wall and began to kill and maim with their long, strangling fingers and vicious teeth. Somewhere in amid the chaos, a few of them found their way to the small northern gate, where most of the guards already lay dead. With their nimble digits they filched the keys from a corpse and opened the gate. The ghauregs were first through, roaring mountains of muscle, and they tore the remaining defenders limb from limb in a frenzy of bloodlust terrifying to behold.

The Aberrants flooded down into the valley, and the Fold's *real* artillery opened up.

The advantage of having the town of the Fold built on a narrow slope of steps and plateaux was that it was highly defensible on three sides out of four. The landscape funnelled the invaders to the valley floor, which lay east of the buildings, and an enemy attacking from that direction was at a disadvantage, for they were fully exposed to the Fold's entire battery of weapons.

The slaughter was breathtaking.

Several dozen fire-cannons released a fusillade into the horde as they pooled at the bottom of the valley, igniting the flammable oil that had been spread there. A section of the valley floor erupted in an inferno, turning everything within it into a flaming torch. The air resounded with a cacophony of animal screams. The charge became a blazing wreck of bodies squirming and thrashing as flesh cooked and blood bubbled. Twenty ballistae fired, flinging loose packets of explosives that came apart in mid-flight and fell randomly on to the horde, geysering broken corpses in all directions.

The Aberrants came up against the eastern edge of the town, where the rise of the bottommost steps formed a natural and impenetrable wall, cut through only by gated stairways. The lifts that were used for transporting things too large for the narrow stairs were raised up and out of the predators' reach. Two hundred riflemen and women were arrayed along the lip of the massive semicircular steps, and they cut the Aberrant predators down like wheat. The Aberrants threw themselves at the wall, at the gates, but the wall was too high, and the gates were so solid that they would not give under any amount of weight. A black pall of smoke churned into the sky, rising out of the valley, as the fire-cannons and ballistae smashed burning holes in the ranks of the Aberrants. Gristle-crows circled and swooped overhead, cawing raucously. At some point, the defences on the southern edge of the Fold collapsed too, and even more Aberrant creatures swarmed in to be massacred.

But the Fold was surrounded now, and still they kept coming.

The Weavers, from their vantage points, extended their influence once again. They did not care about the losses they were suffering. The creatures were expendable, and they were confident that any barrier could be overcome from within by turning the minds of the defenders as they had earlier.

But their confidence was misplaced. This time they were met by the Sisters of the Red Order.

The first contact was nothing short of an ambush. The Weavers were brazen, accustomed to a lifetime of moving unopposed through the Weave. In fact, were it not for the strange and distant leviathans that glided on the edge of consciousness, always out of reach, then they might have believed that the glittering realm was their domain alone. But they were arrogant. Their control of the Weave was clumsy and brutal in comparison to the Sisters, wrenching nature to their will through their Masks, leaving torn and snapped threads in their wake. In contrast, the women were like silk.

Cailin and her Sisters had spiralled along the Weavers' encroaching threads, tracing them to their source, and were unravelling the stitch-work of defences before the Weavers even knew what was happening. They frantically withdrew, marshalling their powers to repel this new enemy, but the Sisters had struck in force and were at them like piranhas, nibbling from every direction at once, feinting and tugging, unravelling a knot here, picking loose a thread there, seeking a way through into the Weavers' core where they could begin to do real, physical damage. Cailin darted and jabbed, dancing from fibre to fibre and leaving phantom echoes of her presence to confuse and delay the enemy. She cut threads, excised knots, opened pathways for her brethren to exploit.

The Weavers desperately repaired the rents that the Sisters opened, batting them away, but it was hopeless. The Sisters worked as if they were one: an effortless communication existed between them that allowed them to co-ordinate themselves perfectly. They were aware of each and every ally in the battle, where they were and what they were doing. Several of them would mount attacks on unassailable positions so that others could quietly work at boring through less protected spots while the Weavers were distracted. Others harried the enemy by confusing them with ephemeral vibrations while their brethren knotted nets to catch the Weavers out.

Cailin evaded the grasping tendrils of the Weavers' counterattacks with disdainful ease, slipping away from them like an eel. She struck at them fearlessly: she had killed one of their number before, and these were no comparison to him. Yet she spared a concern for her Sisters, whose experience was less than hers. She would defend them from the Weavers' attacks, spinning barriers of confusion or clots of entanglement to slow them if the enemy assault should chance to come too near.

The collapse, when it came, was total. Cailin had been carefully weakening sections of the Weave, so carefully that the enemy was not even aware of her, and at her command the Sisters hit those sections all at once. The Weave gave way before them, opening gaping maws in the Weavers' defences. The Sisters swarmed through the Weavers' sundered barricades, sewing into the fabric of their bodies, ripping apart the bonds that held them together. The Weavers shrieked as they burst into flame, a half-dozen new pyres lighting simultaneously across the battlefield to join the blaze that was consuming sections of the valley floor.

But the Sisters' advantage of surprise had been used up now. At least two of the dead Weavers had had the foresight to send calls of distress across the Weave, flinging threads that were too scattered to intercept. A silent plea for help to their brothers who fought elsewhere in the Fold, and a warning.

The swell of outrage was almost palpable, a fury among the remaining Weavers that there should exist *anything* to challenge their authority in the Weave. Fury, and fear. For they remembered the final cry of the Weave-lord Vyrrch before he died, five years ago and more:

Beware! Beware! For women play the Weave!

Threads snaked out across the invisible realm, seeking, seeking. And while men and women and Aberrants both human and animal fought and struggled and died all along the valley, battle was joined in a place beyond their senses. The Red Order had revealed itself at last.

On the western side of the Fold, the stockade wall groaned under the weight of the corpses piled against it.

It was hard to breathe for the stench of burnt and burning meat. Nomoru's eyes teared as she aimed her rifle; she blinked several times and finally gave up. The air was a fog of black smoke and flakes of carbonised skin. The Aberrants' attempts to create ramps of their own dead had been stalled for a time when the folk of the Fold had begun pouring oil over them and setting them alight, but the pause had not lasted for long. The creatures resumed their climbing, squealing and howling as they were immolated. Some of the corpse-heaps were high enough for the invaders to get over the wall now; they burst through in flames and fell off the walkway to smoulder on the ground below, or came flailing onto the swords of the Libera Dramach. But their sheer relentlessness was keeping the defenders occupied, and the oil was not getting to the fires where it was needed. Blazes were already dying, and some Aberrants were beginning to surmount the wall without setting themselves alight in the process.

Further down the line, several dozen creatures had managed to overwhelm some of the men and escape into the streets of the Fold before more swords arrived to seal the gap, and other breaches were happening more and more frequently. The Aberrant army seemed to have no interest in fighting the men and women on the wall: they only wanted to get into the heart of the town.

The line would not hold for long. Nomoru sensed that with a chilling certainty.

She knew what the key to this was. The Nexuses. She remembered how the beasts had stampeded back in the canyons when she had shot several of their handlers. But the Nexuses had learned their lesson from that, and they stayed out of sight now, coordinating the battle from afar. Shooting these foot-soldiers was a waste of her ammunition. She had to get to the generals.

An Aberrant man with a bulbous forehead and nictitating membranes across his eyes rushed past her, paused, and turned back. She gave him a rudely expectant look.

'Why aren't you fighting? Out of ammunition? Here, take some.' He handed her a pouch of rifle balls, then ran on without waiting for the thanks she was not going to give anyway.

Nomoru followed him with her eyes, ignoring the constant din of gunshot and screams and the crackle of flames. Aberrants fighting against Aberrants. If only the people in the cities and the towns might see this, then they might think twice about the deep and ingrained prejudices they bore for the victims of the Weaver's blight. The Weavers, the very ones who had instilled that hatred in the first place, were now using the fruits of their creation to kill other Aberrants. The defining line was not between human and Aberrant, it was between human and animal. The only ones that did not qualify as either were the Weavers. They might have been human once, but they had sloughed off their humanity when they put on their Masks.

Nomoru had no special love for Aberrants, but nor did she hate them. She hated the Weavers. And through that hatred, she rejected all of their teachings, and that made the Aberrants and the Libera Dramach her natural allies. Had she only known it, she had a lot in common with Kaiku, and many other men and women throughout the Fold. She fought for revenge.

Her body was inked with many tattoos, marking moments of a childhood that was as dirty and ragged as she herself was. A baby born to a gang in the Poor Quarter of Axekami, her mother an amaxa root addict, her father uncertain. She was brought up by whoever was around, part of a community of violence in which members came and went, where people were recruited or killed daily. Stability was not a part of her life, and she learned to lean on no one. Everyone she had let herself care about died. Her first love, her friends, even her mother to whom she had some illogical loyalty. It was a vicious, insular world, and only her talents for travelling unobserved and exceptional sharpshooting kept her from becoming another victim of the narcotics, the inter-gang wars, the illness and starvation that led people to thievery and the donjons.

The tattoos marked deals she had made, debts she was owed and had collected, and denoted solidarity with the members of her gang. They sprawled in complex profusion all up her arms, across her shoulders, down her calves and shins. But there was one more prominent than all in the centre of her back, more important to her than anything before or since. That one represented a loathing so pure it burned her every day, a promise of vengeance more powerful and binding than the most sacred lover's oath.

A True Mask, half-completed, with one side inked only as an outline to be filled in when she had completed her vendetta against the Weavers. The bronze visage of a demented and ancient god. The Mask of the Weave-lord Vyrrch.

And had she but known it, the face of Aricarat, the long-forgotten sibling of the moon sisters.

She had been only a little older than Lucia was now when she had been abducted. Those kind of disappearances happened all the time in the Poor Quarter. They were a part of life, and usually went unnoticed except by those close to the one who was taken. The nobles had to feed the monsters that lived in their houses, to keep them appeased, and so they chose the destitute, the poor, the people they saw as worthless. She had believed she was clever enough to stay ahead of them, but that night she had overindulged in amaxa root – little caring that she was going the way of her mother – and she had been shopped to the Weavers' agents by a man she thought she could trust. She had awoken bound up in the chambers of the Weave-lord Vyrrch, deep in the Imperial Keep.

She had no idea what kind of fate had been planned for her. But the knots had been badly tied, and she had slipped free and spent day after terrifying day evading the Weave-lord, searching for a way out of his chambers. Competing for discarded food with the hungry jackal that prowled the rooms, scrabbling a feral existence to prevent herself starving to death or dying of thirst in the swelter. And all the time listening for the key in the door, the *only* door, knowing that if the Weave-lord caught her she would be subjected to unimaginable tortures. She had never known such constant and unrelenting fear.

It had only ended when the Weave-lord dropped dead in amidst the explosions that rocked the Imperial Keep. She later discovered that his death had been the work of Cailin tu Moritat, but that had not concerned her then. She had taken the key from his corpse and escaped the Keep in the confusion of the coup, while Lucia was being rescued by Kaiku and her companions.

Nomoru had gone back to the Poor Quarter only once after that, but she was unable to locate the man who betrayed her. Instead she went to see the Inker, who had put the Mask on her back, and a smaller symbol on her upper arm for the man that had sold her to them.

She left Axekami, shunning the people she had once known. Being delivered to the Weavers had been the last straw. She would not trust anyone again. And so she had wandered, and heard rumours, and eventually followed them to the Libera Dramach and the Fold, where people lived who wished harm to the Weavers. That, at least, was a common cause.

She blinked rapidly as a choking cloud of smoke wafted across her face, her quick mind flitting over options and discarding them. She'd be gods-dammed if she was going to die here in the Fold with so much left undone. There had to be an answer, some way to get to the

Nexuses and disrupt their hold over their army. But they were simply too far away, and too well hidden.

A gust of heated air blew aside the smoke and let the sun shine through. She shaded her eyes and looked up. In the sky above the Fold, wheeling and turning, the gristle-crows cawed. She stared at them for a long moment.

The gristle-crows. They were the key.

Slinging her rifle over her shoulder, she ran along the walkway and began to clamber down the ladders towards the ground. The western wall could not stand for much longer. She only hoped it might stand for long enough.

Yugi hurried through the Fold, his rifle at the ready. Every crooked alleyway, every curve in the packed-dirt lanes was a threat to them now. Behind him went Lucia, Flen and Irilia, one of the Sisters of the Red Order, a narrow-faced, blonde-haired woman left by Cailin as an escort. Bringing up the rear was Zaelis, limping awkwardly on his bad leg, a rifle of his own in his hand.

Predators ran loose in the streets. They had met and killed one already, and passed several maimed and wounded men and women who bore further testimony to the news. Though the defences had not fallen, the creatures had leaked in over the western wall, and that meant there was no sanctuary any more among the plateaux and ledges of the town.

Contingency plans had been laid, but they were being put into effect far too late. The children were being herded into the caves at the top of the Fold, where a network of tunnels housed stockpiles of ammunition and supplies. Yugi had argued that they should have done this before the attack even began, but Zaelis would not hear of it. There were too many entrances and those too large; it was impossible to defend, and once inside the children would be trapped. He had wanted to keep the option open to flee along the valley to the east and scatter into the Xarana Fault, hoping that the army would be content with taking the town and would not disperse to hunt individuals. That in itself was dangerous enough, for the Fault was not a place for children to wander alone; but it was better than the certainty of being massacred. It was a measure of their desperation that they were considering last resorts like these.

The breaching of the barricades to the north and south had made that plan impossible now, for the Fold was surrounded. Sending the children to the caves was only delaying the inevitable, but they had to do *something* to protect their young.

Yugi led them across a wooden bridge that arched over the rooftops of a cramped huddle of Newlands-style buildings, passing a family of Aberrant townsfolk who were inexplicably going the other way. The otherwise clear sky was almost totally hidden by roiling clouds of dark smoke. Lucia coughed constantly, hiding her mouth with her hand, while Flen hung close to her and gave her worried glances. The Sister followed with half her attention elsewhere: the air around her was crawling with the resonance of the battle being fought by her companions, and she was both afraid and yet longing to join them. Cailin would have guarded Lucia herself, but she was needed to lead the fight against the Weavers, so she had left one of her less experienced brethren to look after the disenfranchised Heir-Empress. Irilia was fresh from her apprenticeship, but she had talent, and it would be easily enough to deal with any Aberrant creatures that came their way.

They hurried up a wide stone stairway to a higher tier, turning into a thin and winding street where the haphazard clutter of dwellings leaned in close. Shrines smoked gently with incense and were piled with offerings. Most of them had a small cluster of people praying around them, looking to divine deliverance as the only way to avert the inevitable.

As they headed down the street, a long-limbed, six-legged thing sprang from an alleyway before them, a spidery, emaciated horror with a face that was at once simian and disturbingly human. Yugi had levelled and fired in an instant, but his shot went wide, and the Aberrant disappeared into another alley as quickly as it had come. The people at the shrines scattered, running for what shelter they could find.

Zaelis looked about in dismay, a great weight settling on his heart. For the first time, he was faced with the utter ruin of all he had worked for. All these years spent gathering people, organising and uniting them; all the years those people themselves had spent, building these houses, living their lives. Aberrant folk worked side-by-side with those who were predisposed to hate them, yet the differences had been overcome, prejudices had been torn down, and the Fold had thrived. The people here were fiercely proud of what they had done, the community they had constructed, and Zaelis was too. This place was a monument to the fact that there *was* another way outside of the Weavers and outside of the empire.

But it was all coming down around him. Even if they survived this day, the Fold was over. Now that the Weavers knew where it was, they would be back again and again until it was destroyed. The thought brought a lump to his throat that was painful to swallow.

And then there was Lucia. He felt her actions as a betrayal. How could she have conspired with Cailin to lay a trap like that for the

Weavers, to use herself as bait? She would listen to the Red Order, but she would not listen to the man who had brought her up these past years. She could very well die here, all because she had refused to be taken to safety. Was she doing it only to torment him? Was this merely the rebellion of an adolescent girl? Who could tell with Lucia? But he knew this much: she was punishing him for sending her into Alskain Mar, punishing him because she believed he valued the Libera Dramach above her, that he saw her as a means to an end rather than as a daughter.

Did he deserve that? Maybe. But by the spirits, he had not imagined it would hurt so much.

They made their way up to another tier, nearing the top where the caves were. Women were hurrying their children along frantically, on the edge of panic. As if the caves would provide succour when the walls fell . . .

The Sister came to a sudden halt in the middle of the street, and Zaelis almost went into the back of her. Yugi stopped as well, holding out a hand to indicate that the younger ones should do the same. They were smoke-grimed and sweaty, and all but Yugi were panting with exertion.

'What is it?' Yugi asked, sensing something in the Sister's manner that made him uneasy.

She was scanning the balconies of the houses on either side, their dirtied pennants flapping. The very air seemed to have stilled and quieted, the din around them fading to a distant buzz.

'What *is* it?' Yugi hissed again. A dreadful foreboding was building within him.

The Sister's eyes fell upon a ragged woman and a child walking slowly towards them, and her irises darkened to red.

Zaelis never even saw the furies. They cannoned out of an open doorway and charged right through him, butting him aside and knocking him off his feet to crash in a heap on the ground. Yugi whirled on them with a cry, his rifle already levelled. The massive, boar-like monstrosities were bearing down on him; he squeezed the trigger and took one of them directly between the eyes. Its charge turned into a roll as its legs went limp, but its momentum was too great to check and it barrelled into Yugi. He tried to jump it, but he was not fast enough; it clipped his boots and he somersaulted, landing on his back with a force that winded him.

The second furie was not going for Yugi. It went for Flen instead. The boy was paralysed, too late to run, too weak to fight. The creature was many times his weight and almost as tall as him at the shoulder. It thundered into him, a compact mass of brutality fronted by a tangle of long, hooked tusks, and smashed him down. He went skidding across the dusty street in a chaos of loose limbs, rolling over and over and coming to rest with his unkempt brown hair covering his face.

The furie turned its small, black eyes to Lucia. Lucia looked back at it calmly.

The air erupted in a screaming, shrieking mass of movement, feather and beak and claw. The ravens tore into the Aberrant beast, diving out of the smoky sky and bombarding it, latching on with their talons and stabbing with their beaks. The creature had a thick hide, but its eyes were ripped out in moments and its snout plucked to bloody ribbons. It thrashed and squealed as it was buried beneath a mass of beating wings, finally slumping to the earth where it lay wheezing.

And then, as one, the ravens dropped dead.

Yugi was stunned. He could not credit what his eyes had seen, even as the last few birds hit the ground. They had all died instantaneously, simply falling out of the air. As the breath returned to his lungs and he got up, he took in the scene: Zaelis, struggling to his feet; Flen, lying motionless on the ground; two furies, one dead and one flayed to point of death; Lucia, standing there with a calmness on her face that was somehow worse than the horror she should have been showing; and scattered around, dozens of raven corpses.

Then he looked for Irilia, and he realised that it was not over yet.

She was sprawled a short distance away, her head twisted backwards on her neck. Next to her lay a filthy-looking child, blood streaming from its eyes and nose. And coming towards Yugi now was the woman that he had seen moments ago, a shuffling, hobbling beggar.

As he watched, something happened to his vision, a sudden and violent shift of perspective; and he saw in the woman's place a Weaver, his Mask a shimmering mass of lizard scales that sheened like a rainbow. The dead child had become a Weaver too. Irilia had been overmatched by the two of them, but she managed to take one of them with her. One, however, was not enough, and not even Lucia's ravens could save them now. The people in the street – who had not reacted fast enough to intervene when the furies attacked – ran at the sight of the figure in their midst.

Yugi's blood turned to ice. The Red Order were not infallible, it seemed, and the Weavers were cleverer than they imagined. Somehow these two had slipped past the Sisters.

He heard Zaelis's indrawn breath. Lucia, standing amid all that death, was watching the Weaver.

The Weaver looked back at her, a hidden gaze beneath his patch-work cowl.

Yugi saw Zaelis move on the periphery of his vision. The older man's rifle swung up.

'Zaelis, *no!*' he cried, but it was much too late. The Weaver's Mask turned to the leader of the Libera Dramach, and one hand thrust out, white fingers curled into a claw. Zaelis's attempt to aim was arrested as suddenly as if someone had grabbed the end of the barrel. Yugi felt his muscles lock rigid at the same time. Every part of him cramped agonisingly, rooting him to the spot. His eyes were wide and staring, but his body would not respond, not even to scream.

Zaelis was turning the rifle towards himself. It was clear by the expression of utter and awful horror on his face that the movement was not of his volition, but the muzzle of the weapon was slowly and steadily turning towards him anyway. Yugi, frozen, could do nothing but watch. Lucia stood there, her gaze faraway, and did not move.

The pulse at Zaelis's throat was jumping with the effort of resisting, but it was no good. He had angled the rifle so that the muzzle was pressed into his bearded throat, beneath his chin.

He can't reach the trigger, Yugi thought, with a flicker of futile hope. *The rifle's too long.*

The trigger began to move slowly of its own accord. The Weaver's fingers curled into a fist.

'Gods curse you, you inhuman bastards,' Zaelis croaked, and then the rifle fired and blew his brains out.

The shot rang across the streets and was lost in the distant sounds of battle. The cry of grief that sounded in Yugi's mind was trapped in his throat. Lucia was still and silent. Flecks of her adopted father's blood had ribboned her face. She was trembling, her eyes welling, her mouth open a little.

Zaelis fell to his knees, and then pitched sideways to the ground. A tear broke from Lucia's lashes and raced down her grimy cheek.

The Weaver ignored Yugi, turning his scaled face back to the girl now.

'Tears, Lucia?' he croaked. 'No good. No good at all.'

Yugi made a strangled noise: *Not her! Take me!* But no amount of will could undo the Weaver's power. He wanted to shriek at his own helplessness, but he was not even permitted to do that.

The Weaver took a step towards her; and his Mask shattered.

The report of a rifle reached them an instant later. The Weaver stood blankly for a few seconds, thin blood welling through the cracked fractions of his face, and then he tipped backward and collapsed in a heap.

Yugi's muscles unknotted themselves at once, sending him gasping to his knees. A gust of wind blew a thick cloud of smoke over him, turning the street to a fuggy pall, and he coughed ralingly; but the sheer relief from the pain of the Weaver's grip brought tears to his eyes that were nothing to do with the polluted air. He sobbed once, the shock and terror and grief of the last few moments swamping him; then he swallowed, hitched a shuddering breath, and wiped his eyes with the edge of the rag around his forehead.

Lucia.

The wind changed then. The smoke blew up and away as if sucked back skyward, and there was Nomoru, slowing to a halt from a run as she neared Lucia, her ornate rifle cradled in one arm. She surveyed the scene dispassionately and raked a hand through her messy hair.

Yugi went slowly over to them, his body and mind numb and aching. He met Nomoru's gaze as he came.

'Followed the ravens,' she said.

He stared at her, unable to find words; then he crouched down in front of Lucia, put his hands on her shoulders. She was shaking like a leaf, looking past him, tears running down her face.

'Is that Zaelis?' Nomoru said.

Yugi flinched at her insensitivity. 'The boy. See if he's alright.'

Nomoru did as she was asked. Other people were coming down the street now, running to help, gasping at the sight of the dead Weavers, far too late to do anything. *Where were they when we needed them?* Yugi thought bitterly.

'Lucia?' he prompted. She did not look at him, nor did she appear to have heard. 'Lucia?' he said again.

Then Nomoru was back. He looked up at her: she shook her head. Flen was gone.

Yugi bit his lip; the grief was almost too much to keep inside. He got up and turned away, fearful of losing control in front of Lucia. He was no stranger to murder; there were many things in his past he would rather forget. But gods, all this *killing* . . .

He heard Nomoru behind him.

'Lucia? Lucia, can you hear me? Are there more birds? Are there more ravens?'

He was about to whirl and shout at her to leave the poor child alone, she'd suffered enough; but then he heard a small voice in reply.

'There are more.'

Yugi turned back, saw the scout standing there awkwardly, and the slender, beautiful girl looking up at her with a depth of sorrow written on her features that made him want to cry.

'We need them.'

' Nomoru . . .' Yugi began, but she held up a hand and he subsided.

Lucia pushed gently but forcefully past Nomoru. She walked over to where Zaelis lay and looked down on him. Then she stepped over the corpses of birds to where Flen's broken body was, now turned face-up and staring sightlessly into the afterlife. For a long time, her eyes roamed him, as if expecting him at any moment to get up again, to breathe, to laugh.

She looked over her shoulder, her tear-streaked face unnaturally calm, as if a glaze had been painted over her expression.

'The ravens are yours,' she said, and her voice was chill as a knife. 'What would you have me do?'

Thirty-Five

((*et us out))*
L Kaiku looked automatically towards the source of the sound, before realising that there had *been* no sound. The voice was coming from inside her head, a form of Weave-communication alike to the sort that the Red Order practised, but much cruder.

Tsata stanced ready to receive the approaching shrillings, which were coming down the tunnel, their warbling preceding them. He could see only a dark, stony maw: his night vision had been destroyed by the putrescent light of the witchstone that glowed through the grille at their backs.

'Kaiku, if you have any ideas, now is the time,' he said with a hint of black humour.

((let us out))

The voice was an insistent whisper, hoarse and cracked. It was coming from the creatures that moved behind the bars in the side-tunnels. They stayed just on the edge of the light, allowing hints of their form but no more. The hints were disturbing enough. There was no regular form to them: their shapes were asymmetrical, twisted, some with many limbs and some with tentacles or claws, some with spines or vestigial fins. Most of them had appendages she could not even recognise.

I know them, she thought to herself. *I have seen them before.*

In the Weavers' monastery, deep in the Lakmar Mountains, she had come across creatures similar to this, and similarly imprisoned. They had tried to attack her, thinking she was a Weaver, for she had been disguised as one. Much speculation had been made in the Fold as to what these things were, but theories were all anyone could come up with.

She backed away instinctively from the creature that spoke to her. Her Weave-sense had allowed her to pinpoint the direction. It was coming closer.

But in retreating from one side, she neared the other, and the tunnel

374

was narrow here. Something cold and slimy wrapped around her hand in a tight grip.

She shrieked and spun; the grip loosened, and a thin tendril retreated between the bars. Tsata turned at the sound, to see her staring at the place where it had disappeared. Something was moving closer to the bars now, some small, wrecked thing.

The light fell across it, and Kaiku went pale.

It was a monstrosity, a warped clutter of legs and arms attached around a central torso that was barely recognisable as such. Its yellowed skin was stretched across a hopelessly mangled skeleton, and it jerked and move spasmodically, its multiple limbs waving. There was a kind of neckless head somewhere in the middle of it, little more than a bulbous lump, upon which something like features sat.

But the face it wore was Kaiku's.

The shock of it made her stagger. It was like looking in a distorted mirror, or a sculpture of herself that had been pulled out of shape and half-melted. Flesh drooped from the eye sockets, the mouth was tugged to one side as if by an invisible hook, her teeth in multiple rows . . . but it was still, unmistakably, an approximation of *her*.

((let us out)) the voice came again, insistent.

((What are you?)) she responded, disgust making her forget about the dangers of using her *kana*.

The thing that had copied her face had retreated into the shadows now, and she turned back to the one who was somehow speaking to her. It had come up to the bars, a pathetically runty thing with a flaccid sail of spines and all of its limbs drastically different in size. Gummy odd-coloured eyes fixed her from within a lopsided face.

((What are you?)) she demanded again, needing to make some sense of this.

((Edgefathers)) it replied, and Kaiku was bombarded with images, sights and sensations that hit her all in a disorientating mass, flashing through her mind in an instant.

Edgefathers. The ones who created the Masks for the Weavers to wear. She picked up confused recollections of forges and workshops, deep underground in the monasteries, built to the Weavers' insane ideas of architecture; then, further back, a memory of a family – *gods, this had once been a man, an artisan* – and he was taken, the Weavers coming in the night like evil spirits, stealing him away from his tiny village in the mountains; now he was working, working, crafting the Masks alongside other men – never women – artists and woodworkers and metalsmiths, and always the dust, the dust, the witchstone dust which they put into their work to give it the power the Weavers wanted; and looking around him and seeing what the dust was *doing* to all those men, what it was doing to *him*, beginning as a scaly patch on the heel of his hand, and then some kind of growth on his back, and the changes, the terrible corruption that came from handling raw, untreated witchstone dust day after day; and when they had changed too much they were taken away and not killed – *heart's blood why weren't they killed?* – but imprisoned while they kept changing, even away from the dust; and sometimes like now their prisons overflowed and they were taken elsewhere to be imprisoned because too many together was dangerous, because some *like this one* could do things, strange things brought on by the relentless and unending mutation, and others *like that one* could steal parts from others and copy them and couldn't help it and

((LET US OUT!!!))

The mental force of the sending made Kaiku reel. Torment flooded her in an empathic wave.

'Kaiku!' Tsata said urgently. The shrillings were almost upon them.

She made her decision. Her irises darkened to deep red with the full and unshielded release of her *kana*, her hair stirring around her face as if by some spectral wind. Power leaped eagerly from her, knitting through the golden threads of the air, sewing into the metal of the grille that separated them from the witchstone. With a wrench, two of the columns tore away and went spinning into the lake below, making a gap big enough for a person to pass through. The Edgefathers began to howl.

((NO! NO! LET US OUT!!!))

'Tsata! This way!'

The Tkiurathi had turned at the sound of the tearing metal; now, seeing an escape route, he ran to it, pausing for a moment in front of Kaiku. Their eyes met; his pale and green, hers a demonic Aberrant red. She shoved the sack of explosives into his arms.

'You first,' she said.

He did not question. He simply jumped out into the air, trusting to luck that the water beneath would be deep enough to receive him.

Kaiku heard the splash as he hit. The first of the shrillings raced around the corner of the tunnel, sprinting towards her with its catlike gait. Several more followed a moment later.

She waved her hand, and the bars of the side-tunnels ripped off, clattering to the stone floor. The Edgefathers howled in exultation, pouring out of their prisons; but by that point, Kaiku had already jumped, and was falling towards the lake. The shrillings tore into the Edgefathers, who responded with a mob savagery and overwhelming numbers, careless of their own lives, a furious and insane mass. The rest of the shrillings and the Nexuses that arrived after them found themselves facing dozens of grotesqueries baying for blood.

Their end was as unpleasant as the Edgefathers' lives had been.

The victors rampaged up the tunnel, spreading out into the caverns, sowing havoc where they went. They sought death and vengeance in equal measure, and left destruction in their wake.

The temperature of the water drove the breath from Kaiku's lungs. The cries of the Edgefathers became suddenly bassy and dim as she plummeted into the lake, and her ears were filled with the roar of bubbles; then, as her downward momentum dissipated, she kicked upward towards the foul luminescence of the witchstone. She broke the surface with a gasp, her hair plastered across one side of her face. The tumult seemed suddenly deafening again.

Tsata was already swimming away from her, one arm clutched around the sack of explosives. She called his name, but he did not stop, and so she struck out after him. Behind her, the shrillings were wailing as they were torn apart by the things she had released. Some of the grotesqueries were spilling out from the sundered grille, falling gracelessly through the air into the lake where they swam or sank, depending on the severity of their mutation and the configuration of their bodies. Two of them had clambered out and were crawling up the sides of the shaft like spiders. Golneri were fleeing in all directions, terrified by the sight of the Edgefathers, their boots clattering on the walkways that crisscrossed overhead. What Nexuses and Aberrants there had been here at the bottom of the shaft had gone, following the alarms raised by the sighting of Tsata and Kaiku back in the worm-farm; nobody was here to protect the diminutive creatures, and they panicked. Pandemonium reigned.

Kaiku was a better swimmer than Tsata was, and she caught him as he was clambering out onto a small, rocky hump from which a precarious bridge crossed the water to the central island, where the witchstone lay glowering. Huge scoops continued their procession into and out of the lake in the background, and massive pipes sucked water nearby. She grabbed his good arm as he made to run, and he turned back to her, his tattooed face grim in the eerie light.

'We've got to—' she began, but he shook his head. He knew what she would say: they had to hide, to get away from this place before the Weavers arrived, drawn by her *kana*. But there was no hiding for him.

He clicked his tongue and pointed. Hobbling along a walkway high overhead, a cowled and Masked figure in ragged robes.

'Hold him off,' Tsata said, and then he sprinted across the bridge, towards the witchstone, carrying with him the sodden bag of explosives.

Kaiku had no time to protest, not even time to consider whether the warped Edgefathers that splashed in the water were as much a threat to her and Tsata as they were to anyone else. The Weaver, seeing the Tkiurathi approaching the dreadful rock, sent out a mass of tendrils across the Weave to rip him apart. Kaiku reacted without thought, and her *kana* burst forth to intercept. Their consciousnesses collided, and all became golden.

She was a spray of threads, crashing and entangling with the Weaver's own, using the fractional advantage of surprise to penetrate as deep as she could before the Weaver twisted and closed up like a fist, burying them both in a ball of scurrying combat. Knots appeared before her as she sought to untangle herself and drive onward, insoluble junctions that she sometimes picked at, sometimes avoided. Her mind had split into a jumble of countless consciousnesses, an army of her thoughts each fighting a personal battle amid the churning tapestry of light. The Weaver's fury swamped her, not as intense as the unfathomable malice of the ruku-shai but more personal: woman had invaded man's realm, and her punishment would be extraordinary.

And then suddenly, shockingly, her vision inverted and the diorama went dark. She was in a corridor: a long, shadow-laden corridor. Purple lightning threw bright and rapid illumination through the shutters, flashing strange patterns onto the wall. Moonstorm lightning, like there had been on the last day she ever saw this place. Vases of guya blossoms stood on tables, dipping and nodding in the stir of the breeze. It was raining, though she knew it not by the sound but by the warm moisture in the air. The silence ached in her ears; only the roar of blood could be heard in its stead.

It was her father's house in the Forest of Yuna. The house where her family had died, and where the demon shin-shin had stalked her. She had never quite shed the nightmares from which she would wake up sweating with a diminishing memory of corridors and unseen, stilt-legged things hiding behind doorways and around corners.

But this was no dream; this was impossibly real.

She looked down at herself, and she confirmed what she already knew: she was a child again, in a nightgown, alone in an empty house. And something was coming for her.

She felt its black presence approaching, nearing her rapidly, a thing of rage and wrath. Something that would be on her in moments, a beast so enormous it would engulf her and swallow her whole.

She was a child, and so she ran.

But the night was like tar, thick and cloying, dragging her limbs down. She could not run without turning her back on the approaching monstrosity, but she could not outpace it. And yet she fled anyway, for the terror of that invisible malice was beyond belief, making her want to beg and weep and plead for it to go away, yet suffocating her with the knowledge that nothing she could do would avert it.

Her barefoot sprint was agonisingly slow. The guya blossoms turned their petal-hooded faces towards her, watching her pass with sinister interest. The end of the corridor seemed to be retreating one step away from her for every two she took. Behind her, the creature was coming closer and closer, thundering through the dream-maze of her house, and it seemed perpetually that it must take her at any moment, that it could not *get* any closer without reaching her, yet always the sensation of awful nearness grew, until tears streaked her face and she screamed without noise. And still she fled, and the corridor's end neared with a patience intended to thwart her of her life.

The Weaver! It is the Weaver!

Her thoughts freed themselves from the child-form where they had become momentarily muddled. She reminded herself forcefully that she was in the Weave, that her body stood dripping wet on an island in an underground lake at the bottom of a great shaft in the earth. And yet where was the golden world she had known, the landscape that her *kana* navigated by? Where were the threads?

It struck her then. The Weaver had changed the rules of play. Cailin had told her how the Weavers chose visualisations of the Weave, adapting it to some form that they could understand and deal with, because unlike the Sisters they could not handle the raw element without losing their minds to the dangerous, hypnotic bliss. Her opponent had jacketed her in a visualisation of her own nightmare, had picked up the leaking subconscious fears she was too inexperienced to curb and turned them to his advantage. She was trapped here, a weak and helpless child facing a monster of unimaginable potential.

How could she fight him here? How could she beat a Weaver? It was suicide to face one of them! They were masters of this realm, whereas she had only a few rudimentary techniques and her instinct to guide her. How could she beat her enemy when it was he that was setting the game, he that made the rules?

Despair took her, despair at being a little girl lost in a nightmare, an adult trapped in a hopeless battle. The Weaver would catch her, and it would kill her or worse. And after that, it would kill Tsata.

It was that thought and no other that braked her downward slide into submission.

I cannot run. It is not only my life at stake here.

The purity of that realisation strengthened her. It was no mere attempt at self-persuasion; it was a matter of what she utterly, unarguably *had* to do. Sometime over these last days she had stopped thinking of herself and Tsata as a team, as companions, even as friends; in fact, she was not sure that *friendship* was entirely accurate to describe the bonds that had grown between them, the strange and tentative understanding of each other, the unthinking trust necessary to survive the deadly Aberrant predators that they had hunted and been hunted by. Some subtle osmosis of words and actions had bled from him to her, and she had begun to think of them as a symbiote, a state of existence in which one could not do without the other – a single entity, fused of two independent beings. If she died here, he died. He had placed his life in her hands when he had charged her to hold off the Weaver while he tried to destroy the witchstone. Kaiku had no idea how much time had passed in Tsata's world – she was too deeply immersed in this one – but every moment she could give him might make the distinction between his life and death, between completing their task and failing.

This was *pash*, the Okhamban concept of togetherness and unselfish subversion of personal desires to the greater good. She understood it now, and it put steel in her spine.

She slowed to a stop. The end of the corridor seemed to spring towards her invitingly, urging her onward. The Weaver's advance faltered, and now she was conscious of his presence directly behind her, close enough to touch, making the fine hairs of her back and neck prickle with the intensity of its hunger. She was nearly there, nearly at the corner that would obscure her from that hateful gaze.

But she turned away from it. And as she turned she grew, passing through twenty years in an instant, and it was an adult Kaiku with her irises an arterial red that looked upon the creature the Weaver had become.

It filled the whole of the corridor, an enormous, slavering, six-armed man-beast that loomed over her, its hot and rotten breath stinking of carrion. Its feet and hands were clawed, but the rest of its body was humanoid, lumpen with muscle and covered with thick black hair across the chest and groin. Its skin was red and glistening with sweat, and its face was all snout and horn and fang. Noxious vapours leaked from between its sharp teeth, wreathing it in smoke. Small eyes glimmered fiercely.

It was a demonic exaggeration of one of her most prominent childhood fears, based on the icon of Jurani her father had kept in his study. The six-armed god of fire had two depictions, and statuettes of him were always crafted in pairs – one as a benevolent life-giver, source of light and warmth, and one as a raging creature of de-struction. Kaiku had been scared of the latter statuette as an infant, ever since her mother had told her that Jurani lived in Mount Makara and its perpetual smouldering was the steam from the god's nostrils.

It was the Weaver's mistake. Fear of the gaping dark, of empty corridors filled with nameless dreads . . . that was something that had always been with her, a subtle and primal instinct that followed children into adulthood and old age. But she had surmounted her fear of Jurani when she was young, and his appearance here was incongruous and jarring. The Weaver was manipulating her fears, but it was only picking up resonances and memories, and this was one that was long dead.

She threw herself into the beast, grappling it, and the world burst into a rush of golden fibres again. The Weaver's illusion was shattered.

But she saw now what her enemy had been doing while she was distracted by his ploy. He had used the time she had wasted in fleeing to press the advantage, sewing through her defences, gnawing away knots until the barrier holding him from Kaiku's physical body was threadbare and ready to break. Frantically, she shored them up, spinning new stitches across the battlefield, dancing from strand to strand. The Weaver pressed aggressively, a flurry of jabs and feints intended to distract her from the real damage he was doing; but Kaiku guessed its trick and ignored the false vibrations, skipping rapidly here and there, rebuilding, fashioning knots and traps and tangles to tire and confuse her opponent.

The world shifted again, becoming a long, dark tunnel at the end of which something was tearing towards her, but she knew it now for what it was and she wrenched her perception back into the Weave again, dispelling the scene. Here, she was not hampered by the need to interpret the realm as the Weaver was. She could deal with the raw stuff instead. It gave her an advantage, made her faster than her opponent.

But she was still woefully inexperienced in her art, and the Weaver was clever. She was on the defensive, and quick as she was she could not keep him out indefinitely. The idea of counterattacking was unfeasible while he dogged her like this.

You need only buy time, she thought.

Then she saw it: an opening, a gap in the Weaver's barrier that had frayed from lack of maintenance, pulled apart by the stretching of the strings around it. The Weaver's attention was fixed firmly on her, heedless of defending himself. He was worrying his way towards an insoluble labyrinth that Kaiku had set up to delay him. That would keep him busy long enough for Kaiku to—

She had no time for further consideration. Marshalling her

consciousness to a point, she arrowed it past the glittering tendrils of the Weaver's influence and into the gap.

By the time she saw that it was a snare, she was too late. The gap closed behind her, dropping a curtain of chaotic tangles to prevent her from pulling out. The surrounding fibres pulled tight like a net, constricting her. She struggled desperately, but the bonds were slow to break, and new ones were enwrapping her all the time, like a spider cocooning a fly. In another part of her mind, she sensed the Weaver dodging out of the trap she had set, and realised that he had sensed it all along and had been merely giving her an opportunity to rush into his own trap. He began to bore into her defences again, unpicking them steadily, and she could not disentangle herself to deal with it. She had gone in too eagerly, fallen for an amateurish trick, and there was no way she could get out in time to stop him now. It was a mistake that would cost her her life.

She flailed and screamed soundlessly, fighting to be free, as the Weaver threaded past the last of the obstacles she had laid and sent awful tendrils into her body, into her *flesh*.

Then the fibres of the Weave flexed mightily, a tsunami smashing through them, a wordless, idiot cry that swept both Kaiku and the Weaver up in a riptide and left them spinning in the eddies of its aftermath. Kaiku felt the Weaver's tendrils snapping away from her as she was torn free of her cocoon, all defences blasted aside by the force of the disturbance. She was dizzied and uncomprehending, waiting for her instincts to translate the blare that had stunned them.

The witchstone. *The witchstone!*

It was in distress.

The Weaver was paralysed, battered by the force of the cry and simultaneously drawn to it. His priority was, and ever had been, the welfare of the witchstone in his keeping. It was more than simply a task, it was the very purpose of his being. He did not understand the source of the compulsion that drove him, did not know the source of the group-mind that directed the Weavers. He did not know that what he guarded was not only the fount of the Weavers' power, but also a fragment of the moon-god Aricarat. At the witchstone's cry he was like a mother whose child is threatened, and nothing else but saving it mattered. Not even defending himself.

He did not even realise Kaiku was attacking him until she had burst through the tatter of his barricades and into his core. She was a spiralling needle that tracked along the diorama of the Weave, blooming inside him, anchoring herself until she had the kind of grip she needed.

Even from the start, she had always been able to use her power for one basic purpose: to destroy. She rent the Weaver apart.

Her vision flicked back to reality in time to see the cowled figure explode in a shower of flaming bone and blood on the walkway, burning shreds of robe and Mask and skin sailing through the air to fall hissing into the dark water of the lake. A terrible weakness drenched her, and she was pulled to her hands and knees by its weight, her sodden hair falling across her face, her back rising and falling with heaving breaths. Something felt broken inside her, some remnant damage that the Weaver had managed to cause. The violation of his touch made her vomit, spattering the meagre contents of her stomach across the slick rock between her hands. Dimly, she was aware of the roar of the plunging waterfalls, the echoing moans and howls of the Edgefathers, the clatter of boots on metal as golneri tried to escape up the shaft.

Then it came to her, a thought that rang with triumph and disbelief equally. She had faced a Weaver, and she had won.

But the moment of joy was fleeting. She had drained herself in doing so, overextended her power in the way she used to do before Cailin had taught her moderation. Her *kana* was all but burned out, and her body with it; she was pathetically vulnerable now, and still in the direst danger. She could barely raise her head to gaze at the central island where the witchstone lay, at the foul thing that had unwittingly saved her life.

It was crawling with Edgefathers, chipping at it with rocks and tools and scraping with bare claws. They had snapped teeth and nails on its surface, and bloodied fists and maws bore testament to the insane fury of their assault. The damage they were doing was far greater to themselves than to the witchstone, which was suffering only negligibly under their attacks. She could still sense its wail, resonating across the Weave, carrying over unguessable distance to summon aid. If there were any Weavers left here, they would be rushing to the chamber even now; and Kaiku could not withstand another one.

Then she found Tsata. The Tkiurathi was crouched at the base of the witchstone, jamming explosives beneath it and tamping them with mud from below the waterline. The Edgefathers appeared to be ignoring him, and for his part he seemed focused on nothing else. Had he even noticed the struggle she had been through to save his life? Kaiku felt a surge of resentment at that, and she rode it to her feet, using it as a crutch to overcome the tiredness that had settled upon her.

Somewhere above, Edgefathers and shrillings and Nexuses were fighting on the network of walkways. She was too exhausted to think about anything but stumbling across the bridge towards the central island, towards Tsata. The scoops rotated and the pipes sucked and the furnaces steamed and hissed and rumbled, heedless of her plight, endless in their purpose. The witchstone seethed its foul light, and the very air seemed to crawl as she approached; her stomach shrivelled and began to churn. She staggered to her companion's side, trusting that the Edgefathers would not hinder her, and knelt heavily down next to him. His pallor was even more jaundiced than usual; it was plain that the vile proximity of the witchstone was affecting him too. He spared her a sideways look, then returned to his task.

She knew his ways by now. The most important thing for them all was to destroy the witchstone. That made everything else secondary for Tsata. But spirits, did he even realise what she had just *done*? A word of congratulation, of thanks, even of relief at seeing her . . . that would have been all that was needed. But he was too focused, too rigid in his priorities.

'The fuses are wet,' he said, as the last of the explosives were put into place. 'They will not light.'

Kaiku took a moment to process that, and a further moment for the implication to hit her. What anger she had felt at his uncaring demeanour was swept aside under the force of a new emotion.

'No, Tsata,' she said, aghast. She knew what he was thinking. She knew what a Tkiurathi would do.

'You have to go,' he said, looking over at her. 'I will stay, and make certain the explosives work.'

'You mean you will stay and *die* here!' she cried.

'There is no other way,' Tsata said.

She clutched him by the shoulders, hard, and turned him towards her. His orange-blond hair lay in wet spikes across his forehead, his tattooed face strangely calm. Of course he was *calm*, she thought, infuriated. All his choices had been made for him. That same gods-cursed philosophy of selflessness that had helped to save her life meant that he was going to throw away his, because it was *for the greater good*.

'I will not let you die this way,' she hissed at him. 'A man was killed five years ago because he followed me into something he should not have been involved in, and I still bear his death on my conscience. I will not have yours too!'

'You cannot prevent me, Kaiku,' he said. 'It is simple. If I go, we cannot destroy the witchstone, and all this is for nothing. This is not about us. It is about the millions of people in Saramyr. We have the chance to strike a blow, and my life means nothing compared to those it might save.'

'It means something to *me*!' she cried, and almost instantly regretted it. But it was said, and could not be unsaid.

She fell silent immediately. Something in her wanted to go on, to explain what she felt welling up in her, that in this man she saw a person she could trust utterly, one who was incapable of betraying her as Asara had, someone whom she did not need to fear laying herself bare to. But the healing of her heart after so many wounds was not to be completed in a moment, and as much as she knew that she could not stand the pain of letting him sacrifice himself like this, she knew also that she dared not let herself say it.

He regarded her tenderly. 'There is no time,' he said, and there was something like regret in his voice. 'Go!'

'I cannot go!' she said, swallowing bile as her stomach reacted to the emanations of the witchstone. 'I am too weak. I need you to help me.'

A flicker of doubt crossed Tsata's pale eyes, then disappeared as resolve firmed them. 'Then you must stay too.'

'No!' she shrieked. 'Spirits, this selflessness you hold so dear sickens me sometimes! I will not sacrifice myself for this, and you will not make that choice for me! You are the only one who can carry the message of the danger the Weavers pose back to your people; they will not believe a Saramyr. To kill yourself here is *selfish*! You are thinking of my *pash*, and not of your own, not of your *people*! If they are not told of this, they will be next after Saramyr falls, and you are the only person alive who can warn them! We do not know what destroying this witchstone will do, but we *do* know what the Weavers will do to your land when they get there, and if the Tkiurathi are unprepared then they will all die! The world is *not* so black and white, Tsata. There are many ways to do what you think is right.'

Tsata's expression showed that he was wavering, but when he spoke it brought tears of exhausted frustration to her eyes.

'I have to stay,' he insisted. 'The fuses are wet.'

'*I can do it!*' she screamed at him. 'I am a gods-damned Aberrant! I can ignite them from a distance.'

Tsata searched her eyes, probing her. He was wise enough to know that she would say anything to get him away from there.

'Can you?'

'Yes!' she replied instantly. But could she? She had no idea. She did not know the range of her abilities, nor if there was enough *kana* left inside her. She had never tried anything like it before, and she was at the lowest ebb of her power. But she gazed into his eyes, and she lied to him.

I will not lose you. Not like Tane.

'Then we must go,' Tsata said, springing to his feet and pulling Kaiku up with him. She gasped in both relief and pain – whatever the Weaver had done to her twinged at the movement – and allowed herself to be propelled across to the water and then into it. She had barely the strength to swim, but Tsata supported her with one arm, striking out with the other. She let him take her, not caring where they were going, only that they were getting out, that he had believed her. Whether she could do what she had promised or not was another matter, but she did not allow herself to worry about that now. She clung to him, and he held on to her.

The sounds of the shrillings were all about as they fought with the rampant Edgefathers across the walkways. Some were almost at the central island now. The roaring of machinery filled her ears, getting louder, and she looked up and saw Tsata's reckless plan.

Several metres ahead of them, the massive water-scoops were rising out of the lake, heading upward into the darkness of the shaft. Tsata was swimming right towards them.

'Do not be afraid,' he murmured, seeing her expression; and then one of the scoops passed right in front of them and up and away, and with a few sturdy strokes Tsata pulled them into the patch of water it had just vacated.

Kaiku went limp. She trusted him. There was nothing left to do.

She felt a dip, then something collided with her ankles from beneath, tipping her into the great metal cradle that rose around her. She was submerged and flailed for an instant, banging her hand on something hard, and then righted herself and burst free. They were ascending, the lake falling away beneath them, splashes of water slopping over the lip of the scoop to plunge back to their source. Already, other scoops were following them upward. The awful sinking feeling of being lifted made Kaiku want to panic, but she felt too precarious to dare, and instead she froze.

They were rising past the webwork of walkways, past Edgefathers fighting with predators, past bellowing constructions and glowing furnaces and enormous cogs rotating. A Nexus fell silently from above to smash into a railing, thence to pitch broken-backed into the lake. A shrilling was savaging a golneri, the creature gone wild after the death of its handler. All was chaos, and nobody noticed the scoop and its passengers heading toward the abyss overhead and the beckoning clouds of distant flame from the gas-torches.

She felt Tsata next to her, his steadying hand on her shoulder.

'Now, Kaiku,' he said.

She closed her eyes, searching inside herself for what energy she had left. She would only need a spark, only that. She racked her burning body, eking out reserves, gathering her *kana*.

Just this time, she pleaded, and she realised that it was Ocha she was addressing, Emperor of the Gods, to whom she had sworn the oath that had put her on this road in the first place. *I just need a little help.*

And there it was. She found it, felt it burning in her womb and belly, and she forced it up into her chest and free from her body, a meagre glimmer of energy that seared her on its way out. Her eyes flew open and she drew a shuddering breath, and the world was once again the Weave. She saw the convection of the threads in the lake, the swirl of golden, fibrous blood on the walkways, the curling clouds of steam from the machines. She picked a thread and followed it, down into the lake and then along, and there she found the witchstone.

It was a black, seething knot, a heart of corruption so terrible that she could not bear to look on it. It seemed to writhe in restless anger, and its wail of distress cut across the Weave like a hurricane. And it was *alive*, malevolently alive, its hate radiating out from it, the rage of a crippled god.

But it was powerless to stop her. A last swell of courage sent her onward, finding the mud packed at the witchstone's base, passing through it into the tightly sealed bars of explosive. The threads were coiled and deadly within, throbbing with potential energy.

She found her spark, and threw it.

Thirty-Six

T he battle in the Fold had been carried into the sky. The ravens had launched from the rooftops, from distant trees, from rookeries among the stony nooks to the east, rising in a cloud as thick as the smoke that billowed from the valley. In their small animal thoughts Lucia's call was like a clarion. She regarded them as her friends, and until now she would have done nothing to risk them; but matters had changed, and now she called on her avian guardians and sent them with a single, simple command: kill the gristle-crows.

Black shapes wheeled and shrieked in the ash-darkened afternoon, harrying the much larger and stronger Aberrant birds. The ravens were legion, outnumbering the Aberrants by many times. The gristle-crows slashed and snapped, banking and swooping on their ragged wings; but the ravens were more agile, and they dodged near and raked with talons or beaks before darting away again, reddened with their enemy's blood. Gory clots of feathers plunged through the air to smash onto the uneven rooftops of the town; and for every three of the ravens went a gristle-crow, falling stunned from the air with a bone-splintering impact as it hit.

Cailin tu Moritat was peripherally aware of the conflict going on over her head, but her attention was taken up by the greater conflict in the Weave. She stood on the edge of one of the higher tiers, flanked by two of her Sisters and guarded by twenty men who watched anxiously for predators. Below them, the ledges and plateaux of the town cluttered down towards the barricade and the horde beyond, who were senselessly throwing themselves at the eastern fortifications while the fire-cannons and riflemen destroyed them in their hundreds. Smoke rendered the vista in shades of obscurity, occasionally allowing a glimpse of the streets, where more and more Aberrants ran. The western wall was failing, and the creatures leaked in steadily to prey on those women and children who had not yet found sanctuary in the caves.

The battle in the sky found its mirror in the Weave. The Sisters swooped and struck like comets, evading the Weavers' more cumbersome attempts to strike back. They spun nets of knots, working in co-operation with an ease and fluidity that their male counterparts could not hope to match. The Sisters outnumbered the Weavers now, and the fight had turned to their advantage.

The more experienced Weavers had held out desperately until the great disturbance had swept over them. Cailin knew with a fierce joy what that disturbance was: a witchstone's cry of distress. After that, the Weavers began to make mistakes, distraction ruining the attention to detail that was necessary to keep the Sisters out. Two of them fell in quick succession, erupting into flame as the Sisters dug into them and pulled their threads apart.

Another Weaver was on the verge of crumbling when Cailin felt a terrible chill upon her, like a presentiment of her own death. She braced herself an instant before the shockwave hit them, an immensity of force that dwarfed the witchstone's distress-call. The very fabric of reality flexed and warped, a rolling hump of distortion blasting outward from the epicentre, passing over them and leaving them suddenly becalmed. Instinctively, Cailin quested, tracking the fibres strewn by the blast back to their source.

West. West, where Kaiku was.

It hit her in a moment of triumph. The witchstone in the Fault had been destroyed. She sent a rallying cry to her brethren and they plunged in to attack.

But the Weavers had given up. The souls had gone out of them. Like faint ghosts, their minds drifted, stunned, bewildered by the calamity that had overcome them. The Sisters hesitated, fearing a trick, expecting opposition; but the hesitation lasted only a moment. Like wolves to wounded rabbits, they tore their enemies to pieces.

And then it was done. The Sisters drifted alone in the Weave, disembodied among the gently stirring fibres. Alone, except for the leviathans that glided at the edge of their perception, their movements strangely agitated now. They had felt the shockwave and been perturbed by it.

Gradually, Cailin began to feel strange sensations passing along the Weave. It took her some time to understand what this new phenomenon was. Echoes of their alien language as they called to one another, dull bass snaps and pops that reverberated through her being. She listened in amazement. Never before had the distant creatures ever given a hint that they were even aware of humans in the Weave, other than their seemingly effortless ability to stay constantly out of the reach of the inquisitive; but now they were reacting to the death knell of the witchstone.

Cailin laughed breathlessly as her senses returned to the world of sight and sound. She had wanted to remain there, to listen to the voices of the mysterious denizens of the Weave, but there was far too much to do yet. Though they had defeated the Weavers here in the Fold, it might have been too late to turn the tide.

She looked at the Sisters to her left and right, saw the barely suppressed smiles on their painted lips, the fiery glint in their red eyes, and she felt pride such as she had never imagined she could. These few in the Fold represented only a fraction of the total strength of the network, for she had kept it scattered and decentralised out of fear for her fragile, nascent sorority. Yet here, they had proven themselves as worthy as she had hoped, finally revealing themselves to the Weavers and beating them at their own game. She felt a true kinship then, to all of them, every child that had been born with the *kana*, each one rescued from death. She had always believed they were greater than humans, a superior breed, an Aberration that had surmounted the race that spawned them; and now she *knew*.

Kaiku, precious Kaiku. It was she, perhaps, who had saved them all. Cailin's faith had not been misplaced, in the end.

She sent a flurry of orders across the Weave, distributing her Sisters to where they would be needed the most, and then she swept away. An insidious worry that was growing in her mind, souring her elation. While she had been fighting, she had not the spare time to notice; but now she realised that the Sister Irilia, whom she had left guarding Lucia, was not communicating any more.

The last few gristle-crows were being shredded on the wing when Lucia turned to Nomoru and said: 'What now?'

Yugi gave her a look of grave concern. She was not reacting at all as a fourteen-winter child should. Her father and her best friend had just died in front of her – spirits, she was still splattered with Zaelis's blood, which she had made no attempt to wipe off – but her brief tears had dried and her soot-grimed face was an icy mask. Her eyes, so often dreamy and unfocused, were like crystal shards now, piercing and unsettling.

He cast a quick glance around the street. They were still in the spot where the Weavers had attacked them. The corpses of Flen and Zaelis lay untouched alongside the dead furies, the Weavers, the Sister Irilia and dozens of ravens. Lucia stood in the midst of the charnel-pit. She had ignored Yugi's pleas to get to a safer place, which had been made half out of sympathy for her loss, half because he could not bear to look on his friend and leader Zaelis lying in the dust. Eventually, other soldiers had arrived and Yugi had stationed them all around her position. If she would not move, then he would have to protect her.

He had guessed what Nomoru was doing, even though she had been typically reticent when he asked her. The gristle-crows had taken no part in combat until now, always remaining out of reach, circling high above. With hindsight, it was obvious what their purpose was. They were the Nexuses' eyes. That was the thinking behind Nomoru's plan, anyway. Blind the Nexuses by tearing out their eyes. Put them at a disadvantage. And then . . .

'Find them,' Nomoru said flatly.

Lucia did not respond, but overhead the pattern of the ravens' flight shifted. Those that were not occupied with mopping up the Aberrant birds scattered in all directions, spreading over the battlefield. Searching for the Nexuses.

Lucia listened to the jabber of the ravens, her eyes closed. Nomoru watched her anxiously. A runner came from the western wall, reporting that sections of it were on the verge of collapse, weakened by fire and the weight of the corpses leaning against it.

Yugi bore the news grimly. If the wall fell, it was all over. Even if they could find the Nexuses, he had little hope of getting to them. Perhaps one last, concerted charge might be able to penetrate the Aberrants and reach their handlers, but he doubted it. Still, it would be better than waiting here for death, cowering behind collapsing walls, hiding until the enemy tide came to drown them in a wave of claws and fangs.

Rifles clattered to shoulders as a black shape emerged at the end of the street, but it was only Cailin, striding as tall and unruffled as ever. The guards lowered their weapons, and Cailin passed them without so much as a glance. She took in the scene and then fixed her red gaze on Yugi.

'Is she hurt?'

'She's not hurt,' Yugi said.

Lucia's eyes opened.

'Cailin,' she said, using an imperative mode she had never used before. 'I need your help.'

Cailin walked over to her. 'Of course,' she said, and just for a moment Yugi looked from one to the other and they could have been mother and daughter, so close were they in voice and posture. 'How can I help you?'

'I have found something.'

'The Nexuses?' Nomoru asked eagerly.

'I found *them* some time ago,' she said, with a nasty smile that looked shockingly out of place on her beatific features. 'I have something better.'

★

The Nexuses, unlike the Sisters of the Red Order, had no fear of clustering together. They had taken station some way to the south of the Fold, away from the main battle, and surrounded themselves with a bodyguard of a hundred ghauregs that made them unassailable by any force the Fault could muster. Occasional attacks from small, rogue groups were swiftly repelled, and the only army with sufficient number to threaten them was trammelled in the Fold. Nevertheless, they had learned the merits of keeping their distance, and so they hid at the limits of their control-range and directed the battle from afar.

The loss of the Weavers was not a concern to the Nexuses; they did not have the emotion necessary to respond to the death of their masters. What was more perturbing was the massacre of the gristle-crows, for those beasts had been specialised as lookouts. The Nexuses were not directly linked to the vision of all their beasts, but it was possible to see through the eyes of *some* of them. They prioritised their links; there was, after all, only so much information it was possible to deal with at a time.

They had now switched to skrendel and sent them climbing as high as they could to observe the battlefield, but it was a poor substitute for the gristle-crows.

The spot that they had chosen was a sunken crescent of grassy land banked by a hilly ridge to the west, south and east. They were sheltered from sight from those directions, and as long as they kept their ghauregs off the ridge then they were confident that nobody of importance knew they were here at all. Almost two hundred Nexuses were gathered, an eerie crowd of identical black, cowled robes and blank white faces, looking northward. When the army had first embarked they had been at the limit of their capacity to control the Aberrant predators, for there was only a finite amount that each Nexus could handle. However, as the predators' numbers had been brutally cut down, so the workload had eased. They were comfortably in command now. The ghauregs prowled restlessly around the silent figures, walking low to the ground with their shaggy arms swinging.

The ghauregs were not the most sensitive of creatures, and nor were the Nexuses, which was why they did not think to react to the steadily growing rumble from the south until it was too late. By the time the ghauregs began to look to the ridge with quizzical grunts, the sound was already beginning to separate into something discernible, and a moment before a new and unexpected enemy came into view, they realised what it was.

Hooves.

The mounted soldiers of Blood Ikati burst over the ridge, a battle-cry rising from their front ranks. Barak Zahn was in the midst of the green and grey mass, his sword held high, his voice rising above the voices of his men. The ghauregs' lumbering attempts to consolidate some kind of defence were woefully slow. The riders thundered down towards the enemy, firing off a volley of shots from horseback that decimated the Aberrant line. They switched to blades as they swept into the creatures. The two fronts collided: hairy fists smashed riders from their mounts, blades hacked into tough hide and opened up muscle beneath, horses had their legs broken like twigs, rifles cracked, men fell and were trampled. The ghauregs were fearsome opponents, and the attack became a chaos of hand-to-hand fighting, with the massive Aberrants tackling down the riders.

Zahn danced his horse this way and that, pulling it out of the reach of the beasts and cutting off any hand that came near. In his eyes was a fervour such as nobody had seen in him for years. His gaunt, white-bearded cheeks were speckled with blood, and his jaw was set tight. The riders outnumbered the ghauregs three to one, but the ghauregs held, protecting their black-robed masters who still looked northward as if oblivious to the threat.

Then the second front crested the western ridge, seven hundred men who swept into the sunken crescent of land and crashed into the flanks of the ghauregs. The beasts were faced with overwhelming odds now, and they had no way of preventing the attackers from circumventing them and reaching the Nexuses. The riders hewed the silent figures down from horseback, beheading them or hacking across their collarbones or chests, and the Nexuses stood mutely and allowed themselves to be killed. The men of Blood Ikati did not question their good fortune: they simply massacred their unresisting victims, and drenched themselves in their enemy.

The effect on the ghauregs was immediate and obvious. All coherence in their resistance dissolved. They became frenzied animals, seeking wildly for a way out of the forest of slashing blades and jostling warriors, concerned only for their own survival. It had the opposite effect, making them more vulnerable. They were chopped into bloody meat in minutes.

Finally the last of them had fallen, and the carnage was done. Barak Zahn sat panting in his saddle, surveying the corpse-littered scene. Then, with a breathless grin, he held his sword to the sky and let out a cheer that all his men echoed in one enormous swell of savage triumph.

Mishani tu Koli watched from her horse on the ridge, her ankle-length hair blowing in the breeze, her face, as ever, impassive.

Without the Nexuses, the Aberrants collapsed into disorder. Animals they had been, and animals they became again. On the western side of the Fold, where the stockade wall bowed dangerously inward and where the walkways on the rim were scattered with the dead of both sides, the creatures stopped their suicidal charges and turned on each other, maddened by the smoke and the smell of blood. They left their brethren impaled on the sharp tips of the wall and fell back from the flames, attacking anything that moved in a frenzied panic. The defenders, exhausted and ragged, stared in amazement as the beasts that had been on the verge of breaking through suddenly retreated in the most incredible rout they had ever seen. Someone was hysterically shouting thanks to the gods, and the cry was taken up down the line; for only the gods, it seemed, could have turned back an enemy such as this at the very last minute. They stood on the wall, their swords and rifles hanging on slack arms, and did nothing but breathe, and live, and enjoy the simplicity of that.

The scene at the eastern edge of the town was much the same, but there the Aberrants were penned in by the valley sides and the upward incline discounted it as an easy escape route in the minds of the maniacal beasts. They had no straightforward place to run, and they were still being pounded by fire-cannons and ballistae and rifles. Without the steadying influence of the Nexuses, they went utterly insane amid the explosions, some of them gnawing at their own limbs, others burying themselves under piles of smoking dead, still others simply lying down as if catatonic and being trampled or ripped to pieces by the horde. Some of them managed to escape up the valley, but most stayed at the bottom, trapped in a whirlpool of death until their turn came, by fire or rifle ball or claw.

By dusk, the Fold was quiet again. Smoke drifted into the reddening sky, and Nuki's eye glared angrily over the western peaks of the Xarana Fault. The foul stench in the air had become imperceptible to the survivors of the conflict, so long had they suffered it. Men and women and children wandered the town, battle-shattered and glazed, or roused themselves to slothful and exhausted activity in the knowledge that there was much to be done and little time to do it. Wives wept at the news that their husbands would never return; children screamed for parents who lay sundered in the dust somewhere, and were hastily gathered in by other mothers. Aberrants temporarily adopted non-Aberrants and vice versa, not knowing that their responsibility would become permanent as the dead were identified.

The predators were all killed or scattered, and hunting parties were chasing those that still prowled in the wilds nearby or who hid in houses within the Fold. Against impossible odds, the town had held out; but there was no sense of triumph here, only a weary and broken resignation, a numbness brought on by more horror than they could have imagined. The valley was drowned in gore, choked in corpses. The cost in grief and misery was appalling. And on top of all that was the knowledge that even in triumph they had won only a pyrrhic victory. They had their lives, but the Fold was forfeit. Nobody could stay here now. The Weavers would be coming again, and next time they would not be so reckless. Next time, all the luck in the world would not be enough to save the town.

A dozen troops of Blood Ikati rode slowly into town, with Barak Zahn and Mishani tu Koli at their head. They were as weary as the townsfolk, but for different reasons. Their gruelling ride from Zila had been days of hard travel, pushing their mounts to the limit of their endurance. When Xejen tu Imotu had given up the location of Lucia to the Weaver Fahrekh, Zahn had been finally convinced of the truth behind Mishani's claim. He had taken a thousand mounted men that he had brought to Zila and made all speed to the Fault, following Mishani's lead. They had passed east of Barask, skirted the terrible Forest of Xu on its northern edge, and entered the Fault south of the Fold, where Mishani took them through trails that their horses could travel. Usually, such ways would have been dangerous in the extreme, guarded as they were by hostile factions; but the Fault had given up its petty territorial squabbles in the face of a more extreme danger, and they had made good speed and arrived, it seemed, just in time.

Yet there was no hero's welcome for them in the town. Few even realised that they were responsible for the enemy's ruin. They passed through stares that ranged from curious to accusatory: why were soldiers on horseback here *now*? Where were they when they were needed?

It took all Mishani's strength to retain her composure. With each new corpse she expected to see Kaiku or Lucia or somebody else that she knew. Several of the dead or bereaved she did recognise vaguely, but she dared not allow them sympathy, for she did not yet know how deep her own hurt would be. The sight of her home town destroyed was bad enough, but to Mishani a place was just a place, and she was not so sentimental. However, she dreaded the thought of asking after her friends, what she might hear in response. If she knew Kaiku, she would have been in the thick of it. She always was a stubborn one, who would not back down from anything. Mishani dared not think of what she would feel if Kaiku was dead.

She barely knew where she was leading Zahn's men, only that she had a definite sense of where she should be, a lingering instruction left in her head by Cailin. The shock of having the Sister speak in her thoughts had still not worn off, hours later. She understood how the chain of events had come about – how Lucia's ravens had spotted them from on high, how Cailin had used her *kana* to speak to Mishani and tell her where the Nexuses were and what they had to do – but the sheer narrowness of their margin of victory terrified her. Gods, if the Weavers had been a little quicker off the mark in sending their army here, or if Zahn had wasted any more time with doubt and disbelief . . . if Fahrekh had suspected what Zahn was up to and had kept Xejen's knowledge of Lucia a secret, if Mishani had not been 'rescued' by Bakkara from her father's men . . . if Chien had not insisted she stay at his townhouse in Hanzean . . .

She shivered at the possibilities.

Thinking about Chien brought an image of his face back to her, his blocky features and shaven scalp. She felt little more than a passing regret for his death. He had been a good man, in the end, but she had learned that good men died as readily as evil men. She suspected her father's hand in it, of course; but the assassins were far behind her now, for she had been smuggled out of Zila with all secrecy. At the last, Chien had not managed to fulfil the task she set him, so she did not count herself held to her promise of ensuring his family would be released from their ties to Blood Koli. In other times, she might have been more generous; but she had her mother's welfare to think about, and for now it was best that the pact died with Chien. The world was cruel, but Mishani could be cruel too.

They turned onto a dusty street, and there Mishani saw what lay at their destination. The troops halted, and she dismounted and walked slowly onward, through the carpet of dead ravens and past the corpses of Weavers and furies and the body of the dead Sister. Standing in their midst was Cailin, like a black spike at the hub of all this killing. And crouched over the body of Zaelis was Lucia, her burned neck bent downward and her head hung, face in her hands.

Mishani stopped in front of Cailin and looked up at her, black hair sloughing back from her cheeks as she met the gaze of the taller woman. Cailin's irises had returned to their usual green by now.

'Mishani tu Koli,' the Sister said, with the appropriate bow. 'You have my gratitude.'

Mishani was too agitated to respond with the correct pleasantries. Instead, she asked: 'Where is Kaiku?'

Cailin did not reply for a moment, and Mishani's heart jerked painfully in her chest.

'I am not sure,' she said at length. 'She was on the other side of the Fault. She destroyed the witchstone we found there. It was she, as much as you, that turned this battle around. If the Weavers had still been fighting us, I would not have been able to contact you to direct you to the Nexuses.'

Witchstone? Mishani thought, but did not say. Much had occurred in her absence.

'I cannot reach her,' Cailin continued after a moment. 'She does not respond to my attempts. What that means, I do not know.'

Mishani digested that, processing the implications and coming out only with uncertainty.

Cailin glanced towards Lucia. 'She has not moved for hours. She will not let us take the bodies away. I fear she has taken a wound that she might never recover from.'

Mishani was about to reply, but then a footstep behind her made her look back, and she saw Zahn there, picking his way through the bodies, his eyes only on one person, on—

'Lucia?'

She raised her head at his voice, but no more than that.

'Lucia?' he said again, and this time she turned to him, her face and hair smeared red. He took a shuddering breath at the sight of her. She got slowly to her feet and faced him.

They stood gazing at each other.

Then she raised her arms, palms wet with Zaelis's blood held out to him. Her lower lip began to shake, and her face crumpled into tears. He covered the ground between them in a rush and gathered her up in an embrace, and she hugged him back desperately, her slender body racked with sobs. They stood there, amid smoke and grief and death, father and daughter clutched to each other with a force born of years of secret longing.

For the moment, it was enough.

Thirty-Seven

K aiku stirred and opened her eyes, squinting against the mid-day brightness. Her body ached in every part, and her clothes felt stiff against her skin. Nearby, there was the soft murmur of a fire, and smells of cooking meat. She was lying on stony soil, in a shallow depression surrounded by rock on three sides, a narrow step in the uneven land. Her pack was rolled beneath her head as a pillow. The air was curiously dead and silent; no insects hummed, nor birds flew. She had become used to it over the weeks. It meant that they were still close to the witchstone, still within the range of the blight.

She sat up urgently, wincing as her battered muscles protested their ill-use. Tsata was there, crouching by the fire. He looked over at her.

'Do not exert yourself,' he advised. 'You are still weak.'

'Where are we?' she asked, and found her throat was parchment-dry and she could only manage a thin croak. Tsata handed her a water-skin, and she gulped from it, gasping as she finished. She repeated herself more audibly.

'Several miles west of the mine,' he said. 'I think we are safe, at least for a short while.'

'How did we get here?'

'I carried you,' he said.

She rubbed at her forehead as if to massage life back into her mind. It did seem now that she could recall moments, half-dream and half-waking, dreams of water and being towed through rushing blackness, of being carried like a slain deer across his shoulders.

'We got out the way we came in?'

Tsata nodded. 'We rode the scoops as high as we could, and I ran with you the rest of the way. There were no Aberrants near the top of the mine.' He smiled at her warmly, the tattoos on his face curving with the movement. 'I do not think you noticed, though. That last effort was a little too much for you.'

She snorted a laugh.

'Are you hungry?' he asked, indicating the scrawny thing spitted over the fire.

She tilted her chin at him with a grin. He brought the spit over to her, settling himself by her side. Both of them were bedraggled, having been soaked and dried several times over the last few hours. Tsata tore off a chunk of flesh with his fingers; Kaiku brushed her errant fringe out of her eyes and took the proffered meat. They sat and ate for a time in companionable silence, their thoughts far away, Kaiku happy for the joy of being alive, of the sun on her face and the taste of the meal.

She felt a deep sense of validation, a relaxing of some tension inside her that she had not even known was there. They had destroyed a witchstone; they had struck the Weavers a blow that nobody in Saramyr had ever managed before. It was still a long, long way from the vengeance demanded by her oath to Ocha, but it was enough for now. She had been chafing at her inactivity for so long, driven to *do* something instead of playing this interminable waiting game that Zaelis and Cailin favoured. She could ask no more of herself for the moment. She felt worthy again.

But there was more, even than that. She was not the Kaiku that had set off broken-hearted from the Fold all those weeks ago. That Kaiku had been marvellously naïve, unaware of the potential of the power inside her, content to wield it like a club and control it only as far as preventing it damaging herself. Yet circumstances had forced her to stretch herself again and again, to use her *kana* in ways she had never dared before, and she had risen to the challenge every time. Without adequate schooling, without any experience whatsoever, she had faced down demons, had cleansed a man of poison and saved his life, and most incredible of all, she had beaten a Weaver. Granted, the victory had been a terribly near thing, but it was still a victory.

She had wondered often about why Cailin was so cursedly persistent with her, why she tolerated a pupil so errant that most tutors would have given up. Now she knew. Cailin had told her time and time again, but she was too stubborn to listen; it was only after all this, only after she had learned it herself, that she realised Cailin was right. Her talent with *kana* was extraordinary; her potential was limitless. Spirits, the things she could do with it . . .

She had been too impatient to devote herself to years of study and the Red Order, and so she had squandered her talents on small missions that could have been done by other people. But these past weeks had made her realise at last that her *kana* was more than a weapon. And she also realised that possessing a power and not knowing how to use it well was worse than not possessing it at all. What if she had not been able to save Yugi's life? Or to have destroyed the witchstone? How heavy would the guilt have weighed on her then? She would keep on finding herself in situations where she was forced to use her *kana*, and one day she would not be equal to the challenge, and it would cost lives.

She saw now that the quickest path to fulfilling her oath to Ocha was not the one she thought. Cailin had always said she must go slowly to reach the end faster: that she must master herself to become a more effective player in the game. It had seemed like specious reasoning at the time, but now it made perfect sense. She cursed herself as a fool for not seeing it before.

And in that moment, she came to a decision. She *would* let Cailin teach her. When she returned, she would make her apologies, and ask to begin again as a pupil; and this time, she would hold nothing more important. Her resolve was firmer than ever now that her burning urge for vengeance was temporarily sated. She would join the Red Order. She would become a Sister. And through them, she would fight the Weavers with the abilities that she had once thought a curse, that had once made her outcast.

If, of course, there was any Red Order left when she returned. But curiously, she could not find it in herself to worry about that, nor about the Fold or Mishani or Lucia. She had strange, elusive memories of her time in unconsciousness, of a voice calling to her, and whatever that voice said set her heart at ease. With no clear reason why, she knew that all was not lost, the Weavers had not crushed the last hope, and that both Mishani and Lucia still lived. With that, she was content.

'What will you do now?' she asked Tsata.

'I will return with you to the Fold, then I will make my way back to Okhamba,' he said. 'I have to tell my people what has happened here.' He hesitated a moment, then looked at her. 'You could come with me, if you so chose.'

And just for a moment Kaiku saw how simple that would be, how wonderful, that they might prolong this time that they had spent together, that she would not have to return to the world she knew. How it might be to be with him, this man whom she trusted utterly and whom she believed incapable of guile or deceit or treachery. For that moment, she wavered; but it was only a moment.

'I would like nothing more,' she said, smiling sadly. 'But we both know I cannot. And we both know you cannot stay.'

He nodded, Saramyr-fashion. 'I wish that it were otherwise,' he said, and Kaiku felt a painful squeeze in her chest at his words.

After that, there was nothing that could be said. They finished their meal, and rested for a time, and when Kaiku was strong enough to walk he helped her up. They shouldered their packs and their rifles, and together they set off east, back towards the Fold, and whatever lay afterward.

The temple to Ocha on the top of the Imperial Keep was the highest point in Axekami, excepting the tips of the towers that stood at the vertices of the colossal golden edifice. It was ornate to the point of excess, a circular building supporting a wondrous dome, chased with mosaics, filigrees, intaglios, and inlaid with precious metals and reflective stones so that the sheer wealth it exuded stunned the eye. Eight exquisite statues of white marble broke the dome at the points of the compass, each a representation of one of the major deities, both in their rarely-depicted human forms and with their earthly animal aspects at their feet: Assantua, Rieka, Jurani, Omecha, Enyu, Shintu, Isisya and Ocha himself standing over the entrance, a rearing boar before him. The boss of the dome was most magnificent of all, a cluster of iridescent diamonds visible only from the top of the Towers of the Four Winds, representing the one star, Abinaxis, that had created the universe and birthed the gods and goddesses in the beginning. When Nuki's eye looked upon it, the diamonds blazed like their namesake. That sight was intended for the gods above, in re-compense for the arrogance that had led to the downfall of Gobinda all those centuries ago.

It was no less resplendent within, though redecoration had updated it over the years to make it less gaudy than the exterior and more in keeping with the elegance of Saramyr architecture. Here, tall *lach* sentinels stood in alcoves in the walls, and an ivory bas-relief twisted across the interior of the dome like convoluted vines. The air was cool and moist in contrast to the heat of the day. A raised path was laid from the entrance to the grand altar at its centre, but all else was water, a clear, shallow pool with submerged mosaics and clusters of polished stones arranged artfully to please the eye. No fish swam in the pool, and it was still as glass and restful.

Avun tu Koli knelt on the circular central island, before the ivory altar, a cluster of incense sticks in his hand and his balding head bowed. He mouthed a silent mantra, over and over, time and again. He had unconsciously begun to rock to the rhythm, his body swaying slightly with the imagined cadence of the words. It was a ritual of thanks offered to Ocha, who apart from being the ruler of the Golden Realm was also god of war, revenge, exploration and endeavour. Thanks to the god who had delivered him and his family safely through the fall of the empire.

Once again, Avun had guided Blood Koli into the most terrible peril and brought them stronger to the other side. Blood Batik would be extinguished, without mercy; already none bearing that name lived in Axekami. With its standing army gone, its holdings would soon be seized, and any remaining members of the line hunted down. For five brief years they had held the throne, and Blood Koli had been outcast; but in the end it was Avun that knelt in the temple of Ocha, and Mos who was crushed.

There would be many changes in the weeks to come. Kakre had explained it all to him. The Weavers were too hated to rule, the Aberrants too fearsome to keep order in any way other than by terror. A terrified populace was not a productive one. And so they had needed him, a figurehead. He would be the human face to the Weaver's regime; his men would replace the decimated Imperial Guards with a new peacekeeping force. Once order was established in Axekami, then the Aberrants' presence would be diminished, moved elsewhere where it was needed more. And gradually, the people would come to understand that this was the new way, that their world of courts and tradition and nobility was dead and gone, that *family* meant nothing any more. Avun would be the Emperor in all but name, only subordinate to the Weavers. They would call him Lord Protector, and his men would be the Blackguard.

All it had cost him was his honour. But honour was a small thing compared to victory. Honour had driven his daughter from him.

He thought on Mishani. She was only a face to him now; there was no parental love left in him for his absent child. He had to assume that she had evaded his attempts upon her life, for he had received no word of success. It brought a faint smile to his face. She was her father's daughter in that, at least. Tough to kill. Well, let her do as she would now, for she shamed him no longer. Now that the elaborate politics of the Saramyr courts meant nothing, she had no power to cause him disadvantage. The news of a disobedient child could harm him as a Barak, but it could not harm the Lord Protector, who had no peers to jostle with. He would not waste his time trying to be rid of her now. He would simply forget about her.

He only wished his wife Muraki would see sense and do the same, but it was a minor annoyance.

Footsteps from behind him heralded the arrival of the Weave-lord Kakre, and he finished his round of mantras and stood to bow deeply to the altar. When he was done, he turned to face his new master.

'Prayers, Lord Protector?' Kakre rasped. 'How quaint.'

'The gods have favoured me,' Avun replied. 'They deserve my gratitude.'

'The gods have deserted this land,' Kakre said. 'If ever they existed to begin with.'

Avun raised an eyebrow. 'The Weavers bow to no gods, then?'

'From this day, we *are* your gods,' the Weave-lord said.

Avun studied the corpse-faced grotesquerie in front of him, and made no response.

'Come,' said Kakre. 'We have much to talk about.'

Avun nodded. There was plenty to be done. Even the Weavers could not conquer a land as vast as Saramyr in a day, or a year. They had cut the head off the empire, and seized its capital and several major cities, but the nobility and populace were too widely scattered to easily subjugate, even with the overwhelming numbers that the Weavers possessed and the armies of most of the high families destroyed. The north-west quarter of the continent would be entirely under Weaver control within the month. After that, it would be a matter of sweeping away the disoriented remnants of the nobility, powerless without their Weavers, blinded and crippled. Consolidating and then pushing southward, until all the land was theirs and there was no one to oppose them.

Whether it would be as easy as that, Avun had no idea; but he had a knack for picking the winning side, and in this case he would far rather be with the Weavers than against them.

Kakre's own concerns ran deeper than troops and war and occupation. His thoughts were on what might have happened in the Fault, the loss of so many Weavers, and most abhorrently the destruction of a witchstone. He felt its death like a physical wound, and it had aged him, making him more bent and pain-racked than ever before. What had become, then, of the Fold, and of Lucia?

And what of the entities that had fought his Weavers, the women who dared oppose them in the realm beyond the senses? That was a danger beyond anything he had yet encountered, the most potent threat he could imagine now. If he had been able to spare enough of his forces, he would have sent them rampaging toward the Xarana Fault; but even then, he suspected he would find that his targets had gone back into hiding. How long had they been there? How long had they spread and grown? All these years of killing Aberrant children had been precisely to prevent something like this from happening, and yet despite their best efforts it had happened anyway. How strong were they now? How many did they number?

He thought of the Sisters, and he feared them.

They walked slowly down the raised path across the pool towards the entrance to the temple, where blinding sunlight shone through the doorway. They spoke as they went, of triumph and failure, their voices echoing in the silence until they faded, leaving the house of the Emperor of the gods empty and hollow.

*

The sun was setting in the west as Cailin watched, a sullen red orb glaring through the veil of smoke that still rose from the valley of the Fold. She stood on a high lip of land, a grassy shelf jutting out over a splintered hillside of dark rock. She had been here for some time now, thinking. There were many plans to make yet.

The remainder of the Sisters were scattered around the Fold, helping in the dispersal. The Libera Dramach was breaking up, spreading out, making itself an impossible target; they would regroup at a rendezvous in several weeks' time. The people of the Fold were doing what they could: most were intending to rejoin the others, putting their trust in the leaders who had seen them through good times and tragedy. Others were going their own way, amalgamating into other tribes and factions or heading out of the Fault altogether. The unity of the Fold was shattered, and would never be regained.

Messages had been flashing across the Weave all day, from other cells of the Red Order elsewhere. News of Axekami, of massacres in the northern cities, of the Weavers' daring and unstoppable coup. News of the fall of the Emperor, and with him the empire. The Sisters knew that the game was up now, that the Weavers were aware of them at last, and their silence was broken.

There was a soft tread behind. Cailin did not need to turn to know it was Phaeca. The red-headed Sister walked to the edge of the precipice and stood beside her. She was clothed in black, as all the Sisters were, and she wore the intimidating face-paint of the Order; but her dress was a different cut to Cailin's, her hair worn in an elaborate style of braids and bunches that bore testament to her River District up-bringing.

For a time, they were silent. Nuki's eye was slipping towards the horizon, turning the sky to coral pink and purple, marred by the drifting smoke.

'So many dead,' Phaeca said at last. 'Is this how you planned it?'

'Hardly,' Cailin said. 'The Weavers finding out about the Fold was an unfortunate happenstance brought about by a mob of foolish and misguided zealots.'

Phaeca's silence was response enough. Cailin let it drag out.

'Did we cause all this?' Phaeca persisted at length. 'Hiding, refusing to act, all these years when we could have done something . . . is this the price we pay?'

Cailin's voice was edged with annoyance. 'Phaeca, stop this. You know as well as I why we have not acted these long years. And the lives lost here will be nothing to the lives that will be lost in the months to come.'

'We could have stopped them,' Phaeca argued. 'We could have stopped the Weavers taking the throne. If we had tried.'

'Perhaps,' Cailin conceded doubtfully. She turned her head slightly, looking sidelong at her companion. She was seeking a salve to justify herself. Cailin had none to give. 'But whyever would we do that? There is no sacrifice too high, Phaeca. Do not let your conscience prick you now; it is too late for regrets. This is only the beginning. The Sisters have awakened. The war for Saramyr has commenced.' A sultry breeze stirred the feathers of her ruff. 'We *wanted* the Weavers to take the throne. That is why we have held our allies back, that is why we preached secrecy and told them to hide, that is why we refused to use our abilities to aid them. They can never be allowed to know that. They would call it a betrayal.'

Phaeca nodded in reluctant understanding, her gaze fixed on the middle distance.

'If this is only the beginning,' she said, 'I fear what is to come.'

'As well you should, Sister,' Cailin told her. 'As well you should.'

They said no more, but neither did they leave. The Sisters stood together for a long while in the fading light of the dusk, watching the rising smoke from the valley as the colours bled from the sky and darkness covered the land.